W9-CPI-947

Romantic Times praises Norah Hess,
winner of the Reviewers' Choice Award
for Frontier Romance!

KENTUCKY WOMAN

"A warm, realistic, earthy romance, *Kentucky
Woman* is an Americana love story with the
grittiness of a frontier Western that brings
readers straight into the lives and hearts of the
characters."

MOUNTAIN ROSE

"Another delightful, tender and heartwarming
read from a special storyteller!"

KENTUCKY BRIDE

"Marvelous...a treasure for those who savor
frontier love stories!"

HAWKE'S PRIDE

"Earthy and realistic....Bravo to Norah Hess!"

DEVIL IN SPURS

"Norah Hess is a superb Western romance
writer....*Devil in Spurs* is an entertaining read!"

HEAVEN

Jim's blue eyes studied the slender woman gazing uncertainly at him. Surely there was no other woman in the world so beautiful as Sage Larkin. His eyes ranged over her creamy shoulders, the hint of perfect breasts rising above the dress's round neckline. His pulse picked up as he remembered seeing them in all their bared glory and feeling the shape of them through the washcloth he had used to bathe her.

Suddenly, he didn't want the drunken, crude men in the next room to see her. Their lust-filled eyes would contaminate her loveliness, tarnish her innocence. For she was innocent, despite the fact that she had been married. He could see in the depths of her green eyes that her husband had never awakened the passion he was sure slumbered inside her.

"Well, Jim," Tillie said, "how does she look?"

"She looks," Jim answered in husky undertones, "just like a green-eyed angel come down from heaven."

Sage smiled shyly. "You flatter me, Jim. You know very well that I have no wings."

Jim gave her a knowing smile that made her blush. "Yes, I do know that, don't I?"

Other *Leisure Books* by Norah Hess:
KENTUCKY WOMAN
MOUNTAIN ROSE
KENTUCKY BRIDE
HAWKE'S PRIDE
DEVIL IN SPURS

Sage

NORAH HESS

LEISURE BOOKS **NEW YORK CITY**

To all my fans who wanted Jim LaTour's story told.

A LEISURE BOOK®

April 1994

Published by

Dorchester Publishing Co., Inc.
276 Fifth Avenue
New York, NY 10001

If you purchased this book without a cover you should be aware
that this book is stolen property. It was reported as "unsold and
destroyed" to the publisher and neither the author nor the publisher
has received any payment for this "stripped book."

Copyright © 1994 by Norah Hess

All rights reserved. No part of this book may be reproduced or
transmitted in any form or by any electronic or mechanical means,
including photocopying, recording or by any information storage
and retrieval system, without the written permission of the Publisher,
except where permitted by law.

The name "Leisure Books" and the stylized "L" with design are
trademarks of Dorchester Publishing Co., Inc.

Printed in the United States of America.

Sage

Chapter One

Wyoming, 1872–73

It was a blustery March morning when Jim LaTour waved good-bye to his daughter and son-in-law. He felt himself possessed by a spirit of elation and eagerness. Although his daughter, Jonty, was his whole world, it would feel good not to play father for a while, to be once again the man she knew little about.

The hard-drinking, hard-playing, womanizing Jim LaTour.

While he was still recovering from a near fatal bullet wound he'd been all too happy to stay with Jonty and her husband, Cord McBain. Jonty had fussed over him, preparing special meals that would strengthen his blood. He had played with his grandson, Cody, and he'd had a chance to get to know his son-in-law. There had been bad blood between them for years.

But this past month, as he began to recover

his strength, he'd grown restless and yearned for some excitement in his life.

As his big black stallion, Major, clipped along the valley floor, Jim thought of his saloon in Cottonwood. It would be good to be back at Trail's End with his bartender, Jake, and Tillie, his cook. And he mustn't forget Reba.

Reba was the madam of five girls who plied their trade in the pleasure house next door to his saloon. There had been a time when the ladies of the evening had entertained their men upstairs over the saloon. But Jonty had objected so strongly to that practice that she had finally worn him down, and he had advanced Reba the money to rent the big house next door.

As Jim kept the stallion at a brisk walk, his thoughts lingered on Reba.

Had the voluptuous redhead saved her favors for him while he was laid up? he wondered. She might have, but somehow he doubted it. Reba liked a man in her bed and didn't pretend otherwise. Three months would be a long haul for her to go without the regular pleasuring of a male body.

He knew, though, that if she had taken a replacement in his absence, she would have been very discreet about it. No one would know.

Jim grinned wryly. Reba wouldn't talk, nor would the man, whoever he was. He'd be too afraid of riling big Jim LaTour for poaching on his territory.

Not that he'd really give a damn, Jim mused, rocking along with the stallion's easy gait. He liked Reba well enough, but she held no special place in his heart. He had found that she was better than most in bed, and knew all the ways there were to please a man. But there was a coldness about her, a lack of the gentleness most men wanted and expected from a woman. Sometimes she made him feel like she was the procurer and he the whore.

Far back in the depths of his eyes, a sad pensiveness flickered. He had known many women over the years, but none had been able to erase from his mind his lovely Cleo, the love of his youth . . . the seventeen-year-old who died giving birth to his daughter while he was running from the law.

God, how he had loved her. His eyes squeezed tight as if in pain as he remembered back twenty years.

He had been a wild one then; mad at the world—especially the white man's world that looked at the young half-breed as though he was something dirty, only half human.

He had known logically that he should continue living in his mother's village after she and his white father had died of the white man's disease that had swept through the tribe. His Indian grandmother and his cousin Johnny Lightfoot had tried to persuade him to remain with them, saying that he would find no acceptance in his father's world. But he had felt driven to enter the life his father had turned his back on, to make himself a part of it.

He had taken his time, riding across country, doing odd jobs on the ranches he came across, mostly for meals and a place in the barn to sleep. He would move on after a while, stopping in some small town, hoping for better treatment from the white man. But nothing ever changed much. The only work he could find was sweeping out a saloon or shoveling out stables at a livery.

No one ever asked him his name. From the beginning he was called Breed. He began to hate the word, and to think that his grandmother and his cousin had been right. There didn't seem to be a place for him in the white man's world. But he was stubborn. He would push on a little farther, and maybe find a place where he would be accepted for the person he was.

Jim's lips lifted in a bitter grimace as he continued to reminisce. Within an hour of riding into one small Illinois town, he had known he'd made a wrong decision. He had been looked upon with suspicion by the men, and with disdain by the women. He soon learned that he was expected to step off the wooden sidewalk to let the whites pass, even if the street was ankle-deep in mud.

Stubbornness and pride had kept him among those who referred to him as Breed, who kept him out of their restaurants and taverns, who wouldn't rent him a room, a small place he could call home.

His money had just about given out when he struck a deal with the old man who owned the livery stable. In exchange for a pile of hay and a blanket, plus a dollar a day, he would look after the horses and shovel out the stables.

It had been that same old man who had suggested he cut off his braids. "With your hair short and them blue eyes of yours, you'd be more accepted, LaTour," he'd said. "And maybe leave off the buckskins and get yourself some twills and a shirt and vest, white man's garb."

He had fought the old man's suggestion for a couple of weeks before spending most of his wages on a flannel shirt and twill trousers with a matching vest. It had taken him close to a month to get used to the stiff boots that later replaced his soft moccasins.

And it had taken another two weeks before he allowed his boss to clip off his braids.

He noticed that, with the long black braids gone, there was a slight difference in the townspeople's attitude toward him. He was by no means accepted socially, but occasionally a man would nod to him on the street, and the girls slid him many a coy look when their parents weren't looking. Just as the Indian maids used to do in his village, he'd think with a smug smile. He knew he was handsome. From the time he was fourteen, women had sought him out, slipping into his blankets when the rest of the village lay sleeping. Often he hadn't even known whose body he covered in the black night, and he hadn't cared. He was young and his blood was hot. Release for his throbbing male member was all that had interested him.

For some time, his boss's man-hungry granddaughter took care of him in that department. Almost from the first day he had worked at the stables, he had seen her hanging around. He judged her to be sixteen or seventeen years old, ugly as hell, but always clean.

After a couple of days he had noticed she always watched him as he went about his work, currying horses, shoveling out manure. He had been a long time without the pleasure a woman's body could give him, but he worried that the girl was a virgin. He respected the old man too much to carelessly take her innocence.

Then, one afternoon, he returned to the livery after running an errand for his boss and was greeted by the sounds of grunts and female cries of pleasure in the hayloft above. He stepped into an empty stall and crouched down out of sight. He had no doubt that he had stumbled onto a clandestine meeting; probably a married man and a whore. If that was the case, certainly the man wouldn't want it known that he was carrying on in a hayloft.

Jim could only gape with surprise when a short time later a very much married man climbed down the ladder, followed by the old man's granddaughter, Alice.

When the man said before leaving, "Meet me by the creek at the edge of town tomorrow night," Jim's lips spread in a wicked grin. The granddaughter was no virgin, and he intended to keep her satisfied. There would be no more trips to the creek from then on.

The next day, when the girl showed up at the stable, Jim laid down the currying brush and walked toward her, unbuttoning his fly as he approached. Her eyes watched him avidly, and she giggled when he bared a very large and hard arousal. She licked her lips, then grabbed him by the hand and hurried him up the ladder to the loft.

Finally, he and the girl had worn themselves out. But when he ordered, "Meet me here tonight," she nodded her head eagerly.

And so it had continued. They would enjoy a fast tumble when they could find the time in daylight hours, but they spent at least three hours together every night in the hayloft.

He had always been careful, though, Jim remembered now, to spill his seed into the hay. He knew the heartache of being a breed, and he would never be responsible for the birth of yet another child who could find no place for himself in the white man's world. He only hoped that the other men the girl might run into in the future would be as careful.

One early afternoon, five white men rode up to the livery. They were around his age, ugly drunk and primed for a fight. As he came forward to take their horses, he could read trouble in their faces.

"Look at what we've got here, Red," one of the men had sneered. "A blue-eyed breed." He pulled a pistol from its holster and aimed it at Jim's feet. "Watch me make him do a war dance."

Ready for them, Jim whipped a knife from inside his boot and jumped among them. His lean, whipcord body made no wasted moves as, with lightning speed, his fists and blade and feet struck out. Within a matter of minutes two men lay unconscious on the livery floor, and a third clutched a knife wound in his arm. The other two, suddenly sober, backed away, the desire to tangle with the breed having died a swift death.

While Jim waited on braced feet, the man called Red, who was apparently the leader, spoke. "You're pretty handy with your fists and that knife, breed. We could use someone like you to hang around with us. Are you as handy with the Colt strapped on your hip as you are with that pig-sticker?"

Jim smiled mirthlessly. He'd handled the Colt from an early age. On his fourteenth birthday his father had given him the gun, then spent long hours teaching him how to use it.

At first their targets had been pieces of carved wood hung from a tree branch. When he had been able to unerringly hit each one with a single shot they switched to leaves on a cottonwood. When his father was satisfied that he could hit what he shot at he made him practice a fast draw. Now he could pull the Colt in a motion so fast, it was a blur to the naked eye.

A second after the man spoke, he was staring at his hat lying a couple of feet behind him, a bullet hole in its crown.

"Well, what do you think?" Jim asked coolly.

"I think you're damn good," Red managed to say as he picked up his hat, slapping the dust and hay off it before settling it back on his head. "What about hangin' round with us?"

The five weren't the sort Jim would have chosen for friends. He suspected they were on the wrong side of the law. He knew for a fact that his cousin Johnny Lightfoot would tell him to stay clear of them, that they meant trouble. But he was God-awful lonesome for company, company that wouldn't sneer at him.

But there was his elderly boss to consider. The old fellow had been good to him, had made it possible for him to remain in this town where he wasn't wanted, but was too stubborn to leave. He couldn't just go off and leave him without notice.

He looked at Red and shook his head. "I have this job and I feel obligated to the man who gave it to me."

"Keep your job," Red said. "We've all got jobs of a sort. We get together at night, have a few drinks, raise a little hell, have a good time."

He held out his hand to Jim. "Dick Harlan is my real handle; they call me Red because of my hair. Them two on the floor"—he jerked a thumb over his shoulder—"are Ed and Tex, and the feller holding his arm is Herb." He looked at an older man who leaned against a post, the one who had stood by while his companions were soundly licked. "That there is Rooster."

Jim gave each man a curt nod, and received the same in return.

And so it began. Every evening they met at a small fur post a few miles from town, where they'd engage in drunken revelry, picking fights and raising hell. When their finances became low they would cut a few head of cattle from some rancher's herd, use a running iron over the owner's brand, then sell the animals to the owner of the post. The shifty-eyed man always turned a blind eye to the brand that had been changed.

The weeks passed, and gradually the men began looking to Jim for direction. It had become, "What should we do tonight, LaTour?" He was a natural leader, and the others had unconsciously recognized that fact.

Dick Harlan had put up a token resistance, but no one paid much attention to him. Jim knew, though, that the stocky man resented being replaced as the men's leader. His whole demeanor showed it, even to the sham joking of calling Jim "Breed."

One day around noon, as Jim was currying a horse, waiting for Alice to put in an appearance, a vision walked into the livery. His hand grew still on the horse's back. Never had he seen a lovelier face. She was somewhere in her late teens, he thought, and still an innocent; he could see it in the soft eyes that returned his awed gaze.

She had smiled shyly at him and said that she would like to hire a horse for an hour or so. He had fallen in love on the spot, a love that had lasted for twenty years.

He had chosen for her the gentlest mare in the stables, and with hands that shook a little, he'd helped her to mount. And though she was gone no more than an hour, it seemed to him forever before she returned and he could help her to dismount.

Although he could see from the corners of his eyes that Alice had arrived and was standing back in the shadows, he had kept the lovely young girl beside him, asking her if she had enjoyed her ride. And what were her favorite places to visit when she went riding?

They exchanged names. Then Cleo Rand said that she'd better get home; her mother would be worried about her if she stayed away too long. He had asked her if she'd be going for another ride soon, and she had shyly nodded yes.

He had watched her walk away, admiring her slender body and the graceful way she walked. He gave a startled jerk when a hand landed on his shoulder. "That one will never spread her legs for you, Breed," Alice taunted him. "Forget her. Come on up to the loft with me."

Jim looked down at the hot-eyed Alice as though he had never seen her before. He hadn't the least desire to idle away a couple of hours between her legs. He was as limp as a wet dishcloth.

"Not today," he muttered. "I have too much work to do."

He knew that Alice guessed he was lying, and he wasn't surprised when she gave him a black look and flounced out of the livery. He grinned. She would be making nightly trips to the creek again. There was a never-ending supply of men who would meet her there.

Cleo had shown up every afternoon after that first day. Soon Jim was slipping away from the livery to ride with her. They talked of many things. He told her how he had lost both parents to pneumonia; she told him sadly of her father's death.

One day, when he and Cleo had dismounted to walk along a river, Jim got up the nerve to confess his love for Cleo. She surprised him by saying that she loved him too. Two weeks later, their love for each other led to its natural conclusion.

There was only one cloud in their blissful happiness: Cleo's mother, Maggie Rand. She had come looking for Cleo one day and had found her in Jim's arms. He had flinched at the hatred in the woman's voice when she hissed, "Don't ever come near my daughter again, you half-breed." She had marched her sobbing daughter out of the livery. Watching them disappear down the street, Jim had felt as if the life was draining out of him.

He gave a bitter laugh and walked back into the livery to unsaddle the mounts he and Cleo had just ridden. "Damn-fool breed," he swore under his breath. "What in the hell ever gave you the idea that a girl like Cleo was for the likes of you?"

The next evening, however, when he had finished work and was halfheartedly dressing to go meet the gang, he found a note pinned on the inside of his jacket lapel. It read, "Meet me back of the stables around midnight."

Their courtship had continued in this fashion for a month. Then, one night, Cleo had whispered to Jim that she was going to have his baby. He received the news with mixed emotions. He was happy beyond belief, for now stern Maggie Rand would have to let them get married. But, he asked himself, how was a penniless half-breed going to support a wife and child? He couldn't expect a wife to sleep on a pile of hay, and how was he going to feed her? He could barely feed himself.

That night, after Cleo left him, he lay on his pallet of hay, his mind racing as he considered ways he could support a wife and family. The image of a small, deserted farm a short distance from the village where he had grown up kept returning to him. The buildings were sturdy and the soil rich. It would be perfect for him and Cleo.

A sigh escaped Jim, and the hay rustled as he rolled over on his side and stared blindly out the small loft window. How could he come by the farming implements he'd need, plus a few pieces of furniture and some livestock? And they would have to have enough money to get by on until he could raise a garden and put in some crops that would provide him with money.

In bleak despair, he asked himself how a half-breed was going to get his hands on that kind of money. Then, out of the night, the answer came to him.

For over an hour Jim lay in the darkness, his mind in a turmoil. One part of his brain cautioned, *You're a fool; it will never work,* while the other part urged, *It's the only solution.*

Before he finally fell asleep he'd reached a firm decision. He and his men would rob the bank at the edge of this sleepy little town. He would talk to them about it tomorrow night when they met at the post.

The next night, when Jim laid his proposal before the men, only Rooster hadn't liked the idea of turning bank robber. "If we're recognized, we'll be on the run for the rest of our lives. There will be posters with our faces on them hanging in every town we ride into. There ain't a bit of fun in dodgin' the law."

"Ain't nobody gonna recognize us," Dick Harlan said. "We'll have our handkerchiefs over our faces, fool." He looked at Rooster through narrowed lids. "Well, are you with us or not?"

21

Staring down into his glass of whiskey, Rooster said after a pause, "I reckon. But I feel uneasy about it."

Rooster's worries were brushed aside. Putting their heads together, the five younger men enthusiastically made their plans.

They would hit the bank as soon as it opened, before people started coming in. Ed would stay with the horses, watching the single street, ready to give a whistle should the sheriff appear.

A week later, as they prepared to execute the robbery, Jim gave a last order before riding into town. "There will be no shooting from any of us should anything go wrong. Empty your guns right now."

There was grumbling from some of the men, especially Dick Harlan. "By God," he complained, "if anyone shoots at me, I want to be able to shoot back."

"And that's exactly why I don't want bullets in your side arms." Jim gave him a hard look. "It's one thing to be wanted for bank robbery, but quite a different matter to have a charge of murder hanging over your head. We would be hunted to the ends of the earth and hanged on the spot if we killed someone."

The holdup was a fiasco from the time they entered the bank. Harlan's nervousness was in his voice when he croaked, "This is a stickup! Put your hands in the air!"

The two crusty old tellers had only gaped at him over the rims of their glasses, making no effort to obey his command. Harlan waved his empty gun then, yelling, "You heard me; grab the sky!"

He took a step back in confusion then, for one of the old men was yelling back, "You'd better get the hell out of here, Dick Harlan, and the next time you try a crazy stunt like this, be damn sure you cover that red hair of yours."

As one, they had panicked and bolted for the door. When they ran out onto the street the elderly men were hard on their heels, shouting at the top of their lungs, "Bank robbery! Get the sheriff!" As Jim and the other four piled onto their horses, men came pouring into the street. As they raced out of town, a posse was only minutes behind them, led by the sheriff.

By hard riding, they managed to elude the law, and a week later they crossed the border into Mexico. They came across an old, deserted, three-walled shack, thrown together with odds and ends of wood and tin sheets, and moved in. The question now was, how were they to support themselves?

Harlan came up with the answer. They would cross the Rio and rustle a few head of cattle from the big ranches on the American side. It would be a simple matter to drive them across the river into Mexico, where there would be a ready market for good beef.

The men were quite satisfied with their setup. There was money for tequila, and to hire the services of the *putas* in the cantina just a mile away. Jim never went with the men into the small village. He was saving his share of the money from the rustled herds. Cleo was on his mind all the time. Besides missing her so, he worried about

23

her, and the shame she must bear alone.

After two months of fretting about Cleo, Jim decided he would return to Illinois, slip into her small town, and bring her back to Mexico with him. Property was dirt cheap here, and he had enough money cached away in his saddlebags to buy a nice little farm.

One night, when the men were out, he packed his gear on the stallion, left a note saying he'd return in a couple of weeks, and crossed the Rio, headed for Illinois.

As soon as he crossed the boundary of that state, his high hopes began to fall. Everywhere he went he saw wanted posters with his and his men's pictures on them. Beneath their names was a $500 reward for information of those above.

His shoulders sagged in defeat. He didn't dare enter Cleo's town. He would be slapped into jail before he even got to her house. A week later he was back in Mexico.

For the next five years he and his men remained in the village that was so small it didn't even have a name. But he never ceased thinking about Cleo. He wondered about his child, growing up without a father. And did he have a son, or had Cleo given birth to a little girl?

And all the time knowing he didn't dare go back and find out.

Finally, nearing the end of their fifth year apart, Jim could stand it no longer. He had to know the answers to all the questions that hammered at his brain when he lay sleepless at night.

One day, as he and the others sat in a cantina, he announced that he was returning to Illinois, that he had to find and marry the mother of his child.

"You're crazy, man!" Harlan exploded, removing his hand from under the skirt of a Mexican whore and dumping her off his lap. "We'll be arrested as soon as we ride into that flea-bitten town."

"I don't think so." Jim made wet circles on the table with his glass of tequila. Then he looked up at Harlan. "There's no proof of who tried to hold up that bank . . . except for you and that red hair."

"He's right, Dick," Rooster said, siding with Jim. "And to tell you the truth, I'm tired of this country: the heat, the sand, the rattlesnakes. I'm ready to go back to my own country, to see tall trees, green grass, and eat American food again. My stomach is about ruined from the spicy food it has had to tolerate all these years."

Within the hour, the six of them had crossed the Rio for the last time and were pounding across the country, headed for Illinois. Six days later, when they cautiously entered the small town they had run from, Jim found it little changed. With one exception.

The dirt-poor farm where Cleo had grown up was no longer owned by Maggie Rand. The new owner said that he had no idea where Mrs. Rand and her daughter had gone. The sun had gone down and a fine drizzle was falling when Jim stopped asking the townspeople about Maggie Rand's whereabouts only to receive negative shakes of the head. He was probably only a shadow in Cleo's mind by now anyway, he told himself, heading the stallion down the street to the livery stables he had called home for a short time. The stallion needed a good rest and a generous supper of oats, for tomorrow he planned on leaving this desolate little farming region and pushing on west. If he worked on it, in time he could put Cleo Rand out of his mind.

The old man who had taken pity on the down-and-out breed was happy to see him, and that fact spread a warm glow over Jim. It was a good feeling to be liked and respected. He asked after the old man's health, and his granddaughter Alice.

"As you can see, I'm pretty crippled up with rheumatiz, and Alice run off with a gambler who passed through town. Ain't heard from her in a couple of years."

It was while Jim was unsaddling the stallion that the old man asked, "Did you and the pretty little Rand girl ever come across each other in your travels?"

"No, I've been in Mexico," Jim answered, dragging the saddle off his mount's back. "I was hoping to see her here, but it looks like she and her mother have moved."

"Yeah, they moved to Abilene, Kansas."

Jim dropped the saddle and stared at his ex-employer in stunned disbelief. "I've asked half the people in this town where the Rands have gone and only you seem to know. How come?"

"I just happened to be down at the depot when Maggie asked for a ticket to Abilene. The train chugged in a short time later, and Maggie and the girl boarded it. I never mentioned it to anyone. I figured if Maggie wanted people to know where she was off to, she'd have told them."

Jim gave the old man such a hearty slap on the back, he staggered a bit. "I'll be back for the stallion early tomorrow morning," he said, and started to leave. At the big double doors he paused and turned around. "On second thought, if you don't mind, I'll just spend the night here." His lips twisted in a wry grin. "I don't expect I'll be welcome at the boardinghouse any better now than I was five years ago."

The old man nodded. "Sad to say, that is true."

Jim went looking for his men and found them at the little fur post where they used to raise hell before running afoul of the law. They greeted his news that they would be leaving for Kansas the next morning with loud enthusiasm.

"That city is wild and wide open," Harlan informed his companions, "and they have more whorehouses than any other place in the west, I've been told."

Three days later they rode into Abiline. It was pretty much as Harlan had described it. It was wild, and overrun with houses of ill repute. After the other men entered the first one they came to, Jim walked around the bustling city, wondering how in the world he would ever find Cleo among so many people.

After a week of fruitless searching, covering the entire city, hoping by some miracle he'd run into Cleo, Jim was reluctantly coming to the conclusion that he'd never see her again. She and her mother might not even be living in Abiline. Maggie might have bought a small farm somewhere out in the countryside. Or they might have moved on to somewhere else.

Then, one day, while idling the time away in front of a saloon, his chair tilted back against the wall, a tall, gray-haired woman stepped out from a grocer's across the street.

"Maggie Rand, by hell," he whispered, the chair coming down on all four legs as he left it.

Making sure she didn't see him, Jim followed his old enemy for two blocks before she turned up the boardwalk of a large, unpainted, weather-beaten house. He stopped and stared incredulously at the sign nailed over the door. Printed in large red letters, it read NELLIE'S PLEASURE HOUSE.

What in the hell was prim and proper Maggie Rand doing in a whorehouse? Certainly *she* wasn't entertaining men.

A thought struck him that froze his blood. Was it possible that Cleo was working in that capacity? He shook his head. Even in the unlikely event she would want to prostitute herself, Maggie would never allow it. Jim waited a moment, then followed Maggie as she walked to the rear of the building and unlocked a door there. Then she disappeared inside. He stood on the small stoop, giving her time to deposit her packages, then rapped on the door.

The woman who opened the door to him had aged beyond her years. It showed most in her eyes, pain-shadowed and careworn. She stared at him in stunned horror for a moment, and he feared she was about to faint, her face had turned so white. He automatically reached for her, to steady her as she teetered on her feet.

"You!" she cried, rearing back and stepping on the little child who clung to her skirt. The little one let out a protesting yell, drawing Jim's attention to it. His heart gave a leap as he looked into eyes the exact blue of his own.

"Mine!" he whispered.

When Maggie made no effort to invite him inside he pushed past her and walked into a large kitchen. "I've come for Cleo and my child," he said, coming straight to the point.

Maggie hurried after him, her eyes glittering with hate. "You're five years too late, Breed," she said, her voice trembling with passion. "They are both dead. You'll find their grave in the cemetery at the edge of town."

In all his twenty-eight years Jim LaTour had never felt such tearing pain as gripped him now. "No!" he denied, the blood draining from his face.

"Yes." Maggie watched his grief with grim satisfaction.

Jim sank into a chair, his legs too weak to hold him. The little boy escaped Maggie's hold and came to lean against his leg. He stroked the black curls off the fair forehead and asked gently, "What's your name, little fellow?"

"Jonty Rand." Eyes that could be his own gazed up at him.

Jim looked at Maggie with accusing eyes. "You lied to me, old woman. The child is very much alive." He stood up, swinging the boy into his arms. "I'm taking him and leaving now."

When he strode toward the door Maggie jumped in front of him. "Jonty isn't a boy," she cried. "She's a girl. You can't raise her among a gang of outlaws."

When he hadn't believed her she had, in desperation, stripped the clothes off the child to prove that she was, indeed, female. To his surprise, he had been elated that he had fathered a little girl. A daughter seemed more like a piece of Cleo.

Jim admitted to himself, however, that Maggie was right. An outlaw hideout was no place to take a little girl. He sat Jonty down and said quietly, "I'll leave her with you for the time being, but when she is older I'm taking her away from you."

He left the house where Maggie Rand lived as housekeeper for a madam and her girls, and made his way to the cemetery. As if Cleo was directing him, he walked straight to her grave under a tall, wide-spreading cottonwood. He knelt beside the well-tended mound, and tears he hadn't shed since he was Jonty's age slid down his cheeks as he promised the only woman he would ever love that he would look after their daughter.

Jim and his men hung around Abilene for a week, in which time, in the face of Maggie's disapproval, he visited Jonty every day. By the time he told her good-bye, promising he'd visit again before too long, a warm and affectionate bond existed between them. Jonty loved the man she called Uncle Jim.

The years passed, with Jim visiting Jonty periodically. He began putting aside money against the time he could become a respectable citizen and provide a home for his daughter. But when Maggie died shortly before Jonty's eighteenth birthday he hadn't enough money saved to see the realization of his dream.

He had reluctantly given in to Maggie's deathbed wish that Jonty become the ward of Cord McBain, a horse rancher.

Jonty had had a rocky time of it for a while with McBain; then the rancher had discovered her true sex and had fallen in love with her. In time they had married and become the parents of a little son named Cody. Jim had been on his way to visit them when he was shot by an old enemy and left for dead.

An eagle screamed overhead, jerking Jim back to the present, putting an end to his reminiscing. *I'm glad those days are behind me,* he thought. He had since become a respected citizen in Cottonwood, the owner of the biggest and fanciest saloon for miles around. Men tipped their hats to him on the street, and ladies smiled when he walked by. He wasn't conceited, but he knew that if he half tried he could coax the majority of the single women into his bed, and a good number of the married ones, as well.

But he never tried. The good women of Cottonwood would expect marriage, and that was one thing he would never enter into. It would be a slur to the memory of the one woman who had deserved to be married to him.

Jim had left behind the snowcapped mountains, and suddenly the sun was setting. In a still forest of lodgepole pine, he patted the stallion's neck and said, "Time for us to make camp, Major." When he heard the faint murmur of running water he turned the mount's head in that direction.

Coming upon the small stream, he swung stiffly to the ground with a wry grin. The past three months of idleness had put him out of shape. His bones felt much older than their forty-two years.

He untied his bedroll from behind the cantle of the saddle; then he took the package of grub Jonty had made up for him from the saddlebag. Next, he unrolled the blankets on the ground, dragged the saddle off the stallion, and placed it on the blankets for a pillow. A few minutes later he had a fire going and a pot of coffee brewing.

The beef sandwiches were tasty and filling. He sat in front of the fire, a trail of smoke rising from his cigarette as he sipped a cup of coffee and listened to the moan of the wind in the pines.

When the shadows merged into solid darkness he sought his bedroll, stretching out with a sigh of relief. In a matter of minutes he was sound asleep.

Chapter Two

The slender figure of a woman raced across the valley floor, the young boy with her easily keeping pace. They ran toward a thick stand of lodgepole pine, where they hoped to hide themselves from the man who relentlessly followed them on horseback. All this day and part of the previous one he had been behind them.

Sage Larkin ran not for herself. She knew that her brother-in-law, Leland Larkin, wouldn't harm her in a physical way. It was her nephew Danny who could be in danger from Leland. The youngster was a half-breed, and Leland hated Indians. She had to protect the boy. She was all he had left. His parents and her husband were dead, shot down the day before.

"But I can't think of that now," she whispered, racing on.

Her breath was coming in gasping pants, and there was a ripping pain in her side when finally Sage and the boy reached the trees. She

33

motioned Danny toward a large tree, and they leaned against its trunk, listening and regaining their breath.

Ten minutes or more passed with no sound except that of birds preparing to roost, and the scampering of little feet as small animals moved about among the pine needles.

Had Leland lost their tracks? God, she prayed that he had. She was about ready to fall on her face from exhaustion, and night was fast approaching.

Her eyes scanned the tall trunks of the pines. They must find a spot where they could spend another long, cold night. She shivered in her inadequate clothing as she and Danny fanned out in different directions, looking for shelter. The early spring evenings were still quite cold, and her teeth began to chatter. They had chattered throughout last night when she and Danny had clung to each other in the hollowed-out trunk of a dying tree. She had sneezed off and on all day, and had no doubt that she had caught cold.

Sage gave thanks that Danny was holding up so well as she scoured the area, looking for a windfall tree, or an outcropping of rocks; anything they could crawl under or curl up against.

She had just about given up hope of finding anything remotely resembling shelter when she cocked her head to listen to the call of a whip-poorwill. Only a keen ear would have noticed the difference between that of the real bird and that of a human.

She smiled tiredly. Danny was signaling that

he had found them a spot for the night.

The mournful cry came at short intervals, guiding Sage to her nephew. The sun was a great red ball shining through the pines when she came upon Danny, standing in the bottom of a deep, brush-filled gully. He climbed halfway up the scrub-covered bank and reached up a hand to help her down beside him.

"Over here," Danny said in low tones, and he led Sage to a deep depression in the bank, partially hidden by a jumble of large rocks that gully-washer rains had carried and dumped there over the years.

"This should do just fine," Danny said as Sage dropped to her hands and knees and crawled into the space. It was long enough for her to stretch out in and wide enough for both of them.

"For all your shivering, you feel awfully hot, Aunt Sage," Danny said, crawling in behind her and curling his young body around her back. "Are you feeling all right?"

"I'm fine, honey. Just tired."

Just tired didn't half describe how Sage really felt. Tired to the bone would be a more apt description, not to mention weary to her soul, and gut hungry.

Yesterday she and Danny had eaten a few dried berries that the birds had missed during the long winter, and they had been lucky enough to stumble across a couple of watering holes to quench their thirst. She knew the boy was hungry, too, probably more so than she. His young body was growing and needed an abundance of nourishment.

How was she to provide for this youngster she loved as though he were her own? she wondered wretchedly. She had lost her sense of direction and didn't know if they were headed toward civilization or running away from it. She only knew that this morning they had turned their backs to the rising sun, and now she hoped they had kept traveling westward and not in a circle. If that should be the case, they could very well fall into her brother-in-law's hands.

A shiver of dread ran through Sage's heated body. Leland Larkin wanted her for his wife, and only God knew what he had in mind for Danny. Her husband's brother, although a religous zealot, hated Indians with a fierceness that was a disease inside him. No one knew why. As far as anyone knew, he had never been harmed in any way by the red man.

But the deep hatred was there, glittering in his eyes every time he looked at Danny or the child's mother.

There crept into Sage's feverish mind the tragedy that she had tried so hard to block out. The death of her husband Arthur, her brother Kale, and his Indian wife Mary.

It had been a beautiful spring day the morning before, the air warm and the sun bright, when her menfolk and sister-in-law started making the garden whose produce the two families would share.

Her husband and her brother owned equal parts of the big farm, and they had built their cabins only yards apart from each other. She and Danny hadn't been needed for the preparation of the soil, so they had taken a basket and gone looking for greens in the meadow in back of the cabins. The basket had been half-filled with the tender growth of dandelions when three shots rang out from the direction of the homestead. Alarm had gripped Sage's body. Those had been shots from a handgun, and Arthur and Kale only owned rifles. Dropping the basket, she and Danny had started running toward the cabins. As they neared the top of the small incline that hid the buildings from them, caution made Sage drop to the ground, pulling Danny down with her. They crawled the rest of the way to the top of the rise and peered over it.

A choked cry of horror escaped them at what they saw below.

Her husband and Kale lay crumpled in the garden, with Mary lying a few feet from her cabin door. The awkward sprawl of her body, and the sight of her doeskin tunic ripped from neckline to hem told Sage that the gentle woman had been raped before a bullet ended her life.

Three men who had been out of her range of vision suddenly stepped into the horrible picture. Two walked toward Arthur and Kale, the third man moving to stand over Mary. She would never forget how the sun seemed to set his red hair on fire as he bent over and grabbed Mary by the feet and dragged her into the cabin. He had barely stepped back outside when his companions—one carrying Arthur over his shoulder, the smaller one bent over from Kale's weight—moved into the cabin. A moment later they, too, came back outside, empty-handed.

37

The three men stood talking for a moment; then the man with the red hair took a rag from his hip pocket, struck a match on the sole of his boot, and touched it to the cloth. When it caught fire he tossed it inside the cabin. In moments, before Sage's horrified eyes, the dry timber of the cabin burst into flames. She bit back the scream that tore at her throat and grabbed Danny, pressing his face against her shoulder, smothering his anguished cry. Those monsters must not know that their evil deed had been witnessed.

Leave now, leave; she tried to send the silent message to the three men. *Let me go to my husband and brother to see if there is a spark of life left in them, to drag them out of there.* She knew beyond a doubt that her sister-in-law was dead.

But the three men only climbed on their mounts and sat rolling cigarettes, smoking until the roof of the small building caved in. Only then did they ram spurs to their mounts and ride carelessly away, as though they hadn't just taken three lives.

As in a dream, she heard Danny sobbing, whimpering, "Mama, Papa." She pulled him into her arms and tried to comfort him as she wondered what she was to do. Were the men still hanging around, out of sight? Would they return to the scene of the crime?

Suddenly, Sage grew still. Hoofbeats again. Were the men coming back as she had expected? She whispered, "Shhh" to Danny and, lifting her head, peered down at the smoldering timbers of the cabin. Then she gave a glad cry. Her brother-in-law Leland was galloping up to the smoking ruins of the building.

How ironic, she thought hysterically, that he had never visited the farm before, and now here he came when Arthur was dead.

She started to stand up, to call out to her husband's brother; then a cautioning voice inside her told her to remain where she was. Something was wrong, it told her. Leland was too calm, sitting there, too quiet as he gazed at the smoking ruins that such a short time ago had been a happy home. Could it be he thought no one was inside the charred and smoking ruin?

Then, when Leland cupped his hands around his mouth and began to call her name, a suspicion grew inside her that he knew very well who had been in the cabin. Otherwise, why wouldn't he call his brother's name also?

Questions she didn't want to ask herself burned in Sage's brain. Did Leland really know which bodies lay in the ashes and glowing coals? Common sense told her that he would have had to have seen the men ride away, must have known they were the ones who had fired his brother's home. Why, then, hadn't he used his rifle on them? He was an expert shot, and could easily have shot all three.

Take the boy and hide, the voice inside her spoke again.

She acceded to the unseen advice and released Danny. Laying a finger on her lips for silence, she motioned him to follow her back down the slope. When they were safely out of Leland's sight, Danny turned a tearstained face to her.

"That's your brother-in-law calling you, Aunt Sage. Aren't you going to answer him?"

Sage shook her head. There was no time for explanations. She pointed to a tall pine a few yards away and said in a low voice, "We'll climb that tree and hide until he rides away."

As Sage and Danny crouched in the uppermost branches of the tree, watching Leland ride around calling Sage's name, she wondered if she and her nephew could slip past him and get to the safety of her in-laws' home, five miles away.

Then she gave up the thought. How could she tell those two dear people that she suspected that Leland had been the cause of his brother's death? Losing Arthur would be terrible as it was; to be told that their son had probably hired some men to kill him would be a blow from which they might never recover.

Finally Leland rode off in the same direction the three men had taken, and Sage and Danny climbed down to the ground and ran in the opposite direction.

It was around noon, and they had stopped to rest for a minute. Then Danny spotted Leland's big roan about half a mile from where they stood in the shadows of several tall, projecting rocks. Leland was bent forward in the saddle, studying the ground as he rode slowly along. Fear fluttered in Sage's breast. He had found their tracks and was following them. She grabbed Danny's hand, and they sprinted away.

It was due to Danny and his Indian mother's teaching that they finally lost Leland.

Making a game of it, Mary had taught her son how to move about in the forest and across valley floors without ever leaving a sign of his passing. Their progress was slowed considerably because Sage had to put her feet exactly where the youngster instructed her to.

Stepping upon rocks when possible, walking on fallen tree trunks, they carefully concealed their tracks all the way to a wide, shallow river. Twilight was approaching as they waded across the stream. Staggering from exhaustion, they had found the hollowed-out tree and crawled inside it.

Danny stirred in his sleep, a soft sob escaping him, bringing Sage back to the present. With a shuddering sigh, she tried to relax her body, to ignore the cold and to stop thinking of the past two days. It only made her headache worse.

But her brother-in-law's image persisted in her brain.

The Larkin and Willis children had grown up together, their parents being friends and neighbors. Sage's brother Kale had been quite a bit older than she, and hadn't taken part in the games she and Arthur Larkin had played. Nor had Leland. He was six years older than Arthur and thought it beneath him to play childish games.

And she and Arthur hadn't wanted his company. From an early age, Leland had become a very pious individual. His constant spouting of scripture and verse from the Bible was very boring to them, especially since half the time they hadn't understood what he was talking about.

But, when she was around fourteen, and her

body began to develop, it was no saintly look Leland turned on her when he thought no one was looking. She had caught him several times, and an uneasy shiver had gone down her spine. Her young mind had discerned that evil lived inside Leland, and she knew that she must never be caught alone with him.

Arthur, on the other hand, though a serious young man, was gentle and caring, only goodness looking out of his eyes. It had seemed natural that the friendship between them should turn into love as they grew older.

A coldness passed through Sage as she remembered the evening she and Arthur had told their parents they wanted to marry. Both sets of parents had been happy at their announcement, but not surprised.

Leland's reaction at the news, however, was very different. His face dark and furious, he had jumped to his feet and stamped out of the house. Embarrassed by her elder son's behavior, Mrs. Larkin had murmured that he was probably upset that he was losing a brother.

Sage, however, suspected that Leland had planned on having her for himself. She was sure of it later that night. After Arthur had walked her home Leland had picked a fight with him, beating him unmercifully. Arthur still bore bruises on his face three weeks later when they were joined in marriage.

She hadn't been surprised when Leland hadn't attended the wedding or the small reception.

Kindhearted Arthur had forgiven Leland's attack, and had tried to make his brother a part of their lives, but Leland never visited them in their little cabin, built close to Kale's. They saw him only at family gatherings, which Sage always dreaded.

Every time she happened to glance at Leland, his eyes, dark and brooding, had been on her. When he looked at Mary, though, pure hatred flared in his eyes. He was barely civil to the pretty young woman, and that was only because he feared Kale's temper and his fists. He completely ignored Danny.

"Mary is such a nice person, Leland!" Sage suddenly cried out as, in her fuzzy musings, the past became the present. She tossed and turned in her fever, crying out, "Starting today, you must treat her better."

It was near dawn when she began to whimper and call out to her mother as she relived a spring day five years before. A huge grizzly, just out of hibernation and mean and hungry, had come upon her mother, who was out looking for spring greens. Her terrified screams had brought her husband running to her aid with nothing but a large stick in his hands. In a matter of minutes both had been mauled to death.

It was but a short time later that Danny came awake at his aunt's restiveness and hoarse rambling. He wiped his wet eyes; he, too, had been dreaming, reliving the gunshots and his family lying dead on the ground, and the flames that had eaten his home.

He raised himself up and shook Sage's arm. "Wake up, Aunt Sage; you're having a bad dream."

When Sage made no answer he frowned and

placed a grubby hand on her forehead. "Oh, Aunt Sage," his young voice quivered, "you're burning up with fever." His troubled eyes lifted from the gully and looked at the surrounding trees, which were just coming into focus with the first dim rays of the rising sun. What was he going to do? he silently cried out. He must not lose his only remaining relative.

"If only I could make a fire," he whispered. He knew which barks to gather and from which to make a tea that would bring his aunt's fever down. But a fire might bring the man who trailed them, the man Aunt Sage feared.

The first gray light of dawn was hovering over the Indian village when one of its inhabitants jerked awake.

"What is it, Johnny?" the soft voice of a woman asked sleepily as she turned her naked body to lie close to him.

"I don't know, but I just had a dream that was so real, I feel compelled to go looking for two people who are in desperate need of help."

"But we are supposed to go to Cottonwood today. We are to visit your cousin LaTour, remember?" The wife pressed closer to her husband's body, as naked as her own, the mound at the apex of her thighs meshing with his pubic hair. "Did you not learn that he has returned to his saloon?"

"Yes, that is true." Johnny Lightfoot smiled in the semigloom of the teepee as he stroked the dark head nestled on his shoulder. Nemia wanted his strength inside her, but she would never voice her desire. It would be unseemly for a wife to do so. She would let her body tell him instead.

The soft body pressed closer to the tall Indian, and he felt his manhood thicken and rise. "We will go and visit Jim," he agreed and, nudging his wife over onto her back, he spread her legs and entered her. She smothered a squeal of pleasure against his shoulder as his thrusting pushed her body deeper into their pallet of furs.

Although there had been no foreplay before mating, Lightfoot did not seek his own release until his wife had received hers. Beside caring deeply for Nemia, he was wise enough to know that a contented wife would make her mate's life more comfortable. His meals would be tasty, his buckskins kept clean and mended.

When they both breathed evenly again, they rolled apart. "Make the breakfast maize; then we'll be off to see how Jim is faring," Lightfoot said, reaching for his buckskins.

Dawn broke and the trees in the forest were assuming form and definition as Lightfoot and Nemia rode their mounts at a leisurely pace through the woods. It promised to be a beautiful spring day, and they were in no hurry.

Their near somnolence was broken when the high treble of a youngster's cry for help rang out in the still morning air. They gave each other questioning looks. What child could be out here in the wild when the sun was barely rising?

Lightfoot urged his stallion to a faster pace, but then had to pull him up sharply to avoid trampling a young boy with a tearstained face;

a boy with Indian blood in him.

He slid to the ground and asked gently, "What is a young brave doing out so early, alone?"

"I'm not alone," the boy cried; then he jumped down into a gully. "My Aunt Sage is with me, and I'm afraid she's gravely ill."

Lightfoot motioned Nemia to remain mounted and followed the half-breed boy with the green eyes. He squatted down before the shallow depression and gently lifted the slender female body from it. One look at the fever-flushed face of the white woman told him that the boy was right. The woman was, indeed, gravely ill.

He looked up at the young, anxious face peering over his shoulder. "I'm afraid she has the white man's pneumonia," he said gently, whipping off his jacket and bundling Sage into it. "We must get her to a doctor as soon as possible."

"But is there one near?" Danny's eyes clouded with tears as Lightfoot stood up, Sage in his arms.

"There is one near," Nemia assured him kindly as she dismounted. "Come hold the stallion steady while I help my husband." Danny nodded, and watched as the woman held Sage while her husband climbed up on the snow-white horse. When he was settled firmly on the folded blanket that served as a saddle Nemia part lifted, part shoved·Sage's body into his arms. She looked at Danny then.

"Come on, little brave; you will ride with me."

Danny climbed onto the sturdy pony's back,

and Nemia swung up behind him. As the mounts moved out at a fast pace, she said soothingly, "This doctor we bring your aunt to is very good. Twice he saved the life of my husband's cousin."

"Oh, I pray he can. Aunt Sage is all I have left in the world." Danny's voice trembled.

"And why is that, little brave? Do you not have a mother, a father?"

The tears came then, and Danny sobbed out everything that had happened. "Your aunt is going to be all right." Nemia lifted him to sit sideways in the saddle; then she nestled his head against her shoulder. "Soon we will be in Cottonwood."

Lightfoot looked over his shoulder at Nemia and they exchanged a look of sympathy for the boy.

Jim lifted the stallion into a long, easy lope, relaxing and enjoying the ride. It felt good to sleep under the stars again, breathing the fresh, pine-scented air. He hadn't done that since his outlaw days.

He hadn't always enjoyed those nights of sleeping beside a campfire, he remembered now. Most of the time he had been on the run, ever afraid of a sheriff and his posse riding up on him.

Thank God those days are behind me, he thought, and he kicked Major into a gallop, anxious to get to Cottonwood and his saloon, Trail's End.

An hour later, he rode down Cottonwood's main street. The town was just stirring awake, and there were no more than half a dozen people walking about. He pulled up in front of his saloon and sat a moment, admiring the establishment.

The bat-wing doors were propped open, and through them he could see the chairs stacked on tables, out of the swamper's way as he mopped the floor. His gaze moved to his bartender, and he was pleased to see his friend. Jake worked behind the long bar, stocking the shelves on either side of a large mirror, getting ready for the customers who would begin drifting in before long. He could not see the felt-covered card tables. They were at the end of the long room, waiting to have their covers stripped off later in the day.

Jim gave a nod of satisfaction; then he lifted the reins and steered the stallion around to the back of the false-fronted building. He dismounted there, flipped the reins over a post, and walked over to look through the kitchen window. A smile of affection lit up his face.

His old friend and cook, Tillie, stood at her worktable, her gray-streaked head bent, intent on chopping up vegetables and tossing them into an iron pot. He almost licked his lips. Although Jonty had taught Tillie how to cook, the middle-aged ex-whore made an even better pot of soup than his daughter did.

He quietly opened the door, thinking that it had been a lucky day all around when Jonty took Tillie from the streets and made her a part of their lives. He and his daughter couldn't have a truer friend.

Jim slipped up behind the tall, rawboned

woman and slid his arms around her waist, giving her a hug that made the breath whoosh out of her lungs. She let out a yelp and reached for the lid-lifter on the stove. He narrowly missed being hit on the head with the curved piece of lead as Tillie swung her arm over her shoulder, striking out blindly at whoever had invaded her kitchen.

She recognized Jim's deep laugh then, and gasped, "Jim LaTour, I ought to brain you good. Scarin' the life out of me."

Jim released her and stepped back, a wide smile curving his lips. Tillie scanned his face, finding it still a little pale from his brush with death. "How are you feelin', Jim?" she asked quietly.

"I know I look like hell, Tillie, but actually I'm feeling quite fit. A few days in the sun and I'll recover my color and look my old handsome self again." He grinned at her.

"Well, your self-conceit is as hale and hearty as ever." Tillie grinned back.

She pulled away a chair from the table. "Sit down. I'll pour you a cup of coffee, then make you some breakfast." She hustled over to the big black range, taking a cup from a shelf on her way.

"How's Jonty and that scutter, Cody?" Tillie asked when she had poured the fragrant brew and placed it before Jim.

"Jonty has found true happiness at last, Tillie." Jim reached for the sugar bowl. "Cody is going to have a little brother or sister sometime this coming winter."

"Well, ain't that nice." Tillie beamed, placing

several strips of bacon in a skillet that was already warm on the stove. "I take it that rakehell husband of hers is treatin' her good."

"He couldn't treat her better." An amused grin glittered in Jim's eyes. "He jumps to do her every bidding."

"I like that," Tillie said; then she nodded her head as though putting a stamp on her remark. "Men should jump for women . . . instead of jumpin' *on* them half the time."

"Somehow I can't see a man jumping on you, Tillie," Jim half teased.

Tillie was quiet for a moment; then she said grimly, "I had a husband once who tried to brutalize me. I left the bastard after the first black eye he gave me."

It struck Jim that he knew very little about Tillie's past. She never spoke about it. Come to that, he rarely spoke about his own past. Only Tillie knew about Cleo and the way she had died.

Tillie placed his breakfast before him, interrupting his thoughts. Half an hour later, after consuming six strips of bacon, three eggs, and a mound of fried potatoes, Jim pushed away the empty plate and rubbed his stomach contentedly.

As Tillie poured him another cup of coffee, he asked, "How have things been going while I was away? Have the girls been behaving themselves when they come in the saloon?"

Tillie chuckled. "Jake's been keepin' them in line. If they start a ruckus of any kind he orders them to leave, warnin' them not to come back until they learn how to behave.

"That settles them right down. There's no excitement at the whorehouse, nothin' goin' on."

Jim grinned crookedly and lifted an eyebrow. "Nothing going on in a whorehouse, Tillie?"

"You know what I mean." Tillie swatted at him with her dishtowel. "There's no music or dancin' over there. Just bed work."

Jim took a swallow of coffee; then he asked, "What about Reba; is she still occupying the room upstairs?"

"I think so, but then I don't know what goes on upstairs once I've hit my cot over there." Tillie jerked a thumb at the narrow bed in the corner of the kitchen.

Jim glanced over at the spot where a heavy drape was half drawn, partially showing a neatly made up cot. "How come you haven't moved into Jonty's room right here off the kitchen? It has a nice big bed and everything to make you comfortable."

Tillie shrugged. "I like it here where I can keep an eye on things. Some of your customers ain't above sneakin' in here and helpin' themselves to a slice of beef or a bowl of soup."

"It's up to you, Tillie." Jim pushed back his chair and stood up. "I'm gonna go have a word with Jake, and then . . ."

Tillie laughed knowingly. "Then go see if Reba has been true to you."

"Something like that." Jim laughed, too, as he pushed open the door that separated the kitchen from the barroom. He paused for a moment to say, "Have that Mexican kid take care of Major when he gets here, will you?" Tillie nodded and he walked on through the door.

He was greeted with a face-splitting smile from his big, burly bartender. Jake asked after his health; and then they fell to discussing the saloon, Jake filling him in on what had gone on in his absence.

When Jim's eyes wandered to the stairs a couple of times, Jake grinned. "She's still sleepin' in the same room."

Jim arched an eyebrow at his friend and bartender. "Since when have you become a mind reader, Jake?"

"Weren't no trouble at all, readin' what's on your mind, mister," Jake called after the big man climbing the stairs to the rooms above.

Jim only chuckled in response as he walked past his office; and then he opened the door next to it.

Reba lay on her back, sleeping soundly, one bare shoulder and breast exposed to Jim's view. He had been without a woman for three months, and desire flared in his eyes as he remembered she always slept in the raw. It was a habit of which he heartily approved. There was never any fumbling with a restricting nightgown should he rouse in the night with a hot, fast need for her. Often those couplings weren't even remembered the next morning.

He quietly took off his boots; then he shed his clothing. He lifted the sheet and slid in beside Reba. She was still attractive in a brittle way, considering she was near his own age. He waited a moment; then he bent his head to take a brown nipple into his mouth.

The moment he drew on it, Reba came awake,

yelling, "Who in the hell are you? What do you think you're doin'? Get the hell out of my bed."

Despite all her yelling, Jim noted with no surprise that Reba made no effort to dislodge his working mouth. In fact the nipple had swollen with passion, and he knew that if he ran his hand down to the core of her he would find it moist.

He murmured silkily, "You don't mean that, Reba. You don't want me out of your bed."

"Jim!" Soft curves were thrown against the hard planes of his body. "It's about time you came home. I've missed you."

"I've missed you, too." Jim ran his palm down her soft side. "Should we show each other just how much?" he asked hoarsely, thrusting a hard arousal against her stomach.

Reba flipped back the sheet and looked at his hard, muscled body. Stroking him, she said, "I never cease to be amazed whenever I see you. No wonder the girls used to fight each other over who would sleep with you. You're magnificent. I adore you."

Jim slid his fingers under the hair at her nape and gently pressed. "Show me how much you adore me. I've missed your adoration."

Reba's lips dropped in a jealous pout. "I doubt that you've been true to me all these months. I'll bet there was some young Mexican girl on your daughter's ranch who adored you every night." Her fingers tightened fractionally before releasing him.

Jim came up on his elbows, frowning slightly. Reba was becoming possessive, and she knew better. He had made it plain from the beginning that there would be no strings attached to him.

"Look, Reba," he said coolly, "it's none of your affair if a dozen women slept with me. That was our understanding."

Jim's words and tone told Reba that she had been out of line to probe into his private life.

A mingling of bleakness and anger gripped her. When they had first started their relationship she had known that she meant nothing more to Jim than what she could give him in bed. But as the months had passed and he had continued to let her occupy the room next to his, she had begun to think, to hope, that he was beginning to care for her in ways that mattered.

She knew now that that wasn't the case. LaTour would be hers only as long as she could keep his interest, satisfy him better than any of her girls.

She brought a lightness to her tone that did not reach her heart as she laughingly said, "My, but we're impatient today, aren't we?"

Jim remained on his elbows, watching Reba take his throbbing manhood in both hands and sensually rub a thumb across its velvet-soft tip. He held his breath when she lowered her head and flicked her tongue up and down its length, leaving it wet and shiny. She smiled when he grew tired of her teasing and growled, "Get on with it, Reba."

Reba took special care to please him, knowing now that it was the only way she would keep him. Consequently, several minutes passed before she lifted her head and scooted up beside Jim.

She sighed expectantly as he swiftly entered her.

Reba's expectations were fully realized. An hour passed before Jim was sated and pulled himself free of her arms. He sat up, gave her an affectionate swat on her rump, and swung his feet to the floor. He picked his trousers off the floor, stuck his feet through the legs, and stood up, pulling them past his narrow hips.

Reba watched Jim button his fly, thinking that he still had the muscular body of a man half his age. And she knew from experience that no man in his twenties had any more stamina than Jim when it came to making love.

She stretched lazily and asked, "Are you comin' back later?"

"No; I'm sapped." Jim picked up his boots and the rest of his clothes. "I'm going to my room, wash up and change clothes, then spend the rest of the day looking over my account books, see how business has been while I've been away."

"I'm sure you'll find that Jake has kept the business goin' just fine." Reba scooted down in the bed, pulling the sheet up around her shoulders. "Them eagle eyes of his don't miss nothin'."

There was complaint in Reba's tone, and Jim's lips twisted into an amused grin. She and Jake didn't like each other. Evidently, the pair had locked horns again in his absence. He didn't have to ask who had been the winner. In

Jake's words, "He wouldn't take no sass from a female."

"Yeah, Jake's a good man." He ignored Reba's sour note and, opening the door, stepped out into the hall.

Jim had just finished sponging the cloying scent of Reba's perfume from his face and body when Tillie pounded on his door. There was panic in her voice as she called out, "Get downstairs quick, Jim! Johnny Lightfoot is in the kitchen with a dead woman in his arms."

"What the hell?" Jim swore under his breath, pulling on a clean pair of trousers and buttoning them as he ran down the stairs.

Chapter Three

Jim closed the kitchen door in the faces of the customers craning their necks, curious about all the commotion. He stood a moment, taking in the scene before him.

Tillie and Nemia stood, their faces anxious, on either side of his cousin, who indeed held a dead woman in his arms. And a more beautiful one than he had ever seen before, he thought, gazing down at perfectly shaped features and long, curly brown hair hanging over Johnny's arm in wild profusion. He wondered crazily what color her eyes were and knew a moment's sadness that he would never know.

But hold on a minute, he thought, his pulses beating a little faster; maybe the woman wasn't dead after all. Her face didn't have that grayish-white look the dead wore. Her skin had a pink flush to it, as though of fever. As he looked questioningly at his cousin, he wondered why he felt a wave of relief.

"She's very ill, Jim," Lightfoot said quietly. "I think she has pneumonia."

Jim didn't stop to ask his cousin how he happened to have a half-dead woman in his possession as he flung open the door to Jonty's old room. He would learn about that later. The important thing now was to see what could be done for her.

He strode across the room and swept back the covers on the wide bed. "Lay her down, Johnny," he ordered briskly; then he turned to Tillie, who had followed them inside. "Go fetch John."

Jim stepped back then, to get out of Lightfoot's way, and almost stepped on a small figure peering anxiously around him. He looked down at the small boy and gave a start of surprise at the youngster's dusky skin and high cheekbones. The lad was a half-breed like himself.

An unreasoning anger gripped him. The lovely woman Johnny was carefully placing on the bed had belonged to an Indian, most likely a chief. Had he treated her cruelly? Had she taken her child and fled from him?

But why had she waited so long to escape? The boy must be at least eight years old. Jim cut off his thoughts when hazel-green eyes were lifted to him, eyes that were full of fear. But not for himself, Jim knew. The boy feared for the woman lying like death on the bed.

He laid a hand on the narrow shoulders and said gently, "Your mother will be all right, son. Tillie has gone for my friend, Dr. Stewart. He will know what to do for her."

"Oh, I pray that he does," the youngster's voice quivered. "I mustn't lose Auntie Sage too."

His aunt! Jim felt his heart pick up its beat. He steered the boy into the kitchen and led him over to the stove. Pulling a chair up close to it, he said, "Sit here where it's warm and tell me your aunt's name, where you're from, and how she became so sick."

Danny rubbed his wet eyes, then said, "Her name is Sage Larkin, and we come from a long way away." Tears welled up in his eyes again. "Three men killed her husband, Uncle Arthur, and my father and mother." With a strangled sob, he added, "Then they burned our cabin. Me and Auntie hid until they rode away; then we struck out running. I guess she got sick from sleeping on the ground . . . and we didn't have much to eat." His eyes fastened on the pot steaming on the stove.

Jim stood up. The little fellow looked half starved. They could talk more later. He took a bowl from a cupboard, filled it with the beef and vegetables simmering on the stove, and placed it before Danny.

"Eat up, kid. Tillie makes the best soup in the territory."

"Aunt Sage is hungry too." Solemn eyes looked up at Jim. "She gave me most of the berries we found. She said she wasn't hungry, but I knew she was."

"Don't worry about your aunt. We'll feed her as soon as the doctor looks her over," Jim assured his little guest as he cut a thick slice of bread off a loaf Tillie had baked that morning. Then, placing a spoon next to the bowl, he asked, "What's your name, son?"

"Danny Willis." The answer came through a

mouthful of soup. Jim grinned ruefully. He would ask no more questions until the small stomach was filled.

The soup bowl was half empty when the kitchen door opened and Tillie entered the kitchen, Dr. John Stewart behind her. "Got a sick woman on your hands, Jim?" the doctor said by way of greeting.

"She sure looks like it, John." Jim straightened up from his lounging stance against the table.

"Don't stand there jawin'." Tillie pushed the attractive doctor toward the room off the kitchen. "The woman needs you bad."

Jim's lips curved humorously. It appeared Tillie had found herself another helpless lamb on whom to lavish her care. "Help yourself to another bowl of soup if you want it, Danny Willis," he said over his shoulder, following Tillie and the doctor into the next room.

"She sure is a beauty." Dr. Stewart glanced at Sage's flushed face as he sat down on the edge of the bed and took a stethoscope from the little black bag that always accompanied him, no matter where he went.

Jim felt shame that he envied the doctor his right to undo the woman's bodice. An unconscious woman's flesh wasn't supposed to arouse a man.

But this one, he thought, could arouse a wooden Indian, no matter how sick she was.

The four people hovering around the doctor and the woman held their breath as Dr. Stewart listened to her chest and then her lungs. After several minutes he removed the stethoscope from his ears and looked up at Jim.

"She has pneumonia. Both lungs are very congested. We have a fight on our hands if we are to save her."

Jim saw the grim seriousness on Dr. Stewart's face and was alarmed. He didn't know why, but it was very important to him that this woman live. "How can we help, John?" he asked quietly.

The doctor picked up Sage's limp, fine-boned wrist and frowned at her racing pulse. "To begin with, her fever must be brought down as quickly as possible." He looked across the bed at Tillie and Nemia, standing side by side. "I'll leave it up to you two to sponge her body with cold water until the fever breaks."

Tillie nodded and headed toward the door. "I'll get a basin of water right now."

Unaware that he was going to do so, Jim stepped in front of Tillie. "You've got work to do," he said gruffly, "and Nemia is tired from her long ride. I'll work at getting the woman's fever down."

When Nemia opened her mouth to say that she wasn't in the least tired Lightfoot's black eyes issued her a warning not to speak.

No warning, however, would have kept Tillie quiet. "Jim!" she cried in disbelief, "you can't bathe her."

"Why not?" Jim shot back just as forcefully. "It's not like I've never seen a woman's naked body before. I don't expect she's got anything different from other females."

"It just ain't decent. She ain't one of your whores, Jim LaTour, who don't give a damn

61

what man sees them naked," Tillie argued as Jim ushered her toward the door. "This young woman will be mortified if she learns that a strange man had his hands on her naked body . . . looked at it."

"I'm not a strange man, and who's going to tell her, old woman? You just have that kid, Juan, bring me some water, and keep it coming as long as I need it."

"You're the devil's own son, Jim LaTour." Tillie jerked free of his hand and glared at him before marching out of the room, her chin held high.

With a slight twist of his lips, Lightfoot took Nemia's arm and followed the irate cook.

Jim closed the door behind them and rejoined the doctor, who had taken two small bottles from his bag and placed them on the bedside table. Adding a medicine spoon, he said, "It is a little unorthodox, you bathing my patient; a male and a stranger to her."

"Maybe." Jim looked unconcerned. "But I've had lots of experience in dealing with fevers. In my days of running from the law I was always having to doctor one of my men who had been shot."

He gave John a bantering grin. "Her naked body will mean no more to me than theirs did."

"Bull," John said as he uncorked the two bottles. He let the subject drop as he lifted Sage's head and deftly slipped the spoon between her lips. "That one," he explained of the smallest bottle, "is to help bring down her fever; a spoonful every hour, straight through the night.

"And this one"—he filled the spoon from the larger bottle—"is to break up the congestion in her lungs. Give her two spoonfuls every three hours, also around the clock."

The doctor returned the stethoscope to the bag. "That's about all I can do, Jim. Let's hope she has a strong constitution and can fight her way through this. A healthy body is as important as medicine in curing an illness sometimes . . . that and a strong will to live."

Walking toward the door, Dr. Stewart added, "I'll stop by after my office hours to see how she's doing." Before he stepped through the door, he stepped aside to make room for Juan to enter the room, a basin of water in his hands.

"Thank you, Juan." Jim began rolling up his sleeves as the basin was carefully placed beside the two bottles. "Bring me a pitcher of water and a glass; then hang around the kitchen so you'll hear me when I call for fresh water."

The teenager nodded, and after a quick glance at the woman, who looked near death, he followed the doctor into the kitchen.

Left alone with the gravely ill woman, Jim felt an uneasiness creeping in on him as he listened to her shallow breathing. "Are you basically healthy, pretty woman?" He gazed down at her. "In your feverish mind do you know that there's a youngster who needs you, that you must fight to strengthen that thin thread that is keeping you alive?"

With a determination that she would live, that he would break her fever, Jim took the doctor's place at the edge of the bed and began to undress the woman who had stirred an unwanted interest in him.

The pile of clothes on the floor grew as dress, petticoat, camisole, and narrow-legged bloomers were removed from Sage's body and tossed aside. Finally, only the soft slippers on the narrow feet remained to be slipped off. When they rested on top of the other clothing, Jim, unable to resist, let his gaze roam over the most perfectly shaped woman he'd ever looked upon.

His firm intention to look upon the fever-racked body only in a purely clinical way deserted Jim as his eyes ranged up the long, slender legs, the softly rounded hips, and the curly mound at the apex of her thighs. His eyes lingered there a moment, then moved on up, past the narrow waist to the firm, jutting breasts with their rosy peaks.

Lord above, he thought, there's not a man alive who wouldn't be stirred by this loveliness.

With an unconscious prayer and an order to his loins to settle down, Jim dipped his hands into the basin of water and wrung out the cloth he found there. He gently passed it over her face and throat; then, dipping the cloth into the water again, he bathed her right arm and shoulder.

It was while he was sponging her left arm that Jim saw the wide, gold wedding band on her finger. His hand grew still as he stared at it, a sinking sensation in the pit of his stomach.

Jim finished bathing the arm and shoulder, wondering where she had been running.

What business is it of yours, half-breed? Jim derided himself. *Whatever her circumstances,*

she wouldn't be interested in you. Even uncon-
scious every line speaks that she's a lady, some-
thing you know nothing about.

Jim had gone once over the raging-hot body
and the water in the basin was growing warm
when, unbidden, Juan entered the room with
a fresh pan of water. Jim frowned and yanked
the sheet over Sage's body, hiding her helpless
nakedness from the boy's eyes.

"Don't stand there gawking, *hombre*," he said
gruffly. "Switch the basins and don't come in
here again until I call you."

Tillie's helper jumped to do as he was ordered,
studiously keeping his eyes from the bed. When
he departed Jim flipped back the sheet and
took up trying to sponge the heat from the
inert body.

"I will not look at her with lust," he kept
repeating to himself, and slowly that determination became fact. He was too concerned with
trying to break the fever that was consuming his
patient.

The hours dragged by, with Juan bringing in
innumerable basins of cold water. Her fever
ran so high, the cloth he used on her body
turned the water warm within minutes. Dusk
arrived, and he had given Sage her second dose
of medicine when Tillie entered the room. She
lit the lamp, moving it from the crowded table
to the dresser.

"Go eat your supper, Jim." She walked over
to stand at the foot of the bed. "I'll take over
for a while."

Jim shook his head. He had the overpowering
feeling that this woman's life force was linked

somehow with his own, and that if he left her side it would be severed and when he returned she'd be lying still in death. "I'm not hungry, Tillie, but I'd appreciate a cup of coffee."

Tillie opened her mouth to insist that he eat, then closed it, noting the stubborn lines of his lips. To argue with Jim LaTour once he had made up his mind about something would be like debating Devil Mountain.

She gave one last look at the restless, tossing body on the bed, and said, "I'll send the kid in with the coffee. If you should need me, you know where I am." Jim nodded, and she quietly left the room, trying to remember if she had ever seen this man so concerned about anyone before . . . maybe when Cord McBain got Jonty with child without the benefit of marriage. He had been like a madman then.

Twilight came and passed and the night wore on, the sound of revelry and a heavily thumped piano drifting into the room. An occasional burst of raucous laughter was heard when the door to the barroom was opened by Juan, bringing a sandwich to a customer. Tillie had gone to bed hours ago.

Johnny Lightfoot had knocked on the door earlier in the evening, inquiring how the woman fared. The doctor had stopped in shortly after Tillie had lit the lamp. He had listened again to Sage's lungs and chest, and checked her pulse.

"I don't know, Jim," he had said softly. "She doesn't seem to be responding to the medication. The crisis will come toward morning. We'll know then whether she will live or die."

His voice a feral snarl, Jim grated out, "Don't say die, John. Don't even think it."

It was an hour to midnight when Reba stalked into the room without knocking, her eyes snapping angrily. A dark frown on his face, Jim flipped the sheet up over Sage; then he turned a hard look on the whore. "What do you want, Reba?" he asked sharply.

"Are you goin' to sit here all night?" Reba asked, half whining, half belligerent. "Why ain't Tillie or the squaw takin' care of her?" She gazed down at Sage, her eyes narrowing at the lovely features and rich brown hair spread over the pillow.

There was a chilly glint in the eyes Jim turned to the madam. "Not that it's any of your business, Reba, but Tillie and Nemia aren't here because I don't want them here. Tillie has worked hard all day, and as for Nemia, the woman might become frightened if she should awaken and find an Indian sitting beside her."

"Hah," Reba snorted. "I doubt that she's afraid of Indians. What about that little half-breed asleep in my bed? I'd say . . ."

Her heated words stopped in midsentence at the glower that came over Jim's face. She had forgotten that Indian blood pumped through his veins, too, and the way she had said *half-breed* had hardly been complimentary. She stood a minute, waiting for Jim to speak, but when he ignored her she left the room.

Jim forgot the miffed whore the moment the door closed behind her, and resumed his ministering to Sage. Her soft lips had become dry and cracked, and her raspy breathing filled the room. Again he spooned the clear liquid medicine into her mouth.

At half-hour intervals, between sponging her body, he raised Sage's head and held a glass of water to her lips. Sometimes she drank; other times his offering ran down her chin and from the corners of her lips.

The night wore on, and the high fever persisted in spite of Jim's frantic bathing, and her breathing remained shallow. Sometimes he was afraid that death crouched in the room, waiting to spring. Then her breasts would slowly rise once again and he would let out the breath he had been holding.

Jim's eyes became red-rimmed and his fingers wrinkled from their constant immersion in water. He started to lean back to rest his back a moment; then, his pulse leaping, he leaned forward and peered at Sage in the dim kerosene light. He had caught the sheen of sweat on her pale brow.

The relief that shot through him left his body as weak as a baby's. He wanted to run out into the street and shout, "Hey, everyone, her fever has broken; she will live!"

Jim continued to sit with Sage, watching her breath come easy in a natural sleep. He had changed the sweat-wet bedclothes and put her into one of Jonty's gowns she had left behind. He had even brushed her hair a little, and now it fanned out over the pillow in brown silken waves and curls. He still didn't know the color of her eyes, and as he sat in the chair he had occupied all night, he made guesses at what they were.

The sun rose and shone through the window, making the lamplight unnecessary. He rose wearily and, cupping his hand around the glass chimney, blew out the flame. He moved stiffly as he left the room to tell Tillie she could take over now.

His cook looked up from the stove when he entered the kitchen, a silent question in her eyes. "I think she's going to be all right, Tillie," Jim said with a tired smile. "At least her fever has broken, and she's breathing more easily now."

"I prayed for her last night." Tillie ducked her head shyly. "I guess God listens to old worn-out whores too."

Jim's eyes smiled tiredly. "I guess he listens to ex-outlaws also." He sat down at the table, saying, "I'll have something to eat now; then I'm going to sleep the clock around."

"What are you goin' to do with her, Jim? Her and the boy?" Tillie asked as she bustled around the stove, preparing him pork chops and eggs.

Jim didn't answer right away. What would happen to the woman once she had recovered her health? Had she a destination in mind when she fled whoever it was she had run from, or had she just run, not knowing or caring where she went?

He shook his head. "It's not up to me to do anything with her, Tillie. There's much to learn about Sage Larkin yet, and right now I'm too tired to think about it."

Tillie darted a sidewise glance at Jim and

thought, *regardless of what you may learn about her, Jim LaTour, I'd bet good money that some way or the other you'll manage to keep her with you. When a man works as hard as you did to pull a woman from the brink of death he's not likely to give her up if she can help it.*

With that thought in mind, Tillie put Jim's breakfast before him; then she went to sit with Sage. Twenty minutes later, his stomach replete, Jim left the table and walked through the empty saloon and up the stairs to the rooms above. He opened the door to the room where he had directed that Danny be put to bed, moving quietly so as not to awaken the boy, asleep in Reba's bed. He grinned ruefully to himself, wondering what that one had had to say about being banished back to the whorehouse.

The boy lay on his side, his knees pulled up, his grubby little hands folded beneath his chin. Jim looked at the tearstained face, and for the second time in less than twenty-four hours he knew a feeling of tenderness.

I wish you were mine, boy; the thought flickered through his mind, surprising him. He couldn't recall ever wishing that he had had a son. Jonty had always been enough for him. Was it because she belonged to another man now? he wondered. Was that why he suddenly had this desire to love something innocent and helpless, to have the youngster depend on him?

He rejected the notion that maybe he felt the same way about the woman.

"You're getting maudlin in your old age," he snorted under his breath as he tucked the covers around Danny's shoulders. Why in the hell would he want to saddle himself with a youngster at this late date in his life ... not to mention a woman who wouldn't want any part of a saloonkeeper.

Chapter Four

The cracked voice of an old woman and the deep, rich voice of a man pulled Sage back to the world she'd only been barely aware of for close to two days.

Her forehead creased in confused thought. The man sounded vaguely familiar, as though she had heard him once in a dream. She was sure, though, that she had never heard the old woman before. Sage frowned. If they had company, why was Arthur letting her sleep? And why did she feel so lethargic?

She turned her head toward the window through which the voices continued to drift. Her frown deepened as she gazed in puzzlement at the bright red curtains gently fluttering in a soft breeze. Her home had no curtains like those.

Sage gave a start, her eyes widening. Her bedroom didn't even have a window. Arthur had promised to put one in for her, but hadn't gotten around to it yet.

She grew more confused. Her bed had never felt this comfortable before. She recognized from her premarital days, when she had lived at home with her parents, that she lay on a feather mattress. Alarm washed over her. Where *was* Arthur?

In a blinding flash it all came back to her. Arthur was dead, and so was her brother Kale and her sister-in-law Mary. Again she saw their bodies sprawled on the ground. She saw the cabin set on fire and burned to the ground, those she loved inside it.

Tears washed down her cheeks. She hadn't had the time to grieve over her loss before; she had been too preoccupied with getting away from Leland.

As her tears continued to fall, Sage recalled everything that had happened up to that early evening when she and Danny had hidden themselves in a brush-filled gully for the night. She remembered being terribly cold, and then unbearably hot. After that everything was a blank.

Her eyes flew to the closed door. Had Leland found her and Danny? Were they his prisoners? Where was Danny? She tried to sit up. She must find the boy.

Her weakened body refused to do her bidding. Sweat beading her forehead, Sage sank back against the pillow, calling Danny's name as loudly as she could.

The voices outside ceased, and almost immediately the door opened. Sage stared at the tall, broad-shouldered man who walked toward the bed. In the back of her mind she noted the black hair with the shading of gray and the deep blue eyes, and thought that though his face had a weathered look, he was fiendishy handsome. Her heart skipped a beat when he sat down in the chair drawn up beside the bed.

"So, you've decided to come back to us." The firm lips beneath a thick mustache curved in a smile that showed strong white teeth.

"Who are you?" she rasped from a hoarse throat, jerking the sheet up to her chin.

Amusement flickered in Jim's eyes as he thought, *you're a little late in hiding anything from me, little lady. I've already seen every bit of your loveliness.*

He looked into the sage-green eyes—the same color as the boy's—and said quietly, "My name is Jim LaTour, and you're in a room in back of my saloon. Your nephew is upstairs still asleep."

Jim took a watch from his vest pocket, snapped it open, looked at the time, and then grinned. "He'll be down in about half an hour, looking for breakfast."

Relief flared in Sage's eyes. Danny was safe. "How did we get here?" she asked. "I don't remember arriving."

"That's not surprising." Jim repressed the desire to smooth back a curl lying on her forehead. "You were near death with pneumonia when my cousin, Johnny Lightfoot, came upon you and the boy. He and his wife brought the pair of you here."

Jim leaned forward and laid his palm on Sage's forehead, using the excuse of testing her for fever. "Do you feel like talking; add anything

75

to Danny's story? His was pretty sketchy."

Sage nodded, and as she described the men who had brought her world crashing down on her head, Jim's brow began to darken. When, with clenched fists, she described the leader and his red hair, Jim's lips firmed in grim lines.

He knew those three men. Ed, Tex, and Dick Harlan: all ex-members of the outlaw gang he had once led. They had given him more trouble than all the others put together. Especially Dick Harlan. He was a braggart with a reckless tongue that had brought the law onto their trail many times because of his loose talk with some whore or the other. Because of his ill treatment of the women they had gotten back at him by going to the town's marshal and turning them in.

Jim stared sightlessly at the highly polished boot on his left foot where it rested on his right knee. All three were capable of rape if they happened onto a lone Indian woman. But Sage's sister-in-law hadn't been out by herself, picking berries or digging roots. She had been with her white husband and her white brother-in-law.

He shook his head. Something didn't make sense. Any of the three men were too smart to risk the law by doing murder just to use an Indian woman . . . unless there was money involved. A good sum of money. If that were the case, there had to be a fourth man involved, a man who wanted the two men and the woman dead badly enough to pay for it.

He lifted his gaze to Sage. "In your delirium you kept calling out, 'Please, God, don't let him catch us.' Do you know who you were referring to?"

Sage lowered her eyes and picked nervously at the sheet still tucked under her chin. Jim LaTour suspected that another man was involved in the tragedy. Should she tell him about Leland, of her suspicions that her brother-in-law was somehow behind the killings? She would hate to accuse him if he was innocent.

Her misgivings about Leland wouldn't die. She looked up at Jim. "I imagine that Danny told you we ran from my brother-in-law, Leland Larkin. I don't like to think so, but past events keep niggling at my mind, making me wonder if he had something to do with the attack on my family."

"If it's not too personal, will you tell me what kind of events?"

Sage hesitated a moment; then she said, "Leland flew into a rage when I chose his brother over him. He beat Arthur almost senseless."

Jim gazed down at the lovely face, thinking that, yes, a man could have done murder to get a woman like this one. Keeping his thoughts to himself, he asked, "Do you think he's still looking for you?"

Was Leland still trying to find her? Sage wondered. She recalled the determination and underlying anger in his voice as he had called her name. Yes, she decided, Leland still pursued her. The dread of the day he might find her showed in her eyes as she answered, "He's a very stubborn man. I'm sure he's out there somewhere, still looking."

When she shivered at her words Jim patted her hand, lying outside the sheet. "Don't worry about him. You and the boy are safe here. You just concentrate on getting better. No harm will come to either one of you."

There was still doubt in Sage's eyes, and Jim knew that she wasn't fully convinced about her safety and was amused. She didn't know that Jim LaTour had once been an outlaw and that he still kept in touch with some of his old bunch; those who although riding on the thin edge of the law were still decent men and would come to his aid if he asked for their help. There were also his Indian relatives. Any one of them could slip up on a man and thrust a knife into his heart before he knew what they were about.

Jim kept this knowledge to himself. He felt sure that this girl, up until now, had always led a protected life and knew nothing of the harsher side of life, where men killed men without a second thought.

He stood up and, smiling down at her, asked, "Are you hungry?"

"I'm starving." She smiled back at him.

"Good. Tillie has made a big pot of soup, full of beef chunks and vegetables. I'll have her bring you a bowl of it."

"Thank you, Mr. LaTour, and my thanks are double that you have taken Danny and me in, helped me on the road to recovery."

There was a roughish glint in Jim's eyes as he made a little bow and said, "It was my pleasure, lady."

Sage frowned as Jim left the room, closing the door behind him. She hadn't liked his devilish grin, or the way he had said "pleasure." She had the feeling he was making an indirect reference to something that only he was privy to.

He's very handsome, she thought again, then wondered what she must look like. She tried to comb her fingers through her hair, but it was hopelessly tangled. She ran her tongue over her lips and found them dry and cracked. She wasn't ordinarily a vain person, but she found herself wanting to look her best for the attractive saloonkeeper. She imagined he could have his pick of the women in whatever town this was. Sage's thoughts were interrupted when the door opened again and a tall, angular woman with graying hair stepped into the room, balancing a tray on her hip as she closed the door behind her. The steam rising from the bowl placed in its center sent out a mouthwatering aroma.

A genial smile deepened the many wrinkles on the brown, weathered face. "Jim tells me you're hungry. That's a good sign you're gettin' better."

"You must be Tillie." Sage returned the smile as the tray was placed on the small table.

"That's me." Capable hands lifted her slightly and stacked two pillows against her back. "Jim said to make sure you eat all this."

Sage leaned back against the pillows, feeling drained from the slight exertion. "I feel so dreadfully weak. I must have been quite ill."

"You sure was." Tillie sat down in the chair and lifted the tray onto Sage's lap. "Jim stayed with you 'round the clock, he was that afraid you wasn't gonna make it."

"Mr. LaTour stayed with me?" Sage froze, the spoon halfway to her mouth. She vaguely remembered the cool feel of a wet cloth on her hot body and flushed face. Surely it hadn't been him bathing her. "I assumed it had been you tending me." She looked at Tillie hopefully.

Sage was sorry she'd asked as soon as the words were out of her mouth. She didn't want to know if the handsome man had been with her all that time. She'd never be able to look him in the face if she knew for sure.

But Tillie was saying, "I was too busy in the kitchen. I cook for Jim's customers . . . them that don't drink their suppers." She pointed to a thick slice of bread lying on the tray. "Break some of that sourdough up in the soup. I made it fresh this mornin'."

Tillie sat back in the chair. "I want you to know that when you needed personal help, or somethin' of that nature, Jim called me into the room and sat in the kitchen until I came back out. Jim is a real gentleman," she tacked on.

Relieved at that news, and not thinking to ask who had bathed her, Sage picked up the bread and crumbled it in the soup that was almost as thick as stew. She tried to eat in a ladylike manner, but found it impossible to do. Her stomach had been empty too long.

Tillie watched with a tickled grin as the meat and vegetables and bread rapidly disappeared into Sage's mouth. "Would you like some more?" she asked when the bowl was wiped clean with the last piece of bread.

"I would, but I'm afraid my stomach would burst if I took another bite." Sage laughed. "I've never tasted anything so good."

"Thank you, honey." Tillie beamed. "Jim's

daughter, Jonty, taught me how to make beef soup."

"Mr. LaTour is married?" Sage felt a surge of disappointment. It hadn't occurred to her that the very attractive man might have a wife.

Tillie shook her head. "He's not. Never has been. He loved Jonty's mother and would have married her in time. But the young woman died givin' birth to their baby girl." Tillie pensively gazed out the window. "I don't think Jim ever got over the guilt of not bein' there when Jonty's mother needed him. That happened nearly twenty years ago, and he's never been serious about another woman in all this time. I guess he's a one-woman man."

"Somehow I don't see him as a man who would avoid women." Sage thought out loud. "He has the look of a man who has known many."

"Oh, Jim has. He knows all there is about a woman," Tillie agreed. "But he never lets them get close to him, to know him. That's understandable, though. He never gets involved with a decent woman. He told me once them kind always mean trouble. If a man even so much as holds their hand, they expect him to marry them, he says, and he's not about to wear a dog collar around his neck, heelin' whenever he's told to."

Sage's throaty laughter floated in the room. "Where did he ever get an idea like that?"

"Who knows? He probably just dreamed it up . . . an excuse not to get married. I think he likes his freedom too much. He's forty-two years old and is used to comin' and goin' as he pleases, not havin' to answer to no one. A wife would change all that, and he knows it."

"He probably knows he wouldn't be faithful to a wife, either." Sage sniffed.

Tillie grinned. "I've thought that myself."

The topic of Jim LaTour and his lovelife was dropped when Danny stuck his head around the door. Both women smiled at him fondly when he crossed the floor and climbed up on the bed. Laying a small hand on Sage's brow, he smiled down at her.

"You feel nice and cool, Auntie. How are you feeling?"

Sage took his hand and held it against her cheek. "I feel fine, honey; just weak. How are you?" She looked searchingly into the eyes so like her own.

"Oh, you know. I'm okay." Danny shrugged his shoulders, his lower lip quivering a bit. But, manfully, he held back his tears, and looking at the empty bowl in the tray, turned the subject back to Sage's health. "Tillie will get you strong real quick with her cooking. She's real good."

"What have you been doing with yourself since we arrived here?" Sage smoothed the unbrushed hair off his forehead.

Excitement sparkled in Danny's eyes. "Johnny Lightfoot took me fishing yesterday afternoon, and today we're going hunting. He's making me a bow and arrow."

Anxiety appeared in Sage's eyes. "Danny, I don't think it's wise for you to leave the vicinity of Mr. LaTour's establishment."

"Won't nothin' happen to him if he's with the

Indian," Tillie spoke up. "And he's just as safe with Jim."

"I'd like to meet your friend Johnny Lightfoot, Danny." Sage's face relaxed. "I want to thank him for rescuing us and bringing us here."

"I already did. He just patted my head and said it was the will of the man who rules the Universe. I guess he was talking about God."

"I expect he was. Nevertheless, I'd like to thank him personally."

"He's not here right now. He took Nemia—that's his wife—to a store that sells beads. She wants some bright red ones. I'm supposed to meet him in an hour, right after I've had breakfast."

He looked at Tillie. "Did Jim eat breakfast yet?" When she nodded he looked anxious. "Did he leave anything for me?"

"Danny!" Sage exclaimed. "That's not very polite."

"I'm sorry, Tillie." Danny blushed. "But you know what a big eater Jim is."

"Yes, he is," Tillie agreed, "and I know someone else who can put the grub away." She reached out and gave his hair an affectionate tug. "Your breakfast is keepin' warm on the back of the stove. Go help yourself.

"He's a fine little fella," Tillie said when Danny closed the door behind him. "Jim and the Indian sure are taken with him."

"I think the feeling is mutual." A sadness came into Sage's eyes. "He and his father, my brother, were very close. Do you know if he's been grieving a lot?"

"Yes, he has; I'll not lie to you. That's why Jim

83

and Lightfoot have been keepin' him busy. Tirin' him out so he'll go right to sleep as soon as he hits the bed."

A tear slipped down Sage's cheek. "I can never thank you good people enough. I'm sure I would have died in that gully if Mr. Lightfoot hadn't come along. And God knows what would have happened to Danny then."

"Well, the Indian did come along, and Danny is fine, so think no more about it." There was a short silence, then Tillie asked, "What are your plans . . . when you've recovered your health and strength, that is?"

"I'm afraid I haven't given that much thought." Sage sighed. "I could never bring myself to go back to the homestead. I could never live with what happened there. And even if I wanted to, there's my brother-in-law to consider. Leland would never give me a moment's peace."

Tillie nodded. "Jim told me about him. A real mean one."

"I guess there's only one thing I can do: I must find a job and save enough money to get Danny and me out of the area. I suppose we should go to a big city. Leland wouldn't be so apt to find us among so many people."

Tillie made no response, but she didn't like the idea of this delicate woman trying to live in a city of thousands, trying to provide for herself and an eight-year-old child. The young widow had no idea what she'd come up against. She would be like a dove among a flock of hawks.

A woman like Sage Larkin needed a man's protection.

And what was more, Tillie added to herself, Jim wouldn't like the idea either. The big man might not know it yet, but lovely Sage had gotten under his skin. But she knew he would fight his feelings for this helpless and needing woman like a maddened buffalo. He had boasted so often that there wasn't a woman alive who could touch his heart.

Tillie leaned back in her chair, a gleeful look in her eyes. It would be mighty interesting to watch Jim LaTour fall.

"Do you think that's a good idea?" Sage interrupted Tillie's preoccupation, and she smiled at Sage.

"You've got plenty of time to think of your future. Time has a way of settlin' things for a body. In the meantime, you just concentrate on gettin' your strength back."

"That shouldn't take long with your fine cooking. I feel stronger already."

Tillie's still attractive face broke into a wide, pleased smile. "I can't hold a candle to Jonty. That girl can cook like an angel."

"I can tell you're awfully fond of her. What's she like?"

"Oh, she's just the sweetest thing ever was. She's awfully pretty. She has Jim's black hair and blue eyes. She's about your size." Laughing wryly, Tillie added, "She's made Jim a grandpa once, and is gonna do it again toward winter. He don't look much like a grandpa, does he?"

"Not in the least. How does he feel about being a grandparent?"

"He's pleased as can be. It don't bother him at all when little Cody calls him granddaddy."

"Most men, single and handsome as Mr. LaTour is, wouldn't care much for such a title," Sage said.

"That is true. A lot of men wouldn't. But Jim takes everything in stride. He's that sure of himself."

Unbidden, Arthur popped into Sage's mind. Poor fellow; he'd never had much confidence in himself. There had been times when she had lost patience with his dithering, afraid to make a decision about anything. And, unfortunately, he usually made the wrong one.

She sighed, feeling guilty now about the sharp words she had sometimes said to him, for he had been a kind and loving husband . . . a good man.

Tillie was speaking, and Sage pulled herself out of her gloomy thoughts. "I gotta get back to the kitchen. Can I get you anything before I go? Do you need the chamber pot?"

"No, but I would like the use of a brush, and a basin of water so I could wash my face."

"My goodness, I should have thought of that." Tillie looked at the dresser across from the bed. "Jonty left her comb and brush and hand mirror here when she moved to her husband's place. She left a lot of clothes too; things she couldn't wear around the ranch. You're welcome to use any, or all of them."

"I'm very grateful for the offer, Tillie. As you know, I have nothing but the clothes I arrived here with."

"No thanks needed, Sage. It'll be nice to see them worn again." Tillie stood up and brought Sage the brush and mirror. "I'll get you some warm water and soap now." She picked up the tray and went back to the kitchen.

Sage lifted the mirror and gasped at her reflection. "My God, I look like a dead woman," she muttered. "And this hair, it looks like the old mop I used to wipe the kitchen floor with." She pulled the brush through her hair so forcefully, tears sprang to her eyes.

When Tillie returned a short time later with soap and water Sage had most of the tangles out, but her strength was gone. She smiled weakly when Tillie exclaimed, "My, my, you have beautiful hair."

Sage smiled her thanks and began to soap the washcloth that had floated in the water. Maybe her hair looked all right, but her face was almost skeletal, all eyes. Certainly the handsome saloonkeeper wouldn't think her very attractive.

She impatiently dropped the cloth back into the basin. What kind of woman was she? Her husband dead only four days and here she was fretting that a stranger wouldn't find her attractive.

She wiped her face dry, determined that she would center all her thoughts on remembering Arthur. And she was successful until she fell asleep. Then, a man with a dark, handsome face and deep blue eyes crept into her dreams and stayed there, whispering naughty things as he made love to her.

Her body twisted and squirmed as, with that dream man, she experienced more passion than she'd ever known with her husband.

Norah Hess

When she awakened at a knock on the door she was still held in the aftermath of physical release. When Jim LaTour walked into the room the remnants of passion still slumbered in her heavy-lidded green eyes.

Chapter Five

When Jim walked over to the bed and gazed down at Sage he almost gasped aloud at the pain of his suddenly knotting loins. If he didn't know better, he'd think the lady had just finished making love.

Had she been dreaming of her husband? His eyes unconsciously narrowed. He didn't like that thought, and it irritated him that he would care one way or the other. Sage Larkin was just another woman; more beautiful than most, but nonetheless not anyone for a man to lose his head over.

Still, he couldn't ignore the fact that she made his pulses leap with an eagerness no woman had roused in him before. And that could get out of hand if he wasn't careful.

He drew a chair up to the bed and sat down. "I was beginning to get worried about you." His eyes moved over her delicate features and the wealth of golden brown hair fanned out on the pillow. He ignored the impulse to tangle his fingers in it as he said, "You've been asleep all afternoon."

All afternoon? Impossible. But she noted the burning lamp on the small table, and whipped her eyes to the window. Twilight was almost upon them. "I'll probably be awake all night now," she said crossly. She looked back at Jim. "I hate lying awake at night. Nothing pleasant ever comes to mind in the darkness."

Jim knew exactly what she was talking about. He had spent many such nights in his outlaw days, thinking of Cleo, missing her; then, later, grieving over her death. Later still, he had worried about Jonty. How soon would he have enough money to make a home for her? And then, how was she faring with the hard rancher?

His features tightened. If he wasn't careful, he'd be spending wakeful nights because of this one. His lips twisted wryly. But it wouldn't be his mind that kept him awake and on edge.

"Where is Danny?" Sage's question cut across Jim's thoughts. "I hope he hasn't been a bother to anyone."

"He's no trouble at all. Johnny took him hunting today." Jim grinned. "He's all full of himself tonight. He brought down a dove with the bow and arrow Johnny made for him."

Sage laughed. She could just see her young nephew strutting about, bragging about his first kill. "I wonder how many times I'll have to listen to how he stalked his prey and took careful aim; how the bird was almost as big as a turkey."

Jim laughed, too, liking the musical tone of her laughter.

On a more serious note, Sage said, "I'm still waiting to meet your cousin and his wife. I have so much to thank them for."

"I'll bring them in right after supper, but," Jim warned, "don't make a big fuss over your thanks. You'll embarrass Johnny; make him feel ill at ease."

"I understand. Danny's mother was like that too. So many times I wanted to thank her for something, to kiss and hug her, but she always shied away from too much affection." Sage sighed. "Mary was the best friend I ever had. I'll miss her the rest of my life."

"And your husband?" Jim watched her face closely. "You'd been dreaming of him when I came into the room, hadn't you?"

Sage's face blushed a fiery red. To her embarrassment, in her dream it had been this man who had held her in his arms and made passionate love to her. She felt his knowing eyes on her, waiting for an answer.

"I don't remember dreaming about anyone. What makes you think that I was?"

"Nothing really," Jim drawled, knowing damn well that she remembered her dream. He casually leaned forward and picked up the ends of the pink ribbon hanging from its bow beneath her chin. "It was just that when you opened your eyes you looked as if you'd been having a . . . pleasant dream." He gave the ribbon a gentle tug that undid the perky little bow without Sage being aware of it.

He was still slowly pulling the ribbon when

Sage said coolly, "Well, I don't remember it if I did."

Jim had managed to lay open one side of Sage's gown, revealing a good portion of a firm, ivory-colored breast and showing the hint of a pink nipple. "Yeah, we don't always remember our dreams." His voice was husky as he tried to draw his eyes away from the lovely mound, to keep his hand from stretching out and cupping it. He had meant only to tease her when he had first picked up the ribbon; then, when Sage hadn't noticed the game he was playing, he was helpless to stop. The desire to see her bare flesh again was too strong.

"I've been thinking..." Sage began; then her voice faltered to a halt when she became aware of Jim's staring eyes. *Oh, my God,* she thought in horror, grabbing the garment together, *my gown came open while I was asleep.*

Jim blinked, as though coming out of a daze when the fine muslin was gripped together with a small fist. He slowly lifted his eyes to Sage's red face.

"Don't be embarrassed," he said softly. "You have a beautiful body; nothing to be ashamed of."

Sage's eyes grew round. "You *did* bathe me when I was ill."

"Yes, I did." Jim moved her hand and retied the little bow. "You were burning up with fever and Tillie was busy in the kitchen, and too worn out at night to tend to you."

He gave her a teasing grin as he let his hand rest on her shoulder. "Would you have rather had me call in Jake, my bartender, to sponge you off?"

"Of course not." Sage jerked away from his hand. "But it's still embarrassing to know that a man—a stranger—has looked on my bare body."

Jim sat back in the chair, his eyes intent on Sage's face. "When you say 'man,' does that include your husband? Surely he has seen you without your clothes on."

Sage felt her face grow warmer, and for the first time she wondered if it was unusual for a man never to have seen his wife naked. This saloonkeeper seemed to think it was only natural that a husband should do so.

Avoiding Jim's eyes, she mumbled that of course her husband had seen her in that state.

Jim knew immediately that Sage was lying again. His eyes were the first to have looked upon her loveliness. He grew angry at himself for being pleased about that and abruptly changed the subject.

"I've been thinking about Danny and what you said about your brother-in-law. Johnny is going back to his village tomorrow, and that will mean I'll have to keep an eye on the youngster. I'm pretty much tied up with business during the day and he'd have to stay inside most of the time. That bothers me; a saloon is no place for a boy to hang around."

Jim paused and took a deep breath. He wasn't sure how Sage was going to take his suggestion. "What do you think of him going to my daughter and her husband until you're up and around? They have a big ranch only about two days' ride from here. Larkin would never find him there, and even if he did, my son-in-law would take care of him real quick."

Sage looked up at Jim with troubled eyes. "We are such a bother to you, Mr. LaTour. You're going to be sorry you ever took us in."

Jim stood up, thinking that she was probably right, but not for the reasons she supposed. Never before had he been so attracted to a woman, one who called out to all the protectiveness inside him. He was afraid she meant trouble, all right; trouble to his heart if he wasn't careful.

None of what he was thinking showed on his face when with a crooked grin he scolded, "Now how much trouble could one skinny woman and a tadpole boy cause me?"

"Don't joke about it," Sage said earnestly. "Leland could cause you a lot of trouble."

Jim looked into the fear-haunted green eyes. She didn't know that he had men posted around town already, on the lookout for a bearded man riding a roan. Nor did she know that he had put out the word that he wanted to know immediately if the three suspected members of his old gang showed up.

"Mr. Larkin will find *himself* in a lot of trouble if he shows up in Cottonwood." Jim started walking toward the door. "So put him out of your mind and enjoy the supper Tillie is going to bring you."

He paused at the door. "Do you think you could bring yourself to call me Jim?" His eyes sparkled teasingly. "I'm not all that much older than you."

"I'm sure I can . . . Jim." Sage smiled at the man who seemed to be taking over her life.

As the door closed behind him, Sage stared up at the yellow circle on the ceiling, cast by the kerosene lamp. She liked to think that she was self-reliant, although not aggressively so. She was sensible enough to know that there were times when a woman needed a man behind her, and this was one of those times.

A thought made Sage frown. If she gave herself over to this man's care, how much of herself would she be losing? She knew intuitively that Jim LaTour would demand that the woman in his life be his in all ways.

She felt a pang of guilt. It had never been that way with Arthur. She had always kept a spot inside herself secret, a piece of herself that was entirely hers. But the saloonkeeper . . . he would claim every part of a woman.

But would he be so accommodating with himself? she wondered. Would he share his thoughts, his hopes, his fears?

"Oh, for goodness sake," Sage muttered when she realized where her mind had wandered. "My fever must be returning. There will never be that kind of closeness between me and Jim LaTour. There is absolutely no common ground for us. A few months from now, when I've saved up enough money for Danny and me to move on, I'll never set eyes on the man again."

Her face wore such a scowl when Tillie entered the room carrying a laden tray, the middle-aged woman raised a questioning brow.

"Have you and Jim had words?" Tillie asked, placing the steaming food on the side table, then going to jerk the heavy curtains closed.

"Of course not, Tillie." Sage pushed herself up into a sitting position. "What makes you think that?"

"You kind of had an angry look on your face when I opened the door." Tillie adjusted the pillows behind Sage's back.

Sage gave a little laugh. "Maybe I did at that. I'm irritated at being so helpless. I've never known the feeling before, and I don't like it. I hate being out of control of my life. I feel like a piece of wood floating aimlessly down a river, never coming ashore."

Tillie smoothed a towel over Sage's lap and placed her supper of beef stew on it. "You'll forget those feelings once you're strong again. It's your weakness that makes you think that way. Once you're up and out in the fresh air you'll be your old self and you'll take charge of your life again."

Will I? Sage wondered, picking up her fork and digging into the stew. Jim LaTour's face swam in front of her, and she somehow doubted it. He was a take-charge man, and she would have to be on her toes so that he didn't sweep her along, helpless to do anything but succumb to his dictates.

And that means keeping a distance between us until I can get away from him, she told herself with firm determination.

Tillie rested her arms on the foot of the bed. "I remember how poorly I felt one time, weak of body and soul, feeling that no one in this world cared whether I was alive or dead. I was just about ready to lay down and die when

Jonty came along and brought me to this very kitchen.

"What a sight I was! Dirty and ragged, my hair so knotted and snarled it took two washins' to get it clean and straightened out. Jim was against me stayin' at first. He was afraid, and rightly so, that I was diseased and would pass somethin' on to Jonty.

"But I knew I wasn't. I wasn't like most whores who took on any man who had the price. I took only the men who looked clean. Many nights I didn't make a dime because every man jack who came to the saloon looked and smelled like he'd been rootin' with the hogs.

"I spoke right up to Jim, told him I was not diseased, that if I was, there was no way I'd chance givin' somethin' to a girl as sweet as his daughter. He grudgingly let me stay, and it wasn't too long before we was the best of friends. Jim looks rough and hard on the outside, but inside him beats the best heart you'd ever want to know."

When Sage got over the shock of what Tillie's long discourse had revealed—that as far as she was concerned, Jim LaTour stood at the right hand of God—she said, "Jim wants Danny to go live with his daughter while I'm convalescing. What do you think? Is it a good idea?"

"I think it's a fine idea. There's no better place than a ranch for a youngster to spend some time on. Jonty's husband Cord will teach him how to ride, take him out on the range with him. The boy will love it."

Tillie paused thoughtfully for a moment. "Of course, the boy could go with the Indian to his village. He could learn some about his Indian heritage. Johnny would look after him real good."

Sage shook her head. "Had his mother lived, Danny would have been taught about Indian life. When he became a little older she was going to let him spend some time with his Indian grandparents. But he's in my care now, and I'd rather he know only the white man's world until he is old enough to make his own decision whether or not he wants to learn the ways of Indian people."

Sage caught the disapproval on Tillie's face and hurried to explain. "I have nothing against Indians, Tillie, truly I don't. I loved my sister-in-law dearly. It's just that I, knowing nothing of Indian culture, couldn't help him sort out the different beliefs there are between the races. Besides, I'm afraid his mother's parents would try to take him away from me. I couldn't bear to lose him."

Mollified, Tillie said, "Jim could help him. He spent almost half his life with his mother's people."

Sage poured herself a cup of coffee from the small pot sitting on the tray. "I'd ask Jim to talk about life in an Indian village if we were going to be here for some time, but I'd hate for Danny to maybe get all excited about it and never be able to see his grand-parents."

"So you still plan on leavin' Cottonwood?"

"Yes, just as soon as I can get enough money together. I think it's for the best, Tillie."

"Have you talked to Jim about your plans?"

Sage shook her head. "The subject hasn't come up."

Tillie said no more about it as she stacked the dirty dishes on the tray. "Doc will be here directly to check your lungs and such. I'll bring you a basin of water in a minute and find you a fresh gown."

She gave Sage a teasing grin. "I think the doctor is smitten with you. Jim didn't like the way he stopped in every couple of hours to check on you. Said he only got in his way, feelin' your pulse, takin' your temperature. He claimed John only wanted to touch you."

Sage and Tillie laughed together and agreed to call Jim "Dr. LaTour."

When the doctor arrived half an hour later Sage smelled like roses from the bar of soap Tillie had taken from Jonty's dresser and dropped into the water.

Dr. Stewart thought she resembled a rose; she looked so delicate and lovely in a pink lawn gown with lace-trimmed straps. And he thought that the thick cloud of golden brown hair falling around her shoulders was the most beautiful hair he had ever seen.

"John, meet your patient," Tillie said. "Sage, this is Dr. Stewart." She grinned and added, "The man who LaTour allowed to help him doctor you."

John Stewart gave her a questioning look and she explained, "Just a joke between me and Sage."

"So, how are you feeling today, Sage?" the slender, attractive man asked, picking up her wrist and feeling her pulse. "I must say you're looking fit."

"She's looking more than that," Jim said from the doorway. "She's looking damn good." He advanced into the room and stood looking over the doctor's shoulder.

There was a hint of annoyance in Dr. Stewart's eyes. "I don't know if it's proper for you to be in here while I examine my patient, Jim," he said crossly.

"No?" Jim queried dryly. "How come it was all right for me to be in here when you attended her before? And now you suddenly don't think it's proper."

"It was different then," the doctor answered impatiently. "She was near death, and we were both trying our damnedest to keep her alive."

Sage looked at Jim. Seeing the stubborn curve of his lips, she knew he wouldn't budge an inch from the room, even if the doctor ordered him to do so. To keep them from possibly coming to blows, or at least from a heated argument, she decided to try smoothing the ruffled feathers of the two cocks.

"I don't mind if he stays, Dr. Stewart."

She bit her lips not to smile when Jim, with a look on his face much like the one Danny wore when getting his own way, plunked himself down on the foot of the bed. She had a moment's desire to reach up and slap the smug look off his handsome face, to say that she had changed her mind, that she didn't want him in her room after all.

Dr. Stewart's lips had tightened angrily, but his only response to Jim's action was to move the chair until his back was turned to the person who aggravated him so. Ignoring Jim as if he wasn't even there, he dropped Sage's wrist, remarking that her pulse was a little fast.

"But that's not surprising," he added, "considering a certain person's behavior.

"Can you sit up, Sage, so I can listen to your lungs?" he asked. When it was evident that Sage couldn't readily sit up alone, Dr. Stewart jumped to his feet and leaned over her. "Here, let me help you," he said in soft, murmuring tones.

Jim tensed and almost ordered the doctor to get his pawing hands off Sage when he slipped an arm beneath her shoulders and gently lifted her up.

Jim's lips twisted wryly when he caught Tillie's frowning eyes on him. If not for that castigating look, he probably would have made an ass of himself.

You'd better watch it, hombre, he said to himself. *The little beauty is beginning to get under your skin. You've never been jealous of a woman in your life, and you're too old to start now.*

While Dr. Stewart busied himself, taking the stethoscope from his little black bag, Jim's eyes were drawn to the proud thrust of Sage's breasts pushing against the fine material of her gown. He remembered their beauty, the satin texture of their skin, and the rosy, pouting nipples. There grew a stirring in his loins as he recalled promising himself that one day he would know the taste of them.

He vaguely noted that Tillie had left the room,

but he was too aware of the growing arousal that was bulging the front of his sharply creased trousers to pay much attention. He had to get the hell out of here before his condition was noted. When the doctor bent over Sage to listen to her heart Jim eased off the bed and quickly turned his back to the pair.

"I'll talk to you later, John," he muttered, and hurried from the room, wondering if his doctor friend was being affected by Sage's beauty the same way he was.

When he walked into the kitchen Jim's brooding eyes said that he didn't like that idea at all.

"Well?" Tillie took her attention from the bowl of sourdough she was kneading, preparing it for tomorrow morning's breakfast. "How's Sage comin' along?"

"I don't know." Jim pulled a chair away from the table and sat down. "Dr. Stewart is still checking her out . . . taking his sweet time doing it, too."

Tillie grinned at his surly answer. "Kicked you out, did he?"

"No, he didn't kick me out. I could have stayed if I wanted to."

His tone told Tillie not to pursue the topic. "Do you suppose Jonty will be in tomorrow?" She changed the subject, placing a cloth over the bowl of rising dough.

"She might," Jim answered as Tillie sat down across from him. "I'll look for her some time this week. It depends on when Cord finishes with the spring roundup." After a pause he said, "I'm sending Danny back home with Jonty. It will help Sage not to worry about him so much."

Tillie nodded. "I think that's a good idea. A saloon is no place for a youngun."

"It's not safe for the boy to stay here either. I look for Sage's brother-in-law to show up in Cottonwood one of these days, and I don't want to worry about the kid as well as about his aunt. I can't keep an eye on both of them at the same time."

"You do know Sage's plans, don't you?" Tillie asked when Jim grew silent, staring through the window at the darkness.

"What plans are you talking about?" He brought his attention back to his old friend. "She hasn't mentioned any to me."

Tillie shifted uneasily. It wasn't up to her to tell Jim what Sage had in mind to do, but now that she had opened her big mouth she was a little late in thinking about it. Jim would drag it out of her if he had to sit there all night. She gave a startled jerk when Jim growled, "Well, out with it, Tillie."

"When she gets her health and strength back Sage wants to find a job. She intends to save her money until she has enough to take her and the boy to some big city to live."

"That's the most ridiculous thing I've ever heard." Jim jumped up and grabbed the coffee-pot off the stove. "How does she plan on making a living for herself and the boy once she gets there?"

"I don't know. She probably expects to get a job as a maid or a cook in some wealthy household. Her main interest right now is to get as far away as possible from her brother-in-law. I don't think she's thought much further than that."

She looked across the table at Jim's frowning face, bent over a cup of coffee. "I don't think we have to worry about that too much, though. She's gonna have a hard time findin' work around here; at least work that would pay very much. She'd have to save a great deal in order to move on. There's coach fare; then she'd have to have money to live on until she can find a job in whatever city she lands in."

Jim relaxed visibly, and his face lost its glower. Why hadn't he thought of that before? Of course Sage wouldn't find a job in Cottonwood. Not the kind she would take, at any rate.

He was smiling pleasantly when Dr. Stewart walked into the kitchen. "How's your patient, John?" he asked as Tillie poured his friend a cup of coffee and refilled his own cup.

"She's coming along fine, considering she was half dead the first time I saw her. She certainly had the will and determination to live. Something made her hang on."

"Her nephew, Danny," Tillie spoke up. "She's scared to death something will happen to him."

"You're probably right," Dr. Stewart agreed. "Half the battle is won when your patient has a reason to fight Old Man Death. Usually it's the young, with a full life ahead of them. But the old ones, they're often too tired to fight; most times they're tired of living."

Tillie nodded solemnly as the doctor emptied

his cup in one long swallow. Setting the cup back on the table, he said, "Sage's lungs are mostly clear now. Tomorrow, if she feels like it, she can get out of bed and sit in a chair for half an hour." He looked at Tillie and smiled. "Keep feeding her that good soup of yours. It's as beneficial as medicine to her now."

He rose and picked his bag off the floor. "I'll drop in tomorrow," he said, and passed through the door and on into the saloon.

Jim frowned after John Stewart, opened his mouth to speak, and then closed it. Lightfoot and Nemia had entered the kitchen through the back door. He gave his cousin his usual welcoming smile and motioned the pair to sit down. "Will you have some coffee and pie?"

Johnny shook his head. "We have come to meet your woman; then we leave for the village. We are needed there to help plant the seeds."

"Hey, wait a minute, hold on there," Jim exclaimed in denial. "Where did you get the idea that Sage Larkin is my woman?"

"She became yours the moment you took over the care of her. She lives because of you. She is now yours."

Jim threw back his head and laughed disbelievingly. "You've been smoking loco weed in your pipe, Cousin. That may be an Indian custom, but try telling that to the lady in the other room."

He rose from the table and motioned Lightfoot and Nemia to follow him. "Come say hello to her. She's been anxious to meet you both."

* * *

Sage could see the resemblance between Jim and his tall relative, although there were differences too. Beneath his mustache Jim's lips were softer than the Indian's, and his hair, although a rich black, was of a finer texture. Then there were the startling blue eyes. She'd never seen bluer in another human being.

Sage returned the steady gaze turned on her, aware of the inner strength in Johnny Lightfoot. She stretched a pale, thin hand to him and, remembering Jim's warning not to thank his cousin too effusively, she spoke simply: "I hope that someday I can return the help you gave me and my nephew."

Lightfoot gave her hand a firm shake; then he pulled forward Nemia, who stood behind him. "This is my woman, Nemia."

Sage offered her hand again, looking into soft brown eyes. Where Nemia's husband was tall and broad, she was of slight build. Sage thought her quite beautiful, with her raven-black hair and smooth, dusky skin.

"Danny has told me much about you, Nemia." She smiled at the shy young woman. "He tells me that you can catch more fish than he and your husband can, and that you tell wonderful stories."

Nemia lowered her lids, not used to praise. "There is nothing special about my stories. They were only about the people in my village."

Jim leaned in the doorway, taking no part in the conversation between the three. He was pleased with the way Sage was getting along with Johnny and Nemia. There had been no

condescension in Sage's manner, no patronizing from Johnny because Sage was only a
woman. Evidently, he saw something in the
beautiful woman that he liked and respected.

He straightened up from his lounging stance
and walked over to the bed. "She looks a little
different from the first time you saw her, eh,
Johnny?"

The Indian nodded. "I did not think she would
live through the day."

"It was nip and tuck there for a while," Jim
said soberly, remembering the times he'd been
afraid Sage wouldn't draw another breath.

Lightfoot slid his cousin a look from beneath
lowered lids. Seeing a softness on the hard
features, he thought that after all these years
Jim LaTour had found a woman who wouldn't
be so easy to cast off once he had taken her to
bed. This one would linger in a man's memory
for a long time. He laid a hand on Nemia's
shoulder.

"We go say good-bye to little brave now; then
we must leave. The wolves will be coming out
soon and I don't care to fight with them in the
dark." He lifted a hand in farewell to Sage, and
Nemia, after giving her a shy smile, followed
him toward the door.

"I'll see you to your horses," Jim said, and left
the room with them.

Sage wondered if he intended to return to
her room. He hadn't said good night to her.
Wishing that he wouldn't, she raised herself
up and, leaning over, blew out the lamp.
He made her nervous, made her feel things
she didn't understand but felt that a decent

woman shouldn't. It made her feel wanton, like the women who plied their trade in the house next door to the saloon.

A faint breeze rustled the curtains, drawing her attention to the window. The heavy gray twilight was deepening. She wondered if Lightfoot and Nemia would beat the wolves home; then she wondered if Danny had remembered to wash his face and hands before going to bed.

A burst of ribald laughter penetrated the thin walls, followed by the shrill cackle of a whore. When heavy fingers began to pound out a tune on the tinny piano she thumped her pillow, knowing she would never get to sleep.

But the next thing she knew it was bright morning, and Tillie was shaking her shoulder, announcing that she had brought in her breakfast.

Chapter Six

Sage stepped outside the kitchen door and blinked her eyes against the bright light of the sun. Last night Dr. Stewart had agreed that, after being confined for two weeks, she could go outside and sit in the sun for an hour.

Walking over to a bench placed alongside the kitchen's outer wall, she sat down and leaned back against the rough-planked building. She breathed deeply, filling her weakened lungs with fresh air and the bracing scent of pine. How wonderful it smelled; how warm the sun felt. She was an out-of-doors person, and she had grown to hate the two rooms that had hemmed her in.

The recovery from her illness had been slow at first, causing Jim and Tillie to worry about her. But the doctor had claimed, and rightly so as it turned out, that fretting over her nephew and her future was keeping her from a fast recovery.

His pronouncement had proven true when, four days later, Danny had gone away with Jonty and Cord to stay with them while she regained her health. She had relaxed then and quickly grown better. Although Leland didn't like the little boy, she doubted he would go out of his way to hunt him down. It was her he was intent on finding.

A soft light came into Sage's eyes as she remembered the morning Danny had prepared to leave her. Concern had been in his eyes as he asked, "Are you sure you don't mind me going off and leaving you, Aunt Sage? You won't get too lonesome for me?"

"Oh, I'll miss you, honey." Her hand smoothed his unruly hair. "But I'll be happy at the same time. I think it's wonderful that you're getting a chance to live on a ranch for a while. And you won't be gone all that long."

"And when your aunt is strong enough to ride I'll be bringing her out to the ranch to spend a couple of days with you," Jim spoke up. Danny's face brightened then, and his eyes gave away his eagerness to get to the ranch he had heard so much about.

Sage leaned her head back against the wall and stared into space as she remembered meeting Jim's daughter. Her first thought had been of how much she looked like her father. She had felt keenly the blue eyes that had studied her, weighing her. She had known just when she passed judgment by the warmth that gathered in Jonty's eyes. The young woman's hand had come out, gripping hers firmly.

"Dad and Tillie tell me you have been gravely

ill," she said in her throaty voice.

"More than I realized at the time." Sage returned the warm smile directed at her. "I have so much to thank them for."

"I'm sure that's not necessary. Tillie loves to fuss over a person, and Dad would never find it a hardship tending to a beautiful woman. Isn't that right, Dad?" She grinned at her father, lounging in the doorway.

"I've been accused of it." Jim advanced into the room, his lips curved in a crooked grin. "I must say, though, Sage hasn't responded like the others. She never pays a bit of attention to my compliments."

"Probably because she's smarter than the others," Jonty said, a teasing note in her voice. "She knows a scallywag when she sees one."

Sage wondered how the conversation had shifted from her illness to Jim's relationship with women. And there had been many in his life, she suspected. She was aware of one who had his interest now. Her name was Reba. Danny had mentioned her in very disapproving tones.

"That Reba woman," he'd begun sourly, "asked Jim real meanlike, 'How much longer is that kid gonna sleep in my room?' "

When Danny hadn't continued Sage, anxious to know Jim's response, forgot that Danny had been taught not to gossip, and asked, "What did Jim answer?"

"First he glared at her real fiercelike; then he growled, 'It's none of your damned business how long the kid sleeps there. Now just get the hell out of *his* room and stay out until you're invited back again.' Boy, was she mad. She gave me a look that was meaner than some Leland used to give me."

Sage directed a disgruntled snort at herself now. Her heart had given such a happy little skip at Danny's words, she forgot to chastise him for repeating swearwords.

Later, as she sat quietly thinking back on the words Jim had flung at Reba, the last part of his last sentence—"stay out until you're invited back again"—stayed with her. There had been no reason for her pulse to give that silly leap. The simple truth of the matter boiled down to the fact that Jim wasn't about to be dictated to by any woman, especially a whore. Sage had learned from Tillie the woman's occupation.

Sage stared unseeing at a little lizard that darted across her line of vision. Now that Danny was gone she had no doubt that Reba had been invited back to her room, that Jim visited her there every night.

When that thought bothered her she gave herself a mental shake. Why should she care how many women he slept with? He meant nothing to her, and she was sure that she was of no interest to him. No two people's lives could be so dissimilar, so contrary to the other. Hers had been a quiet, orderly life, whereas Jim, from what she could make out from a word dropped here and there, had led a reckless, sometimes dangerous life. Where there had never been spirits of any kind in her and Arthur's home, nor in her parents', Jim LaTour owned a saloon.

And drank freely from that which he sold to

the cowboys, miners, and trappers who came into his place night and day. She had smelled it on his person several times.

If the two of you are so unsuited, an inner voice broke into Sage's thoughts, *why is it he's on your mind so much?*

He's not! she denied. *It's just that ...* She paused, searching for the words that would describe her exact feelings for Jim LaTour.

The only answer she arrived at was that she had never been so physically aware of a man as she was of the saloonkeeper. Even Arthur, whom she had loved dearly, had never made her pulse race, her heart hammer.

The crunch of stones underfoot brought Sage out of her disquieting soul-searching. She turned her head to see a shriveled-up little old woman coming toward her. Deep wrinkles mapped the brown, wrinkled face framed by straggles of white hair that had escaped the loose knot at her nape.

My goodness, she must be a hundred years old. Sage blinked a little when the black-clad, slightly bent body stood before her. But for all the years the worn face revealed, the eyes that peered at her were as bright as those of a baby bird peeking from its nest.

The smile with which Sage meant to greet the old woman died on her lips when the aged person cackled with glee. "I heard Jim had a new woman. What does his old woman, Reba the whore, have to say about that? Watch out for her; she's a mean bitch."

As Sage stared blankly at the gnomelike figure, at a loss what to say, a male voice rapped out, "Janie, are you up to mischief so early in the day?"

Janie spun around so fast she lost her balance, and Jim had to hurry from the kitchen door to catch her before she hit the ground. "I should have let you fall and break your scrawny neck," Jim growled, steadying her on her little feet shod in black, scuffed shoes. "Whose woman did you say Reba was?"

Janie's sharp little eyes shot a fast glance at Jim's stern face; then speaking very fast, she said, "Oh, she's nobody's, everybody's, just a plain old whore."

Sage looked at Jim to see how he was taking the unkind description of his present bedpartner. Surprise jumped into her eyes. From the quirking of his lips, it was all he could do not to burst out laughing. She watched him control his features and bring a scowl to his face, and then speak gruffly to the bent, white head as he released the birdlike arm.

"You remember that from now on, you old harridan. Now scoot back to your shack and see if you can mind your own business for a change. If I tell Tillie that you've been running off at the mouth again, there won't be any more supper plates for you."

As if to have the last word, Janie snorted, "Huh!" Then, chin in the air, she hobbled her way to a patched-up wooden shack a yard or so behind the saloon. Sage and Jim grinned at each other when she tried to slam the sagging door behind her and ended with having to tug it closed.

Trying for a nonchalance he was far from

feeling, Jim said, as he rolled a cigarette, "No one pays any attention to what Janie says. It's well known that she makes up stories to pass the time. Many times Jonty could have wrung her neck because of her mischief-making."

It was on the tip of Sage's tongue to remark, *But I bet sometimes the old lady tells the truth*, then thought better of it. If Jim wanted to pretend the woman Reba meant nothing to him, so be it. Hadn't she told herself it was no business of hers how Jim LaTour led his life?

Jim sat down beside her, and she returned his smile when he said, "You're looking chipper this morning. How are you feeling?"

"I'm beginning to feel almost like my old self again." Sage moved over a bit, putting more room between them, so that their thighs weren't touching. "It's so nice to be outside again. One reason I hate winter so is because one is cooped up inside for weeks on end. The long monotony of gloomy gray days almost drives me crazy."

"That's because you've always lived on a farm, with nothing to break your boredom. It's different in a town. There's always people around, and something going on."

"Yes," Sage agreed, "I can see how that is true. I heard a church bell ringing last Sunday. I'm planning to go to church this week, and meet some of the ladies; join some of their clubs."

Jim adjusted his hat to hide his eyes. Sage didn't know it, but she would be snubbed by the "good women" of Cottonwood. Word had already gone out about LaTour's *new woman*. Old Janie wasn't the only female in town who thought Sage was sharing his bed.

And dammit, he could stand in front of a preacher with his hand on a Bible while he swore that there was nothing between him and the recently widowed woman and not a soul would believe him.

For the first time in his life his reputation as a womanizer bothered Jim. The beauty sitting beside him could very well end up hating him when she discovered that her good name was in shreds because of him.

"Are you sure you want to hobnob with those old biddies?" Jim asked finally. "It doesn't look to me like they get much joy out of life . . . except for gossiping, that is. They do seem to get a lot of pleasure out of that. You see three women talking together, you can bet they're slicing up some poor soul."

"Now, Jim, you're just imagining that. Good Christian women wouldn't talk mean about anyone," Sage scolded in an assured voice.

Jim gave Sage a pitying look. What a shock she was in for next Sunday. It was clear she wasn't used to the kind of churchgoers who inhabited Cottonwood.

The least he could do, he decided, was to attend church with Sage; be on hand to lend her moral support when her attempt at meeting the *ladies* was met with cold stares. He laughed to himself. The shock of seeing him walk into church just might make the females of the congregation forget to turn their noses up at Sage.

In the following days Jim made a habit of sitting with Sage when she took her hour outside.

As they talked together, he learned that she was thirty-two and not in her mid-twenties, as he had imagined. When this pleased him he directed a cynical laugh at himself. What difference was there if she was thirty-two or twenty-two? She was not his type of woman. He liked his women to be tough and lusty, ones who wouldn't expect more from him than a good tumble in bed.

Sage Larkin, a lady to her very bones, would expect much more from a man. More than Jim LaTour was willing to give. Cleo had received the best of him; there was nothing left over for another woman.

And yet, he had never wanted another woman as he wanted the beautiful widow. Every time he looked at her desire ran through him like a fire burning out of control.

In those days before the arrival of Sunday and church, Sage grieved for her lost relatives; gentle Mary, fun-loving Kale, and quiet, steady Arthur, her husband of fourteen years.

With Arthur and Kale, it was almost like grieving for two brothers instead of one. She had known and played with Arthur since she could walk and talk. They'd had a good marriage, if not an exciting one. Their one big disappointment had been that she couldn't conceive. There had been no sons for Arthur, no daughters for her.

Sage imagined now that it was lucky there hadn't been any children. It would be difficult enough to provide for Danny, much less two or three other children.

She sighed as she sat at her usual place

outside. To provide for her nephew she must find a place of employment. She mustn't impose on Jim's hospitality much longer. He had been more than generous, providing a roof over their heads, food, and even clothing. Fortunately, Jonty's clothes fit her as though they had been made for her. But Danny had needed to be clothed from the skin out.

Her eyes sparkled with amusement as she remembered the day Jim had bought him a pair of boots "just like the cowboys wear." He had strutted about, wobbling a bit in heels higher than he was used to, equally proud of the twill trousers shoved into his boots and the red flannel shirt hugging his small shoulders. Always before he had worn homespuns, faded from many washings.

But running a close second to the high-heeled boots was the wide-brimmed hat that never left his head except when he sat down to a meal or went to bed.

She had so much to thank the big man for. Above all else, she owed him for the time he had spent with Danny, helping him to begin to get over the pain of losing his parents.

A pensive frown marred Sage's forehead. The affection her host had for her nephew was evident, but how he felt about her she hadn't been able to decide yet. In his actions and words he was always a gentleman, but sometimes the way his knowing eyes flicked over her body made her blush uncomfortably. He had, after all, seen her nakedness in all its completeness. Was he remembering that when his hot gaze swept over her?

She stirred uneasily, reluctant to admit that those fleeting looks always caused a warmness to grow in the pit of her stomach. Arthur had never made her feel that way and this troubled her; made her feel guilty.

Her soft lips firmed into a determined line. She must find a place for herself and Danny as soon as possible. If she stayed much longer under Jim's protection, she might very well end up as the old woman had called her: "Jim's new woman."

Sunday morning arrived, bright and clear, and Sage hummed a little tune as she prepared to dress for church. How nice it felt to be going to church again. She had missed it. All her life, Sunday had been the one day that had broken up the monotony of the daily grind of farm chores.

Would the women in Cottonwood be as friendly as the women she had known all her life? she wondered, taking a green sprigged muslin dress from Jonty's wardrobe. Maybe not at first. She took a camisole, a petticoat, and a pair of narrow, midthigh bloomers from a dresser drawer. If not today, in time they would nod and smile at her.

Sage took off her robe and gown and, laying them across the foot of the bed, went to stand in front of the dresser mirror. At home she'd only had a small one, hanging from a nail beside the kitchen window. She was acquainted with her face, but she had never had an all-over view of her body before. She studied it closely.

From the hard work she had done all her life,

every line was firm and smoothly toned. Her breasts stood high and proud, her waist small and lean, her hips softly rounded. She'd had no children, so her body was free of the marks of childbirth. Sage nodded her satisfaction; then she donned her underclothing and pulled the dress over her head.

As she buttoned the close-fitting bodice up to its square neckline, an uneasiness settled over her. Again she asked herself, would the women like her, accept her? But why shouldn't they? she thought as she brushed her hair back and formed it into two loose coils at her nape. She looked respectable; she *was* respectable.

Sage's hand hovered over a rouge pot. She could use a hint of color in her cheeks. Then she dropped her hand. Everyone must know that she had been ill, and they would expect her to look pale. She picked up a small, lacy bonnet and, using a long hat pin, secured it to her hair. Two green streamers of ribbon fell almost to her shoulder.

She stood in front of the mirror for a last moment, turning her head one way and then the other, admiring the fancy little creation. The only headgear she had ever known before had been a slatted bonnet in the summer and a woolen shawl in the winter.

With a happy little sigh, Sage pulled a pair of white gloves over her long, slender fingers. She slipped a small bag over her wrist and, taking a long breath, left the room and stepped into the kitchen.

"My, but you do look pretty," Tillie exclaimed, noticing her first. "Ain't she just lovely, Jim?"

Jim switched his gaze from staring out the window to looking at Sage, and several moments passed before he expressed himself. *Lovely* and *pretty* were such tame words to use to describe the woman who stood shyly under his inspection. Even the word beautiful wouldn't truly do justice to how Sage Larkin looked.

She had lost weight with her bout of pneumonia, and her features were like that of a finely carved piece of translucent porcelain: clean and pure. The green eyes beneath the wide, smooth forehead were fringed with thick brown lashes that fanned her cheeks as she looked down to escape the fire in his gaze.

Jim finally stood up and, taking Sage's hand, he raised it to his lips. "She is a vision, Tillie," he said, his voice husky, "exceeding a man's wildest dreams."

Tillie took pity on Sage, who blushed red in confusion at the unexpected compliment. The only time Arthur had ever remarked on her appearance had been to say that she looked tired and should rest awhile. Brother Kale had often teased her, claiming that she looked as pretty as a baby's pink ear, or some other nonsense. Consequently, she had always been serenely unconscious of her beauty.

With a short laugh, Tillie quipped, "I'm sure you know all about wild dreams, Jim LaTour."

"Hush up, woman." Jim laughed and crooked his elbow for Sage to slip her hand into it. As he escorted her through the kitchen door, Tillie stepped outside behind them.

"I'll be listenin' for the noise of the church

fallin' down when you step inside it, Jim," she teased.

Jim's lips twitched in a nervous grin. The church roof might very well cave in. To his knowledge, he had never been inside one before. If his white father had ever taken him to church, he had no remembrance of it.

And wouldn't his presence draw gaping stares from the congregation? He grinned to himself. Jim LaTour, half-breed and owner of a saloon, would be the last person they'd ever expect to see occupying one of their pews.

As Sage clung to Jim's arm, her long legs easily keeping pace with him, he tried to remember if he had ever before walked down a street with a woman holding on to him. He couldn't recall it ever happening. He had ridden in fringe-topped buggies often enough with whatever *fancy* woman he might have been interested in at the time—Reba, for instance— but he had never escorted one on foot.

Amusement sparkled in his blue eyes. Another first for him.

He glanced down at Sage and wondered what she was thinking about. Was she remembering going to church with her husband? Was she still grieving for him?

The church bell began to ring, and halfway down the wooden sidewalk Jim could see the people filing into church. He felt Sage's hand tighten on his arm, and he covered it with his own, gently squeezing it, sending the message, *Don't be nervous, I'm with you.*

Chapter Seven

When Jim and Sage turned their footsteps onto the narrow, rough-planked walkway that had been laid so that the ladies' skirts wouldn't drag in the dust or mud or snow, those of the congregation who hadn't yet passed into the church turned as one to gape at them.

Jim chuckled softly. He could imagine what was going through their minds. What in the world was a rakehell like Jim LaTour doing, walking into a house of God? And Reverend Ketch, standing on the small stoop greeting his parishioners, was going to catch a horsefly in his mouth if he didn't close it pretty soon.

The procession into the small building came to a halt as those bringing up the rear paused to get a closer look at LaTour's new woman; to decide for themselves if she was as beautiful as rumored.

There was surprise in the women's eyes as they stole cold looks at the young woman, who smiled shyly at them. Not only was she beautiful but she looked very much the lady, not a painted-up hussy like the saloonkeeper was usually seen with.

Nevertheless, she was living with LaTour, a well-known womanizer, and didn't that say that her morals must not be of the highest quality?

When the Reverend Ketch came out of his benumbed state and nudged his flock to pass on through the door, not one woman had returned Sage's smile.

"Well, this is a surprise, though a pleasant one." The man of the cloth stuck out his hand to Jim when he and Sage stepped up beside him. With a glint of humor in his kind blue eyes, he added, "I'd given up hope that you would ever come listen to me preach fire and brimstone."

"I'm shocked myself to be here." Jim grinned back; then he looked down at Sage, standing beside him, a smile frozen on her face. "My young friend, here, is a regular churchgoer." He looked meaningfully at four women who, although they had passed inside, still gawked over their shoulders at Sage. "I thought it best I come with her; she might need protection from a few old crows."

None knew better than the preacher that there was a certain clique of his parishioners who weren't as Christian as they should be, and he smiled kindly at Sage when Jim introduced her. Her clear, steady gaze told him that she was not Jim LaTour's woman. He feared, though, that very few would believe it. Some of the women wouldn't mainly out of jealousy. There wasn't a woman in Cottonwood who could hold a candle to the widow when it came to good looks.

Tobias mentally shook his head. Sometimes beauty was a cross to bear.

Sage would have sat down at the first bench she and Jim came to, she was so bewildered at the cold treatment she had received. But Jim would have none of that. He ushered her midway down the row of benches and curtly ordered a fat lady to move over, to make room for them. He exchanged a wide grin for the irate lady's dark scowl.

The pleasant lifting of his lips hid a smoldering rage inside Jim, however. How dare these so-called God-fearing women turn their noses up at the woman sitting quietly beside him, fighting back tears, confused at their treatment of her. Bygod, just wait until their husbands showed up at Trail's End. They'd get a damn good earful. They'd straighten out their bitchy wives or he'd call in the notes most of them owed him. And Tobias had better have a talk with his female members too. Otherwise there would be no more large contributions from Jim LaTour the next time he came begging money for the church.

The whispering of women and the restless movement of children ceased when the preacher stepped up to the pulpit. He looked out over the congregation a moment, then gave a slight nod of his head. There followed a rustling of starched petticoats and shuffling feet as everyone rose and opened their songbooks. He raised his hand, and the beautiful words of "Abide With Me" swelled through the room.

One full verse had been sung when Jim gave

a start and looked down at Sage. She had begun to sing in a clear, rich contralto that rose above all the others. He shook his head in wonder. In his travels across most of the western states he had heard many professionals sing, in barrooms and onstage, but never had he heard any who could compare with the sweet notes coming from Sage Larkin's throat.

It soon became evident that Jim wasn't the only one aware of the new voice among them, for toward the end of the song only a few others continued to sing along with her. Most had left off singing just to listen to Sage.

Although she sang like an angel and looked and acted like a perfect lady, when the services were over and everyone stood around outside talking in groups Sage continued to be snubbed. Jim saw the tears that hung on her lashes and swore savagely to himself. He knew what she was feeling. Hadn't he been made to feel the same way practically all his life?

He stood a moment; then he led Sage to the shade of a tree. His voice rough with his anger, he said, "Wait for me here, I won't be but a minute."

Sage watched him stride away, every line of his body furiously stiff. She wanted to call him back, to tell him that it didn't matter how she was treated, but she didn't want to call attention to herself. She didn't think she could bear to face one more sneering look. What was he going to say to the women? She chewed her bottom lip, sorry that she had attended the service.

Jim, however, walked past the women, not even glancing at them as he continued on to the knot of men who waited for their wives to join them. Their welcoming smiles died on their faces when Jim began to speak.

Neither Sage nor the others standing around heard what Jim said to the men. But whatever it was, they took his words to heart. As soon as he stalked away from them, each man approached his wife, and he wasn't gentle in his handling of her as he marched her away from the churchyard.

Jim watched the women being hustled along, a wide smile of satisfaction on his face. Then, offering his arm to Sage, he said, "Let's go home."

Midway up the street, Sage's tears spilled over. "Why were they so cold to me, Jim?" She fumbled blindly for a handkerchief.

Jim pressed his own white handkerchief into her hand, the cold blue flame in his eyes like a winter storm. "I should never have exposed you to those bitches' cruelty. Forgive me for that, but I thought they would at least be polite to you . . . all claiming to be such good Christians. They're nothing but a bunch of damn hypocrites."

Sage mopped at her wet eyes; then she looked up at him. "So you knew all along that they wouldn't treat me kindly."

Jim couldn't meet the bruised look in the green eyes and turned his head from Sage before he answered. "I suspected you wouldn't be greeted with open arms. After all, you have taken up residence in a saloon. I'm sorry as hell, but I'm afraid your name has already been linked with mine."

"I don't understand." Sage stopped in mid-stride and stared up at Jim. "What do you mean, my name linked with yours?"

Jim nudged her to walk on, saying bluntly, "It's all over Cottonwood that you're Jim LaTour's new woman."

Sage caught her breath, a pallor spreading over her face. "I must leave the saloon. As soon as possible."

Jim's expression softened as he looked down on the scrap of bonnet riding on top of the rich brown hair. "Where would you go, Sage?" he asked gently.

"There must be a respectable boardinghouse in Cottonwood where I can find a room to rent. Of course, I'll have to borrow some money from you until I can find a job."

Jim ignored the last part of her sentence. "There is a boardinghouse in town, but it's run by Agnes Bridewell, the biggest gossip in town. She tells her little clique what to think, what to say, how to act. I'd bet my saloon she's the one who started the talk about us."

"But that's so unfair, Jim." Tears brimmed again in Sage's eyes. "Those women don't even know me. How can they decide what kind of person I am?"

"I know, honey." Jim gently squeezed the slim fingers clutching his arm. "But you're a very lucky lady if this is the first time you've discovered the unfairness of life. You must forget about the Agnes Bridewells in this world. There will always be people with small minds and malicious tongues. You have to rise above such; know them for what they are."

They had reached the saloon as Jim talked, and he directed Sage down the alley, coming up behind the kitchen. Tillie closed the oven door on a pan of biscuits and straightened up as they walked inside. She took one look at Sage's tearstained face and took a step toward her.

"Sage, you've been cryin'. How come? Did some of them old biddies say somethin' to you that wasn't nice?"

"Hah!" Sage snorted, throwing herself into a chair. "They didn't say a word to me, nice or otherwise. They just gave me looks like I was something dirty." She bent an elbow on the table and rested her chin in her palm. "It was just awful, Tillie."

"Them holy bitches." Tillie's eyes snapped. She awkwardly pressed Sage's shoulder. "Let's have a cup of coffee and forget about them. You don't need that lot."

"I've been trying to tell her that, Tillie." Jim sat down at the table. "It seems she don't want to believe me."

"I do believe you, Jim." Sage looked earnestly at him. "It's just that I'm afraid now I won't be able to find employment. Who's going to hire me when everyone thinks I'm a loose woman?"

"Loose woman?" Tillie hooted with laughter. "Just because them tongue-flappin' women claim you're LaTour's woman don't make you a loose one. There's very few of them in Cottonwood who wouldn't be proud to be considered to be his woman."

Jim squirmed a bit at his cook's high praise; then he looked at Sage, a crooked smile twisting his lips. "I pay her extra to say things like that."

Sage smiled at his attempted levity, but the troubled look remained in her eyes. On a serious note, Jim said, "I wish you'd stop worrying about getting a job and moving. It's going to be quite a while before you're strong enough to work, and leaving Trail's End won't stop the gossip that's making the rounds. You'll be forgotten as soon as something else comes along for those vultures to get their teeth into.

"Meanwhile, work at regaining your strength and stop worrying about your future. I have a half-planned idea for how you can earn the money you'll need to make your move to that big city you've got your mind set on."

"And what is that, Jim?" Tillie joined them at the table after pouring three cups of coffee.

"I'm not going to say yet, Tillie." Jim pulled the sugar bowl toward him. "I still have to work out some details."

"Can't you give us a hint?" Tillie pressed, and Sage looked hopefully at him.

"No," Jim answered firmly, drinking the last of his coffee and standing up. Before going through the door into the saloon, he looked at Sage and said, "Danny told me that you play the guitar."

Sage nodded. "A little. My father taught me chords. He was very good on the strings."

"Why did you want to know that, Jim?" Tillie asked. "Does it have anything to do with your idea?"

"You sure are full of questions today, old lady," Jim chided, a teasing smile taking away the sting from his words. "But if you must know, I have in mind to stand Sage out in front of the saloon with a guitar and a tin cup. If she strums the strings real fetching, I'm sure passersby would toss a coin into it."

Tillie laughed at the alarm that jumped into Sage's eyes as Jim left them. "He's teasin', honey. You can stop worryin', though. He's got some plan runnin' through that brain of his. You're gonna be just fine."

Sage felt suddenly that everything was going to be all right. She gave Tillie a wide smile. "I'm going to my room and lie down for a while; maybe take a little nap." The emotional upset brought on by the unfriendly churchwomen had drained her fragile strength. As she walked into her room and closed the door behind her, Tillie wore a pleased look.

But what was Jim up to? she wondered. He was very taken with his beautiful guest. She could see it in his eyes every time he looked at Sage. He'd be in no hurry to see her leave Cottonwood. Maybe never, she hoped. He deserved to finally have a good woman in his life.

Of course, he would fight any such thoughts like the very devil, Tillie reminded herself as she gathered up the empty cups and carried them to the dry sink and pumped water over them.

Chapter Eight

The bearded man sat his mount on a small hill, looking down on a canting shack sitting in the misty gloom of a narrow valley, a thin spiral of smoke rising from its chimney. There was a dark broodiness on the man's face, an aura of evil about his tall, sparse frame clad in rough homespuns.

He gave a cruel jerk of the reins when the horse grew restless, wanting to move on. The animal had been in the same spot for ten minutes or more while its rider sat cursing and muttering on its back.

It tossed its head uneasily when Leland Larkin cried out, "It's all your fault, Sage! I would never have become involved with that red bitch if I hadn't been on fire with wanting you."

Sage's brother-in-law sat on, his mind going back sixteen years, to the day he had left his home in a rage after seeing his brother holding

Sage in his arms, kissing her. Only fear of his father had kept him from attacking his brother; beating him senseless and then throwing Sage on the ground, ripping off her clothing, and driving himself inside her; taking her again and again until his seed had taken root. No one could take her away from him then. She would be his to use any time he wanted her.

His driving lust for Sage was still driving him when, two days later, he came upon a young Indian girl, alone, gathering roots and greens for her mother. She had jumped to her feet at his approach, and an arousal rose and pressed against his fly as he watched the pulse in her throat beat like that of a small frightened rabbit.

He smiled down at her terror-stricken face and said softly, "It is a beautiful morning for a beautiful maid to be out gathering food for her mother . . . or is it for a husband you do this?"

His gentle tone had calmed her fears, and there was trust in her soft brown eyes when she answered, in a shy voice, "It is for my mother. I have not taken a husband yet."

"Then I am in luck." He had widened his smile and swung to the ground.

They had spent over an hour together, he doing most of the talking as they sat beneath a tree. He told her he had a farm and a snug little cabin, and that he had been searching for the perfect wife to share it with him. When he had asked her if she would do him the honor of becoming his woman she had readily agreed, saying softly that he was so handsome, so gentle, unlike the men in her village; what more could a young woman ask for in a husband? It was hard for Leland to keep the satisfaction from his voice when he asked, "What is your name?"

"I am called Brown Sparrow," she answered shyly. "It was that small bird I first looked upon when I opened my eyes after birth."

"Well, then, Brown Sparrow, shall we be on our way?"

"Oh, I would have to tell my parents first, and say good-bye to them," the young girl protested.

Leland looked down at the ground to hide his anger and irritation. Was he going to lose the bitch at the last minute? This one wasn't the run-of-the-mill slothful Indian maid. She had been gently reared, and her parents would be too wise to let her go off with him.

Hiding his displeasure, he picked up her hand and, stroking its back, he said in a sorrowful voice, "You know in your heart, Brown Sparrow, that they would never give you permission to go away with me."

He turned her hand over and kissed its palm. "It saddens me that you won't be sharing my little cabin. We could have been so happy."

He rose to his feet and started walking toward his horse. He wasn't too surprised when he heard her running after him. "Wait, mister . . ." She caught up with him when he was about to swing into the saddle.

"My name is Leland," he said gently, giving her a sad smile. "What is it you want?"

"I will go with you . . . Leland," she said, a little breathlessly. "I have scratched out a message to my parents on the forest floor."

"You have made me a very happy man," he said, and he swung her onto the horse's back.

Leland Larkin's lips pulled back in a wolfish grin as he sat his mount on the hill. Those had been the last kind words he had spoken to the red bitch in thirteen years.

In his overwhelming lust, when he had felt they were a safe distance from the Indian village he had reined in the horse, slid out of the saddle, and jerked Brown Sparrow to the ground. Pushing her onto her back, he had fallen on top her, ripped open his fly, jerked her legs apart and driven himself inside her. When a pain-filled scream ripped from her throat he slapped her across the mouth, cutting her lips.

He had taken her three times within an hour. When finally he was finished with her, her spirit was broken. She was afraid to open her mouth, cowering every time he looked at her. When they came to a deserted shack he told her that this was her new home. Dismay had flickered in her eyes, but she had said nothing of what she was thinking.

He had stayed with her a week, taking her often on the sagging bed that bore only a musty mattress of moldy straw. The day before he left the shack, he went to a small town nearby that he had visited before to purchase what food they would need. He bought a large supply of dry beans, salt pork, and hard tack. That should do the bitch until he returned or she went back to her people.

The next morning, he had left Brown Sparrow without a word. His lust sated for the time being, he hated himself and the young Indian girl he had rutted with.

He had stayed away from the shack for six weeks, until his sexual desire drove him to visit it again. That Brown Sparrow was still there surprised him a bit. But he reckoned that she was too proud to return to her people.

He spent two days and nights with her, replenished her supplies, and rode away again.

Five months had passed before he noticed on one of his visits that Brown Sparrow was expecting. He was gripped in a towering rage. To his shame, he was to become the father of a heathen half-breed. He had ridden his young squaw hard several times, hoping to make her lose the baby. But it had survived his pounding, and on the day Sage married his brother, Brown Sparrow gave birth to a baby boy. What she named the child he didn't know, nor did he care.

There had followed two miscarriages; then, when the firstborn was five, another son had been born. Over the years there had been other miscarriages; then after thirteen years his hated squaw had died giving birth to a stillborn baby boy.

He hadn't been there when it happened. Her two whelps had buried her and the baby in a grove of cottonwood.

"Damn your soul, Sage." Leland Larkin came back to the present. "You knew how much I wanted you, but you had to choose my weakling brother and force me into a life of shame."

A mirthless smile twisted his thin lips as he

lifted the reins and jabbed the mount with his heels. The horse rolled its eyes and started down the sloping hill, the man on its back still muttering to himself. He'd find her before long. He had lost her trail a few miles back, her and that breed nephew of hers, but she was in the vicinity somewhere. The town of Cottonwood wasn't too far away. She might have made her way there. He'd have his three henchmen scout around, see if they spotted her.

A dark scowl came over his face. They'd be looking him up any day now, demanding to be paid for the job he'd hired them to do. "But they'll not be getting it all," Larkin muttered. They had only done half of what he had hired them to do. They hadn't delivered Sage to him yet.

Leland's oldest son, fifteen-year-old Lisha, saw the rider coming. His mouth went dry and dread clutched his heart. The hand that smoothed down his ragged homespuns trembled a bit. When the weary horse came to a halt in front of the shack he turned from the door, whispering urgently, "Our father is here, Benny. Tidy yourself."

Their stomachs fluttering with nervous tension, the teenager and the ten-year-old waited facing the door as though they were standing in front of a firing squad.

The flimsy door banged open, slamming against the wall, and Leland stood there, the usual scowl on his face. His gaze ranged over the neat, sparsely furnished room, his eyes missing nothing.

Although the boys never knew when their

father might pay them a visit, and it had been two months since the last time he had been around, they always made sure the shack was as clean and neat as they could make it. That also went for their persons. The cruel-faced man used the smallest excuse to punish them.

Without any greeting to the boys, Leland threw himself down on the single bench pulled up to the table. "What kind of slop do you have cooking in the pot?" He looked at Lisha with mean eyes.

"Venison stew," the boy answered in a small voice. "I shot it yesterday; a young doe. The meat is very tender."

"I'll decide that," Leland growled. "Fetch me a bowl of it."

Neither boy said a word, hardly breathing, as Leland shoveled the stew into his mouth. His hunger sated at last, he lifted his head and bent a cold look on Lisha.

"Have you had any company while I've been away?"

"Just those three men who were here before."

"What did they have to say?"

"The redheaded one was mad that you weren't here. He said to tell you they'd be back."

"Yeah, I just bet they will," Leland muttered, scraping the bench away from the table. As he flopped down on the bed, he ordered, "Tend to my horse."

In just seconds, it seemed to the boys, he was asleep. They looked at his sprawled body, hatred in their eyes. How long would the brutal man stay with them? they wondered, praying that he would leave as soon as he woke up.

Chapter Nine

The bartender left off talking to the three men lined up at the bar and walked its length to grin at Jim. "Reba has been askin' for you. She called me a lyin' bastard when I told her you'd gone to church. She wanted to go upstairs and wait for you. Cussed me out real good when I told her no dice. She said you'd give me hell when she told you. When I told her I'd take my chance on you not givin' a damn, she flounced her ass out of here."

"It's time I had a talk with her." Jim frowned his annoyance. "She's been told not to go upstairs unless she's invited." Then, dropping the subject of the madam, he asked, "Where's the key to the storage room?"

Jake reached under the bar, picked up a long skelton key, and handed it to Jim. "It's a pure mess in there. Watch where you're walkin'."

Jim unlocked the heavy door behind the bar and stepped through it. He stood a moment, letting his eyes become accustomed to the gloom, enough that he could make his way to the shuttered window at the end of the room. When the slatted covering was opened and the sunlight flooded the room, he grimaced. A pure mess didn't half describe the room. Sundry items had been pushed and shoved into every available space; only the bar supplies were stacked neatly beside the door.

There were numerous saddles, rifles, guns, and holsters; a glass case with a lock, holding rings and pocket watches. Everything in the room was the possession of men who had pawned it for needed cash.

With a long sigh, Jim began pawing through the accumulation of saddles, blankets, guns, and rifles. There were even two pairs of boots. All were tagged, waiting to be redeemed.

He had about given up hope of finding what he sought when he spotted the guitar half-hidden in a corner by a large framed picture of a naked woman reclining on a sofa. It had hung over the bar when he first purchased the saloon.

The guitar had been there, gathering dust, for over a year. Its owner, a young cowboy, had been trampled to death in a stampede one stormy night, and no relative had come forward to claim it.

He picked his way to what had been a young man's most prized possession. He knew it had been highly valued, for even beneath the film of dust covering it the instrument's highly polished wood shone through. Fastened to its slender neck was an ivory pick. As he strummed his fingers across the strings that were badly in need of a tuning, he wondered how well the cowboy had coaxed a tune from it.

The feeling of contentment was still with Sage when she awakened from her nap. The odor of cooking wafted under her door, and a glance out the window showed that twilight was settling in. She had slept all afternoon.

She stretched lazily; then she turned over on her side to gaze out the window. What was Danny doing at this hour? she wondered. Was he missing her like she was missing him? Probably not. He'd be so involved with his new life at the ranch, he'd never give her a thought.

And that is why I must make a home for us as soon as possible, she thought; and then she wondered what Jim had in mind for her. He seemed to think she could make money at whatever it was.

A minute later she heard her benefactor enter the kitchen and speak to Tillie, so she hurriedly rose from bed. She smoothed down her skirt, tidied her hair, and then walked quickly to the door. Jim might knock for entry at any moment, and she had developed a reluctance to be alone with him. The slide of his blue eyes over her person made her feel sensations she didn't understand.

No, she corrected herself, her hand on the doorknob. She fully understood what he made her feel, and a widow of less than a month shouldn't be feeling that way about a man so soon. Especially about a man like Jim LaTour. Any woman with half a brain would know not to pin any hopes on him; not for a long period of time, at least. Not only did he have a dozen women to choose from, but according to Tillie, he still loved a dead woman.

Sage pushed the door open, her smile including both Tillie and Jim as she stepped inside the kitchen. "It smells awfully good in here, Tillie," she said.

"A beef roast." Tillie indicated the big roasting pan she had just removed from the oven. "As soon as the biscuits are done, we'll eat."

"May I help you with something? I feel so lazy, sleeping all afternoon. I'm not used to doing that. There was always some chore to do on the farm."

"No, everything is ready but the biscuits." Tillie motioned her to join Jim at the table. "You know what Doctor Stewart said. You need lots of rest and good food to regain your health and strength."

"When did John say that?" Jim's eyes narrowed.

"When he dropped by yesterday to visit with Sage for a while," Tillie said with satisfaction, having seen the look of annoyance that crossed her boss's face. Maybe a little competition would stir him up.

Jim kept his face bland, however, and his lashes lowered, hiding the jealousy that jumped into his eyes. Does the doctor have courting in mind? he asked himself. Of course he does, he answered derisively. He and Sage were perfectly suited. They were near the same age; John was a gentleman, and Sage a lady. He tried to tell himself that it would be a good thing if they fell in love and got married. It would solve Sage's dilemma of finding a home for herself and Danny.

He assured himself that he would be happy for them.

But as he watched Tillie place a bowl of mashed potatoes alongside the roast, he found himself giving a scornful grunt and remarking caustically, "I hope John isn't getting his professional feelings mixed up with his personal ones again."

"What do you mean?" Sage gave him a puzzled look while Tillie hurriedly wiped a tickled grin off her lips.

"I mean falling in love again," Jim answered. "Less than a year ago he was in love with Jonty, and wanted to marry her in the worst way."

"So what if he did?" Tillie put a plate of biscuits on the other side of the roast before sitting down at the table. "Most men fall in love many times before the right woman comes along. Each new love can be as strong as the one before it." She slid a look at Jim, wondering if he'd gotten her message.

"Not if the first one was a true love." Jim forked two thick slices of beef onto his plate; then he passed the roast to Sage.

Sage helped herself before passing the meat to Tillie. She looked at Jim and asked, "Do you mean like the love you had . . . have for Jonty's mother?"

Jim gave Sage a startled look; then he shot a reproachful look at his cook, who was studiously helping herself from the bowl of potatoes. When Tillie refused to look up he turned his gaze on Sage, who was gravely watching him and answered shortly, "Yes."

The meal continued in a heavy silence, the only sound the click of flatware as supper was eaten.

The tension eased somewhat when Tillie brought an apple pie to the table and poured each of them a cup of coffee. Conversation picked up, and they talked about other things.

It was after Jim had rolled a cigarette and smoked it that he rose from the table, walked over to a corner, and returned carrying the guitar. He had rubbed away all traces of dust, and Sage exclaimed in delight when he handed it to her.

"It's beautiful, Jim. Not at all like my dad's old battered one."

"Can you pick us a tune, Sage?" Tillie asked eagerly. "I've always preferred the guitar and fiddle over the piano."

Sage strummed her fingers over the strings and grimaced. "Let me tune it first; then we'll see what I can do. It's been a long time since I've played the guitar."

It didn't take her long to adjust the strings. Then, for the next half hour, she entertained Tillie and Jim, picking out tunes and softly singing the words.

When her fingers became sore and she put the guitar aside, Tillie was wiping her eyes on the hem of her apron. "I've never heard the likes before, Sage," she said. "You sing like an angel."

Sage smiled shyly at her praise. "My family always liked to hear me sing, but they never

146

made much of my voice." She laughed softly. "Certainly they never said that I sounded like an angel. In fact, brother Kale used to tease me by saying that I sounded like a cackling hen that had just laid an egg."

She glanced at Jim, who'd had nothing to say yet, and forgot all about Tillie's enthusiastic praise. From the abstract look on his face he hadn't been all that impressed with her singing.

She blinked when he said, "I've come up with an idea of how that marvelous voice can make you a lot of money, Sage. Enough to enable you to get out of Cottonwood . . . if that's what you still want to do."

"You mean giving singing lessons?" Sage and Tillie chorused together, one voice excited, the other one doubtful.

"Come on, ladies." Jim shook his head. "Who in this town could she teach to sing? The cowboys out on the range? The whores next door? The *good wives* around here wouldn't send their younguns to Jim LaTour's woman for any kind of instruction."

Sage flinched at Jim's description of her but didn't say anything. That was the gossip going around. "Well, then, how can Sage make any money with her singin'?" Tillie asked before she could. "I know you wasn't serious 'bout her standin' on the street with a tin cup."

"She can sing for my customers."

While Sage stared at Jim in disbelief, Tillie demanded incredulously, "You want Sage to sing in front of drunken cowboys, whores and men who are just a few steps from the law. That

147

bunch would be all over her. It would be like throwing her to a pack of wolves."

"Do you think I'd let any man so much as lay a finger on her?" Jim shifted indignantly on his chair. "I thought you had more faith in me, Tillie."

"Well, I do," Tillie began weakly. "If you was always there with her they wouldn't, I guess."

"Even if I wasn't there, not one man would dare touch Jim LaTour's woman."

"I reckon," Tillie agreed grudgingly. She and Jim looked at Sage then, and read from the stony look on her face that she, unlike Tillie, hadn't been swayed by Jim's heated assurances that she would come to no harm. To her way of thinking, the chance of being pawed by drunken men was only a part of what was distasteful to her. What she couldn't get past was the thought that she, Sage Larkin, properly raised, a churchgoer all her life, should stand in a saloon and sing to a bunch of ogling, leering men.

It made her cringe to think that she had fallen so low. Was it the devil's work that had put her under Jim LaTour's roof, made her indebted to him?

But even as she resented the plan he had for her, and felt a pain that he more or less put her in the same class with the women who entertained his customers in another way, she didn't lose the thought that she owed this man who watched her so intently. He had saved her life, provided a haven for Danny, and if she could repay him by singing a few songs she would somehow find the courage to do it.

And in the process, she reminded herself, if

what he claimed turned out to be true, she would earn enough money to take them to a safe place where Leland wouldn't find them.

Yet, when Jim asked quietly, "Is it yes or no, Sage?" she couldn't put any enthusiasm into her answer.

"If that's what you want, Jim, of course I'll do it." She held his blue gaze for a moment; then she looked down at the table. "I doubt if the men will like my singing, though. I don't know any bawdy songs."

A sigh of relief feathered through Jim's lips. He hadn't thought it would be that easy to bring her around to his way of thinking. "Don't worry about them not liking your type of songs, Sage." He smiled at her reassuringly. "Believe it or not, those men out there weren't born hellions and outcasts. There was a time when each and every one of them had the love and guidance of parents . . . or at least a mother. Your songs will remind them of those times, and they will shower you with silver dollars and greenbacks."

Unaware of the wistfulness in his eyes, Jim added, "Before you know it, you'll be able to leave us."

"Jim," Sage said earnestly, "it's not that I want to leave you and Tillie. You've been so good to Danny and me, made us feel safe. I don't know what I would have done without your help. But I feel that I must move on. I can't help feeling that Leland is out there somewhere, just waiting to pounce on me.

"I firmly believe there is a sickness in my brother-in-law's mind, and what he might have once called love could turn into hate at any time. I have a real fear of him, Jim."

"Dammit, Sage," Jim swore heatedly, "why can't you believe that I can keep that man from hurting you, that you are safe here? Safer than anywhere else in the world."

Yes, Sage agreed to herself. *I would be safe as long as I stayed here with you. But what would staying with you involve? That I, in truth, become Jim LaTour's woman? And what would happen when you tired of me and went on to some other woman who had caught your fancy? I'd have to move on then. So to save myself heartache I might as well leave as soon as possible.*

She laid her hand on Jim's. "I know that you believe that, Jim," she said quietly, "but Leland isn't like the normal man who goes for what he wants out in the open and accepts rejection. His way is to slip around, to wait for weeks, for months, if necessary, to accomplish what he sets out to do. Look how long he waited to get revenge on his brother."

Jim shook his head resignedly. There was no arguing with her. Her fear of the man kept her from thinking straight. He turned his hand over to lace his fingers with hers. "I hope you will at least feel safe in the saloon. If Larkin is as sly as you claim, he's not likely to try anything in a room full of men."

"I'll feel safe." Sage smiled at him.

"Good. You can start tomorrow night. Go through Jonty's wardrobe and pick out whatever dresses you want."

Sage sat staring at Tillie after Jim rose and left the kitchen. "Oh, Tillie," she wailed, "do you think I can do it?"

"Yes, you can, and you'll do just fine," Tillie answered with a wide smile.

Chapter Ten

Sage had been sorting through Jonty's dresses for at least twenty minutes. In any other circumstances she would have been filled with excitement at wearing something so fine as these garments. The dresses that had hung on pegs in the small cabin she had shared with Arthur had been of homespun, calico and linsey-woolsey, all sewn by her own hand. These creations of silk, taffeta, dimity and fine muslins had been made by a professional seamstress . . . made to Jonty's measurements, which, luckily, were close to her own.

She paused and rubbed her tired eyes. Her sleep had been fitful last night; half asleep, half awake, she had turned from side to side, kicking the covers into a wadded mass at the foot of the bed.

Half-formed dreams had plagued her, where she had stood in front of hot-eyed men whose gazes had stripped off her clothes piece by piece.

When they would reach their hands out to her she would jerk awake, trembling with dread and revulsion.

Sage pushed a heavy fall of hair away from her face as she tried again to choose between a dark green brocade and a blue taffeta. She had washed her hair first thing this morning, wondering why she bothered. When she appeared before her audience this evening they would be so bleary-eyed from drink, they wouldn't even know what color her hair was.

A heavy sigh lifted her chest as she listened to the kitchen clock strike the hour. The time was drawing near for her debut as a saloon songbird.

She sat down on the edge of the bed. Her life had taken such a drastic turn these past weeks. She looked down at her clasped hands. Even they had changed, growing smooth and soft during her time of idleness. Her nails were shiny now, no longer chipped and broken from scrabbling in the dirt, planting seeds, pulling weeds and tending to the many chores that had to be done on a farm. Even the calluses on her palms were gone; those thick, hard patches of skin she had thought to carry to her grave.

A knock on the door pulled Sage's attention from herself and she called, "Come in, Tillie."

It was not the tall, angular cook who stepped into her room. "Oh, it's you, Jim," she said nervously, conscious of her scantily clad body that was covered only with the thin cotton robe she had pulled on after bathing.

Jim closed the door and advanced into the room, and Sage's heart thudded. He looked

Sage

so handsome in his black broadcloth suit, the
black string tie making the texture white of his
shirt almost blinding. No wonder women's eyes
followed him on the street; with his dark skin,
collar-length hair, and deep blue eyes.

What would it feel like, she wondered, to wrap
her arms around those broad shoulders and feel
the chiseled lips on hers? When a warmth began
to spread in her lower regions Sage looked away
in confusion. What in the world was wrong with
her, having such thoughts? She had never asked
herself such questions about Arthur.

Jim's knowing eyes hadn't missed Sage's
disconcertedness, and he knew that in some
way he was the cause of it. His composure
was disturbed also. Every lovely line of her
body was easily discerned beneath the clinging
cotton, and it was evident by the way her breasts
bounced when she walked across the floor that
she wore nothing beneath the robe.

Shoving his hands into his pockets to conceal
the arousal that had risen and pressed against
his fly, he looked down at the two dresses Sage
had spread out on the bed. "Have you decided
which one you'll wear?" he asked, his voice a
little husky from the desire that had leapt into
his loins.

Sage shook her head and turned from the
dresser, where she had been fiddling with the
hairbrush and several little porcelain pots with
red roses painted on them. "Why don't you
choose for me," she said, walking over to
the bed.

He knew which one he preferred, but it took
him a minute to calm his pulse, and to order

his thick tongue to speak in a normal tone. Finally, after pretending to look over both dresses carefully, he said, "I think the green one. It almost matches your eyes."

He looked down at Sage and saw her nervousness, the tightness of her features. He lifted a hand and stroked the curls lying on her shoulders.

"Don't worry about tonight," he said gently. "There's nothing to be afraid of. That wild bunch out there is going to love you."

Sage wanted to turn her cheek against the hand that smoothed her hair, to draw strength and comfort from it. But he might read the action wrong, think that she was inviting more than friendship from him. And that she must never do. By his own admission, he still loved Cleo. He would never involve himself in a lifetime relationship, and she would have nothing less.

When Jim realized he was fingering the softness of Sage's hair he dropped his arm and stepped away from her. "I've had a little stage built for you," he said. "It sits well out of the reach of the customers." His white teeth flashed in a smile as he placed his hand on the butt of the Colt in the holster riding on his hip. "Not only this will be ready to look after you, but there's Jake, too. He wields a heavy club of solid oak."

"Now," he said, turning to the door, "Tillie has a bowl of soup waiting for you. She'll help you get dressed and will fix your hair when you're ready. She's a pretty good hairdresser. She used to do Jonty's when she dealt poker for me."

"Jonty used to deal poker in Trail's End?" Sage's eyes widened at Jim.

"Yes, she did." Jim's lips twisted wryly. "She did until that wild husband of hers came and took her back to his ranch."

"How was she treated by your customers?"

"She was treated fine. Wouldn't nobody dare lay a hand on Jim LaTour's daughter." His eyes teased Sage as he added, "There won't be a man out there who will dare lay a hand on LaTour's woman, either."

Sage felt her face blushing. She didn't know if she liked or disliked the idea that everyone thought she was sleeping with the handsome saloonkeeper. In this instance, she guessed it was just as well that the carousing men she could hear through the thin walls did think that she belonged to Jim.

"I'll come for you in an hour or so to introduce you to the gentlemen," Jim said, putting a derisive emphasis on the word *gentlemen*.

Sage was sitting in the kitchen rubbing a cloth over the guitar when Jim came for her.

Not twenty minutes ago Tillie had helped her into the green brocade and piled her curls on top of her hair, fastening them there with a satin ribbon the color of the dress. She had often heard the expression "fine feathered bird," and as she had looked into the mirror she had smiled thinly. This nervous songbird was at least fine feathered; never mind that she might not be able to sing a note once she left the security of the kitchen and Tillie.

She looked up at Jim to see what his expression would tell her. Would he approve of how she looked?

Jim's blue eyes studied the slender woman gazing uncertainly at him. Surely there was no other woman in the world so beautiful as Sage Larkin. His eyes ranged over her creamy shoulders, the hint of perfect breasts rising above the dress's round neckline. His pulse picked up as he remembered seeing them in all their bared glory and feeling the shape of them through the washcloth he had used to bathe her.

Suddenly, he didn't want the drunken, crude men in the next room to see her. Their lust-filled eyes would contaminate her loveliness, tarnish her innocence. For she was innocent, despite the fact that she had been married. He could see in the depths of her green eyes that her husband had never awakened the passion he was sure slumbered inside her.

"Well, Jim," Tillie broke the silence, "how does she look?"

"She looks," Jim answered in husky undertones, "just like a green-eyed angel come down from heaven."

Sage smiled shyly. "You flatter me, Jim. You know very well that I have no wings."

Jim gave her a knowing smile that made her blush. "Yes, I do know that, don't I?"

Sage made no response. What could she say? He probably knew her body as well as he knew his own.

She lowered her eyes, unable to hold his gaze.

As though he took pity on her, Jim said in his normal tone, "Shall we go, then, Sage? Give them hell-raisers a treat."

Sage's nerves grew tight and her hands trembled as she picked up the guitar. "Relax, honey." Tillie patted her on the back as Jim took her arm and led her toward the door. "Just pretend you're singin' for me and Jim."

Sage was barely aware of her feet moving as she followed Jim into the saloon. When he paused to have a word with Jake, her uneasy gaze skimmed over the smoke-filled room. The long bar was lined with men, and the several tables scattered about were filled. Cordoned off by itself was the gambling area, where more men sat or stood, playing games of chance. Several garishly painted whores danced with some of the customers to a tune pounded out by a thin young man at the piano.

Overwhelmed by the noise, the smell, everything that was alien to her, Sage spun around, crying, "I can't go through with it, Jim."

Jim caught her arm, drawing her to him. "Yes, you can, Sage," he said firmly. "There is nothing for you to be afraid of." He lifted her chin, forcing her to look into his eyes. "The word has gone out that a woman is going to sing in Trail's End tonight. If you don't get up there on that stage and sing, I'm going to have a full-scale brawl in here. They'll wreck the saloon."

Sage's shoulders drooped in resignation. She couldn't allow that to happen. She owed Jim too much.

Calling on every shred of courage within her,

she pulled herself together and said in a small voice, "I'll try."

I'm a no-good coyote, Jim told himself as he took Sage's arm and felt how she was trembling. But dammit, how was she to hold on to her pride if she had to depend on him much longer? These drunks would shower so much money at her feet, she could be independent of everyone. She could make her move to a big city in a short time. And with that voice of hers, plus her beauty, she could choose among the fanciest places in any large metropolis.

His heart was unexpectedly heavy as he helped Sage up on the stage, settled her on the tall stool, then walked away.

A sharp intake of breath came in unison from the men at the bar when they became aware of the proud beauty LaTour had placed before them. "Wonder can she sing?" one man asked another.

"Who cares?" he was answered. "Just lookin' at her will be enough for me."

The entire room grew quiet as gradually everyone picked up the excitement emanating from the bar area. Cards were laid down, the clink of chips ceased, and the roulette wheel stopped turning.

Her legs trembling from nervous tension, Sage slipped the guitar strap over her head and settled it on her shoulder. She ventured a look out over the faces staring up at her and her fingers faltered on the strings at the hunger in the men's eyes.

Her gaze fell on Jim then, sitting alone at a table just below the small stage. The soft encouragement she read in his eyes steadied her hand. She took a deep breath and began to sing as she picked and strummed the chords learned from her father.

By the time her rich voice had finished singing the words of "The Old Folks at Home" the eyes of many of the rough men had grown suspiciously bright. The room burst into an uproar of clapping hands, stamping feet, and calls for more as silver dollars rained at her feet.

Sage looked down at Jim, and pride shone in his eyes. She smiled at him, a comfortable feeling coming over her. No male hand had reached out to paw her and, to her surprise, they approved of her singing.

She had to restrain herself not to jump off the stool and gather up the mound of silver dollars at her feet.

Tillie, though, had advised her not to when the subject was brought up. "You must always act the lady in front of them drunks," she'd said. "Even they know a lady is above scramblin' around on the floor to pick up her money. Let the whore snatch the coin that is tossed at her. Jake will gather it all up after you've left the stage."

Sage idly strummed the strings a moment, then began to sing "Camptown Races," a rollicking song with which the men, as well as the whores, joined in. All the time as she sang two more songs, she managed to ignore the money that continued to fall at her feet.

As she finished the last notes of "My Old Kentucky Home," Jim signaled that she should leave the stage. Disappointed cries were raised when she stood up and smilingly said, "Thank you, gentlemen." Jim took her arm in a possessive manner to help her down the two steps that wasn't missed by the customers. Their eyes followed them until they passed through the connecting door to the kitchen.

"I guess it's true," one man muttered. "She is LaTour's new woman. The lucky bastard."

Tillie waited for Sage, her wrinkled face all smiles. "They loved you, honey," she exclaimed, pulling a chair away from the table and pushing Sage down onto it. "I've made a pot of herb tea for you. It will soothe your throat."

And so the pattern was set for the new phase in Sage Larkin's life.

Sage grew used to singing in front of the rough men, for never by word nor look was she ever bothered. She was highly respected by those who listened to her every night, who even cried at some of her songs. Everyone, with the exception of Tillie, was sure she and LaTour were lovers.

"The blue-eyed breed," they said among themselves, "can't keep his hands or eyes off her." They all agreed enviously that no one could blame him. There wasn't a man among them who wouldn't sell his soul to the devil to be in LaTour's boots.

Reba was also sure that the songbird had taken her place in Jim's affections. Since the widow's arrival not once had he sought her out. Fact of the matter, he practically ignored her these days. He gave her no more attention than he did the girls who worked for her.

Reba chose not to remember that from the very beginning of their relationship Jim had warned her that there would be no future for her with him. He had told her honestly that he tired easily of his women, and if his eye caught one more to his liking, he would move on.

The madam's ire grew as night after night she watched Sage make more money in two hours of singing than she did in a month of catering to the whims and demands of those same males. Reba began to hate the woman she blamed for being the cause of her having to ply her trade again.

And her devious mind began forming plans.

Sage couldn't hide her surprise when one day, while sunning herself on the bench in back of the kitchen, Reba walked outside and sat down beside her. The woman had only barely acknowledged her one time: when Jim had introduced her as the one who ran the business next door. The madam's girls had given Sage a friendly smile and asked if she was feeling better. But Reba had given her a black look and stalked away.

"A beautiful day, isn't it?" Reba said, leaning her head back against the wall.

"Yes, it is," Sage answered; then she waited for the attractive, though hard-faced woman to reveal why she had sought her company. She had come to discuss more than the weather, of that Sage was sure.

Reba knew she couldn't attack Sage directly. If word got back to Jim, he would bar her and the girls from the saloon, and that she did not want. Most of her business came from the patrons of Trail's End. Before Reba had approached Sage she had decided that the best way to break up anything that might be going on between Jim and the singer was through the beauty's pride. Sage Larkin was not the type to share her man with another woman.

She set her plan in motion by giving Sage an innocent look before telling her lie. "I told Jim last night that we should get out in the fresh air more often." She giggled. "Not stay in bed all day."

Sage could not believe how much Reba's remark affected her. She had actually flinched at the woman's words. And though she was furious with herself for caring one way or the other, she waited in dull misery for Reba to continue. She knew there would be more. The madam wanted her to know beyond a doubt that Jim belonged to her.

"Jim agreed, of course." Reba laughed softly. "He agrees to most anything I want. I expect we'll go for a ride later on today."

Sage forced a smile to her face and managed to say calmly, "That will be nice"; then she added her own lie. "I may do the same with John. But most likely in his buggy. He thinks it would be too strenuous for me to go horseback riding just yet."

Reba turned a surprised face to Sage. "I didn't know you and Doc were . . ."

"We're good friends," Sage broke in. "He's a very nice man, you know. A gentleman in all ways."

"Yes, he is a nice fellow," Reba agreed. "It's

too bad he's keepin' company with that Mae Denton, the proprietor of the boardinghouse where he lives. It's said that he sleeps with her."

Reba was quite friendly now and warned, "The woman has a terrible temper. If she sees you ridin' round with Doc she's liable to go after you with a broom. She's not above spreadin' lies about a person either. She's got a tongue like a viper."

Sage shrugged. "I can't help her talking about me, and I doubt that John would let her harm me."

"What if he wasn't around when she attacked you?" Jim said coldly from the kitchen doorway.

Both women turned to look at him in startled surprise. Sage knew that despite his lounging stance Jim was raging inside. How long had he been standing there? she wondered. Had he heard their entire conversation, or just that bit about her and John?

But why should any part of what they spoke of make him angry? If he was involved with Reba, why should he care if she was involved with John?

Reba was concerned, also, with how much Jim had heard. Very flustered, she rose to her feet, hurriedly explaining, "I was just passin' the time of day with Sage, chattin' a little bit. We was remarkin' on the weather; what a beautiful day it is. A perfect day to go ridin'. I was just tellin' . . ."

"Forget about going for a buggy ride with John, Sage." Jim cut across Reba's babbling.

"John would do his best to protect you if the occasion arose, but I doubt he's ever held a gun in his hand or been engaged in a rough-and-tumble fight. If you want to take a buggy ride out into the country, I'll take you."

Sage's eyes dropped to the deadly looking Colt strapped around his hips. Tillie had told her how fast he could draw the gun. And that tough, lean body had been involved in many fights, she imagined. There was no doubt he could protect any woman he might be with.

She glanced up to see the sullen pout on Reba's face and remembered the relationship between the madam and Jim. It was cruel of him to invite another woman to go riding with him in front of the woman he slept with.

She ignored his invitation and remarked, "I suppose I'll have to be content with going to dinner with John occasionally. It is unlikely he would want to handle a gun or engage in fisticuffs." After a short pause she added, "After all, it's his job to save lives, not take them."

Jim slid Sage a dark look. "Sometimes the killing of a polecat will save lives also."

As soon as the words had left her mouth, Sage wished she could recall them. It had been an unfair remark, and she didn't know why she had made it. Here in the untamed west, a fast gun probably saved more lives than it took . . . provided the weapon was handled by a man who didn't take life lightly.

There was an apology in the gaze she lifted to Jim. "You are right, of course."

Jim allowed himself to return her coaxing smile even as he wondered if she knew about his outlaw days, if that had caused her to make the slighting remark about taking lives. He had wounded many men, but he had yet to take a life.

Not that it bothers me one way or the other what she thinks, he told himself, *but I might as well test the lady today.* He would invite her to ride with him, and along the way he would tell her about his past. If she refused his invitation, he would know that she was aware of those days and how she felt about them.

He opened his mouth to speak, then closed it. There was an uneasiness about Sage. Why? His gaze drifted to Reba, whose presence he had forgotten. He frowned at her sullen face and wondered what devilment she might have been up to. What had she and Sage been discussing when he paused in the doorway? He didn't trust Reba as far as he could throw his stallion.

"Reba," he said, "the girls are looking for you"; then he stepped out of the way, pointedly waiting for her to leave. Her face like a summer storm cloud, Reba flounced into the kitchen, making Tillie jump. The madam slammed the saloon door behind her so hard, it shuddered.

Jim hid his amusement as he took Reba's vacated seat beside Sage. "How do you feel about taking that buggy ride today?" He smiled down at her. "We can take the river road, where it's cool and shady."

Sage hesitated. "Will Reba be coming with us?"

Jim shook his head. "She'd spoil the whole

outing. Reba never stops talking. She goes on and on and never says a word worth listening to."

Sage had her first uncomplimentary thought of Jim. How could he spend his nights with Reba and then treat her so shabbily once he left her bed? She would have never thought him that sort of man.

But even as she dithered back and forth, Sage knew that she would take the buggy ride. Something, against her will, pulled her toward the man. It was if she had no control over her mind or actions where he was concerned.

Jim stood up and reached a hand down to Sage, pulling her up beside him. "I'll go hire a two-seater and meet you at the end of the alley in fifteen minutes."

Sage nodded helplessly and went to her room to tidy her hair.

Less than fifteen minutes later, Jim was assisting her into the lightweight buggy and helping her to arrange the full skirt of her dress. Was that necessary? she asked herself as Jim picked up the reins and slapped them over the horse's rump. Arthur had never performed such an intimate act for her . . . before or after marriage.

Actually, Sage admitted to herself as they whirled down the dusty street, she knew nothing of what was proper outside her small world. Jim, however, understood the ways of society in Cottonwood, and probably helping a lady with her wide skirts was the proper thing to do.

As they rode out of town, headed for the tree-lined river, neither of them noticed the pair of angry eyes watching them from an upstairs window of the house next door to the saloon.

Chapter Eleven

Sage sat comfortably in the buggy, relaxed and enjoying the scenery as she and Jim rode along at a leisurely pace. Until now she hadn't fully realized how she hated being cooped up inside. She thought of Danny and almost envied the little fellow's everyday outdoor activities. She missed him dreadfully but was thankful that he was with Jonty and Cord. As Jim had said, a saloon was no place for a youngster.

But was a big city the right place to bring a boy who had never known anything but open spaces and blue skies? As for that, what else had she ever known? They would both be out of their element.

Sage sighed. There was no other answer. If she and Danny were to escape from Leland, it must be in a place where they could hide themselves among a lot of people.

The bright sun cast a dappled pattern through the leaves of the cottonwoods, occasionally highlighting the gray sprinkled in Jim's dark sideburns.

He is the most handsome man I've ever seen, Sage thought, studying his strong profile, the firm, straight lips beneath the thick mustache, the lashes black and stubby.

When she realized she was staring she quickly looked away before he could catch her at it. "Have you always been in the saloon business, Jim?" She broke the easy silence between them.

Well, Jim thought, *she doesn't know about my past after all*. He flicked the whip at a fly on the horse's rump and answered, "Hardly. I've owned Trail's End for just a couple of years."

"I'm surprised. You run the place so well. What kind of business were you in before?"

Sage had given him the opening to tell her about his wasted years, but now Jim hesitated. Should he tell her of his past, from the beginning, when the harshness of life had begun to twist itself around him, making him a fugitive from the law? Should he chance making her think less of him than she did now? He knew she wasn't too impressed as it was with the way he earned his living.

But hell, what difference did it make what Sage Larkin thought of him? She would be out of his life as soon as she was able. It wasn't like they had a future together.

Jim leaned back in the seat, the reins held loosely in his hands. "From the time I was twenty until I was forty, I was an outlaw, Sage. I lived by my wits on the wrong side of the law. It was only a couple of years ago that

I realized how badly my daughter needed me. I couldn't take her on the outlaw trail, so there was only one other alternative. I had to become a repectable, law-abiding citizen, make a home for her. I know that running a saloon isn't the most respectable business in the world, but it beats the hell out of running from the law."

Other than a sucked-in breath, Sage had made no sound as Jim revealed his unsavory past. He looked down at her, dreading to see the scorn that would surely lie on her face. But though she looked a trifle stunned, he saw no contempt, no drawing away from him.

But what was she thinking? he wondered.

He learned some of her thoughts when she asked in a small voice, "Have you ever shot anyone, Jim?"

Jim took several moments before saying, "I have shot men, Sage, wounded them. But always in self-defense. Either I shot them or they shot me. Self-preservation is a man's strongest sense.

"As for lawmen, I've never shot at them. I always figured a man with a star on his vest had a right to shoot at me if I had broken the law."

"Those men you shot at," Sage said after a while, "you must not have been very angry at them. A raging anger can make a person kill. The day those men killed my family, I'd have shot them in the blink of an eye if I'd had a gun."

So, Jim thought, she understands two basic passions, at least: anger and hatred. He still doubted, though, that she had ever experienced that driving, all-consuming passion for a man's body coupled with hers.

He fell to musing on how he'd like to be the man to awaken those fires in her. The only sound that broke the silence between them was the whirring of wheels and the clomping of hooves.

The buggy rolled out of the timber and onto a level stretch of rough bunch grass. Jim and Sage gave a startled jerk of surprise when a streak of lightning zigzagged its way across the sky and a crack of thunder assaulted their ears. Jim glanced up at a sky that seemed to boil with swiftly rolling clouds.

"I'm afraid we're in for a storm, Sage."

"But not half an hour ago there wasn't a cloud in the sky." Sage clutched the sides of the seat as Jim whipped the horse into a run.

"Storms come up real suddenlike in these parts," Jim said. "There's a barn not far from here. Maybe we can make it there before the rain comes."

They had traveled less than half a mile when the clouds opened up, sending down a torrent of water. A high wind came with it, blowing and slashing against the horse's eyes. It whinnied and broke stride.

"Damn," Jim muttered, standing up and popping the reins over the animal's back, which only seemed to confuse the animal more. "He's getting panicky because he can't see," Jim yelled over the wind and the rain and the roll of thunder.

A minute later the horse came to a dead stop, tossing its head and squealing its fright. "I'm going to have to lead him," Jim shouted to a worried, drenched Sage.

"But can you see how to go?" she called anxiously as Jim jumped to the ground.

"I don't know, but I'm sure as hell going to try. It's dangerous to be out here in this lightning," he shouted back, grabbing the slippery-wet bridle and giving it a tug.

The nervous animal calmed down immediately at the human touch and willingly walked alongside Jim, who led the way by instinct alone.

The rain slackened a bit just as the buggy topped a gentle rise. In the distance Sage was able to make out the black bulk of a barn sitting in a grove of spruce and cottonwood. It had the look of a building that had stood empty a long time.

As they neared the shelter, she noted a burned-out house a few yards to the left of the barn. Who had lived here? she wondered. Whose hopes and dreams had burned to the ground? Whoever they were, she sympathized with them. She knew the heartache of seeing one's home burn to ashes. She hoped there had been no lives lost here.

Sage's gaze came back to Jim, who had wrested open the wide barn door and was holding it open with some difficulty in the whipping wind. She grabbed up the reins and drove the horse into the dry, hay-smelling structure. Jim reached up and, grasping her slim waist, swung her to the floor. They stood looking at each other for a moment; then they burst out laughing.

"We look like a couple of drowned prairie dogs." Jim removed Sage's wet floppy hat and tossed it on the floor. He lifted a hand and smoothed a strand of wet hair from her face. When she grinned up at him he lightly stroked her cheek.

"You are so beautiful," he rasped, the playful look gone from his face.

His fingers stroked her throat; then his hand raised her chin so he could look at her soft lips.

Sage's eyes wavered, then shifted. Jim was going to kiss her. Did she want him to? Before she could make up her mind his arms were around her, drawing her tight against his chest. He whispered her name; then his lips were descending on hers. As the kiss went on and on, he cupped her small rear end, bringing it up to mold her body against his rising arousal.

She felt her breasts swell, and the lower region of her body grew weak. She had to cling to him to keep from falling. Jim made a growling noise in his throat and slid a hand between their bodies. His fingers undid buttons until he could bare a breast.

Sage stiffened at his touch on her bare skin. This must go no further. Tonight he would be sleeping in Reba's bed, and she wasn't about to be a quick tumble in the hay, to be as quickly forgotten.

Shame engulfed her. Arthur was dead such a short time, and here she was in the arms of another man, feeling a passion she'd never known before. Although her breasts ached and her body trembled with unfulfilled desire, she moved her head, dislodging Jim's devouring lips.

Jim looked down at her as if in a daze, his eyes clouded with a craving that made her catch her breath. Then he was releasing her, the thick look of passion leaving his features.

"I'm sorry, Sage." He stepped away from her. "I couldn't help myself." He walked over to lean against a supporting beam from which hung bridles, bits, ropes, and branding irons. Also hanging there was a fringed doeskin jacket. It was old and worn, but it would hide the temptation of Sage's body. He took it down and, walking back to Sage, held it open for her so she could slip her arms into the sleeves.

He gave her a rakish smile as he laced the garment up to her chin. "Maybe I can control myself now that your beautiful body is hidden from me."

Her heart still racing and her pulse fluttering, Sage managed to speak with a calmness she didn't feel. "I wonder who the jacket belonged to."

"It belongs to Johnny Lightfoot," Jim answered, walking over to the wide door that still stood open. He stood there in the damp air, hoping to cool his blood, to ease the aching in his loins.

"This place belongs to your cousin?" Sage followed him, but kept some distance between them.

Jim shook his head. "It belongs to me. Before an old enemy of mine burned the house down Jonty, with Johnny's help, ran some cattle here."

"That's terrible," Sage exclaimed, remembering her own home going up in flames. "I hope the culprit didn't get away with it."

"He didn't." Jim's voice was as hard and cold as chipped ice.

They grew silent, gazing out at the rain, which had picked up again. Behind them, the horse snatched mouthfuls of the hay that was hanging down from the loft and made a grinding sound as he chewed contentedly.

"I see Jonty's cattle have multiplied," Jim said after a while as he watched the lightning flash over a sea of horns down by the river, a quarter of a mile away. "Looks like there's been a lot of calves dropped this spring."

"What do you intend to do with the cattle?" Sage also watched them milling around, bawling their fright each time the thunder rolled.

"To tell the truth, I'd forgotten about them." Jim sounded surprised. "I guess I'll have them rounded up and sent to market."

As he spoke, another idea came to Jim. Now that his old enemy Paunch lay six feet under, why not rebuild the house and hire a couple to run the place? His mind went further. What if he sold the saloon and became a rancher . . . maybe even a cattle baron. Wouldn't that make the citizens of Cottonwood sit up and look at the breed with different eyes?

He'd have to think on that some more, Jim told himself, liking the idea.

"When I was a little girl I used to dream of living on a ranch." Sage smiled as she remembered. "There was a large spread near our farm. If I climbed to the top of a tall tree I could make out the ranch buildings and the cowboys herding the cattle."

"And when you grew up, did those cowboys come courting you?" Jim teased.

Sage shook her head, her lips curving upward. "We moved when I was around six years old. That's when I met Arthur. He was the only man who ever courted me."

But, Sage reminded herself, Arthur had never courted her in a romantic sense. They had drifted into marriage.

For a brief moment she wondered what she might have missed in not being courted.

Jim saw the pensive look on Sage's face and wondered what she was thinking about. He knew a twinge of jealousy. Was she remembering her husband? Did she still grieve for him? She seldom talked about him.

Why do you care one way or the other? his inner voice asked. Jim frowned in irritation at himself. When he saw that the rain had slowed to a fine drizzle he said, in a voice that was gruff, "We'd better head back to town if we want to get there before dark."

"Should I leave the jacket?" Sage asked when he had backed the horse and buggy outside.

Amusement flickered in Jim's eyes. "You'd better keep it. If any of the men saw you, their eyes would bug out of their heads. That wet, clinging dress leaves nothing to the imagination."

"Oh," Sage exclaimed in a small voice, clutching the jacket closer to her body. "I'll give it to Johnny the next time I see him."

A red sun was setting and the street was ankle-deep in churned-up mud when Jim pulled the horse up at the alley running alongside the saloon. "Get out of those wet clothes and into some dry ones," he ordered Sage as he helped her out of the buggy. "I don't want you catching pneumonia again." She was picking her way around puddles of water when he called after her, "What if I took you to dinner in that new restaurant in about an hour?"

Sage paused and turned around. "I'm sorry, Jim, but I've already promised John I'd go there with him tonight."

"Oh, and when did the good doctor issue his invitation?"

"Last night. Right after I finished singing."

"I see old John isn't letting any grass grow under his feet," Jim managed to say calmly, although he was fuming inside.

"I'm afraid I don't know what you're talking about, Jim." Sage frowned.

"Cut it out, Sage. You know that John is courting you . . . asking you to have dinner with him, inviting you to go buggy riding with him. Aren't those the same things your husband did before you married him?"

Arthur had never done any of those things, but she wasn't about to tell Jim LaTour that. Instead, she asked him a question: one that startled him and made him fumble for an answer.

"I want to get this straight Jim. You have taken me for a buggy ride, kissed me, and now invited me to dinner. Are you, by any chance, courting me?"

Jim stood poised, one foot on the buggy's small iron step, ready to resume his seat and drive away. Was he courting Sage? he asked himself. When a man courted a woman he had marriage on his mind. He was sure that wasn't the case with him. He didn't want to marry anyone. But looking at it honestly, his actions could very well cause Sage to think that he was courting her, had honorable intentions toward her.

"Look, Sage," he finally said, "I'm sorry as hell for grabbing you back there. I had no idea I was going to do it, but I promise it won't happen again. The buggy ride and the offer to take you to dinner were only friendly gestures."

Jim let out a slow breath after telling his lie. The truth was, friendship didn't enter into it. He wanted Sage Larkin with a gut-deep ache that kept him awake nights. The only solution to his problem, as far as he could see, was to stay well away from her.

"I'm sorry I misunderstood you, Jim." Sage wanted to curl up and die from embarrassment. Of course handsome Jim LaTour wasn't trying to court her. Whatever had made her ask him if he was? Before he could answer her she turned and continued dodging mud puddles as she made her way to the kitchen door.

Jim watched Sage turn the corner of the saloon, his whole being wanting to call her back. But for what purpose? he derided himself as he climbed into the buggy. If ever there was a woman a man should leave alone, it was Sage Larkin. She could take a man and tear him inside out with wanting her, and before he knew it he'd be standing in front of a preacher with her.

Tillie looked up from stirring a big pot of soup and frowned. "My goodness, Sage," she exclaimed, "you look half drowned. Go get yourself dried off and then come have a bowl of soup before it's time for you to sing."

In her room, Sage stripped off the wet clothing and briskly dried her body with a large, soft towel, one of many in a tall cabinet across from the dresser. She had found that Jim had spared no expense in supplying his daughter with anything she could possibly need: like the scented soaps, the hip tub for bathing, and the silk, lace-trimmed underclothing she was now sliding over her body.

Why had Jonty left them behind? she wondered, attacking her hair with another thick towel. Hadn't she liked all the feminine gewgaws?

Sage grinned at her image in the mirror. Sage Larkin liked them. She liked it all: the silk against her skin, the soft nightgowns and clinging robes with their ruffles and lace.

As she pulled a comb through her curls she recalled when she used to pull on her coarse homespun camisoles and petticoats, she had dreamed of silk against her skin.

The clock in the kitchen struck the half hour, and Sage muttered, "Goodness." Her heavy hair was still damp, and she had to be dressed and in the saloon in another half hour. She hoped there would be time for Tillie's soup as she pulled a black taffeta dress over her head and settled the skirt over her hips. She remembered as she adjusted the wide ruffle around her shoulders that she hadn't eaten since the morning. It would be a long stretch before she and John had dinner at the restaurant.

She fashioned her damp hair into a loose chignon at her nape, smoothed her arched eyebrows, and pinched her cheeks to bring more color to her face. She was still pale from her illness, but she refrained from using the rouge pot. Whores painted their faces, and there was no way she wanted to look like them.

Chapter Twelve

As usual, Sage was greeted with loud cries of welcome when she stepped up on the small stage and climbed on the tall stool. " 'My Old Kentucky Home,' Sage," a man called as she picked up the guitar that always leaned against the stool when she wasn't using it.

As her eyes roamed over the smoke-filled room, she smiled and nodded to some of the faces she recognized. Then her gaze drifted to the table where Jim usually sat. He wasn't there! Instinctively, her eyes skimmed the room, looking for Reba.

Reba wasn't there either. Her pick struck a wrong string, giving out a sour note. They were together somewhere . . . upstairs in Jim's bedroom.

Sage felt she had never spent a longer two hours in her life. Her lips hurt from forcing them to smile; her throat ached from holding back the hurt she wanted to put into her songs.

It didn't help at all to scold herself, to point out that it was none of her business where Jim was or with whom.

Finally she sang her last song of the night, and after she had thanked everyone she stepped off the stage and hurried to the kitchen.

Dr. Stewart sat waiting for her, and Sage was forced to smile again. She'd give anything if she didn't have to go out among people, have to talk and laugh and pretend that she was having a wonderful time. *But you have to do it,* her conscience ordered. *The doctor is too nice a man to disappoint.*

"I'll be with you in just a minute, John." Sage smiled at the doctor. "I want to check my hair."

"There's no hurry, Sage; take your time." John had risen when she entered the kitchen, but now he sat back down.

Sage's hair had dried, and she tugged it around her face into tiny, tight curls, the whole time her mind on Jim and Reba. *He wouldn't be with the redhead now if you hadn't rejected him in the barn,* her mirrored image pointed out.

Yes, for one night. Sage gave her hair a final pat and turned away from her accusing face. *You're not thinking about the nights to follow. Nights when he would choose Reba over me. I would be miserable, and I don't need anything else on my plate right now. Worrying about Danny, afraid of Leland finding me . . . that is about all I can handle at present.*

Sage picked up her small reticule and left the room, promising herself that she wouldn't give Jim LaTour another thought. She would sing her songs, hoard her money, and leave Cottonwood as soon as possible. Her rough audience was very generous with the coins they showered at her feet, and another couple of months should see her and Danny on their way.

Jim turned the horse and buggy over to the teenager who worked at the livery and was about to leave when someone called his name. He looked over his shoulder and grinned. Coming toward him was Rooster, one of his old outlaw gang, who he had kept in touch with.

Rooster called, "Hold up, Jim. I got some news for you." Jim waited for the tall, slim man, who was in his mid-fifties, to catch up with him. "Harlan, Tex and Ed are camped down by the river, a couple of miles away," Rooster said.

"How'd you find that out?"

"I overheard one of the whores complainin' about a new man in town abusin' her while she entertained him in bed. When she called him a redheaded devil I had me an idea it might be Harlan. As you know, he's got a reputation for treatin' his women rough. I figured Tex and Ed was with him, so I moseyed out to the edge of town and picked up three sets of tracks and followed them. They led me straight to them."

"I don't suppose there was a stranger with them—a tall, bearded man?"

"No, just them, passin' a bottle of whiskey among themselves."

"Come on; let's go see what the bastards are doing in Cottonwood." Jim turned around and headed back toward the livery, Rooster at his heels.

Jim and Rooster galloped their mounts the first mile and a half; then they slowed to a walk, so as not to alert the three men camped by the river. A short time later Rooster swore a string of angry oaths when they came upon a deserted campfire.

"They ain't been gone all that long," he said as he squatted beside the dead fire and ran his fingers through the gray residue. "The ashes are still warm." He stood up, dusting off his hands. "Do you think they heard us comin'?"

"Most likely. Sound carries on water," Jim answered, then steered the stallion to follow the hoofprints leading along the river.

He had gone only about a hundred yards when the tracks disappeared into the river. He sat looking down at the shallow flowing water. Had the three men gone up the river, or down? He shook his head in aggravation. Even if he knew which direction they had taken, they could stay in the middle of the stream for miles before wading ashore.

Jim turned the stallion around, heading him toward town. "There's no use trying to tail them, Rooster. It's going to be dark in another fifteen minutes."

Rooster kicked his horse into motion. "Why do you think Harlan sneaked into town just to visit a whore? He prefers Indian women, and there's no scarity of them around."

Jim didn't answer for a minute; then, with an angry glint in his eyes, he said, "I think he's after my new singer, Sage Larkin. I think

Harlan has been hired by her brother-in-law to snatch her, to bring her to him. The man is wild to get his hands on her and will go to any length to do it. It's a pretty sure thing he's already had his brother, her husband, killed in order to have her.

"I believe Sage is in grave danger from the man, and when I'm not around I want you to keep a close eye on her. In fact, I've been thinking about asking you if you'd sleep nights in the kitchen until I can take care of the bastard."

Rooster grinned. "Do you think Tillie will let me?"

Jim grinned in response. "Ordinarily she wouldn't, but when I explain to her why I think it's necessary, she won't complain."

"All right, then; I'll bed down in front of Sage's door, starting tonight," Rooster said, and they lifted their mounts into a gallop down the river road.

As Jim climbed the back stairs to the rooms over the saloon, he could hear Sage's throaty voice singing a love song. He paused in front of his bedroom door to listen to her. Had she missed his presence tonight? he wondered. Should he change clothes and go take his usual seat?

No, he decided. She's so damn anxious to leave here, to be on her own, it might as well begin now. He would go down to the kitchen and have supper; then, after Sage finished singing, he'd spend the evening playing poker.

Jim was ready to descend the stairs and make his way through the silent men who would be crowded around Sage's stage when he remembered that she was having supper with the doctor after she finished singing. He paused on the top step. What if Harlan had sneaked back into town? John wouldn't be able to keep the outlaw from taking Sage.

As badly as he hated to do it, he'd have to go to the restaurant and keep an eye on her. Maybe he could sit at a corner table and she wouldn't even know he was there. He sure as hell didn't want her thinking that he had followed her . . . out of jealousy.

As he opened his bedroom door and stepped inside, a nagging inner voice sneered, *That's not the real reason you're going to the restaurant. You know that Harlan is miles away by now.*

"Shut up," Jim growled, stripping off his clothes and then pouring water from a pitcher into the plain white basin. Fifteen minutes later he had washed up, changed into a white shirt and his black, broadcloth suit, and stamped on his best boots. He picked up his gunbelt and strapped it around his lean hips. Checking to see if the holster flap was unsnapped, he took a seat beside the window. From there he would be able to see Sage and John when they entered the restaurant.

Although it was a quagmire underfoot as Sage and John made their way across the street, the sky was clear of all clouds. It bore no resemblance to the one that had poured down rain a few hours back. Sage refused to let herself dwell on what had happened between her and Jim during the deluge.

Sage had never been in a restaurant before, and as she followed John to a table off in a corner, her eyes skimmed over the room that was lit by several kerosene lamps suspended from the ceiling. Three teenage girls wearing long white aprons over gray and white dresses moved among the diners, taking their supper orders.

John was greeted with smiles as they wended their way through the tables, but Sage was coolly ignored by the wives and daughters sitting beside the men, who gave her quick smiles before hurriedly looking away.

Hypocrites, Sage thought, giving those men scorching looks. She knew them all. They came to the saloon every night to ogle her as she sang. And all but one of them often escorted a whore out a side door and across the alley to enter the back door of Reba's pleasure house.

Sardonic amusement flashed in Sage's eyes. Wouldn't the noses of their gossiping wives come down a few inches if they knew their husbands preferred prostitutes to them.

She forgot about the women and their treatment of her as John seated her at a table covered with a fine white cloth with matching napkins. The light from the lamp hanging directly overhead reflected off the shiny china and silverware. Having only ever eaten in kitchens, Sage was quite impressed with it all.

"How are you this evening, Dr. Stewart?" One of the young waitresses approached their table, a wide smile on her face. "Welcome to our establishment." She turned her back to his companion. "We have roast beef or fried chicken tonight, along with mashed potatoes and new peas. For dessert we are serving peach cobbler and cream."

"Come back later." John's tone was short and cool; he was angry at the way Sage was being snubbed. "After Mrs. Larkin and I have decided what we want."

The young woman gave an audible sniff, spun on her heel, and flounced away. John looked compassionately at Sage's flushed, embarrassed face. "I'm sorry, Sage. That's Agnes Bridewell's daughter, and I'm afraid she's just like her mother. Agnes is the self-proclaimed leader of the ladies of Cottonwood, and the biggest gossip. The others wouldn't be so bad if it wasn't for her sharp tongue and trouble-causing ways. They're all afraid if they don't go along with Agnes, they'll be her next target."

Sage lifted pain-filled eyes to John. "All of Cottonwood thinks I sleep with Jim because I sing in his saloon."

"Did you ever consider getting a different job?" John asked, toying with his spoon. "That would stop a lot of tongue-wagging."

Sage gave a bitter laugh. "No one would hire me, John; you know that."

Her eyes widened in surprise when he said quietly, "You could work for me."

"Work for you?" Sage continued to gape at John. "Doing what? Don't you live with . . . have a room at the boardinghouse?"

John flushed and looked down at his plate. He should have known that she would have heard the gossip about him and Mae, he thought angrily, cursing the town's busybodies.

"I had in mind your working in my office." He raised his head and looked at Sage. "Doing such things as writing down the patients' names, when they visited me, what their illnesses were." He smiled a little boy's grin. "I'm not very good at that sort of thing."

At first Sage was gripped with excitement. Working in a doctor's office . . . That would be a very respectable job, one that no one could turn his nose up at.

Her elation began to cool then. She was afraid that would only be the beginning of something else. John acted like a man in love, and she was afraid that later on he would ask her to marry him.

John was a very nice man, Sage thought. He was gentle, considerate, always the gentleman. She sighed silently. Arthur had been all those things, too, but she knew now that much had been lacking in their marriage. There had been no fire between them, no excitement, no thrilling of the blood. She tried to push away the thought of how Jim LaTour's very presence sometimes sent her blood to singing.

But then, Jim wasn't for her either. Even if he wanted her, she wouldn't be able to bear sharing him with another woman. She lifted her eyes to John.

"I need to make a lot of money fast, John," she said gently. "You know my plans. I'm afraid you wouldn't be able to pay me what I make from singing in the saloon."

"You still want to leave Cottonwood, then?" Disappointment was heavy in the doctor's voice.

"I'm afraid so." Sage laid her hand on his.

The reappearance of the waitress stopped John from making a response. The girl noted Sage's hand on his and sniffed her disapproval. Irritation snapped in her eyes when she learned that the couple still hadn't decided what to order.

With soft laughter directed at Miss Bridewell, but unbeknownst to the young lady, Sage and John finally settled on fried chicken. "And bring us a bottle of wine while we wait," John added.

The waitress flashed Sage a look of scorn before walking away stiffly.

Sage smiled thinly. "By tomorrow morning it will be all over town that besides being a fallen woman, I also drink."

"Don't let it bother you, Sage." John reached across the table and gently squeezed her hand. "You'll be leaving her kind before long."

"That's true, but still I'd . . ." Sage broke off at a shrill laugh she recognized. She looked over her shoulder and felt the blood draining from her face.

Just sitting down, two tables away, were Jim and Reba.

Jim sat at his window for close to an hour before he saw Sage and John cross the street and head for the restaurant. Sage clung to John's arm, laughing at something the doctor had said. His face hardened and an erratic pulse worked at his jaw. Did Sage care for John, after all? Did she feel more than friendship for him?

No; Jim shook his head. If she cared for John,

she wouldn't have responded to his own kiss the way she had back at the barn.

But he began to have his doubts again when, a few minutes later, he left the saloon and crossed the street. He had remembered that Sage had been married for some time, and that her husband had been dead for two months. Wasn't it logical that she would miss that part of her marriage, need the feel of a man's body again? And if that was the case, John could probably rouse the same passion in her that he had. And John could offer her something that he couldn't, or wouldn't: marriage.

There was a surly look about Jim when he reached to open the door, where on the other side people laughed and talked as they ate their evening meal. His face grew darker, and he frowned his irritation when his arm was grabbed and Reba's shrill voice rang out: "I was just going in to have my supper, too. We can sit together."

"Oh, hell," Jim swore under his breath, his eyes scanning Reba's bright red satin dress, the neckline scooped so low her nipples were barely covered. And that awful-looking black feather she had stuck in her hair: where in the world had she found that? All in all, she looked exactly what she was: a painted whore who was fast leaving her youth behind.

Cottonwood's society would have something to chew over tonight, Jim thought grimly, pushing the door open. He could almost hear them. "The songbird has transferred her favors to the doctor, and LaTour is back with his whore."

He cringed as Reba's shrill voice exclaimed, "My, my, ain't this grand, Jim"; then she let loose an equally shrill laugh, making everyone turn their heads and stare at them. He gritted his teeth and followed her and the waitress to a spot only two tables away from Sage and John.

What little appetite Sage had deserted her. Jim was telling her, and the whole town, that Reba was still very much a part of his life; that nothing had changed between them. And what would the townfolk think of that, she wondered, staring down at her plate, her face flushed. Would they tell each other that the saloonkeeper slept with both of them?

That she was helpless to make the people in this room think otherwise caused an anger to grow inside Sage. But was she really helpless? A glimmer of an idea came to her. What if she could make them think she was only interested in John, that she cared nothing for Jim LaTour? It wouldn't be fair to John, but she was going to put on a performance that would convince everyone here that she was very interested in the handsome doctor.

She became so animated that the diners watching them had no idea she was describing to John how once her father's bull had chased her up a tree.

John sensed that although Sage might not realize it, the soft laughter and the touching of his hand were a display for Jim and not for him. But though it pained him, he went along with her. It was time Jim LaTour knew the bite of jealousy.

John smiled into her eyes and appeared to

be murmuring very intimate things to her, but actually he was saying, "Let's rile the hell out of him."

Surprise leapt into Sage's eyes for a moment; then she giggled. She slapped playfully at John, exclaiming, "You naughty boy," just as Jim raised his head and glared at her.

"Oh, hello, Jim and Reba," she called sweetly, pretending she hadn't seen them until now. "Would you like to join John and me?"

When Jim only continued to glare at her with no answer, Sage smiled and shrugged her shoulders. "I guess the lovebirds want to be alone," she said, loud enough for Jim to hear. She hid her glee at the killing look he sent her way.

Sage and John's fried chicken was served then, and they attacked the meal with hungry appetites, continuing their soft laughter and softer looks at each other.

Jim watched them through lowered lids, eaten up with jealousy. It was an emotion he had never experienced before; and one he didn't like at all. It gripped him in the pit of his stomach, tying him in knots. He wanted to leap to his feet, rush over to John, and plant his fist in the man's smiling face.

He turned a snarling face on Reba and barked, "What!" when she put her hand on his arm and spoke.

"I said, Sage and Doc seem to be havin' a good time. I never seen Sage laugh so much before. Usually she's on the quiet side." She slid Jim a look from the corners of her eyes and asked, "Did you know they was courtin'?"

"No, I didn't know it, and you don't either. They're only having a friendly supper together."

"Well, it seems more than a friendly supper to me," Reba observed. "I bet Doc gets farther than the kitchen tonight. I bet he gets to see Miss Fancy's bedroom again." She snickered. "And not for doctorin' this time."

The sly look slid from her face as Jim's icy stare bored into her. "Why don't you just shut up," he grated, "and keep your mind on who's going to visit your room tonight."

"Will it be you, Jim?" Reba looked at him hopefully. "It's been a long time."

"It won't be me, Reba." Jim softened his tone. "You knew from the beginning that there would be nothing permanent between us. Our time together is over and done with."

Reba's temper flared. "It wouldn't have been over if that damn, skinny widow hadn't come along, and you know it. It's her you want now, but I'll lay you odds you won't get her. She's not one to sleep with a saloonkeeper."

"I'm not planning on sleeping with her," Jim retorted, annoyed. Reba's pronouncement was too close to the truth. He sighed his relief when their food arrived.

Chapter Thirteen

Sage awakened to two different songs: the trill of a meadowlark perched in a lodgepole pine outside her window and Tillie singing a bawdy song from her days of entertaining men.

She rolled over on her back and flung an arm across her red-rimmed eyes. She hadn't slept well last night, and the joyous song of cook and bird was a source of annoyance, adding to a headache that threatened to pounce upon her.

Sage was more annoyed with herself, though. Why did she let it bother her, keep her awake, that Jim was still very much involved with Reba? What had made her think that he wasn't? Just because he spent some time with his singer in the daytime didn't have any bearing on how his nights were spent. Once she finished singing to his customers she didn't see him until the next day. If she had given it any thought, it would have been obvious how, and where, he spent his nights.

Sage sat up and slid off the bed. She and John had made plans last night to ride out to the McBain ranch to visit Danny. Her spirits picked up as she washed her face, and then dressed in a divided skirt of Jonty's and slipped her arms into a red-checked shirt. She had been missing Danny dreadfully and couldn't wait to see his sunny, freckled face. She stamped on her boots, brushed her hair, tied it back with a red ribbon, and then swung open her bedroom door.

The breath left her lungs with a whoosh when she stepped into Jim, ready to knock on the door. His hands shot out to grab her arms to steady her. She gazed up at him and thought to herself that he looked worse than she felt. From his haggard-looking appearance, he hadn't got much sleep last night either.

Reba had seen to that, she thought bitterly, and pulled herself free of Jim's hands.

"Good morning," she said coolly; then she smiled a greeting at Tillie, turning her back on Jim and sitting down at the table.

Jim followed and sat down opposite her. "I see you're dressed to go riding," he said as Tillie poured them both a cup of coffee. "I'm afraid I'll be too busy today to ride with you, but I'm sure Rooster will be thrilled to keep you company."

"That won't be neccessary," Sage said, reaching for the sugar bowl. "John is taking me out to the ranch to spend the day with Danny."

"Like hell he is," Jim exploded, making Sage jerk and spill a spoonful of sugar on the table. "Unless you ride like the wind you can't make it to the ranch without camping out one night. And you're not going to be camping out with

Dr. John Stewart. Tongues would really wag about that."

Sage brushed the sugar into her palm and carried it over to the dry sink. "I didn't know Jonty's ranch was that far away," she said in disappointment as she resumed her seat. "I had so hoped to see Danny."

"And so you will." Jim gave her a wide smile. "I'll take you."

Sage stared at him, not believing what she'd heard. "Won't tongues wag if I camp out with you?"

"No." Jim shook his head. "Nobody will think a thing about it. Everyone already knows that you're my woman."

"I'm no such thing, Jim LaTour!" Sage glared across the table at the smug-looking handsome face.

"Let me rephrase that." Jim grinned. "Everyone *thinks* you're my woman."

"I doubt that," Sage snapped. "Not after last night. The room was buzzing with speculation when you escorted Reba into the restaurant."

"I didn't bring Reba with me," Jim barked loudly, bringing his fist down on the table and making Tillie draw back for a moment before placing bacon and eggs before him. "She invited herself just as I was ready to go inside. What was I supposed to say: 'Reba, you can't sit with me. I don't want you to?'"

"You could hardly say that," Sage sniffed, "considering you'd be sleeping with her later on in the night."

"Sleep with her? Where in the hell did you get that notion?" Jim was practically shouting now.

"Everybody knows you sleep with her. It's hardly a secret." Sage's voice had risen too.

"Everybody knows I *used* to sleep with her. They *think* they know that I now sleep with you."

"Damn you, Jim LaTour," Sage shouted, looking like she was going to spring across the table and attack him. "Everybody in this miserable town thinks you're sleeping with both of us after last night."

"I can't change their way of thinking," Jim said unconcernedly as he opened a steaming biscuit and slathered it with butter.

Indignant color flared in Sage's face. He reacted so casually even though her good name was ruined in Cottonwood. *Why do you care what these people think?* her conscience asked. *You'll be leaving here soon, never to lay eyes on any of the gossips again.*

Still, when a little later Jim remarked that they could leave for the ranch whenever she was ready, she nearly retorted that she had changed her mind; she didn't want to go after all.

But, as the old saying went, she would be cutting off her nose to spite her face. She badly wanted to see Danny, and if it meant camping out one night, Jim was probably the only man she knew who could safely take her to her nephew. Truthfully, she wouldn't feel all that safe with John in case Leland was lurking around, maybe following them.

She looked at Tillie, hovering near the table, and read encouragement in her eyes. With an inward sigh, she said, "I'll be ready to go as soon as I write John a note."

"Fine." Jim nodded, then looked at his cook.
"I know." Tillie grinned. "Pack some trail
grub."

Jim returned her grin, then attacked his
breakfast. Sage watched him a moment, wanting to slap the complacent look off his handsome face. As usual, he had gotten his own
way.

As Sage and Jim rode along the river road
for a couple of miles before cutting across
country, heading toward the distant Devil's
Mountain where the McBain ranch was situated
in the foothills, a comfortable silence existed
between them.

It was a glorious day, Sage thought; the air
was dry and warm, the cloudless sky so deep
blue it hurt your eyes to look at it. Underfoot
lay a carpet of wildflowers, stretching as far as
the eye could see. *I love this beautiful land,* she
thought as she gazed out over the grandeur of
flowers and grassland. *It will be hard to leave
it, to live in a dirty, crowded city with strangers
who will care nothing about me, no one to
call on if I needed help. I can't even think about
what such a move might do to Danny.*

But it had to be done if they were to live free
of her brother-in-law.

As Jim's stallion, Major, clomped along, Jim
kept his eyes on the mount's ears. They would
alert him quicker than anything else if someone
was trailing them. In open country like this,
though, a man would be a fool to try tailing
someone. It was when darkness set in and they
were camped that was the dangerous time.

While they were sitting around a campfire, a sniper could stand back in the shadows and blast a man to kingdom come. He was a fool, he knew, taking this trip, but Sage was a very determined young woman when she made up her mind to do something.

Like leaving Cottonwood and his protection.

He understood her desire to see her only remaining relative, though. He looked forward to seeing his daughter and grandson.

I'll just have to keep on my toes and have the Colt ready. Jim's lips firmed grimly. *And keep Major nearby.* The stallion was almost like a dog when it came to warning him of danger. In his outlaw days he had been nudged awake many times by a snorting nose on his shoulder, warning him that a stranger was approaching the camp.

It was a little past noon when Jim reined in beside a waterhole. Sage came up beside him, and while the horses quenched their thirst Jim rummaged in the grub bag and brought out two sandwiches wrapped in oiled paper.

He handed one to Sage, saying, "If it's all right with you, we'll eat our lunch as we ride along."

"I don't mind in the least." Sage unwrapped a hearty beef sandwich. "But why not stop to eat?"

"This trip can be made with one night's camping only if you don't tarry along the way. Like not stopping to eat the noon meal, or making a fire and brewing a pot of coffee. Otherwise, you're forced to camp out two nights."

"Then, by all means, let's keep riding," Sage

said with a shiver. "Camping out doesn't appeal to me at all. I had enough of that when Danny and I were running from Leland."

"You'll find sleeping out quite different tonight. You'll have a nice warm supper, and you'll sleep cozy warm. And," he assured her, "you'll not have to worry that your brother-in-law is sneaking up on you."

"That's good to know." Sage smiled, then bit into her beef and bread.

Dusk was not far off when Jim pulled up the stallion beneath a large lodgepole pine. "This is my halfway point," he said, swinging to the needle-strewn ground and motioning to a fire pit beneath the spreading branches of the tree. "I don't know who originally fashioned it, but as you can see by the ashes piled around, it's been used many times."

He helped Sage to dismount, his hands lingering a moment on her waist before releasing her. When she gave him a startled look before walking away from him he dragged the saddles off the mounts and then tethered them to the tree. Hungry wolves would be roaming around tonight, and the horses would look tasty to them.

He spread the cinches and stirrups over a large rock; then he folded the saddle blankets and placed them on the ground to sit on while they ate their supper. Later they would be used as a foundation for their bedrolls.

Jim walked over to the fire pit. Hunkering down beside it, he raked together the burnt ends of a previous fire, most likely his own, and tossed a couple handfuls of pine needles beneath them. When he struck a match and held its flame to the oil-filled spines it took only seconds to have a crackling fire going.

Sage, who had been watching his efficient movements, asked, "What can I do to help?" when he dumped the cooking gear and bedrolls onto the ground.

"Nothing, nothing at all." Jim gave her his crooked, handsome grin. "Just sit there and look beautiful. I've done this so often, it's second nature to me."

Sage blushed at his reference to her beauty but made no response. What could she say— that she wasn't beautiful, making him feel that he should add another compliment? After all, she wasn't some giggling young girl who didn't know the difference between an honest compliment and insincere flattery. If Jim said she was beautiful, that was what he thought.

She sat quietly watching as he started a pot of coffee to brewing, taking the water from his canteen, and then started thick slices of salt pork to sizzling in a blackened skillet.

In moments, it seemed, the sun dropped behind the distant mountain and night was upon them. In the vast land of darkness Sage thought their fire was tiny and insignificant. But the smell of wood burning somehow brought a friendliness to it. She looked over her shoulder, hoping the fire was big enough to keep away the wolves she was sure roamed the area.

Jim saw her nervous action and smiled reassuringly at her. "Don't worry about any critters sneaking up on us, Sage, be it four-legged or two-legged. Major will let me know if there's an enemy of any kind within a mile of us."

He patted the Colt. "If I have to use this, I never miss what I aim for."

Sage gazed into the fire with a certainty that she was quite safe with Jim. He would protect her against any danger. She was fully relaxed when he handed her a tin plate containing crisp fried meat, heated baked beans, and a slice of Tillie's sourdough bread.

"You're a fine cook, boss." Sage grinned at him as she scraped her plate clean of the last bean and leaned back against the rock behind her with a sigh of contentment.

"Thank you, peon." Jim grinned back at her as he poured them each a cup of coffee. "The secret was in how I heated the beans."

Sage laughed softly at his nonsense, then carefully sipped the hot coffee as Jim rolled himself a cigarette. As they sat staring into the fire, there was no sound in the night but the rustling of the pine and the cropping of grass as their mounts ate their supper. When a yawn escaped Sage Jim rose to his feet, bent over, and picked up their bedrolls.

Sage stood up and unfolded the blanket she'd been sitting on, and he unrolled the sleeping gear on top of it. While he was smoothing it out, she picked up his blanket, then stood, uncertain where to spread it out. On the other side of the fire? That would be the proper thing to do. But she didn't want him that far away from her!

There was amusement in Jim's voice when he said, "Place it next to yours, Sage. How else can I keep a protective eye on you?"

Feeling like a fool, or an old maid, Sage made no response, only shook out the blanket and spread it next to hers. Her face blazed red when Jim said, "I'm going to take the mounts to a waterhole a few yards away for a drink. You can . . . ah . . . have a little privacy for ten minutes or so."

Thank God, Sage thought. *Another minute and I'd have embarrassed myself.* Swaying along on a horse all day didn't help a full bladder.

She had answered nature's call and was snuggled in her blankets, having only removed her boots, when Jim returned, leading the horses. She pretended to be asleep as Jim scoured out the cookware with pine needles. She didn't open her eyes until she heard the rustling of his blankets as he settled into them.

It's not bad, sleeping out, when you can do it in comfort, Sage thought, staring up at the countless stars dotting the sky, shedding a soft light over the area. She was warm, her stomach was full, and she had protection. She wished, however, she had placed Jim's blanket a little closer when off in the distance the yowl of a wolf sounded wild in the night.

She gave a startled jerk when Jim said quietly, "Relax, Sage; they won't come near the fire."

Taking him at his word, Sage drifted off to sleep, rousing once to see Jim roll out of his blankets and replenish the fire; and then, half asleep, he sank back into his bedroll.

How did he know the fire was almost out? she wondered; then she fell back to sleep.

The new day began with bright, warm sunshine, but a cool, brisk wind had risen sometime during the night, making Sage shiver and pull up the collar of her jacket. She was thankful that she had taken Jim's advice about taking it along.

"The wind is cold because it's coming off the mountain," Jim explained as he cooked the same kind of breakfast they'd eaten for supper. "There's snow still lingering in the high reaches. It won't all melt until the latter part of next month."

The morning meal was eaten in short order; then Sage packed up the camping gear while Jim saddled the horses. Her movements were a little stiff, her body unused to long hours in the saddle. She dreaded climbing back on the mare Jim had rented for her. But after a few minutes of the mount's easy gait she loosened up and felt fine.

At noon another of Tillie's sandwiches was handed to Sage, and again it was eaten as they rode along. "I hope Jonty isn't serving beef for supper." Jim finished off his lunch with a swallow of water from his canteen. "I'm a little tired of it; how about you?"

"Oh, I don't know. I'm not a fussy eater," Sage answered. "I like beef, actually. Living on a farm, a person mostly eats pork and chicken."

"I'd like to hear about your farm . . . unless of course, it's too painful to talk about."

Sage gazed out over the plains. Could she talk about the farm where she and Arthur had spent their married life and worked so hard together? In her mind she saw Arthur's dear, kind face, and she thought, yes, she would like to speak of the place where she had thought she'd live out her life.

"It wasn't too large a place," she began, "only about fifty acres, and ten of those woodland. But Kale owned fifty acres that abutted ours, so the two farms together gave us enough land to keep the four of us working from sunup to sundown. Although cash was always scarce, we made a good living off the place. We always ate well."

But you never had any of the nice extras of life, Jim thought. *Never a fancy dress or a silk bonnet, or a piece of jewelry, except for that wide band of gold on your finger.*

Jim remembered Sage's rough, workworn hands the night he'd bathed her, fighting desperately to keep her temperature down. How at odds they had been with her soft white body, he remembered.

Suddenly, he wanted to give this woman all the pretty things she deserved but had never had.

The thought had barely entered Jim's mind when his face darkened with a frown. What in the hell had he been thinking? A woman like Sage would only accept expensive gifts from her husband, and Jim LaTour would never be a husband to any woman. He had no heart to give. And though he desired Sage with an aching hunger, she was too decent to be used casually. She deserved a good man, one who would love her, marry her.

John Stewart's face swam before his eyes, but he pushed it away. He didn't want her to marry a man from Cottonwood. He would have to see her all the time, know that she belonged to someone else. So let her leave whenever she was ready and find a stranger to marry.

It was around two hours before sunset when Jim pointed westward and said, "There's the ranch—there at the beginning of the foothills."

Sage shaded her eyes against the glare of the sun and peered at the group of buildings in the distance. "It looks like quite a large place."

"It is. One of the largest spreads in this part of the west, I'm told."

Together they lifted their reins, sending the horses into a gallop toward the mountain. Sage gave a ringing, glad cry when she spotted a little Indian pony racing toward them, a small figure on its sturdy back.

"It's Danny." She smiled excitedly at Jim.

"And look how that little dickens can ride," Jim called back. "It's the Indian blood in him," he said proudly. "There's no finer rider than the Indian."

The three mounts met, their hooves throwing up a cloud of dust as they were pulled to rearing halts. Danny and Sage were out of the saddles and flinging their arms around each other before the swirling dust had settled. Jim smiled his pleasure, watching them laugh and hug, so happy to see each other again.

Sage finally held her nephew away from her, her eyes hungrily moving over his face. "My goodness, Danny, you've grown like a weed while my back was turned."

Danny's head nodded eagerly. "Cord says two inches at least. He says that if I keep growing like that, pretty soon he'll make me into a ranch hand."

"It sounds like you'd approve of that." Sage smiled, but inside she was alarmed. This little fellow wasn't going to like living in a big city. She looked at his tanned, glowing face and his clear green eyes, used to looking out over unobstructed distances, and felt her heart sink. All the joy would go out of that dear little face, penned up in a place of noise and dirt, with nowhere to play or ride a horse. And probably there wouldn't even be a clear view of the sky.

Jim was thinking along the same lines. It would be almost criminal to take the boy from a life he plainly loved to one that would crush the vibrancy from his entire being.

When he switched his gaze to Sage Jim realized from the worried frown on her face that the same thought had occurred to her. He swung to the ground and gave Danny a wide smile of greeting.

"What do you think of my mustang, Jim?" Danny patted the little horse's neck. "Cord gave him to me. I call him Hero because he's so brave. He stamped a rattlesnake to death one day when we were out riding."

"He's a fine-looking animal, Danny, and I can tell you've been taking real good care of him," Jim complimented him, making the boy's face glow. "We'll have to . . ." He broke off at the sound of galloping hooves coming toward them.

"Jonty!" he cried, the happiness of seeing his daughter fighting with a worried frown.

"What a nice surprise." Eyes so like his own

gazed down at Jim as he lifted Jonty from the saddle. "I didn't expect to see you for at least another month."

"It's a good thing I've come when I have." Jim gave her a slight shake. "What do you mean by riding like that in your condition? Are you trying to lose my grandchild?"

"Oh, Dad, a short run isn't going to hurt the baby." Jonty laughed; then she turned to Sage. "Welcome, Sage. Danny has been missing you."

"I've certainly been missing him." Sage hugged the boy's narrow shoulders, then gasped in alarm. Trotting toward them was the largest wolf she'd ever seen. She grabbed Jim's arm and pointed. "There's a wolf, Jim! Shoot him!"

Everyone laughed, and she thought she'd faint when Danny ran to meet the animal and throw his arms around the thick neck.

"It's all right, Auntie Sage," he called, leading the wolf up to them. "He's Jonty's pet. Johnny Lightfoot gave him to her. His name is Wolf."

"Johnny didn't give a lot of thought to coming up with an original name, did he?" Sage laughed weakly, still clutching Jim's arm, her heart still pounding.

Sage spent half an hour with Danny in his room. He told her about the exciting life on the ranch, his speech peppered with Cord's name. When he yawned in the middle of a sentence she told him good night. Dropping a kiss on his forehead, she left to join Jonty and the two men in the large family room.

A fire burned in the fireplace, taking away the

chill of the evening. As she took the chair left for her next to Jim, he noted her preoccupation. Something to do with Danny, he imagined.

As conversation went on around him, Jim stared into the flames, taking no part in it. He had his own anxieties about the boy, as well as a tinge of jealousy. He had grown fonder of Sage's nephew than he had realized. Seeing the boy hang on every word that came out of his son-in-law's mouth hadn't set at all well with him. Back in Cottonwood he had received all the adoration from the lad. Was it possible, he asked himself, that all this time he had unconsciously wished he had a son?

Don't be an idiot, he snorted silently. Sage will be taking the kid away before long and you'll never see him again. Nevertheless, he found himself imagining Danny riding his little Indian pony over *his* range, riding alongside *him*, emulating *him*, sitting the saddle the same way, walking like him. He grinned. Maybe even swearing a bit, scandalizing his aunt.

Jim drifted on to visualize the house he would have built on his property. It would have a big family room like this one, and a kitchen with a big window that Sage could look out of as she prepared meals or washed dishes.

A log in the fireplace burned through and fell with a thud, showering sparks onto the hearth and bringing Jim out of his daydream. He threw an uneasy glance at his companions. Could they read what had been on his mind?

He relaxed. Nobody was paying any attention to him. Sage was bringing Jonty up to date on the news in Cottonwood.

"Janie can be a pain in the neck sometimes," Jonty said, "but I do hope that Tillie remembers to give her a plate of something for supper every night."

"Don't worry about that old hag." Jim snorted. "She's always there to remind Tillie what sweet little Jonty always did for her. Tillie grinds her teeth, but she always feeds her." He looked at Jonty and teased, "Just like you feed her old friend, Thadeus."

"I know." Jonty grinned sheepishly. "And he's a pain in the butt also. The man never stops talking."

Jim yawned widely, then apologized. "I guess all that fresh air made me sleepy. I'm not used to it."

"I'm sleepy, too," Cord said, flipping his cigarette butt into the fire. He looked at Jonty with slumberous eyes. "You ready to go to bed, wife?"

Jonty blushed at Cord's obvious meaning, and gave him a chastising look that only made him grin at her. She turned her head away from the mischievous smile. She had other things than making love on her mind. Should she give Sage and her father separate rooms, or would they want to share the same bed?

Although they seemed to get along exceptionally well, she didn't think there was anything romantic between them. It was true she had caught her father looking at Sage as if he'd like to devour her, but Sage never seemed to notice.

That disappointed Jonty. She liked the young widow. She was the first decent woman her father had ever shown an interest in. Jonty's dearest wish was for him to fall in love and get married.

Jim stood up and stretched, then took the decision away from Jonty. "Will I be sleeping in the same room I had before?"

"Yes," Jonty answered at the end of a long, silent sigh of relief. She looked at Sage. "Your room is next to mine and Cord's, Sage. At the end of the hall to your right."

Good nights were said and beds were sought. Jim was awhile falling asleep. His hunger for Sage was tying him in knots.

Sage didn't fall asleep all that quickly either. The rhythmic squeak of the bed next door made her think of Jim and how his kiss had affected her. She found herself wishing that he was with her, doing with her what Cord was doing with Jonty.

"I wish you could stay longer," Jonty said the next morning as she packed Jim's saddlebag with fried chicken and biscuits. "You weren't here any time at all."

"We've got to get back, honey. My customers will be howling to hear Sage sing, and there's a carpenter in town I want to talk to before he leaves."

"Are you going to have some work done on the saloon?" Jonty asked as she pushed a platter of cookies out of Cord's reach.

"No. I'm thinking about having a house built on the burned-out ruins of the cabin."

"When did you decide to do that?" Jonty asked, surprised.

"When Sage and I rode out there the other day and I saw how the cattle had multiplied. I should either turn the place into a working ranch or sell it."

"Build on it, Dad. It's so beautiful there in the valley. Didn't you think so, Sage?"

"It's one of the most beautiful places I've seen," Sage answered, an unconscious wistfulness in her voice.

Jonty could hardly conceal her pleased smile. The day was approaching when her father would realize he loved his songbird.

Chapter Fourteen

Jim and Sage didn't talk much as they rode along. Both were occupied with thoughts of the future.

Sage's musings were uncertain and disturbing. She was planning to move into a world she knew nothing about, and it frightened her. And, after seeing how happy Danny was, living on the ranch, she worried more than ever about transplanting him.

It frightened her more, however, to think of staying much longer in Cottonwood. She had the uneasy feeling that Leland was not far away, that it was just a matter of time before he learned of her whereabouts.

Jim was thinking about the house he wanted to build; he would buy more land, purchase more cattle. He asked himself if he should sell the saloon and decided that maybe he would. It kept him indoors too much. Sometimes days would pass without him stepping outside once.

The long night hours kept him sleeping the days away.

Then again, the saloon brought in a lot of money. Maybe he'd keep it and let Jake run it for him while he ran the ranch. As he dithered back and forth, he ignored the fact that the beautiful widow might have a lot to do with his decision when the time came for him to make up his mind.

The day wore on, and Sage and Jim left off their separate ponderings when they came to the spot where they had camped before. It was nearing twilight as they swung out of the saddle, and Jim immediately began setting up camp. When he took the mounts to the watering hole Sage set out to answer nature's call.

She had arranged her clothes and was walking back toward the brightly burning campfire when she stopped short, so frightened she couldn't cry out.

In her path stood a huge gray timber wolf, his jaws slavering, his eyes a malignant red. As she stood staring, terrified, the animal bared its fangs in a hideous grin, as though it mocked her, daring her to try to escape him.

Sage made no move. If she made the slightest motion, she knew the beast would spring at her. Her heart pounding and her nerves stretched to the breaking point, she kept her eyes steady on the great beast.

Then the tense silence was broken by the snapping of a twig. The wolf's head shot up, his ears erect as he looked past her. The fur on his back bristled as he stood on braced feet. Then, with an angry snarl, it wheeled and leapt away from her. While its body was in the air, there came the sharp report of a gun, and the gray body dropped to the ground, landing on its side, jerking spasmodically.

Sage wheeled around. Jim stood behind her, the smoking Colt in his hand. He ejected the empty shell and reloaded before returning the gun to its holster.

"I expect old Lobo has been following us," Jim began, then sprang forward to catch Sage's limp body before it hit the ground. "By God if she hasn't fainted," he said under his breath as he scooped her up in his arms and carried her to the fire.

Supporting her back with one hand, Jim managed to shrug out of his jacket and bunch it into a pillow for Sage's head. When he had stretched her out he began to chafe her cold hands and call her name, his voice sharp with alarm. Never before had he had to deal with a fainting woman.

He gave a deep sigh of relief when Sage's eyes opened and she looked at him blankly. "What happened?" she asked in confusion.

"You fainted." Jim continued to rub her hands.

Sage stared up at him for a moment; then enlightenment widened her eyes. "Oh, Jim!" Her face blanched. "It was terrible. I was only inches away from death and I was too paralyzed with fear to call out to you."

Jim pulled her into his arms, stroking her head as he held her trembling body. "You don't have to be afraid now," he murmured softly. "He's dead."

Sage remained in the warm safety of Jim's arms a moment longer; then she pulled away from him. "I'm terribly embarrassed," she said. "You must think I'm an awful coward."

"I would never think that," Jim denied, wishing he could have held her a little longer; she had felt so good in his arms. "A wolf that size could shake up the bravest man," he said, standing up. "I'm going to get a pot of coffee going and make us some supper. You'll feel better after you've eaten."

Sage watched Jim start the coffee brewing and then laid out the remainder of Jonty's fried chicken and biscuits. Her nerves gradually settled back to normal. Only a weakness in her limbs remained from her encounter with the wolf.

But Jim's blood still raced hot in his veins. How he wanted the slim body he had held in his arms such a short time. He could still feel the ripe breasts smashed up against his chest. It had taken every bit of his willpower not to take advantage of her vulnerable state and seduce her on the spot. He felt sure he could have, but what would have happened later, when the passion had drained away and Sage had come to her senses? She might hate him, might pick up and leave as soon as they arrived back in Cottonwood.

And what if she did? he asked himself. Wouldn't it be better if she did move on? Out of sight, she wouldn't be a constant temptation, this woman who made him want her with every beat of his heart yet frightened him to the core of his being.

Slowly Jim's blood cooled and he was back to his usual calm, cool self when he smiled across the fire at Sage and announced that supper was ready.

Neither had much to say as they ate the tender fried chicken and drank two cups of coffee each. The day's ending had been too traumatic, shattering nerves, taking away the desire for conversation.

When Sage looked over her shoulder several times, peering into the darkness, Jim said, "He was alone, Sage. Most likely he had become separated from the pack. There won't be any more coming around."

"If you're sure, I think I'll go to bed." Sage commanded herself not to look into the darkness again.

"I'm ready to turn in too." Jim stood up and began spreading their bedrolls.

Sage was soon snuggled between her blankets, gazing up at a full moon. She dimly heard Jim moving about; adding more wood to the fire, rinsing out the coffee cups. Her lids grew heavy and she drifted off to sleep.

It was around midnight, according to the movement of the moon, when Jim jerked awake at the sound of his name being called in a panic-stricken voice. As he threw off his blanket and moved the couple of feet to where Sage lay thrashing about, he knew she was dreaming about the wolf. He had expected that she might. He knelt down beside her and gently shook her shoulder.

"Sage, wake up, honey. You're having a nightmare."

Her eyes flew open, staring at him wildly. "Oh, Jim!" She sat up and threw herself against his chest. "He was ready to spring at my throat and I couldn't move. It was just like it happened before."

"Shhhh," Jim soothed, his arms coming up around her. "It was only a dream. I killed the varmint, remember?" He felt her head nod against his shoulder and was relieved. If he didn't pull away from her soon, he'd be crawling in beside her.

"Go back to sleep now," he said softly, taking his arms from around her. "Nothing is going to harm you now."

Before he could move, Sage clutched his arm, crying out a protest. "Don't leave me yet, Jim. Stay a while longer."

His heart pounding and his voice strained, Jim groaned. "Sage, don't ask that of me."

"I'm sorry for being such a baby." Sage ignored his plea, pressing herself back into his arms. "I'm such a bother to you, practically afraid of my own shadow."

Jim wanted to answer, *Yes, you're a bother to me. Everything about you bothers me . . . your beauty, your slender body, your firm breasts. It bothers me the way you make me go around in a near state of arousal all the time. In other words, you bother the hell out of me, lady.*

He said none of that as he smoothed the tousled hair off Sage's forehead and gazed down at her moonlit face. "You could never be a bother to me, Sage," he said softly, "not in the sense you mean." Without any warning to either of them, he bent his head and settled

A Special Offer For
Leisure Romance Readers Only!

Get
FOUR
FREE
Romance
Novels
A $19.96 Value!

Travel to exotic worlds filled with passion
and adventure —without leaving your home!
Plus, you'll save $5.00 every time you buy!

Thrill to the most sensual, adventure-filled Historical Romances on the market today...

FROM ■ LEISURE BOOKS

As a home subscriber to the Leisure Romance Book Club, you'll enjoy the best in today's BRAND-NEW Historical Romance fiction. For over twenty years, Leisure Books has brought you the award-winning, high-quality authors you know and love to read. Each Leisure Historical Romance will sweep you away to a world of high adventure...and intimate romance. Discover for yourself all the passion and excitement millions of readers thrill to each and every month.

Save $5.⁰⁰ Each Time You Buy!

Six times a year, the Leisure Romance Book Club brings you four brand-new titles from Leisure Books, America's foremost publisher of Historical Romances. EACH PACKAGE WILL SAVE YOU $5.00 FROM THE BOOKSTORE PRICE! And you'll never miss a new title with our convenient home delivery service.

Here's how we do it. Each package will carry a FREE 10-DAY EXAMINATION privilege. At the end of that time, if you decide to keep your books, simply pay the low invoice price of $14.96, no shipping or handling charges added. HOME DELIVERY IS ALWAYS FREE. With today's top Historical Romance novels selling for $4.99 and higher, our price SAVES YOU $5.00 with each shipment.

AND YOUR FIRST FOUR-BOOK SHIPMENT IS TOTALLY FREE!

IT'S A BARGAIN YOU CAN'T BEAT! A Super $19.96 Value!

■ LEISURE BOOKS   A Division of Dorchester Publishing Co., Inc.

GET YOUR 4 FREE BOOKS
NOW—A $19.96 Value!

*Mail the Free Book
Certificate
Today!*

4
FREE
BOOKS

A
$19.96
VALUE

Free Books Certificate

YES! I want to subscribe to the Leisure Romance Book Club. Please send me my 4 FREE BOOKS. Then, six times each year I'll receive the four newest Leisure Historical Romance selections to Preview FREE for 10 days. If I decide to keep them, I will pay the Special Member's Only discounted price of just $3.74 each, a total of $14.96. This is a SAVINGS OF $5.00 off the bookstore price. There are no shipping, handling, or other charges. There is no minimum number of books I must buy and I may cancel the program at any time. In any case, the 4 FREE BOOKS are mine to keep — A BIG $19.96 Value!

Offer valid only in the U.S.A.

Name _____

Address _____

City _____

State _____ *Zip* _____

Telephone _____

Signature _____

If under 18, Parent or Guardian must sign. Terms, prices and conditions subject to change. Subscription subject to acceptance. Leisure Books reserves the right to reject any order or cancel any subscription.

494FF

A
$19.96
VALUE

4
FREE
BOOKS

Get Four Books Totally FREE— A $19.96 Value!

▼ Tear Here and Mail Your FREE Book Card Today! ▼

PLEASE RUSH
MY FOUR FREE
BOOKS TO ME
RIGHT AWAY!

Leisure Romance Book Club
65 Commerce Road
Stamford CT 06902-4563

AFFIX
STAMP
HERE

his lips hungrily over hers.

Sage made a soft sound of protest, but Jim ignored it as he deepened his kiss. She breathed in the heat and scent of him and became lost to everything around her. Her lips parted on a soft sigh as she felt the warmth and strength of his body follow hers back onto the blanket.

Jim groaned his satisfaction when Sage threw her arms around his shoulders in surrender. "Sage," he whispered against her lips, "I want you so much I ache from it. With you I feel the passion I thought had died forever. Please let me make love to you."

A small voice cautioned Sage not to give in to the husky plea, that it would only bring heartache in the end. But she mentally shook her head in dismissal of the warning. She didn't care about later; she didn't care that her husband had been dead such a short time. She didn't remember that Jim was involved with Reba. All she knew at this moment was that she wanted Jim LaTour's possession, his lovemaking.

Her answer was to arch herself against the hard planes of Jim's body. With a shuddering sigh, his fingers divested her of the red-checked shirt and riding skirt. The fingers that had moved so swiftly before slowed when only the camisole remained. Inch by inch, as though he was opening a birthday present, he eased it over her head. He sat back on his heels then and feasted his eyes on her full, firm breasts. His gaze lingered a moment on the aroused nipples before lowering his head and slowly running his tongue across each one. When she

moaned and softly called his name he opened
his mouth over one, swirling his tongue over
her mounded flesh.

Sage gasped her delight when he slid his lips
up to her nipple, took it between his teeth and
sucked long and hard. Sage wanted to cry out
her delight at his drawing lips. Arthur had
fondled her breasts in the early months of their
marriage, but never had his lips touched them.
She had ached for him to, but had been afraid
he would think her wanton if she asked it of
him. She gently took Jim's head in her hands
and transferred his lips to the other breast,
waiting for attention.

Sage thought she couldn't bear it when Jim
began to buck a very hard arousal in time with
his pulling lips. She caught his rhythm and
thrust back at the same time, trailing a finger
around his working mouth.

The erotic action brought Jim rising to his
knees. He began tearing off her narrow-cut,
mid-thigh bloomers. When he again ran his
gaze over her Sage felt herself blushing under
his scrutiny. She knew that he had seen her in
her entirety when her body had been racked
with fever, but she had been unaware of it at
the time. No other man had seen her thus, not
even her husband.

She and Arthur had only made love upon
retiring for the night, both undressing in the
dark. Arthur always kept his underwear on,
and she a long nightgown. Beyond a kiss
or two, there had never been any foreplay
between them.

She wondered now if that fact had any

bearing on the reason she had never known the thrill of the marriage bed.

From the cover of lowered lids Sage watched Jim hurry out of his clothes, even stripping off his underwear. Having never seen the completely naked body of a man, she was fascinated with the way the muscles rippled over his arms and back, and his flat, firm stomach.

Her eyes shyly traveled down to the apex of his thighs and her green eyes widened as they found his full, hard arousal. He looked so much larger than what she was used to. Of course, she had never seen Arthur's private parts, but she had felt him inside her and she was sure he hadn't been nearly as large as Jim.

Rid of his clothing, Jim lay down beside Sage and pulled her into his arms. A tingling began in her lower regions as she felt his bare length pressed against her, one long leg pushed between hers, the thigh pressing against the curly hair protecting her woman's core. The tingling became a throb when his lips descended on hers with the heat of a branding iron, and her breasts were crushed against the furry pelt on his chest.

Sage's hands restlessly stroked over Jim's back, his waist, his narrow hips, as the kiss went on and on, his tongue slipping in and out between her lips in the rhythm of his moving thigh.

When Jim slid his lips away Sage gave a small, protesting cry and lifted a hand to pull him back, to continue the kiss. But he had only abandoned her lips to settle his mouth over a taut nipple. Soft sighs and little moans escaped her as Jim worked his tongue on both nipples until they were swollen with passion.

Raising his head, Jim took her hand and whispered, "Touch me, Sage. Touch me all over."

He was surprised at how timidly, how awkwardly Sage touched him. Hadn't she ever caressed her husband? He found himself hoping that she hadn't. This was one thing he could teach her.

Jim took Sage's wrist and moved her hand down the flat plane of his stomach. "Touch me like this, honey," he whispered, moving his palm over her hand, which lay only inches from the black mat surrounding a manhood that jerked spasmodically with its need.

His hand still covering hers, he guided it to his hardness. Curling her fingers around him, he encouraged, "Squeeze me, Sage, stroke me. The way you've done it in my dreams."

Sage was unsure at first just how to go about doing what Jim wanted. She never had, nor expected to hold a man's male organ in her hand. It felt so very nice, though, like velvet stretched over iron. And though she felt its strength throbbing in her palm, it still seemed very delicate. Would she hurt it if she exerted pressure, the way she would like to do?

When she cautiously tightened her grip a bit Jim closed his fingers around hers. Squeezing them hard around his length, he began to slide her hand up and down. He whispered encouragement and she responded.

Sage learned quickly what pleased Jim, and he had to stop her after a short time for fear he'd spill his seed into her palm.

He raised up and climbed between the soft thighs that opened eagerly for him. With his broad shoulders blocking out the moon, he slid his hands beneath her hips. Lifting them off the blanket, he whispered hoarsely, "Put me inside you, Sage."

When she guided him to the opening Jim held still a moment before, with a groan, he drove himself deep inside her.

As Sage had expected, Jim's largeness filled her, stretched her. He leaned up on his elbows and gazed down at her in wonder. "God, but you feel good. So smooth and tight, almost like a virgin."

Sage traced a finger around his lips. "And you," she said with slumberous eyes, "are so hard and large, almost like a stallion."

"I feel like one." Jim groaned and began a slow in and out thrusting in the tight, moist well that sucked at him like drawing lips.

It's coming too fast, Jim grated to himself, when after only a few minutes he felt his manhood stiffen, warning that soon there would follow that release that stopped a man's breathing for a while and sent him to heights where he felt cut off from the world. He had so wanted Sage to make that trip with him, their first time together.

Then he felt Sage's body go tight, heard her give a small gasp of surprise as her release approached as fast as his. He quickened his drive, deepened it until they moved as one.

Their joyous cries of release startled the mounts, which turned to look as Jim continued to thrust a few more times before falling forward onto the body he held so closely.

Sage cradled Jim's shuddering body, her own still trembling from a pleasure she had never known before. She knew she had been made love to by an expert and she wanted more.

It was with wonder and much satisfaction that Sage felt Jim slowly hardening inside her, filling her again. When he slid his hands beneath her rear and lifted her up to fit into the well of his hips she looked at him hopefully and whispered, "Again?"

"Yes, again." Jim gave her a teasing thrust. "Don't you want to?"

"Oh, yes." Sage bucked her hips back at him. Jim laughed softly when she added, "All night long."

"We may just do that." He kissed her soft shoulder; then, setting a slow, rhythmic pace this time, he thrust deep inside her, almost withdrawing completely before driving forward again.

Long, wonderful minutes passed as Jim continued to work over Sage, she rising to meet each slow downward shove of his hips. Sweat glistened on both their bodies as they worked together, intent on making this time last, building to a climax that would make them explode when it arrived.

It came with a power that shook them, almost frightening them. They were gripped so hard they didn't have the breath to cry out their release. The two bodies could only cling to each other, wonderment on their faces.

This time, when the shuddering stopped and

their breathing was almost normal, Jim withdrew from Sage and rolled over on his back. Cradling her head on his shoulder, he said in awe, "I'm an old hand at this mating game, but never, ever, have I experienced the wonder I felt with you, Sage, the complete fulfillment."

Sage snuggled closer to him. "It's for sure I never have. I was a little frightened there for a while. I felt like I had left my body and was floating away."

Jim chuckled as he pulled the top blanket up over their moist bodies. "Let's rest a while before trying it again. I'm drained."

The small death wasn't achieved again that night. Exhausted, Jim and Sage fell into a deep, contented sleep that lasted until morning.

Chapter Fifteen

Sage awakened to the sun in her face, and a feeling of well being; she had found something that had been missing in her life for a long time. While she furrowed her brow, trying to think why this should be, the memory of her lovemaking with Jim rushed back to her.

A softness came over her face as she remembered how it had been between them. Never had she imagined how wondrous it could be between a man and a woman. It had seemed that not only their bodies but their souls had melded together. She had suspected before, but now knew for certain, she was deeply in love with Jim LaTour. And that he returned that love she had no doubt. No man could make such love to a woman if he didn't truly love her.

When Sage smelled freshly brewed coffee she realized that she lay in the bedroll alone. She lifted her head and looked at the firepit, where flames danced. A frown etched itself between her eyes. Jim stood staring into the fire, his face still and brooding, as though he was worried about something.

Sage felt a tightening in her chest, a feeling that her contentment was going to have a short life.

Jim was also reflecting on the events of last night, but not in the same manner that Sage had. Although his loins stirred every time he remembered what they had shared, although he admitted that never had a woman made him feel so complete, so fully satisfied, he knew it must never happen again. As he had so sternly told himself before, Sage was not the type of woman a man could treat lightly. She would never involve herself in an affair that would lead nowhere.

How was he to convey to her that she mustn't put any importance on what had happened, that it was a moment of weakness on his part, and probably hers as well. She had been very vulnerable last night, terrified from her nightmare. He had been a bastard for taking advantage of her when she was so open to seduction.

Jim sensed Sage's eyes on him and turned to look at her through shuttered eyes.

Sage's heart beat with heavy, sickening thuds. She knew that when Jim spoke his words were going to hurt her, cut her to the heart.

Don't let him know it, pride whispered to her. *Don't for one moment let him see that your world is tumbling around you.*

Her face showed no emotion when Jim came toward her, carrying a cup of coffee. When he hunkered down beside her and held out the steaming cup she brought out a bare arm from beneath the blanket and took it from him, smiling her thanks. "With the exception of times when I've been sick, I can't remember ever having been served coffee in bed."

"I thought it would help you wake." Jim smiled back, fighting to keep his eyes off the smooth bare shoulder and arm. He glimpsed a love mark he had put on her throat and hurriedly looked away.

He squirmed uncomfortably. Damn, but he'd like to crawl into the blankets with her, take her into his arms, make love to her one last time.

Why don't you do it? his inner voice derided him contemptuously. *Use her, then tell her there will be no more lovemaking between you. That would make her really think highly of you.*

Sage drank the last of the coffee and, as she placed the empty cup on the ground, she wondered at the angry, shamed look that fleetingly crossed Jim's face. She waited, gazing up at him, and after awkwardly clearing his throat he spoke.

"About last night, Sage . . . I'm sorry I took advantage of you. My only excuse is that I was half asleep. I promise it won't happen again. It was just . . ."

"That lust overtook you," Sage finished for him, her voice light, the twinkle in her eyes hiding the pain that lay so close to the surface. "Your excuse is more honorable than mine." She lowered her lids to hide the lie she was about to tell. "I can only say that I had been without a man for two months and your kiss set fire to me."

She looked up him, her features calm. "Why don't we just forget it happened?"

Jim's eyes narrowed on her face. The cavalier attitude she was taking about what he had thought so wonderful cut deep into his male ego. To her, it had been just an action that gave her body the release it craved. Maybe he had been mistaken about her husband, he thought sourly. Evidently he had been quite adept in bed.

Was he also wrong in thinking that she wouldn't enter into a light love affair?

Something told him he wasn't wrong. Sage Larkin was a strong-minded woman. If she told her body to behave itself, it would. And knowing her pretty well by now, he knew she wouldn't put herself in temptation's way by being alone with him again.

But what about John? Jim asked himself. Sage and the doctor were often alone together. Had John kissed her yet? Had he set her pulse afire?

He didn't think so; not yet at any rate. Sage had been as hot as a Wyoming summer breeze blowing across the plains. Look how they had both exploded that first time. He had barely entered her and they were both reaching toward heaven. She hadn't acted like a woman who had recently been made love to. In fact, she had acted like it was her first time with a man in a very long time.

But now, a few hours later, she was acting as though it hadn't meant that much to her, had even told him that they should forget all about it.

Well, that was fine with him, by God, Jim told himself. Still, when he looked at Sage and said, "I'm glad you feel that way," there was a hint of reproach in his voice. He picked up the empty cup and stalked back to the fire.

Sage and Jim rode toward Cottonwood in a strained silence, occasionally speaking of trivial matters to keep up the pretense that nothing of importance had happened between them, that everything was still the same.

But it wasn't the same and never would be again, Sage thought as she left Jim at the livery and walked down the alley to the kitchen door. A few hours of lovemaking had changed their relationship for all time.

"So, how was your trip?" Tillie asked as soon as Sage stepped into the kitchen. "How did you find Danny, and how is Jonty and little Cody?"

"It was a long, tiring ride." Sage dropped into a chair, knowing she had to sit and visit a while before she could escape to her room and let the tears she had withheld all day have free rein.

Tillie poured them both a cup of coffee and sat down, her eyes shining, waiting to hear all about her beloved Jonty.

When Sage had repeated almost every word Jonty had spoken and finally was able to escape to her room, surprisingly, no tears came. They had been replaced with the firm determination to put Jim LaTour out of her mind. She would put all her energy into singing and hoarding her money. She would not waste another thought on a man who was sorry he had made love to her.

Walking across the room to the wardrobe, Sage took out Jonty's most daringly cut gown of black satin. From now on she was going to play up to the men who crowded 'round to hear her songs. She needed to make a lot of money, and fast. The sooner she got away from Jim LaTour, the better it would be for her.

Sage almost took the dress off when she stood in front of the mirror and saw how much of her breasts were revealed in the low-cut bodice. Jonty wasn't as busty as she, and had probably shown no cleavage wearing it.

She kept the dress on, however, ignoring the hateful little voice that taunted her. *You want LaTour to see how the men will lust after you in that shameful dress, and do a little lusting himself.*

Jim did not see Sage in the daring gown that night. He was upstairs in his office with a Mr. Paul Applegate. The men had been there for a couple of hours, drawing up the blueprints of the house Jim wanted the carpenter to build for him. When they had first sat down Jim told the builder exactly what he wanted.

"It's to be two stories high, and the rooms should be large, with big windows. I want to be able to see the countryside from whatever room I might be in. There will be four bedrooms, all upstairs, and downstairs a large parlor and kitchen, plus a dining room and a room for my office. There will be a curving staircase to the rooms above."

Applegate, short, gray-haired, and in his mid-fifties, looked at Jim in surprise. "That's a

mighty big house for a single man, LaTour."
He raised a questioning eyebrow at Jim. "Are
you planning to get married and have a big
family?"

"No, marriage is not in the cards for me, I'm
afraid," Jim answered. "I do have a daughter,
though, and a son-in-law. And one grandson,
with another on the way. I expect them to visit
me often, and stay overnight. I expect there
will be friends stopping by occasionally to stay
overnight."

Applegate nodded his understanding, then
said, "You mentioned a bunkhouse too."

"Yes, after the house is up I want you to build
a good, tight building for about a dozen men,
with a cookhouse attached to it."

"You understand I'll be a while building the
house. It will take some time getting the lumber
delivered just for the framework. All the doors
and windows and hardware will have to be
ordered from Cheyenne."

"How much time are you talking about?" Jim
scowled down at the paper on which he'd been
figuring, annoyed with himself that suddenly
he wanted the place to go up so swiftly. He'd
only got the idea of building a week ago. He
dismissed the notion that Sage had anything to
do with it, that he wanted it finished before she
left Cottonwood. She had nothing whatsoever
to do with the place.

When Applegate said he'd bring extra men in
on the job, that he could have the house up in
a couple of months, Jim reluctantly agreed to
the set time. By the time Applegate shook his
hand and departed Sage had finished singing.

"Not that I planned on seeing her anyhow," Jim muttered to himself, leaving his office. That young woman wasn't going to be seeing much of him anymore. He went downstairs to the saloon, had a drink with Jake, lent a cowboy some money, and then retired to his bedroom.

It took Jim a while to fall asleep, though. Green eyes and a soft, smooth body haunted his mind.

It soon became clear to Sage that Jim was avoiding her. She was both hurt and angry. She was hurt that he had taken their night of lovemaking so lightly and angry that she had allowed herself to be used; angry that she missed seeing him at his table while she sang and helping her off the stage when she finished. Jake did that now, shooting hard looks at any man who looked like he might approach her.

Sage was aware that Tillie thought it strange that Jim never joined her for supper anymore, and she worried about what she'd say to her friend when asked the reason. She couldn't very well say, "I was foolish enough to let him make love to me one night, and now he wants nothing more to do with me."

The days passed, and Sage continued to puzzle over why Jim had turned away from her. At night, when she lay wide awake in bed, she asked the question over and over again. He'd had a long relationship with Reba, but after only one night of love spent with *her*, not even friendship was left.

Of all the reasons that came to her mind, none made any sense except for one: She had evidently disappointed him that night. Reba probably knew a dozen different ways to please him.

Out of loneliness, Sage began to see more of the doctor, often having supper with him after she finished singing, even though she knew tongues wagged with speculation every time she and John entered the restaurant.

One day, as she and Rooster walked down the street—it seemed the man was always around these days—they passed Mae Denton, the woman gossip claimed was John's lover. From the deadly look she received from Mae's hate-filled eyes, she felt sure the rumor was true.

You must not see John socially anymore, her conscience ordered. *There is no future for the two of you, and it is cruel to continue hurting the woman who obviously cares so much for him.*

Sage's good opinion of John Stewart began to slip that day. He wasn't as honorable as she had first thought. It was plain that he was using his landlady while he looked for another woman to marry. She would like to give Mae Denton a good shaking for allowing John in her bed. Someday he would choose a suitable woman who would agree to marry him and Mae would be left with a broken heart and bitter memories.

Two weeks passed before Sage learned why Jim hadn't been around. She was rolling out dough for the raisin pie Tillie was making for supper when the cook said, "It's too bad Jim's not here to have a big slice of this. It's his favorite dessert."

"Where is he, by the way?" Sage asked, lifting the flat, round piece of dough and fitting it into a pie tin. "He's never around anymore."

"I thought you knew." Tillie looked at Sage in surprise. When Sage shook her head Tillie said, "He's out at his ranch, watching his new house go up. The dang fool has been livin' in his barn. The Mexican kid takes him out supplies every few days."

Tillie poured the raisin mixture into the pan and shoved it into the oven. After wiping her sweating face with the edge of her apron she grumbled, "Probably has his stomach all messed up, eatin' his own cookin'."

Sage's heart gave a joyful leap. Maybe Jim hadn't been avoiding her after all. Her tone was light and her eyes sparkled when she said, "He mentioned something about rebuilding the cabin that burned down, but I didn't think he meant to do it so soon." She formed another round of dough and picked up the rolling pin. "I'm curious why he's doing it now."

"So am I," Tillie said. "At first I told myself that he had finally found a woman he wanted to marry." She slid Sage a meaningful look that went unnoticed; then she sighed and said, "But I guess that's not the way of it. I guess he meant it when he said he was tired of the saloon and wanted to try his hand at ranchin'."

"Jim will never settle down with one woman, Tillie. You should know that by now."

Tillie sighed. "I know. For twenty years he's been carryin' 'round the guilt that he wasn't with Jonty's mother when she died, that it was his fault for gettin' her in the family way. And that foolish notion that he still loves Cleo."

"I'm afraid nothing is going to change his mind about anything. Besides, I think he's been a bachelor too long." Sage finished preparing another tin and, wiping an arm across her damp forehead, remarked, "I'm stepping outside for a minute. This kitchen is like an oven."

Outside, Sage took her usual seat on the bench and stared unseeing at the small patch of yard that was mostly taken up with Tillie's herb garden. Leaning her head back against the wall, she let Jim's valley slip into her mind. She thought of the cabin he was building, how she and Danny would love living there if only they could.

But two things made that an impossibility. One, Leland was sure to find her, and two, Jim would never invite her to live in his cabin. He would have women out there, she knew, but none would take up permanent residence.

"Howdy, Miss Sage." Rooster's gravelly voice broke in on Sage's moody thoughts. "Gettin' a breath of fresh air, are you?" he asked, sitting down beside her.

Sage wasn't surprised when the big rough man followed her outside. If she set one foot out of the kitchen, he was right behind her. But why, she couldn't determine. He didn't ogle her like the other men did, never touched her unless it was to take her arm to help her cross the street or climb onto her mount's back when they went for a ride. He was always the gentleman, always attentive to her needs.

But Rooster's almost constant presence was beginning to get on her nerves. She never had any privacy unless she went to her room and closed the door. And it was blasted hot in there, these humid days of July.

Knowing that Rooster would sit there until she went inside, Sage turned her head to him and asked, "Do you think it's too hot to go for a ride?"

"Naw; we'll ride along the river. It's always cooler there under the trees. I'll get our horses and meet you here in about ten minutes." He stood up but didn't walk away until Sage had reentered the kitchen.

She smiled, shaking her head. "My shadow and I are going for a ride, Tillie." She took a couple of cookies from the cookie jar. "I don't know what he finds so entertaining in my presence."

"You make good company, Sage, and maybe he's lonesome. Besides, he's had orders from Jim not to let you out of his sight."

Sage almost choked on the bite of cookie she had just put in her mouth. "Jim told him to watch me?"

"Yeah, he seems to think you're in danger from your brother-in-law."

As Sage changed into her riding clothes, she pondered the mystery of Jim LaTour. He never sought her out anymore, yet he had a man seeing to it that she didn't come to harm.

When a little later the ex-outlaw arrived at the kitchen door, riding his mount and leading hers, she had come to the conclusion that Jim was the type of man who took his responsibilities seriously. He had taken on the care of her and he would see to her welfare as long as she lived in Cottonwood. Once she left the small cowtown she would be on her own.

When Rooster handed her onto the mount's back she wasn't all that happy at the decision at which she had arrived. She only wished that Rooster watched over her because Jim cared for her.

It was several degrees cooler, riding alongside the river with the shade of the willows overhead. Sage and Rooster rode at a leisurely pace, speaking little. Being in each other's company so much, a comfortable friendship had grown between them. Neither were the garrulous sort, not given to meaningless, excessive talk. When the crack of a rifle rang out it was an ominous sound in the silence.

Sage cried out Rooster's name when he clutched his shoulder and reeled in the saddle. When she swung off the mare and ran to help him dismount he yelled, "Get down on the ground, Sage."

As she threw herself down, the rifle spoke again, kicking up dirt and gravel at the feet of Rooster's horse. Rooster fell, more than dismounted, grabbing his rifle from its sheath as he went down. "Come on," he panted, crawling toward a big cottonwood. As they lay in the shelter of the tree, Sage saw the blood seeping through Rooster's fingers.

"Oh, Rooster," she cried, "are you badly hurt?"

"It's just a flesh wound, I think. Be quiet now."

Minutes passed, with the only sound the flowing of the river, as they waited for the next shot to come from the sniper. Blood had spread over Rooster's shirtfront, making a big, dark stain on the flannel material. He felt himself growing weaker by the minute and prayed he wouldn't faint, leaving Sage unprotected.

It was a great relief to him when a few minutes later the silence was broken by the sound of hoofbeats racing away. "Something scared him away," Rooster said over the pain that burned into his flesh like a hot branding iron.

"Thank God," Sage whispered. "Look," she exclaimed, "there's a couple of riders down in the valley. They must have scared whoever it was away. Give me your rifle. I'm going to shoot, and get their attention."

"Maybe you'd better not, Sage. The less people who know I've been shot, the better. Help me to mount."

Sage hurried to bring the horses up to the tree; then she helped Rooster to struggle to his feet. His great weight sagged against her, almost bringing her to her knees.

"Sorry, honey," Rooster gasped, and fell against his mount. The horse whinnied at the smell of blood and sidestepped away. Sage grabbed at the reins, caught them, and pulled the animal back. Rooster managed to get a foot in the stirrup and Sage, exerting all her strength, boosted him into the saddle. With a lithe swing of her body, she was up behind Rooster, pulling him back to rest against her. She dug her heels into the horse, thankful they were less than half a mile from town.

Tillie was standing in the kitchen doorway

when Sage rode around the corner of the building, her arms aching from the dead weight of Rooster, who had passed out. "Good Lord, Sage, what happened?" she cried, starting toward the sweating mount and calling over her shoulder, "Juan, get out here!"

"He's been shot, Tillie, and he's lost so much blood, he might be dead."

Tillie's face turned as pale as Rooster's. "No." She shook her head. "He ain't dead. He's too tough to die."

The teenager came running, and between the three of them they got Rooster out of the saddle and stretched out on Tillie's cot. "Hurry, Juan, go get Dr. Stewart," Sage cried, bending over Rooster. She ripped his shirt open and peeled it over his shoulders, gasping at the ugly wound high on his chest. She grabbed up his wrist and felt for his pulse. She found none. "Oh, Tillie." Her eyes filled with tears. "I'm afraid he's dead."

Tillie pushed her away and laid the side of her face on Rooster's chest above his heart. She listened a while; then her face brightened. "He's alive, but barely." She stood up, her fingers gripping each other nervously. "Where in the blazes is Doc? This bleeding must be stopped."

"I'm here, Tillie." Dr Stewart came through the door, and the women stepped away from the bed, making room for him to bend over Rooster.

Stewart had no need to examine the older man Tillie and Sage had grown so fond of. The jagged wound pumping out blood said Rooster was in a grave way. He sat down on the edge of the bed and began rolling up his sleeves. "Tillie, get me a bottle of whiskey and some hot water. I've got to get the bullet out."

Tillie practically ran to the stove, saying in an undertone to wide-eyed Juan, "Go fetch Jim."

The bullet was dug out of Rooster and seven stitches were taken to close up the hole the flattened piece of lead had left. Though drained of all color, he was resting comfortably when Jim's stallion thundered up behind the saloon. He was out of the saddle almost before the animal came to a full stop.

"Did he make it?" he demanded of Tillie as he burst through the door.

Tillie turned from the pot of chicken pieces she had just started to simmer on the stove. "Yes"—she put the lid on the pot—"but just barely. The wound wasn't bad, but the bullet hit an artery and he liked to have bled to death. I'm makin' some broth to help strengthen him."

Jim and Tillie turned and looked at Tillie's curtained corner when Rooster called weakly, "Is that you, Jim?"

"It's me, hoss." Jim went swiftly across the kitchen floor and pushed aside the heavy hangings that had been pulled closed so that Rooster could sleep. "What happened?" He drew a chair up beside the cot and sat down. "Who winged you?"

"I got no idea, Jim. Me and Sage was ridin' along and all of a sudden a rifle cracked and I got this burnin' jab in the chest. He shot at me again, and me and Sage crawled behind a tree.

"Whoever it was, he sure as hell wanted me

dead. He'd have got me, too, if a couple of riders hadn't come along and scared him away."

"So you didn't get a look at the bastard?"

"No, not even his mount. Do you think it was one of the fellers workin' on Larkin's orders?"

"Them, or Larkin himself."

"What about Sage's safety, now that I'm laid up and you're gone all the time?"

"I don't know yet, but don't worry yourself about it. I'll think of something. Are you in much pain?"

"Naw. Doc gave me some laudanum. I can't hardly keep my eyes open."

"Go to sleep then." Jim stood up. "I'll go say hello to Sage; see how she's doing."

"You'll see she's doin' just fine. She didn't get hysterical once. She managed to get me up on my horse, then held me all the way here. I don't know how she managed it."

"She's not very big, but she's all grit," Jim said proudly before drawing the drapes again.

"Is Sage in her room?" he asked Tillie, who was sitting at the table, snapping a pan of string beans.

Tillie nodded. "She's resting. She's blamin' herself for Rooster bein' shot. She thinks her brother-in-law is back of it."

"I think she's right. Larkin is a crazy man who intends to get his hands on her. I don't know what his intentions are, but I'm sure they're nothing good. He may even have in mind to kill her. Sage tells me he's a religious fanatic, and that type is liable to do anything."

"Them's the worse kind, all right." Tillie rose and set the pan of beans on the workbench;

then she poured Jim a cup of coffee before sitting back down. "Who's goin' to keep an eye on Sage now that Rooster is laid up?"

"I've decided to stay in town until he's up and around. A week should see him out of bed. Thanks for small mercies, his wound is on the left side. He can still handle a gun."

"Speakin' of beds, can he be moved upstairs? You know how I like to keep my eye on my kitchen all the time."

"Don't worry about your kitchen, old lady," Jim teased. "Jake and I will get him upstairs by bedtime." Jim looked toward Sage's door. "I wonder if she's still sleeping."

"I don't know. Why don't you go knock and find out?"

"I'd hate to disturb her if she is sleeping. Why don't you go take a look."

Tillie nodded, stood up, and then sat back down. Sage had just opened her door.

As usual, Jim's heart leapt at first sight of Sage. *She is so beautiful, it's almost sinful*, he thought, his eyes devouring her face before drifting over her slender body, encased in a robe that clung to her every curve. *She's lost weight*, he worried, and wondered why. Did John Stewart have anything to do with it? He knew a jealous pang as he rose to his feet.

"Hello, Sage." He smiled at her. "I hear you've had a bad scare."

"Yes, quite a scare," Sage answered as Jim pulled a chair away from the table and assisted her into it. "Someone was trying his best to kill Rooster."

"Who do you think that someone was?" Jim resumed his seat.

"I can only think of Leland, or his henchmen. I don't think Rooster has any enemies."

"None that I know of. As you say, it was either Larkin or one of those three lowlifes from my old gang." Jim stared thoughtfully out the window. "I don't think it was them, though. They'd be too afraid to try something like that with me being so close . . . unless, of course, they knew I wasn't in town."

Sage shook her head. "I've come to the conclusion that it was Leland. He's a crack shot with a rifle. Look how close he came to Rooster's heart."

His face grim, Jim ordered, "You're not to set foot out of this building until I've satisfied myself that Larkin isn't hanging around town."

A wry grimace twisted Sage's soft lips. "You don't have to worry about that, Jim. I'm half afraid to go out there and sing tonight. I'm afraid he'll be out in the darkness, watching me."

"You don't have to fear that. I'll be patrolling the streets while you sing."

"Thanks, Jim." Her smile made his pulse leap and his heart race. He had forgotten what her smile always did to him. When she asked, "How have you been? How's the new cabin coming along?" he had to swallow a few times before he could answer.

"The frame is up and the roof on. I'm expecting five hundred head of cattle to arrive any day; added to my present five hundred, I'll be running a thousand."

"My!" Sage's eyes grew round, as did Tillie's. "That's a lot of cattle. You'll have to hire quite a few men to ride herd on so many."

"Maybe. Sometimes the cowboys who deliver the steers stay on and work for the new owner of the critters. I'll wait and see how many stay before I hire new men."

A sadness passed across Sage's face. Jim was so in control of his future, while hers was so up in the air. She had no idea where life was going to lead her. Before today's events she had begun to think that maybe Leland had decided he didn't want her, that he had returned home. She knew better now. She was back to being a virtual prisoner, not daring to set foot out of the saloon alone. And she was not about to ask anyone to escort her anywhere. They would run the risk of being shot and killed. She thought of Rooster and shivered. Never again would she chance another person's life.

"Why the sad look, Sage?" Jim hadn't missed her preoccupation.

"Oh, nothing and everything." Sage laughed bitterly. "I feel like I'm living in limbo, just waiting for something to happen. I have this awful feeling that when it does happen, it won't be good."

Jim had never before so wanted to take a woman into his arms to console her, to promise that everything was going to be all right, that he'd always be there to look after her. But he'd be lying if he told Sage that. Such a promise would mean marriage, the one thing he would never consider.

He said the only thing he could honestly say.

"Put aside your fears of Larkin, Sage. I'll see to it that he never bothers you again."

Jim's words were so sincere, Sage almost believed them. She knew he would try his best, but Leland hadn't the scruples that Jim possessed. He'd never face Jim in a clean shoot-out. He'd hide in the dark, or skulk behind a tree to shoot a man in the back.

She was suddenly very afraid for Jim. She reached over and laid a hand on his arm. "Promise me you'll be careful of Leland. He's a devil and will do anything, wait as long as it takes, to get his way."

Jim patted her hand. "That's strange, Sage. I'm pretty much the same way when I set my mind to doing something."

Sage searched his blue eyes, and after a while she smiled. "I believe you are, Jim. Suddenly I feel quite safe."

"Good girl." Jim gave her hand a quick squeeze and stood up. "I'm going to go talk to Jake awhile, see how things have been going. I'll see you at suppertime."

Chapter Sixteen

A full week had passed since Rooster had been shot, and he had been out of bed and moving around on three of those days. The wound had healed nicely, and his shoulder was only a little stiff.

"I can start lookin' after Sage again," he said to Jim one night as they stood at the end of the bar, having a drink with Jake.

The saloon was beginning to fill up with its usual customers. Soon Sage would appear and touch each man with her songs. Some of the men would laugh, some would cry, and all would remember a more innocent time of their lives.

"I expect you're anxious to get back to the ranch, Jim," Jake said, splashing more whiskey into their glasses.

"Yes, I am. My new cattle will be coming in any day now. They may be there already. I left Lightfoot there to keep an eye on things."

"You can leave anytime you're ready, Jim." Rooster picked up his glass of whiskey. "I'm feelin' good as new, and my shootin' arm never was affected." He grinned. "Anyway, I don't think Sage will be wantin' to go on any more horseback rides."

"Just make sure she doesn't. In fact, I don't want her setting foot outside the saloon until that bastard has been found. I've got a couple of Arapaho friends trying to pick up his tracks in the area where he hid to take a shot at you."

"So, when will you be leavin', Jim?" Jake leaned an arm on the bar.

"I think tomorrow morning. And by the way, Jake, you're doing a fine job tending to business here. I appreciate it." After Jake nodded his thanks, a pleased smile on his rough-hewn face, Jim added, "I've been thinking to make you a partner, if you're interested."

"You mean that, Jim?" In his excitement, Jake knocked over the bottle of whiskey sitting at his elbow.

"Yeah, I mean it. Are you interested?"

"I sure as hell am, and you won't ever be sorry, Jim." He stuck out a hand. "Shake on it."

The men lining the bar and those sitting at the tables suddenly grew quiet, and the three who had been drinking steadily for the past hour knew Sage must have put in an appearance. Jim turned his head to see her standing just inside the door and felt the usual leap in his loins. He swore softly to himself. It was past time he got back to the ranch. He couldn't be around her much longer without making love to her. Every night he dreamed of their one time together and woke up aching with the need to repeat those hours.

He had a strong desire to hear Sage sing one last time before he returned to the ranch. He turned to Rooster. "You want to watch outside tonight while I listen to Sage sing? I haven't heard her since I've been back."

"Sure thing, Jim." Rooster pushed away from the bar. "I'll be back when she's finished."

Jim walked over to where Sage stood and, taking her arm with a smile, helped her up the two steps to where her stool and guitar waited.

With Jim's touch sending a tingling all through her body, the smile of thanks Sage gave him was slightly strained. When she was seated Jim returned to the bar and motioned to Jake to fill his glass again.

Jake arched an eyebrow at him but made no remark as he silently tilted the bottle again. He had never seen Jim drink so heavily. He wondered what was bothering the big man.

Jim thought that Sage had never looked lovelier, or more desirable. She seemed to seduce every man there with her throaty voice. He suddenly wanted to grab her off the small stage and take her away from the ogling, worshiping male eyes. He almost wished she'd leave Cottonwood tomorrow—go someplace where he wouldn't be tortured by seeing her, knowing that he mustn't touch her.

His eyes narrowed in slumberous desire as he watched Sage and snapped open when she laid aside the guitar and thanked the audience of men and whores. When she stood up amid the money raining at her feet, Jim moved to the stage and lifted his hand to assist her down the steps.

Sage looked down at him, a frown between her eyes. He seemed a little unsteady on his feet. She had noted as she sang that he seemed to be drinking quite a bit. It had appeared that every time she glanced his way he was raising a glass of whiskey to his lips. She smiled good night to Jake as Jim led her out of the saloon.

In the kitchen, Tillie was snoring softly in her corner. She had left the lamp, turned down low, on the middle of the scoured-clean table. When Jim closed the door behind them Sage whispered, "Thank you, Jim," and walked across the floor toward her room. She lifted the latch, stepped inside, and gave a startled gasp when she discovered Jim right behind her.

"Jim." She gazed up at him. "I thought you had left. Do you want to talk to me about something?"

"Yes, I want to talk to you about something," he whispered back, his voice gruff and aching. "I want to talk about wanting you so bad it's ripping me apart."

Before Sage could catch her breath he had snatched her into his arms and his mouth was on hers, hungry and demanding.

And though the old familar rush of blood, the pounding pulse, enveloped her, Sage pressed her hands against his chest and tried to wrench her mouth away. Jim had weakened her once with his coaxing lips and his stroking hands, and he wasn't about to do it again.

Sage was trying so hard to ignore her body's

clamoring to know Jim's again, she wasn't aware at first that all the time he had been backing her across the floor, coming closer and closer to the bed. She made a smothered sound against his lips when she suddenly found herself on her back, Jim's lean frame pressing her into the mattress, his hard arousal pressing against her stomach. Bucking slowly and suggestively in the well of her hips, Jim moved his lips to whisper beneath her ear, "God, Sage, it's been pure hell not seeing you, wanting you all the time, desperately needing to make love to you again."

Sage turned her face away, refusing to let him capture her lips again. "Jim," she panted, "we agreed this must not happen again, and it still holds true." She tried to wiggle free of the body that was setting her blood on fire. "Nothing has changed."

"I know, I know." Jim nuzzled her throat and trailed his lips down to her breasts, which rose slightly above the cut of her bodice. "My brain tells me that, but the rest of me doesn't pay any attention. It's like I'm two different people and it's tearing me apart."

As he whispered his need for her, Jim slid the wide-cut neckline over Sage's shoulders, taking the camisole straps with it. He stared down at her bared breasts, bathed in the moonlight; then, with a low groan, he bent his head and caught a passion-hard nipple in his mouth.

His lips drew so urgently, Sage's whole being turned to water. "Jim," she whispered, "please don't do that."

"I must," he whispered back, his hands bunching her skirt up to her waist, his breath harsh as his hands stroked her velvet-soft thighs and flat stomach.

When ripples of passion began to spread through her body Sage moaned, "Please, Jim, stop."

"I can't." He moved his mouth to the other yearning nipple, at the same time taking her hand and shoving it between their bodies.

Sage made one last effort to stop the madness that was about to happen. But when she tried to pull her hand away Jim's grip tightened, holding it still while his other hand undid his trousers. He pressed her hand downward, and his rock-hard maleness seemed to jump into her palm, clinging to it lovingly.

Without conscious thought, her fingers curled around it, making Jim quiver and cry out his gratification. When she would have released him, determined to bring everything to a halt, he gasped a pain-filled, "No!" curling her fingers around him again. "Please, honey, touch me . . . like I showed you how."

Don't do it, Sage, her conscience warned her. *He's not to be trusted. He's in love with a dead woman. He'll never belong to you.*

But even as the good advice sounded in her head, Jim slid his hand down to the apex of her thighs, his finger parting the golden hair there and slipping inside her.

All was lost, Sage knew, when he began to stroke the little nub of her femininity. She moaned his name and arched up against his hand, at the same time stroking him feverishly.

Sage made a protesting sound when a little later he removed his hand from her and removed her grip from him. "Let's get out of these clothes," he whispered huskily, climbing off her and pulling her to her feet. "I want to feel your nakedness against mine."

Sage stood half dazed from the release her body was crying out for as Jim practically tore the dress off her in his hurry. When she stood bare before him he stepped back and feasted his eyes on her firm breasts, her tiny waist, and her long, slender thighs and legs. He put his hands on her shoulders and eased her down to sit on the edge of the bed.

As she sat with slamming pulse, waiting for him to undress, he gently pushed her back onto the bed; then he knelt on the floor between her legs. She came up on her elbows in surprise and then caught her breath when he parted her thighs and lowered his head between them.

"Jim," she cried softly, "what are you doing?"

"What I've been wanting to do for a long, long time."

"But," she began, then got no further as his tongue began to flick in and out of the moist core of her. She grew so weak with passion, she fell back on the bed. Surely men didn't do this to women; she clutched weakly at his head, trying to pull him away.

A second later, however, her fingers relaxed and mindlessly stroked through his hair as wave after wave of warmth engulfed her, making her toss her head from side to side and moan his name.

Her eyes flew open when Jim suddenly lifted

his head and stood up. Was this it? Was he going to leave her now, empty and aching? She sat up, and a sigh of relief feathered through her lips. He would be back to her; he was only undressing.

She watched each article of clothing come off, the shirt nearly ripped off and tossed on the floor, the belt unbuckled, the trousers pushed down over slim hips, leaving him standing in his underwear. His eyes never leaving hers, he sat down on the edge of the bed and yanked off the only remaining article of clothing. He stood before her then, in all his magnificent maleness, his hard arousal straining against his stomach.

As though mesmerized by the throbbing length of male strength, Sage couldn't take her eyes off it. There grew inside her a desire to do to Jim what he had done to her. Slowly, her hands came out to grasp his hips and draw him to her. She heard Jim catch his breath as she bent her head and laid her face in the hollow of his hip, her lips only inches away from that which needed her so badly.

Would she? Jim wondered, hoping with everything inside him. He stood stock-still, hardly breathing as he waited. Finally her pink tongue darted out and flicked across the tip of his readiness, then again, and yet again, driving him to distraction. When he groaned, "Sage, please don't tease," she took him in both hands and opened her mouth over him.

His head bent, watching Sage, Jim stroked his fingers around the mouth that worked on him so delightfully, repressing as long as he could the climax that battled to find release.

Finally he had to ease away from her. Lifting her up, he laid her lengthwise on the bed. When he hung over her, her hands reached eagerly for his wet, slick length and guided it inside her.

Both gave a deep sigh as he thrust deep into the moistness that awaited him. "God, you feel so good," Jim whispered hoarsely, sliding his hands beneath her small rear and lifting her several inches off the bed.

Sage made no response. She was unaware of anything except that long, stroking manhood.

Neither was aware of the shadowy figure that stood outside the open window, watching them as they made love through the night.

It was near daybreak when Jim, completely exhausted, raised himself off Sage. "I'd better get out of here before Tillie starts stirring," he whispered. Giving her a swift, hard kiss, he left the bed and gathered up his clothes. Sage watched him a moment out of drowsy green eyes, but was asleep before he finished dressing and left her room.

When Jim quietly closed the door behind him the bearded figure skulking in the predawn shadows silently slipped away. As Leland rode out of town, cruelly using his riding quirt on the mount, a dark rage burned in his eyes. The woman he had loved all his adult life was nothing more than a common whore, wallowing in the sins of the flesh.

"She'll pay for her wanton behavior." The rushing wind threw the hissed words back in his face. "Oh, yes, she will pay." His maniacal laughter trailed behind him.

* * *

Sage awakened to the song of a meadowlark in the tall pine outside her window. "You sound almost as happy as I am," she murmured as the bird hit a long trilling note.

She stretched, then hugged herself. After last night there was no doubt in her mind that Jim loved her. Before the day was over he would ask her to marry him, to share his life in the cabin he was having built. At last everything was working out for her. Danny would be beside himself, living on a ranch, and she, besides being deliriously happy, could relax and stop worrying about Leland. Jim would never let him harm her.

She lifted her head and looked at the small clock on the table next to her bed. She couldn't believe it was only a few minutes to noon. Was Jim asleep in his own bed? she wondered; then she grinned. Probably; he had worked hard last night. Her grin widened. He hadn't seemed to mind, though. In fact, he had seemed to delight in his labor.

Her face soft with memories of last night, Sage rose from the bed and padded across the floor to gaze at herself in the dresser mirror.

"Oh, dear," she exclaimed, leaning closer to her reflected image. "How am I going to cover all of these."

Love marks were scattered all over her throat and down onto her breasts. She examined her body for more tale-telling marks and found them—some in the most embarrassing places. She hurried to pull on her robe in case Tillie walked in, thinking that she was still asleep.

The aroma of simmering stew wafted under the door, and Sage was suddenly ravenous. She hadn't lain idle last night either. She had worked right along with Jim, rising to meet his thrusts. And she had done all the work a couple of times when he had lifted her on top of him, whispering, "Ride me, Sage."

What a night, what a night; her blood sang with the memory as she walked into the kitchen.

"Good morning, Tillie," Sage said gaily, walking over to the stove and picking up the coffeepot. "Isn't it a beautiful morning?" She filled the cup waiting next to a clean plate and flatware.

"Hah!" Tillie snorted, "It's more like afternoon." She watched Sage's face narrowly as she added, "I must say you're in a high good humor."

"Oh, I am," Sage agreed happily, returning the coffeepot to the stove, then sitting down at the table. "And I'm so hungry I could eat anything that isn't alive."

"I'll fry you up some bacon and eggs. How many do you want, half a dozen?" Tillie teased.

"I'm not that hungry." Sage grinned at the cook. "Two will do."

All the while Tillie made her breakfast, Sage kept glancing toward the door that led into the saloon. Jim should be getting up soon, and she could hardly wait to see him, to hear the tenderness in his voice when he spoke to her.

A few minutes later her whole world went dark and empty. Tillie had said, as she placed the bacon and eggs before her, "He's gone, honey."

"Gone?" She looked at Tillie blankly. "Gone where?"

"Back to his ranch," Tillie answered gently. "He left about an hour after daybreak."

Her face paled to absolute whiteness, Sage asked with a tremor in her voice, "Did he leave me a message?"

Tillie shook her head. "I'm sorry, honey. He just said that he had a lot of work to do at the ranch and that he probably wouldn't be back for a while."

Sage stared blindly into her cup of coffee. Used again, used again—the refrain beat against her brain, shaming her as she had never been shamed before. She had been as naive as a young girl, thinking that because Jim seemingly couldn't get enough of her, that meant he loved her. She should have remembered that he was drunk, and that he had been two weeks without a woman while watching the construction of his cabin. And being as virile as he was, he'd be as randy as an old ragged-eared tomcat prowling the alleys looking for a mate.

"Sage, honey." Tillie sat down at the table. "I tried to tell you about Jim. I warned you that he'd allow no strings attached to him."

"I know, Tillie." Sage rearranged her flatware, then played with the spoon, too embarrassed to look at her friend. "I've been all manner of a fool. I actually thought that I could be the one woman who could make him forget the girl who has been gone for twenty years."

She forced herself to look up at Tillie. "I'm beginning to wonder if he doesn't use Jonty's mother as an excuse not to settle down with one woman."

Her appetite gone, Sage stood up. "Jim LaTour has taught me one thing at least, and that is never to depend on a man, to make sure you never need one. I'm going to go get dressed, and when I come back I want you to help me decide what city I should move to."

"But, Sage," Tillie started to protest; then she closed her mouth. Sage had disappeared into her room.

Swinging between dull misery and sharp pain, Sage paced the floor for several minutes before getting dressed in the highest-collared dress she could find in the wardrobe. The garment would be much too warm for the scorcher the day promised to be, but she wasn't going to walk around with red marks showing on her throat, glaring proof of what she had been up to last night.

She was ready to go back into the kitchen when she heard the stagecoach pull in at its usual time. She hoped to be departing Cottonwood in it before too long. First she had to talk to Jonty, though, and get her permission to leave Danny at the ranch until she could get settled.

Tillie still sat at the table when Sage walked into the kitchen, as though she was waiting for her. "I've made a fresh pot of coffee," she said, rising to her feet. "Would you like a cup?"

"Yes, that sounds fine, Tillie, thank you." Sage sat down at her usual place at the table and waited for Tillie to resume her seat. When the coffee was placed before her she spooned sugar into the cup. Then she spoke what was on her mind.

"What is the largest city in the Wyoming Territory, Tillie?"

Tillie thought a minute before answering. "Cheyenne, I reckon. Why do you ask? Do you plan to go there?"

Sage nodded. "To check it out, at least. I'll see if I can find a place to sing."

"Sage, I wish you wouldn't." Tillie looked earnestly at her. "There must be another way. I hate to see you go off alone. Who will look after you and the boy?"

"I'm not helpless, Tillie. I can look after us both." She took a long swallow of the bracing coffee, then set the cup down. "Surely you understand that I can't stay here now. After last . . ."

"After last night," Tillie finished for her.

Sage's face flamed. "You know?"

Tillie grinned crookedly. "I knew you wasn't makin' all that noise by yourself. Besides, I was awake when Jim came slippin' into the kitchen. I pretended to be asleep when he shook my shoulder and told me to wake up." She laid her hand on Sage's. "I was hopin', too, honey."

Sage shrugged tiredly, afraid if she spoke she would start crying. She and Tillie sat in silence, pondering the selfishness of men, consigning them all to hell. Both jumped when the door opened and Jonty stepped into the kitchen, Danny, carrying Cody, following behind her.

"Look who's here!" Tillie exclaimed, rising and embracing Jonty.

Danny set Cody on his feet and, crying out,

"Hi, Aunt Sage," launched himself at her.

Excited chatter took over as everyone talked at once. "How have you been?" "We didn't expect you so soon. How is Cord?" "How long are you going to stay?" "Can I have a cookie?" "Where is Jim?"

"Jim left this mornin' to go back to his ranch," Tillie answered Danny's question as everyone but Cody took seats at the table. Cody was too busy poking around the kitchen, looking for cookies.

Jonty's face fell in disappointment. "I can't believe we just missed him. And we're staying a couple of days, too. Cord's down at the livery unhitching the carriage and hiring a stall for the horse."

"Well, since you came in that fancy contraption, why don't you ride out to the ranch and visit him there?" Tillie suggested.

Jonty's face brightened. "Of course. Why didn't I think of that? I'd like to see the ranch again . . . although I do have some very unhappy memories of it." At Sage's questioning look, she explained, "I was living there when an old enemy of Dad's raped Johnny Lightfoot's wife, then set fire to the cabin. I barely got her and Cody out before the place burned to the ground."

"How awful, Jonty," Sage exclaimed in sympathy.

"Yes, it was." Jonty nodded soberly; but then she smiled gently. "There were a lot of good things, too, though. Cody was born there."

She looked from Sage to Tillie. "Do you know what kind of cabin Dad is having built? Is it good-sized or just big enough for him?"

"He's never mentioned it much," Tillie answered. "He mostly talks about the cattle he's expecting to come in any day. I guess he's goin' into the ranchin' business in a big way."

"I'm glad." Jonty smiled. "I never liked him owning the saloon." She looked at Sage. "What he needs to do now is find a nice lady to marry."

Sage pretended not to catch the younger woman's not-too-subtle hint and, looking at Danny, she said, "Let's go to my room and have a long chat. I've missed you," she added, her arm across his shoulder as they left the table.

Tillie saw the droop to Jonty's lips and patted her hand. "I had my hopes, too, but you know your dad. He's still got it in his head that he's in love with your mama."

"I know, and it's ridiculous, after all these years. I bet he can't even remember what my mother looked like." Sage rose and pulled Cody away from the stove and onto her lap.

"You know what I'm going to do, Tillie? While we're visiting with him, I'm going to ask him to tell me about my mother, describe her to me."

A tickled grin spread over Tillie's face. "I'll be anxious to hear what he has to say."

"I will, too, because my grandma told me many times what her daughter looked like. He'd better give me the same description."

Chapter Seventeen

Jim had been trying to beat out the storm that had started brewing when he was halfway to the ranch, but it had caught him half a mile away from his destination.

He kicked Major into a flat-out run as the rain peppered down on his head and shoulders. Lightning slashed across the sky, thunder rolled, and the rain increased. It slashed him across the face, blinding him. The stallion suddenly snorted and veered to his right, almost upsetting him.

"What in the hell is wrong with you, Major?" Jim righted himself, peering through the wet curtain that obscured a yard ahead of him. "By damn," he exclaimed, blinking water out of his eyes, a wide grin on his face. His cattle had arrived, and he and Major had almost run them down.

By sound, rather than sight, Jim skirted the herd of bawling cattle. He dimly made out the

271

shape of a horse and its rider, the man's face ducked down against the slash of rain as he kept the cattle moving, giving them no chance to turn tail and stampede. When the next flash of lightning lit up the area he saw several other riders alongside the herd.

A worried frown creased Jim's forehead. He prayed the animals didn't decide to run. More cowboys were killed by lightning and stampedes than any other way, though pneumonia ran a close second.

When Jim was close enough to the cowboy to be heard over the storm he called out, "You're on LaTour's range now. You can start milling them if you can."

"I don't know if we can," the cowboy yelled back. "They're spooky as hell."

"Turn them to your right. There's a river there nearby. It will help you hold them."

Slowly the lead steer was turned right, the rest of the herd blindly following him. Then, as if Mother Nature took pity on man and animal alike, the rain slackened; then it slowed to a fine drizzle. Jim got a clear look at the drivers, then, and liked what he saw.

There were eight of them, mostly Texans, he realized; quick and wiry, clear-eyed and honest. They would mostly be good-natured and loyal to the outfit they worked for. They'd be willing to follow their foreman through hell if need be, providing that man was deserving of their support. He noted that bringing up the rear of the herd were a couple of Mexican *vaqueros*.

The cattle were settling down and milling quite nicely when the chuck wagon hove into view, followed by a wrangler driving about twenty head of horses. The cowboys changed horses two or three times a day.

Jim nudged Major into a trot and rode out to meet the chuck wagon. Bringing the stallion up alongside the wagon, he looked into the sun-weathered face of a man somewhere in his mid-fifties. In all probability, the man had been a cowboy until either busted up from a bucking horse or caught in a stampede and crippled.

"The handle is Jessie, Jessie Brown," Jim was told in a gravelly voice after a stream of tobacco juice was sent over the wheel, away from Jim.

"Howdy, Jessie." Jim nudged the stallion closer to the wagon, enabling him to stretch out a hand to the thin, rangy cook. "I'm Jim LaTour." He waved his hand toward a small rise several yards ahead. "There's a barn over that little hill. The men can sleep dry tonight, and you can set up camp there and get a hot meal started for them."

Jessie nodded and whipped up the team. Jim watched it roll away, noting the barrel of water strapped to one side of the vehicle, a heavy toolbox fastened on the other side. Underneath the wagon a cowhide hammock affair swayed, full of kindling wood. At the rear of the wagon, facing him now, was the chuck box, which, he knew from past experience, carried such items as coffee, sugar, bacon, beans, flour, and salt.

Satisfaction gleamed in Jim's eyes. It looked as though his agent in Cheyenne, Henry Crystal, had taken the time to find a cook with a good sturdy wagon. And now, if the cook could cook and the cowpunchers could punch cattle, he was well on his way to seeing a dream come true.

He reined Major around and rode over to where five men stood in a group, water dripping off their hat brims and trickling down their black slickers. The tallest of the group urged his horse forward. "I'm Clem Trowbridge, LaTour, trail boss of this outfit."

Jim nodded and accepted the hand held out to him. "You have much trouble on the trail?"

"Not too much. Had a couple of run-ins with low-down cattle rustlers. One of our men got a flesh wound in the arm. A bunch of renegade Indians made off with a dozen steers, and we lost about twenty in a river crossing."

"That's not bad," Jim said. "I expected a bigger loss. The man who got shot—is he all right now?"

"Yeah, Cookie doctored him up. His arm was stiff for a couple of days; that's all."

They rode over to the other four men, who were relaxed in their saddles. As Clem introduced them, Jim didn't try to remember their names. If any of them remained with him, he would put names to faces in time.

After the introductions were over, he said, "I pay thirty a month to my cowhands, more to the ranch foreman. Do any of you men want to stay on and work for me?"

As one, all five men answered that they were looking for jobs, as were the three who were herding the cattle.

"That's good." Jim grinned. "I need a full outfit. Clem, you wanna be the foreman?"

"Damn betcha," the tall Texan agreed at once. "I like this country."

"That's settled, then." Jim nodded, then hurried to add, "You men will have to bunk in the barn until I can get you some quarters built. I'll be sleeping there with you until my house is finished. I was burned out a year or so ago."

"If the barn is good enough for you, boss, it's good enough for us," the youngest of the group declared.

"Thanks, kid." Jim smiled at the young man. "Now, if you men want to follow me, I'm going over to the barn to change into some dry clothes. Jessie more than likely has a pot of coffee going by now."

The aroma of fresh-brewed coffee hung in the damp air as the horses splashed through mud and water. Jessie had backed his wagon up to the wide barn door and let the tailgate down. Both it and the firepit he had built were just inside the barn, out of the drizzle. When the men rode up he was mixing a bowl of sourdough.

Jim and the men swung to the ground and grabbed tin cups off the makeshift table as they hurried to the steaming coffeepot. Wide grins of pure pleasure spread across their faces as they sipped at the hot, bracing brew.

Jim carried his cup to the back of the barn, where he kept his clean clothes hanging on pegs. As he drew on dry clothing he could hear the men, who had shed their wet slickers, ragging the cook. As Jessie limped between fire and tailgate, he gave back as good as he got.

Feeling human again, Jim returned to the fire. "Why don't you fellows stop jawing at Jessie and go spread out your bedrolls back there in the hay?" His smile was genial as he hunkered down by the fire and poured himself another cup of coffee.

Someone agreed that was a good idea, and rolled-up blankets were taken from the back of the wagon. A minute later Jim looked at the cook and shook his head. "Listen to them," he said.

The cowhands were arguing good-naturedly over spots in the hay. "I don't wanna sleep next to Clem; he snores loud enough to stampede the cattle."

"Oh, yeah," Clem came back, "I don't make half the noise you cowpokes make when you bring a couple of whores into camp. Chauncy squeals like a stuck hog when he gets off. Like to have scared the soup out of Cookie one night with his carryin' on."

"And I guess you're real quiet when you're ridin'. The coyotes howl when they hear your huffin' and puffin'.'"

The good-natured insults went on until everyone had spread their blankets and returned to the fire. The wrangler, a young man not quite twenty, Jim judged, entered the barn, shucking off his slicker.

"This is Cal, my son," Jessie said to Jim, pride in his voice. "Been takin' care of horses since he was sixteen."

Jim stood up and shook the hand that was offered to him. "I take it you found the corral back of the barn."

"Yes, I did. We're gonna need a bigger one, though. The horses get ornery and fight each other when they're all crowded together."

"Did you take care of our mounts, kid?" Chauncy asked.

"You know damn well I did," Cal answered, and poured himself a cup of coffee.

Everyone lazed around then, sipping their coffee and having a smoke. Their hard day was catching up with them.

The rain had stopped altogether and a damp dusk was settling in. Cookie was filling plates with beans and bacon when the lightweight carriage was spotted coming down the small incline. Jim stood up and peered, then exclaimed, "Damn if that don't look like my son-in-law and daughter."

He stepped out of the barn, a wide smile on his face, as the vehicle was brought to a halt. "Jonty, Cord, what in the blue blazes are you two doing way out here?"

Cord jumped to the ground; then he helped Jonty to climb down beside him. While Jim gave his daughter a careful hug, Cord grouched, "She came in to see her *daddy*, and when he wasn't at the saloon, nothing would do her but to make the trip out here. I thought we were either goin' to be drowned or struck by lightning."

"So, I'm a daddy's girl." Jonty grinned up at Jim; then she sniffed the air. "Something smells awfully good, and I'm starved."

"You're just in time for supper. Come meet my cook and some of the hands. Three of the men are riding herd."

The men who hadn't seen a woman for three weeks or more smiled shyly at their boss's daughter as they mumbled their howdys. They were their regular selves when they shook hands with Cord.

"I see you've left Cody and Danny with Tillie," Jim said as he and Jonty joined the line to have their plates filled.

"Yes. Tillie insisted. She said a barn was no place for younguns to be sleepin'. Sage is going to help keep an eye on Cody. And she naturally wanted to spend all the time she could with Danny."

Jim looked away from Jonty at the sound of Sage's name, and Jonty had to repeat the question she put to him a moment later. "How many head of cattle did you buy? It looked like hundreds as we rode by the herd."

"I did buy hundreds. Five hundred, to be exact."

"My!" Jonty exclaimed; then she said no more as their turn came and Cookie shoved a heaping plate into her hands.

For the next ten minutes or so the only sound heard was the scraping of flatware against tin plates. Clem stacked his tin with the others, then named three men to go relieve the three riding herd.

Jim rolled a cigarette and reached a hand down to Jonty. "Come take a look at your old man's house that's going up."

In the dusk the shape of the incomplete house rose majestically, its wet timbers somber against the darkening sky. Jonty stopped and stared. "I thought you were only building a cabin, Dad. This is darn near a mansion. Why such a big one for an old bachelor?"

She gave him a teasing look. "Could it be that

that status is going to change? Has a certain beautiful widow caught your eye?"

Jim ignored the last two questions. "I know it's foolish to build such a fine house just for me, but I've always dreamed of having such a home. I've got something to prove to the folk who used to look down on the poor, rootless half-breed."

Jonty squeezed her father's arm sympathetically, then got back to Sage. "Sage is a lovely person, Dad. I bet if you tried, she'd look on you kindly as husband material."

Jim gave her a stern look. "Get married at this late time in my life? I loved your mama, Jonty. She's still in my heart."

"Describe Mama to me, Dad. Was she short or tall, slender or plump? What color were her eyes, her hair? Was she a serious young woman, or fun-loving?"

Jim gave a start, a look of confusion coming over his face. His brow furrowed in thought as he pulled a blurred image to mind. "Cleo's hair was brown in color, and she had greenish eyes. She was tall—came up to my chin—and she was slender. As for her personality, she was a mixture of seriousness and gaiety."

Oh, Dad, Jonty thought sadly, *you don't even remember what she looked like.* According to her grandmother, Cleo's hair had been a dark blonde and her eyes had been light brown. And instead of coming up to Jim's chin, she would have struck him midchest. He had said that she was slender, but actually the young woman he had loved had still carried baby fat. The only thing he had gotten nearly right was that her mother was fun-loving.

She slipped her hand through Jim's arm as they started back toward the barn. Her father didn't realize it, but he had just described Sage Larkin.

Just before they came to the barn Jonty said, "I wish you'd give some thought to getting married. I don't like to think of you being out here all alone in your old age."

"You mean you wouldn't take me in?" Jim arched a teasing brow at his daughter.

"You know I would, but you wouldn't like it."

"Don't worry about me, honey." Jim patted her hand. "I can always get me a pretty young housekeeper."

Later that night, when the men lay snoring around him, with Jonty and Cord asleep in the hayloft, Jim lay awake, going over the conversation he and Jonty had had. It had shocked him that he could no longer recall a clear picture of Cleo. He had loved her so dearly. How could he have forgotten what she looked like?

Jim stared into the darkness, thinking back over the years. He mulled over questions that had never entered his mind in this time. He was stunned a little at some of the answers he came up with.

His love for Cleo Rand had been that of a rash young man; his first love, a love that had burned hot and fierce. He wondered now, had it been given a chance, if it would have burned itself out. Could it be that because that young girl had given him a daughter, someone of his own to love, he had put her on a pedestal? And there was also the guilt he felt that Cleo had died giving birth to that child. How had that affected his feelings for Cleo?

Jim was still wrestling with the confounding thoughts when he finally fell asleep.

"Isn't it time you got to bed?" Sage ruffled her nephew's hair as the saloon door closed behind her and she moved into the kitchen.

"I'm getting ready to." Danny smiled up at her, a rim of white around his lips. "Just as soon as I finish these cookies and milk."

Sage smiled at Tillie. "I see you got Cody in bed." She glanced at the crib Rooster had found somewhere and set up next to Tillie's cot.

Tillie smiled fondly at the freckle-faced boy swinging his legs as he chewed a cookie. "Danny got him to go to bed. The little scutter will do anything his friend asks him to do. He won't hardly let Danny out of his sight."

"It's nice of you to help out with Cody." Sage sat down beside the eight-year-old she loved with all her heart.

"It ain't nothin'." Danny drank the last of his milk. "He's a nice little kid." He stood up and gave Sage a wet kiss. "I'll be goin' to bed now." He smiled at Tillie. "Thanks for the milk and cookies."

When he had closed Sage's door behind him Tillie said, "He's a fine little youngster. So polite."

"Thank you, Tillie. I think his parents were

doing a fine job of raising him." Tears stung Sage's eyes.

"Yes, they did." Tillie reached across the table and squeezed Sage's hand. "Try not to look back, Sage."

"I do try, Tillie, all the time. Sometimes it's very hard, though."

"I know." Tillie rose and picked up the coffee-pot and cups.

Sage waited until her friend had filled the cups and resumed her seat. Then, not looking at Tillie, she said quietly, "I'm leaving for Cheyenne after Jonty and Cord go home."

"Oh, Sage, I wish you wouldn't." Tillie leaned anxiously toward Jonty. "Can't you stay a little longer? I can't help but feel your future lies here in Cottonwood."

"Tillie, you know better," Sage scolded gently. "My reputation here is ruined. Danny and I would always live under that cloud. For more reasons than one, I must start all over again somewhere else.

"And you can bet I will be very careful not to get myself in the same fix I did here. There will be no more men in my life."

"You're awful young to feel that way, Sage, and with your looks I think it will be impossible to keep men out of your life."

"I can do it, and I will," Sage answered firmly. "Now, my biggest problem will be getting out of town without being recognized. I don't want anyone but you to know I'm leaving. I will keep in touch with you through letters, but there will be no return address on them.

"I figure to get settled and return for Danny in about three weeks."

Tillie sighed in resignation. "If you're bound to go, I'll help you. Let me think a minute," she said, idly stirring her coffee, gazing out the window.

Sage watched her intently, and when Tillie laid her spoon in the saucer, she sat forward.

"You must dress like a widow lady," Tillie began, "and wear a heavy black veil to hide your face. Tie a scarf around your head before putting on your bonnet. Your hair would give you away right off. There ain't nobody in Cottonwood got hair like yours."

Tillie paused and tapped her teeth thoughtfully. "The dress must be big and full-skirted. You can pad the bodice and hips . . . give you a matronly look.

"And since the coach arrives around noon, hang back in the ticket office until just before it leaves town."

"I think you've pretty well covered it, Tillie." Sage looked at the older woman, her eyes bright. She chewed at her bottom lip then, a small frown marring her forehead. "Do you think Jonty will mind if I take some of her gowns with me . . . just until I can buy my own?"

"Naw, she wouldn't care if you took them all. A rancher's wife has no need for fancy duds."

"Well, I guess that just about does it," Sage said and, standing up, she took her empty cup over to the dry sink. "I think I'll go to bed now. Tomorrow is going to be a very busy day for me."

"I'll go to the store down the street and buy

Norah Hess

your dress and bonnet," Tillie said, rising also. "I'll say it's for me. I don't think anyone will question me buying a veil."

Sage hugged the woman she had grown to love. "Tillie, I am going to miss you so much."

"Now don't start blubberin'," Tillie grouched, trying to hide her own wet eyes. "Get on to bed so's I can turn in. Like you said, tomorrow is goin' to be a busy day."

Just outside the kitchen window, standing in the shadows, Reba had heard every word spoken between Tillie and Sage. She drew in a delighted breath. At last the songbird was leaving. Jim would come back to her now.

Chapter Eighteen

The kitchen clock was striking nine when Sage awakened the next morning. She turned over on her side and gazed at her nephew, sleeping beside her. A wistfulness shadowed her eyes. He looked so young, so vulnerable. *Please, God,* she prayed silently, *help me to make a good, decent home for him. He's all I have in the world.*

She eased out of bed so as not to awaken the boy, and slipped on her robe. She walked into the kitchen just as Tillie bustled through the outside kitchen door. The cook laid a paper-wrapped package on the table and grinned mischievously. "Here's your new outfit. You're gonna love it; it's real stylish."

"I just bet it is." Sage's lips curved in a crooked smile as she opened up the heavy brown paper wrapping and looked down at the black garments.

She laid aside the black bonnet and veil and picked up the dress folded beneath it. Holding it at the shoulders, she gave it a snap to smooth out the wrinkles from being crushed in the package; then she held it out to look it over.

"My, my." She laughed. "What a beautiful creation."

The dull black article, at least two sizes too big for her, couldn't have been plainer. It buttoned up the front, right to the chin, without any adornment. The skirt was long and full.

Both women giggled, trying to imagine Sage wearing the dress. Sage picked up the bonnet and pulled it on over her uncombed hair and, after smothering their laughter at the sorry-looking picture she made, Tillie said, "Before I went to bed last night I fixed some paddin' for your hips. You can fill out the top with anything that's handy."

She went to her corner and quietly, so as not to rouse Cody in his crib, lifted the lid of an old trunk. She rummaged around inside it for a moment; then she returned to the table with a black scarf. "To bind your hair in," she explained, placing it on top of the dress.

"That should do it, I guess." Sage half sighed and picked up her widow's weeds and took them to her room. The first step of her departure had begun. The rest would be up to her. There would be no Tillie guiding her along.

Both boys were up shortly, and while Danny took Cody to the outhouse in back of the saloon, Sage helped Tillie prepare breakfast. Only Tillie noticed that Sage ate very little as the boys chattered away.

Sage could not eat for thinking that this was the last time she'd eat at this table, that never again would Jim have a meal with her in Tillie's neat and orderly kitchen.

When the two youngsters finished their pancakes and went out in the back to play Sage sighed and stood up. She still had her clothes to pack. When Tillie asked softly, "Can I help you with anything, honey?" she shook her head, too near to tears to speak.

In her room, Sage opened the doors to the wardrobe and took from its bottom a portmanteau. She carried the suitcase to the bed and folded back its double lids. Then, going back to the wardrobe, she began going through the many dresses hanging there. She carefully selected what she felt was suitable wear for a stage or theater, a couple of street dresses, and three to wear at home, wherever that might be. After picking up the soft slippers she wore with the beautiful dresses, she carried everything to the bed and spread the things out.

She moved to the dresser next. Pulling out drawers, she took from them a week's supply of underclothing and hose, setting aside what she would put on later. She stood undecided, staring down at the dressertop at the fancy jar of rice powder and the rouge pot. Should she take them with her? In the end she scooped them up. In a large city the use of cosmetics would probably be expected of her.

Apprehension built inside Sage as she carefully folded the dresses and laid them inside the portmanteau. All her life she had been protected. She had never been to a city and had no idea what to expect. Pray God everything would turn out right for her.

Before snapping the two lids together and locking them with the key that had lain in the bottom of the portmanteau, Sage went back to the dresser and opened its bottom drawer. From beneath the two blankets stored there she took up a thick packet of bills. Every night when Jake collected the silver showered on her he exchanged it for greenbacks. She tied a ribbon around the money and slipped it between her undergarments and dresses.

Carrying the bag across the floor and setting it next to the door, Sage looked at the small clock. It was almost eleven o'clock. In a little over an hour the coach would roll into town. She heaved a deep sigh. It was time to call in Danny, to explain that she was leaving Cottonwood, and why.

Danny gave Sage a questioning look when she closed the door against the inquisitive Cody. "I have something important to tell you," Sage explained, "and the little fellow can be very distracting with his chatter, and forever getting into things." She sat down on the edge of the bed and patted the space beside her. "Come sit beside me."

Danny sat down and smiled at her. "What do you want to talk about, Auntie?"

Sage picked up the loosely clasped hands lying in his lap and held them between her own. "Danny, remember how Leland followed us, how we hid from him?" When he nodded she continued. "I'm afraid he's traced us here, so I have decided to move to a larger city where he won't find us."

Danny's green eyes became troubled. "Where will we go, Aunt Sage?"

"I'll have to tell you when I get settled." She avoided a straight answer. "But I won't be taking you with me at first." She squeezed his hands gently as he gave her a startled look. "But it shouldn't be more than a few weeks before I come for you."

"Will I be going back to Jonty and Cord's ranch until then?" His eyes grew sadly pensive. "I like living on a ranch, and I'll miss Hero."

"I know, sweetheart." Sage blinked back a tear for the child. "Just as soon as I can save enough money, I'm going to buy us a small farm where we can work the land, and be outside all day, if we wish. And of course I'll buy you a horse. Another little mustang, if you like."

Sage knew Danny was trying hard not to cry, and she hugged him when he threw his arms around her waist and choked out, "I'll miss you, Aunt Sage."

"And I'll miss you, honey." Sage squeezed her eyes shut against the unhappiness in the boy's voice, thankful that last night she had made arrangements with Rooster to take the boys for a buggy ride this morning. It was cowardly of her, she knew, to slip away without saying good-bye to Danny, but it would be easier on both of them.

She looked at the clock, thinking that Rooster should be coming any minute; then she breathed in relief when at that moment she heard him talking to Tillie in the kitchen. She held Danny away from her. "I've arranged a surprise for you. Rooster is going to take you and Cody for a buggy ride to see some of the area. How would you like that?"

"Hey, I like that fine." Danny knuckled his wet eyes. He was off the bed like a shot, heading for the door. Sage followed him, kissing his cheek before opening the door for him. A few minutes later she stood at the window and watched the big man and two boys ride away in the whirl of dust stirred up by the buggy wheels. She drew a ragged breath and began to don her disguise.

Throwing off her robe, Sage stepped into her narrow bloomers and pulled a camisole over her head. With a grimace, she strapped the saddle-bag affair that Tillie had created for her. Filled with feathers, one side lay on either hip, making her look at least twenty pounds heavier. She pulled the ugly black dress over her head next, and laughed at the extra material she plucked away from her breasts. It was going to take a lot of padding to fill out the bodice. What to use? She frowned; then her face brightened. She brought the carrier back to the bed, unlocked it, and took from its side the seven pairs of clean hose she had put there.

Relocking the portmanteau, she carried it back to the door; then she gathered up the stockings and moved to the dresser, where she began shaping them around her breasts. When she was finished she lifted her eyes to the mirror and stared in surprise at the matronly figure reflected there. "I must make sure I never gain weight," she muttered, before turning away from the unattractive image.

Sage looked at the small bedside clock. It was almost time to leave. She quickly bound her hair in the black scarf, then set the ugly bonnet on her head, dropping the veil over her face. She gave one long last look at the room where she had known the completeness of Jim's lovemaking, and then the pain of realizing that it had meant nothing to him. "Good-bye, Jim," she whispered and, picking up her bag, she left the room.

The big kitchen was empty, and Sage understood. Tillie didn't like good-byes either. Looking neither to the left nor the right, she walked out the back door and proceeded down the alley; then she crossed the street to the ticket office.

The ticket master asked no questions as she asked for a ticket to Cheyenne. If he wondered who the stranger was, he did not ask. She put the stub in her wrist bag, then moved to a far corner to await the coach's arrival.

Sage had to wait only about ten minutes before the big vehicle swayed into sight, coming to a loud, creaking halt in a cloud of dust. She picked up her suitcase and hurried outside, keeping her eyes straight ahead. As she climbed into the coach she saw the McBain four-wheeler coming down the street. Her heart raced. She had barely missed being seen by Jonty and Cord. Jonty's eagle eyes might have recognized her.

Sage squirmed uncomfortably on the hard, unsprung seat. The heavy veil was smothering hot, but if she lifted it back, her face would soon be covered with the dust that rolled into the coach. And she did not want to attract the attention of the black-frocked gambler sitting across from her, or the whiskey salesman sitting next to him. Both men had been in the saloon last night when she sang. The gambler had wandered over from the poker table and watched her through slitted lids. The salesman had tried his best to catch her attention, requesting songs, some of them quite bawdy. Their regular customers had applauded when Jake finally escorted the man to the bat-wing doors and shoved him outside.

She remembered that the man's face had been beet red with anger and embarrassment. If he should discover that he was riding with Trail's End's songbird, she had no doubt he would make the ride as uncomfortable for her as he could.

Sage's body ached from the two days of jostling it had received. The coach had seemed to hit every hole and rock in the road, and her eyes burned from the lack of sleep. The obese woman sitting next to her, on her way to visit her son in Cheyenne, had snored through the night, her large, lax body edging ever closer to Sage's slender one. Finally Sage had been pushed into a corner by the great weight. She had shoved at the woman, even jabbed her with an elbow, but the woman had only grunted and slept on.

But the trip was coming to an end soon, thank God, Sage thought. The driver had said this morning that they would arrive in Cheyenne around noon, and the great red ball of sun now hung directly overhead.

It was twenty minutes later when the coach

rolled into Cheyenne. It came to a jarring halt in front of a large false-front building bearing the name Wintercorn Hotel. The driver immediately began to toss down the luggage piled on top of the coach, making the salesman flinch as he heard his whiskey samples clink together. Sage was barely in time to catch her guitar before it hit the ground.

The two men had departed the coach first, not offering to help a fat lady and a matronly widow to descend from the tall reach to the ground. Sage's lips curled as she watched them hurry away, remembering how both the men had ogled her two nights earlier. She lost sight of them as they merged with other people on the street.

Mrs. Fat's son came running up to her, and after a boisterous greeting they took off down the street. Sage was left alone, standing beside her suitcase, her guitar in her hand, wondering which way to go. She looked up the street, down the street, and across the street, and was very disappointed at her first sight of the city.

Cheyenne sat in a treeless, windswept prairie. It was made up of false-front buildings with outside stairs leading to second stories. She learned later that it was cheaper to build them outside than to construct them inside. The street was ankle-deep in dust, and when possible everyone avoided walking in it. Consequently, when she stepped out onto the wooden sidewalk Sage was jostled by bearded miners, cowboys, and men of the gentry escorting their elegantly clad wives.

She had covered a full block and her arm felt like it was going to be pulled from its socket from the weight of her bag dragging at it, when she saw a young boy around Danny's age. He stood in front of a saloon, holding the reins of a horse. She hurried toward him.

"Young man." She lifted the heavy veil from her face. "Can you direct me to a respectable boardinghouse?"

The barefoot boy looked at her beautiful face and smiled widely. "Yes, ma'am, I can. I would take you there, but I'm watchin' this gentleman's horse. He promised me a quarter. But the place is easy to find. Just go down another block, turn to your right, and you'll see it right off. It's the only building that's painted. It's yellow."

Sage reached into her wrist bag and handed the boy a dime. "Thank you, son." She smiled at him and walked away. The boy was too surprised to utter his own "Thank you."

As soon as Sage turned the corner, she saw the yellow building. It was like a light in a window, sitting with its gray, weather-beaten companions. She climbed the two steps to the front door and lifted the knocker placed in its center.

The door was opened almost immediately by an old man, who peered at her through wire-rimmed glasses. When he asked, "Can I help you, missy?" she knew he must be nearly blind. No one with good eyesight could mistake her for a young girl. She looked every inch the matron her disguise meant her to look.

"Yes," she answered. "I'm looking to rent a room."

The old man opened the door wider and stepped aside. "Come on inside. A gentleman left us this morning. You can have his room. Just follow me."

Sage was led through a large sitting room that sparkled with a cleanliness that made her spirits rise a little. When the old gent opened a door after a short walk down a narrow hall, saying, "This is it," she wasn't surprised to find it scrupulously clean.

The room was of a good size, containing a large bed with a table beside it, a washstand with a pitcher and a basin sitting on it, a small dresser, and a rocking chair. There were curtains at the window, plus heavy drapes that could be drawn for privacy.

Sage set the heavy portmanteau on the floor and walked over to the window. She parted the lacy covering and gazed outside. She frowned. The window looked out on an alley. She ran her fingers along the top of the window, searching for a lock. Not only did she find one, she also discovered that the window had been nailed shut. She was relieved; she would be able to sleep easy here.

She let the curtain fall back into place and turned to the old man standing in the doorway. "I'll take it." She smiled. "How much are you asking?"

"Five dollars a week, including breakfast and supper."

Her money wouldn't last long at this rate, Sage thought, digging into her small bag again. She must start looking for employment immediately.

When the friendly old man handed her a key to the front door and hobbled away Sage locked her door behind him and jerked the hated bonnet and veil off her head. She tossed them on the bed, next to the guitar. The black scarf followed, and with a sigh of relief she shook loose her mane of long hair.

She felt several degrees cooler after pulling the black dress over her head and removing the hip padding and the hose that had increased her bust size. She moved about the room in the freedom of her underclothing as she unpacked her bag, hung her dresses on pegs fastened on a board, and placed her intimate items in the dresser.

Sage checked the water pitcher next and found it full. Twenty minutes later she had washed away the dirt and grime from her face and body, changing the water twice, and dressed herself in clean clothing. She picked up her brush and, sitting down in the rocker, brushed her hair until it shone like rich brown silk. She started to fashion it into a loose bun at her nape, then decided to let the curls lie loose on her shoulders. It felt so good to let the air move through her hair after having it contained so long under the black scarf.

She rose from the chair and returned the brush to the dresser. What should she do now? she asked herself. She was too tired to go job hunting now. She would do that tomorrow morning after a good night's sleep. She glanced at the bed with its colorful quilt. Maybe she would lie down awhile and rest her tired body.

Only a few minutes had passed when Sage's eyes drifted closed and she fell into a deep sleep. The sun was sinking when she was awakened by the sound of male voices. For a moment she was disoriented, unable to place the unfamiliar surroundings. Everything came back to her then, and she sprang off the bed. The odor of cooking drifted under her door, and she hurriedly smoothed her dress and ran the brush through her hair again. It must be supper time, and she was starving.

Was she supposed to wait for someone to call her, to say that the evening meal was ready, or should she go into the big front room and wait there? She would do the latter, she decided.

Three men sat in the large room, each with his nose buried in a newspaper. Three pairs of eyes looked up as she closed her door with a click. The printed word was forgotten as the men gaped at the beauty standing uncertainly before them. Finally the oldest of the three stood up and asked politely, "Are you looking for someone, miss?"

Sage shook her head. "No; I live here. I rented a room a few hours ago."

All three of the men were on their feet at this news. They welcomed her, asked her name, and told her theirs. Tim O'Brian, in his mid-twenties, worked as a grocery clerk; Peter Swanson, around her age, was the proprietor of a barbershop, and Dr. Wesley Brent was the man who had spoken to her first. One of the men had asked her if she was a schoolteacher when the loud clearing of a throat sounded behind them.

Sage turned around to face a stern-faced woman who could have filled out the black dress she had discarded in her room. Taking a deep breath, she said, "My name is Sage Larkin. I expect it was your father who rented the room to me. You seem surprised to see me." She crossed the floor and held out her hand to the big woman.

It was gripped firmly and her face closely scrutinized. "I see you wear a wedding band." The words were short and clipped. "Where is your husband? You're not running away from him, are you?"

"Oh, no. I'm a widow, Mrs. . . ."

"I'm a widow too. Folk call me Widow Baker."

Sage smiled at her. "If you don't mind, I'll call you Mrs. Baker. I've been referred to as the widow a few times, and I don't like it. It made me feel as though I was different from other women just because I had lost my husband."

There was a softening in the coal-gray eyes that gazed at her. "I don't care for it either, but the name has stuck. I have a couple of lady friends who call me Carey. You can call me that." Before Sage could respond to that gracious offer, Carey Baker said gruffly, "Supper's on the table."

All three men tried to seat Sage in the dining room, the barber winning out. The landlady provided a tasty-looking, generous meal of chicken and dumplings, string beans, and sliced tomatoes. When all the bowls had been passed around Dr. Brent asked, "Are you a schoolteacher, Mrs. Larkin?"

Sage's grip on her fork tightened. *Here's where everyone's friendly attitude toward me changes,* she thought, remembering how the ladies of Cottonwood had scorned her for singing for a living. Her lips drew into a firm line. She would not be ashamed of the voice God had given her. She had done nothing to besmirch that gift.

She lifted her chin defiantly and said clearly, "I am a singer. I will be looking for work tomorrow morning."

She waited for Carey's eyes to turn cold, and for a salacious leer to appear on the men's faces. She was at a loss for a moment when the eyes upon her showed only a lively interest.

"You have come to the right town if you want to sing," Carey said. "There are five theaters in Cheyenne. Some present burlesque dancers, but there are three respectable, legitimate places where you are sure of finding employment. Those places are always eager to hire beautiful women."

Sage blushed at Carey's compliment, but she frowned slightly at the notion that she would be hired for her looks, regardless of how she sang. If she couldn't be hired on her singing ability alone, she would seek a job doing housework.

She was about to say so when Peter Swanson offered to show her around Cheyenne the next morning. "I'll point out the theaters and other places of business; then you'll know your way around when you decide which place you'd like to sing in."

"That's very kind of you, Mr. Swanson." Sage sent him a grateful smile. "I confess I've been dreading venturing out alone for the first time. I've never been in a large city before."

Her dinner companions waited for her to

expand on her comment, but when she said no more they refrained from asking why she had come to Cheyenne in the first place.

"Cheyenne isn't very old, is it?" Sage asked after an awkward moment or two.

"No, it's not," Carey answered her. "Actually, it's just a baby. I came here in the spring of '67, when it was just coming into existence. It was a town of tents. My first establishment was a large tent. I had ten beds, and I charged a quarter a night. I'd give the men breakfast and supper for another fifty cents. I cooked outside over an open fire.

"Most of my customers were men who worked for the railroad that was coming through Cheyenne. The Union Pacific. That fall, in November, the first passenger train arrived."

"And don't forget there wasn't much law here then." Dr. Brent picked up the story of Cheyenne's growth. "We had to contend with a gang of men the railroad had hired on as a construction crew west of the Missouri. They were known as Hell on Wheels, and they caused a lot of trouble, with their drinking and fighting."

"Then saloonkeepers and prostitutes and gun-toters began arriving, always ready to help the hardworking miners spend their money," Peter Swanson said.

Carey nodded. "Finally it got so bad, General Dodge, who sort of looked after the town, asked the commandant at Fort Russell, General J. E. Stevenson, to help him bring order to the town. General Stevenson rode in with some soldiers and chased everybody out of town, and wouldn't let them come back in until each man swore to behave himself."

"Cheyenne started picking up then," the doctor said. "A passenger depot was built, and a freight house and a stockyard to hold the herds of cattle that would ride the rails to Abiline and Chicago."

"But we still didn't have much law in those days." The barber spoke next. "Justice in Cheyenne was handled by vigilance committees. Not everybody liked the method, but those men were neccessary in a raw frontier town."

"It wasn't until 1868 that the police and courts put the vigilantes out of business," Carey said. "Then, in 1869, Cheyenne became Wyoming's temporary capital. We've come a long way since those days. We now have a mayor, five councilmen, a city attorney, a city treasurer, a city clerk, and a city marshal." Pride was evident in Carey's voice.

It felt to Sage as though a great weight had been lifted off her chest as she learned of the law and order in the town in which she had chosen to live. She would be safe from Leland if he did happen to discover where she was.

A few more stories were told about early Cheyenne; then, when Carey rose from the table and started gathering up the dishes, Sage and the men left the dining room, each going to his own room. Peter Swanson reminded Sage that they would go for their walk right after breakfast the next morning.

Although the small clock on her bedside table said it was only a few minutes after eight, Sage couldn't stop yawning. The bed looked so inviting. She disrobed, washed her face and hands and, after donning a nightgown, turned back the bedcovers. She was asleep almost before she pulled the sheet up around her shoulders.

Chapter Nineteen

The first week and a half following Jonty and Cord's departure, Jim was too busy during the day to give Sage more than an occasional thought. He was occupied overseeing the erection of a bunkhouse and a cook shack. He figured that after twelve hours of herding ornery, longhorn cattle, a man had a right to expect a bunk to sleep on and a table to eat his grub off of. And Cookie was probably tired of cooking over an open fire, fighting dust and flies.

No one had grumbled yet—the Texans were a happy-go-lucky bunch—but if things displeased them too long, they would let their dissatisfaction be known, loud and clear. That was why Jim worked from sunrise to sunset, helping in the hasty erection of the buildings. It bothered him, though, that the house had to wait for completion.

Although Jim didn't think of Sage much

during the busy days, it was a different story when he lay down on his pile of hay at night. Guilt-ridden, he would think of her, cringing at how she must have felt on awakening and finding him gone without a word to her. It had been a cowardly act, slipping away from her. That it had been the hardest thing he'd ever done in his life didn't make it right. But had he stayed until morning, he'd have taken the chance of never leaving her. Having a mate for life didn't fit in with his scheme of things.

Still, Sage haunted him. Awakening in the middle of the night, hard and needing, was a common occurrence. He would lie in the darkness, remembering how it had been, her soft, warm arms wrapped around his shoulders, her long legs around his waist as he moved inside her. Only when his hand had brought him an unsatisfactory release was he able to go back to sleep, only to dream of her again.

Each new morning he swore that he would put the woman out of his mind, cease to need her.

When the day came that the roof was almost completed over the cookshack and the bunkhouse, Jim was almost giddy as he swung onto Major's back. He had a bona fide excuse to ride into Cottonwood. He needed to buy a cookstove, didn't he? Not to mention a heating stove for the men, and furnishings for the long building.

He kicked his heels into the stallion's sides and rode off toward town, vehemently denying to himself that Sage Larkin had anything to do with the elation he felt. He was only looking forward to seeing Jake and Tillie, to catching up on what had been happening in his absence.

Jim halted to breathe the stallion occasionally before lifting him into a gallop again. It was a couple of hours before sunset when he pushed open the kitchen door, startling Tillie, who was sitting at the table, peeling a pan of potatoes.

"Jim!" She exclaimed her pleasure. "I didn't expect to see you for some time. I hope you ain't run into any trouble at your ranch."

"It's just the opposite, Tillie. Everything is going along fine. The builder and his helpers are putting the roof on the cookshack and bunkhouse, and I'm here to buy a cookstove and whatever else I need."

"Well, ain't that fine. Pour yourself a cup of coffee and tell me all about what's goin' on out there."

"Well," Jim began, after pouring himself a cup of Tillie's strong brew and sitting back down, "I've been working my butt off, helping with the building. I expect Jonty told you that my cattle arrived, and that all the men who drove them in have hired on with me."

"Yes, she told me. Said they seem like a real nice bunch of young men." Tillie sent him a look that was almost reproachful. "She also said that you're havin' quite a fancy house built for yourself. I figured you was just havin' a cabin built, like the one that no-good Sly burned down."

She watched him from the corners of her eyes when she asked, "Won't you feel lost, rattlin' 'round in a big house like that, all by yourself?"

Jim grinned to himself. Tillie was trying to

pump him, to find out if he was hiding something. She couldn't believe he would want a big house all for himself. But he did . . . didn't he?

He let his grin come to the surface as he answered. "I thought I'd move you out there with me. Unless, of course, you want to stay here, and keep on cooking for a bunch of drunks."

"You're joshin' me, ain't you, Jim?" Tillie's eyes widened at him.

"No, I mean it. I'll need someone to look after me. Keep me in line, chew me out once in a while." His eyes teased her. "Rooster's moving out there too."

Tillie's face reddened. "Bah, what do I care what that old gray lobo does? I'd be pleased to live in your grand house, Jim, although it should have a young mistress to look after it, one that would chew you out when you got ornery."

"I'd take your jawing over any other woman I know, Tillie," Jim teased affectionately. "And speaking of the woman you have in mind but won't mention, where is the lady Sage?"

Tillie looked down at the pan of potatoes in her lap. "She ain't here, Jim."

Jim straightened up from his slouching position. "Are you telling me that she's crazy enough to go riding again?" he almost shouted.

"No, I'm not telling you that," Tillie answered in a low voice. "She's left Cottonwood, Jim. She left the day after you went back to your ranch."

She looked up in time to see Jim swallow, to see the tightening of his cheek muscles. His voice was rough as he said, "I see"; then he followed with, "Where'd she go?"

"I don't know." Tillie looked back at the potatoes as she told her lie. "She's gonna write to me just as soon as she gets settled. She hopes to come back and get Danny in a few weeks."

When Jim only sat silently Tillie said, "I sure hated to see her go, all alone, no one to look after her. As you know, she's too pretty for her own good. I'm afraid some no-account will take advantage of her."

Jim sighed and heaved himself up from the table. Suddenly he felt like an old man who was nearing the end of his days, alone with no one to comfort him. "We knew she would be leaving us sooner or later, Tillie. It just happened sooner than we expected."

There was a slight droop to his shoulders as he crossed the kitchen and disappeared into the barroom. "Damn fool," Tillie muttered, and picked up a potato and her paring knife.

Jake spotted Jim as soon as he leaned on the bar. He left off talking to a cowboy and hurried over to him. "What are you doin' back in town so soon, Jim? You get lonesome for some female company?"

Jim laughed halfheartedly. "Believe it or not, I'm here on business. Come to pick up a cookstove mostly."

"So, how's everything goin' out there?" Jake asked, placing a glass in front of Jim and tilting a bottle of bourbon over it.

"Everything is going along fine." The elation that had been in his voice when he had said the same thing to Tillie was gone. "Got me a thousand head of cattle now, and some fine young cowboys to herd them." He took a hefty swallow of the bourbon; then he asked, "How are things going here? Been having any trouble?"

Jake shrugged. "Nothin' I can't handle. The men raised a little hell the night they learned Sage wouldn't be singin' for them anymore. A few chairs was broken up and a couple of hangin' lamps was shot out. I soon put a stop to that. I just waded in with my club, knockin' whatever heads I could reach."

The two men shared some laughter; then Jake nodded his head in the direction of a table in a far corner. "That Reba has been givin' me her usual trouble. Wantin' to use the rooms upstairs now that you're gone. She's a trouble-causin' bitch if ever I seen one."

"Who's the stranger she's sitting with? I've never seen him around here before."

"He came in a couple of days ago, and him and Reba have been thick as molasses ever since."

As Jim watched the pair, Reba leaned her red head against the stranger's brown one. She smiled and said something to him, at the same time stroking a hand over his heavy beard. The man returned her smile and, taking her hand in his, kissed her palm.

Jim turned back to Jake and drawled cynically, "Looks like a love match to me."

"Well, now, maybe you shouldn't scoff," Jake said. "Reba's been tellin' everyone that the man has asked her to marry him."

"The hell you say. You reckon it's true?"

"Could be. Men have married whores before."

"I hope it's true in Reba's case." Jim finished his drink. "She's wanted out of the business for a long time."

"I think she had her sights on you for a while." Jake offered the bottle again, but Jim shook his head.

"That was foolish of her if she did. She knew from the beginning how I feel about marriage." Jim pushed away from the bar. "I'm gonna go take care of business now, and then head back to the ranch. Keep your club handy, and I'll be seeing you."

Jake laughed; then he frowned at the menace in the stranger's eyes as he watched Jim walk away. Should he call Jim back and tell him? He decided that Reba had probably mentioned her previous relationship with Jim to her new lover, and that it was jealousy glaring out of the man's eyes.

As Jim went through the bat-wing doors, he met Rooster entering the saloon. "Howdy, Jim. I didn't know you was in town."

"I got in just an hour ago. Come in to get some things for the ranch. Come along with me to the store."

"I guess you've heard Sage has left us," Rooster said as he fell into step with Jim. "Nobody knew she was gone until Tillie told us. She just up and slipped away. It kinda hurt my feelin's. I thought me and her had become good friends."

Jim made no response as their boot heels rang sharply on the wooden walk. Rooster looked at his set face and said no more.

The sun had set by the time Jim had made

his purchases and had made arrangements at the livery to have them delivered the next day. "Will you be staying the night, Jim?" Tillie asked him later as they sat in the kitchen having their evening meal.

Jim shook his head. "I'd best get back to the ranch; keep an eye on things."

Half an hour later he said good-bye to Tillie and headed out across the plains. The grooves on either side of his mouth were a little deeper as he rode Major at a walk. He didn't have that feverish rush to get back to his land that he had had when he rode away from it. He admitted now that the thought of seeing Sage had put that leap to his blood, the increase to his pulse. He had never felt so let down in his life as he had on discovering she had left Cottonwood.

As the stallion clomped along, Jim began to deride himself for not being at the saloon when Sage took the foolish notion to go looking for her future. He could have talked her out of it, or at least gone with her, to see that she was properly settled and working in a decent place wherever it was she had chosen to move to. Alone, she would be like a lamb amid a pack of wolves.

Jim's grip tightened on the reins. In his mind's eye he could see men flocking around Sage, their eyes hot and hungry as they mentally stripped the clothes off her. Hadn't he done the same thing himself a hundred times?

"Cut it out," he muttered to himself, lifting the mount into a gallop. "Why should I care how many men flutter around Sage Larkin?"

But to his chagrin he did care as he rode

through the night, guided by a full moon. He was mentally and physically exhausted when Cookie's cookfire came in sight. He rode Major up to the black bulk of the barn and swung to the ground.

Jessie looked up from his tailgate worktable. "You hungry, boss? I've got some real good stew left in the pot. One of your calves stepped in a gopher hole today and broke its leg. It had to be shot, so we had part of it for supper."

"Damn." Jim swore to himself. What other bad news was going to clobber him over the head?

The next morning, after a hearty breakfast of ham and eggs and fried potatoes, Sage and Peter Swanson started out, the barber proudly escorting her down the raised wooden sidewalk. Every man who saw them would envy him as he showed the young widow around town, Peter thought, for never had there been a woman so beautiful in the whole of Cheyenne.

As they went down one side of the street, the first building of interest Peter pointed out was the hospital, on the second floor of a big wooden building. It had been built by two doctors, he informed her, and had forty beds.

Peter smiled crookedly. "Most of the patients are ones who have been shot or knifed in a fight. In the winter, though, there are a lot of pneumonia cases. Especially cowboys."

A post office was pointed out next, which Sage was happy to see. She hoped to get a letter off to Tillie within the week.

She and Peter came next to a volunteer

firehouse. "There's always a fire breaking out around here," Peter said, "and they're mighty dangerous. The buildings are built so close to each other, the flames jump from one roof to the next. If it wasn't for those men who volunteer to fight the fires, the whole town would burn down. We're mighty proud of them."

Some distance from the other buildings but still on the main street, Peter pointed out the schoolhouse. "There's around thirty children who attend . . . mostly to make the teacher miserable," he added with a grin. "We have a hard time keeping teachers here in town. The kids aren't like the ones who go to school out in the country. The minute a teacher turns her back on city students, she's peppered with spitballs or anything else that's handy, even buckshot bullets. The poor teacher can't do much about it. The older boys are usually bigger and stronger than the teacher."

Sage was glad she had chosen singing for a career as they turned down a side street. "We call this Church Street, and you'll discover why as we walk along," Peter said, amusement in his eyes.

Sage was amazed when she counted seven different churches. She was pleased to see one that was of the Methodist persuasion. She would attend services tomorrow, and hopefully she wouldn't get the same reception she'd received in Cottonwood. She felt a twinge of pain in her chest, remembering how Jim had escorted her to the rudely constructed church and had stood beside her, glaring at those who had snubbed her.

She forced Jim out of her mind as Peter took her arm and guided her across the street, where family dwellings stood. The small yards were neat and orderly, with flower beds flanking wide porches. Several women called out greetings to Peter, their curious eyes on Sage. He returned their friendly greetings but ignored their desire to know who he was escorting around town.

When Sage and Peter came to the edge of town he guided her across the street to view the stores opposite the ones he had shown her already. He paused in front of a dressmaker's shop so that Sage could gaze at the beautiful bonnets displayed in its wide window. "I have never seen such beautiful creations," she exclaimed in awe.

A haberdashery came next, then a drugstore with Dr. Brent's office above it. On the next block Peter proudly pointed out his barbershop, situated between a grocery store and a butcher shop. There was a bathhouse next to that, with several men waiting to make use of its tubs and hot water.

Crossing another street, Peter guided their steps to where most of Cheyenne's social life took place in saloons, hotels, and theaters. Sage counted five variety theaters, and one that presented burlesque. She'd stay away from that one, she promised herself.

When they came to two places, side by side, that advertised musical shows, Peter said, "You should apply at one of these places. They have many well-known performers here; troupes that stop here for a short time, on their way to San Francisco, where the really fancy places are.

You'd do real good in either of these two places."

"Peter." Sage laughed. "How do you know that? You've never heard me sing."

"It wouldn't make any difference if you couldn't carry a tune. The owners of these houses would be happy just to have you as a decoration."

"Well, I certainly wouldn't care for that," Sage snapped, irritated. "I want to be hired for my ability to sing, not to be ogled at by men."

"I didn't mean to hurt your feelings, Sage," Peter apologized. "But what I said is true, nevertheless. You are a beautiful woman, and men will enjoy looking at you."

When Sage made no answer to his overtures Peter asked, "Which one do you want to try first?"

"You mean right now?" Sage gave him a startled look.

"Sure; why not? I see no reason to put it off . . . do you?"

"No, I guess not," Sage replied, and scrutinized the two buildings. "From the outside they look pretty much the same. I guess it doesn't make much difference."

"Then let's try number-one first." Peter took her arm and walked with her to a double door entrance. He turned the doorknob and, when it gave, they stepped inside.

Sunlight, coming through narrow transom-like windows near the ceiling, shone on rows of seats leading downward to a wide stage. The big room appeared empty of humans, and after they stood in the doorway Peter called out, "Is anyone here?"

"Back here," a distant voice to their left called back, "In my office."

A short, stockily built, balding man looked up from a desk on which was spread many sheets of paper. When his eyes fell on Sage first he didn't bother to look at her companion. "How can I help you, my dear?" He rose and came toward her.

"I'm a singer, and I'm looking for employment." Sage smiled at him.

"You've certainly come to the right place." The man beamed at her. "Would you like to start tonight?"

"But . . . but you haven't heard me sing yet." Sage frowned.

"Oh, I'm sure you sing like a bird." Avid eyes ran over her face, then moved down her body.

"Maybe I sing like a crow in a corn patch." Sage's voice was sharp with annoyance.

"I'm sure you don't." The man waved his hand dismissively. "One so beautiful couldn't possibly sound like a crow." He mentioned a sum of money that staggered Sage. She would be earning more than enough to provide a good home for Danny. She could even add to the hoard of money she had saved at Trail's End, and before the year was out start looking for that small farm she wanted.

It still irked her, though, that she was being hired for her looks. *Go ahead and take it*, her inner voice advised. *The audience will soon discover that you can sing. You will earn your wages honestly.*

Peter had watched the way the short man ogled Sage and didn't like it one bit. Finally he spoke up. "My name is Peter Swanson, and I'm Miss Larkin's manager. You deal with me from now on."

Hard dark eyes were turned on Peter, quickly followed by a wide, ingratiating smile. "Claude Jefferson," he said, holding out his hand. "Is everything agreeable to you?"

"Nothing was mentioned about Sage's days off. I only allow her to work five days a week. The voice needs a rest, you know."

Claude Jefferson was careful to keep his displeasure from showing. This beauty would draw men like honey drew bears. Every night she didn't sing meant less money for him.

Still, he didn't want this Swanson person taking her next door to his competitor, who was sure to snatch her up. He bared his teeth in a facsimile of a smile. "It goes without saying the young lady will have time off. What about Mondays and Thursdays?" Those were slow nights.

"Is that all right with you, Sage?" Peter asked.

"That will be fine." Sage gave Peter a grateful smile. She hadn't expected any time off. She had sung seven days a week at Trail's End. She turned to Jefferson. "What time should I be here?"

"Our shows start at seven. Come a little earlier, though, so I can show you your dressing room and you can meet the other entertainers." When Sage nodded and she and Peter turned to leave, Jefferson added, "You understand that

316

you'll have to paint your face a little. So the m . . . audience can see your face better."

Sage nodded again, thinking to herself that she would paint her face, but she would not dress up like a whore. She would wear her own . . . Jonty's lovely gowns.

She and Peter were at the door, ready to go outside, when Sage remembered something. "I forgot to mention one thing, Mr Jefferson. I accompany my singing with a guitar. Will you please have a stool for me?"

Jefferson frowned but agreed that he would. Did he have a prima donna on his hands? She probably couldn't sing worth spit.

Out on the boardwalk again, Sage gave in to the case of nerves that had gripped her during her talk to the theater manager. A fine film of sweat gathered on her upper lip, and her knees began to shake. "I hope I do all right tonight, Peter," she said as he took her arm and guided her across the street. "I've only ever sung in a saloon where the audience was male and always mostly drunk. Maybe sober men and women won't like me at all."

"Don't worry about it, Sage. You'll do just fine," Peter assured her. "And don't be nervous. Me and Corey, and Doc and Tim, will be there, right in the first row, cheering you on. Just pretend that you're singing for us. That we're the only ones there."

Sage smiled her thanks, and a minute later they arrived at the barbershop. Three men were waiting for Peter to open up; nevertheless, none went inside until Sage was out of sight.

*   *   *

It seemed to Sage that every nerve cell in her body was shaking as she sat in the rather shabby dressing room applying color to her face. The theater was called the Gilded Cage, and she felt just like a helpless little bird about to be locked up in it. She remembered how Mr. Jefferson's beady little eyes had skimmed over her when she arrived earlier and wondered if later she would have trouble with him.

I wish Jim were here, she thought with a sigh. She had always felt so safe when he was nearby. *But he is no longer a part of my life,* she reminded herself. And he wouldn't have been a permanent part of it for long even if she had remained in Cottonwood. In time he would have tired of her and moved on to another woman.

The clock over the dressing table showed she had fifteen minutes before her turn on the stage when Sage gave one last look in the brightly lit mirror. Her gown of green dimity brought out the highlights in her dark brown hair and increased the green in her hazel-colored eyes. Its bodice hugged her ribcage and molded her firm breasts, only a hint of them rising above the wide cut of the neckline. The sleeves were short, merely little caps on her shoulders. The skirt stood out from around her narrow waist, helped by two stiff petticoats beneath it.

She had painstakingly gathered the curls to the top of her head and fastened them with green ribbons. She looked at her face then, and wondered what her mother and Arthur would think if they could see her painted face.

There would be condemnation on her husband's face, of that she was sure, and probably a sadness on her mother's.

With a ragged sigh she turned away from her image. She would do what she had to do. For the time being singing was the only way she could provide for her nephew. She picked up the guitar and went to stand behind the heavy blue curtains until it was her turn to walk out onto the stage.

Chapter Twenty

The Gilded Cage theater had opened with a juggling act, followed by seven scantily clad young dancers. The men in the audience yelled and stamped their feet as the dancers did their high-kicks in the can can. Two burly bouncers were kept busy keeping some of them from bounding onto the stage and grabbing the girls.

It was the first week in July and swelteringly hot in the theater. The audience grew restless when a big-bosomed, middle-aged woman replaced the dancers and sang a cappella in a wavering soprano. Long sighs of relief rose from some when the aria was finally finished.

There was a polite clapping of hands as the opera singer sailed off the stage; then Jefferson announced that he had a treat for those attending tonight.

"She is not only lovely to look at but she sings like an angel." His voice carried all the way to the back of the room. "Please welcome Miss Sage Larkin."

Gripping the guitar with suddenly damp palms, Sage took a deep breath and, parting the heavy drapery, stepped out onto the stage. As she stood waiting for her stool to be brought out, the room grew so quiet, one passing by on the street would have thought the theater empty of people.

A teenage boy arrived with a long-legged stool and placed it directly under a brightly burning chandelier suspended from the ceiling. Sage seemed to float in her wide skirts as she approached the stool and climbed up on it. The heavy silence continued as she settled the guitar in her lap and slipped the strap over her head and across one shoulder. Every man watching her would have been quite content just to sit and gaze at her. Never before had such beauty graced the theater.

Sage picked a few chords, giving her nerves a chance to calm down, then began to sing "Jeanne With the Light Brown Hair." As she crooned the beautiful words of the song, she noted that this larger, more sophisticated audience was reacting with the same rapt attention as had the rowdy bunch back in Trail's End.

When she came to the end of the song the silence lasted a moment; then the room seemed to erupt. Everyone was on their feet, clapping their hands and yelling, "More, more!"

Sage looked down at her new friends and gave them her stunning smile; then, softly strumming the guitar, she sang "Beautiful Dreamer." Again cheers and applause rattled the rafters.

It was time she settled down her admirers, Sage thought. She decided to sing them something that would lull them back to the days of their youth. She sang her third and last song of the evening, "My Old Kentucky Home."

The words were like a soothing drug on the listeners, who barely breathed as the words floated out to them. She finished the song, slipped off the stool, and was walking away before those who seemed mesmerized were aware that she was leaving. No silver was rained at her feet, but as the drapes closed behind her there sounded a thunderous applause.

Mr. Jefferson, the jugglers, and the dancing girls stood waiting to congratulate Sage. They crowded around her, exclaiming, "What a beautiful voice you have! I loved that last song, even though it made me cry. Every man out there was ready to fall at your feet."

"You are my new star," Jefferson declared. "You shall have a dressing room all to yourself."

"But what about Madam Louise?" Sage asked. "Doesn't she occupy the private dressing room?"

Jefferson waved a negligent hand. "She can take your place with Ruby."

What a callous, unfeeling person you are, Sage thought of the theater manager, and although she hadn't met Ruby the dancer yet, she shook her head at the short, squat man.

"I'll not do that to Madam. I'll share with Ruby."

Sage knew she had done the right thing by the pleased smiles that curved everyone's lips.

The new performer had declared herself one of them.

Carey and her boarders waited for Sage in the small dressing room. Again she had to listen to words of praise for her voice, and how much they had loved her songs.

"We waited to escort you home," Carey said when everyone had settled down. "And we'll sneak out the back door. There will be a horde of men waiting out front, clamorin' to take you to supper, to come callin' on you. Some can be pretty persistent."

"Thank you, Carey." Sage smiled her thanks. "You don't know how safe you make me feel."

" 'Tain't nothin'." Carey looked embarrassed for showing a tender side of herself. "Anyone can see you're like a lost lamb."

Sage had to smile. She felt like a lost something.

"What if we took you to the Grand Hotel next door for coffee and a piece of cake, to celebrate your successful night," Tim suggested shyly.

"That's a marvelous idea," Sage agreed. "That's just what I need: to relax with friends. I don't mind telling you how awfully nervous I was up there on that stage. I didn't know if my simple songs would please a sophisticated audience."

Carey snorted. "All those people listening to you were simple folk at some time in their lives. Beneath all their fancy trimmin's, they're still the same."

As Carey had predicted, when they passed down the alley a glance up the street showed several men loitering in front of the Gilded Cage.

"Didn't I tell you?" Carey took Sage's arm and hurried her along.

The Grand dining room was packed, every table taken with people waiting to be seated, when Sage and her friends arrived. "Shall we go on home?" Carey suggested. "I have enough of my peach pie left for a slice each. It won't take long to brew a pot of coffee."

"I'd enjoy that much more," Sage said. "I can't wait to get this paint off my face."

And so it became the custom to return to the boardinghouse to have coffee and dessert every night when Sage finished singing. The three men, however, didn't attend Sage's every performance. Tim was courting a young lady; Dr. Brent sometimes had patients to see; Peter liked to drop into a saloon two or three times a week and have a few drinks, and then visit the redlight district a short way from town.

But Carey was always on hand to walk her to and from the Gilded Cage. It hadn't taken the more persistent men long to realize that Sage was slipping out the back door. Mr. Jefferson had been forced to have his two big bouncers escort her partway home, one on each side of her, and Carey trailing along behind.

The dancers were more than a little envious of Sage's popularity, but they tried to keep it from showing. Despite the fact that she attracted the men they used to draw, Sage was still very well liked. It was agreed by everyone that she was definitely the star performer at the Gilded Cage, yet the lovely widow never put on airs or demanded special treatment. And she never went out with any of the men who chased after her.

Although Sage liked all the girls—even Madam Louise, who felt that she was above Sage and the dancers—Sage's favorite was Ruby, who shared her dressing room. A friendship had grown between her and the black-haired, vibrant twenty-seven-year-old. She lived with her mother and was the sole support of her two youngsters: a boy of seven and a girl of five. And though the children's grandmother was with them while she worked, Ruby worried about them. Sometimes her mother drank.

It was an unspoken rule among theater performers that no one pried into the affairs of others. But Ruby had let scraps of information drop occasionally that enabled Sage to piece together what had happened to the father of Ruby's children.

One day he had walked away and had never returned. The little girl had been six months old at the time. It was no wonder Ruby had no use for men, and did not trust them at all.

Sage had openly revealed the reason she had come to Cheyenne, omitting, of course, any mention of Jim or her fear of her brother-in-law. She told them that with the exception of her eight-year-old nephew, her family had been killed by three outlaws.

Tears had sprung up in her eyes at the telling, and Ruby had put her arms around Sage and held her while she cried—weeping not only for Arthur, Kale, and Mary, but for the loss of Jim. *I never lost Jim*, she thought bitterly, wiping her eyes when her tears were spent, *I never had him.*

Sage pulled away from Ruby and spoke of a worry that nagged at her. "Danny's mother was an Indian, Ruby. How do you think Cheyenne society will accept my nephew when I bring him here to live?"

"Well, Sage, I won't lie to you. The big mucky-mucks will turn their noses up at him, as well as at you. But the common people, the workers, won't pay any attention to the Indian blood in the boy." Ruby paused a moment, and then asked, "Wouldn't the boy be better off if you had stayed in Cottonwood? You've mentioned how happy he is on that ranch. Didn't singing in the saloon pay enough for you to provide for him?"

Sage couldn't give Ruby the real reasons she couldn't stay in Cottonwood; that she had been afraid she would become Jim LaTour's new whore, afraid that her brother-in-law would find her. So she lied. "There's not all that much money in a small town."

It was Sage's day off and she still lay in bed, even though her small clock showed it was nearing ten. She had remembered the conversation she'd had with Ruby a week ago and it had triggered her longing to see Danny. Reluctantly, she admitted her desire to see Jim too. She missed his easy, relaxed company, and the way he had of looking at her through narrowed, slumberous eyes, sending the message that he wanted to make love to her.

She remembered the last time they had

soared the heights together, the time that had sent her rushing to Cheyenne. Did he know yet that she had left Trail's End? she wondered. And if he knew, did he care? Although he had enjoyed the use of her body, his later actions had shown that it hadn't meant as much to him as it had to her.

Sage sighed and threw an arm across her eyes. What she had given him any woman could have done, and probably even better. Reba, for instance. That one would know a dozen different ways to please a man.

"Stop it!" she whispered fiercely, sitting up in bed and swinging her feet to the floor. "You are not to give that man another thought. Do you think for one minute that he's mooning over you like a sick calf? You know good and well that by now another woman has replaced you in his thoughts, as well as in his bed."

Sage was mistaken about Jim forgetting about her. She was also wrong in thinking that he had taken himself another woman. He hadn't looked at nor touched one since making love to her.

Jim found himself thinking of Sage almost constantly, worrying about her. She had been gone three weeks now, and a dozen times a day he asked himself if there was a man in her life yet. One minute he told himself that Sage wasn't the type of woman who fell into bed with a man after knowing him a week or so; the next minute he was reminding himself that she had been that way before he made her aware of her sexuality. Now she knew the pleasure a man's body could give her, and maybe the urge for fulfillment was a driving force within her.

One thing bothered Jim more than anything else, something that had slowly sneaked up on him. Recently his dreams of Sage weren't always sexual. Many times she had only lain in his arms, her warm, soft body nestled in the curve of his, her curly head on his shoulder. Sometimes she was on the stage at the saloon, singing her sweet songs, and he was so proud of her, he thought he'd burst.

But mostly he saw her in his new house, arranging furniture, cooking his meals. And Danny would be there also, like a son, riding the range with him, helping to herd the cattle.

Each time he had such a dream Jim would be angry with himself, would call himself all manner of fool. But that didn't stop the same dream from occurring again the next night. It had gotten to the point where he hated to stretch out on his pile of hay. Whether he dreamed of Sage as a helpmate or his sleep images had him making wild love to her, he always awakened in a state of unrest, unfulfilled and a little bewildered. He was slowly going out of his mind.

To escape the teasing memory of Sage, Jim had involved himself in whatever was going on around him. But soon the bunkhouse was finished, and the cowboys moved in. The cookhouse, too, was in operation, with Cookie preparing tasty meals on the big black range.

At odd times, when he was idle for a moment, Jim would remember that day when the cookstove was delivered. He had begun to help Jessie set it up. But after getting in the cook's way, stepping on him a couple of times, the man had groused, "Boss, don't you have somethin' else to do somewhere else?"

He had taken the hint and drifted over to his new house, nearing completion. He had pitched in to help put on the roof, and after a half hour the builder had muttered more or less what the cook had, only more to the point. "LaTour, why don't you get the hell out of my way? Go help someone else."

Only the cowpunchers had welcomed his help, and that had been his salvation. Chasing stubborn, mean, longhorned cattle for twelve hours at a stretch left a man so exhausted, when he hit his blankets he immediately fell asleep.

Jim's men had outfitted him for the rough riding from their own saddlebags. He was donated a floppy hat, its brim pinned back with thorns, a pair of woolen pants with buckskin sewn over the seat and inner thighs. He was informed that without the leather the saddle would soon have the pants' material worn thin.

One man gave him a vest with deep pockets that would save him the trouble of reaching into his pants pockets while on horseback. His trail boss, Clem Trowbridge, lent him a pair of knee-high boots that would keep out the dirt and pebbles. He had his own spurs.

Cookie continued to serve good, hearty meals. Jim had told him not to stint on grub, and Jessie had taken him at his word. Every morning at daybreak, before the men rode out, they were served bacon and pancakes. At dusk, when the men rode in, either a roast or steak or stew waited to be served at the long table. His biscuits were light, his coffee strong, and his pies and cakes were delicious. Jim knew that if nothing else, good food and plenty of it would keep the cowboys working for him. It was a known fact that cowhands would choose good food over higher wages.

One evening, when everyone had sat back with full stomachs and was rolling cigarettes, one of the men looked at Jim and said, "Boss, some of us men ain't had a woman for some time, and we're gettin' real itchy. We was wonderin' what you'd have to say about one of us ridin' into Cottonwood and bringin' back a couple of whores for a night or so."

Jim grinned as he rolled his own cigarette. He understood their need. He was in need himself, but only for Sage. He struck a match on the underside of the table and held it to the white cylinder between his lips. After exhaling a stream of tobacco smoke through his nostrils, he answered the waiting cowboy.

"I expect it's all right, providing no fights break out over them. I won't tolerate my men fighting among themselves. If anyone starts anything, he's fired on the spot."

A half dozen voices assured him that there would be no trouble. "None of us are gonna fight over a whore," one young man added.

When the men started arguing over who would make the ride into Cottonwood, Jim made the decision. He looked at his ramrod. "You go, Clem. I know you won't get all likkered up and forget to come back for a couple of days."

There was some good-natured laughter then everyone rose and headed for the bunkhouse. Except for Clem. He went to the barn to saddle up and make the trip to Cottonwood.

Breakfast was almost over the next morning when Clem returned with two of Reba's youngest and prettiest girls. The men all rushed out to help them dismount. Jim, leaning in the doorway, wondered at the subdued look on the female faces. Hadn't they wanted to come with Clem? If that was the case, he'd take them right back to Reba. Whores or not, he'd have no unwilling women on his ranch.

He noted that his ramrod also wore a sober face as he walked toward him.

"Something's wrong here, Clem," he said, stepping out onto the narrow porch. "What is it?"

"The madam, Reba, has disappeared, clothes and all."

"What do you mean disappeared?" Jim asked. "She probably left with that stranger who came to town. She spread it around that they were getting married."

"I don't think so," one of the girls spoke up. "He was still at the saloon the next day." She looked at her companion. "After he spent the night with Mazie."

"And a more brutal man I never entertained before," Mazie said with a shiver. "I got the feelin' he hated women. I know for a fact he hates Indian women. I heard him say so many times."

Something clicked in Jim's mind. Sage had said once that her brother-in-law had an unnatural hatred of Indians, and that was why she feared for her half-breed nephew. His heart gave such a leap, pounded so hard, it pained his chest. He knew as well as he was sitting here that Reba's beau and Leland Larkin were the same man. He had courted Reba just to get information about Sage's whereabouts. If Reba had that knowledge, and he didn't doubt for a moment that she had, she had told Larkin.

And that meant the man had a long start on him.

The chair scraped on the floor as Jim shot out of it. Larkin's start would become much longer since he had no idea where Sage was. Pray God that Tillie did.

"You girls go on down to the bunkhouse and get some sleep," he said as he rushed to the door. "I'm ridin' to Cottonwood."

The stallion's breath was coming in pants, his sides heaving, and lather flecked his broad chest when Jim pulled up in front of Trail's End. He threw the reins to a young boy passing by, handing him a silver dollar to walk Major to the livery, give him a pail of water, wipe him down, and give him some oats. Then, with a pat on the stallion's sweaty rump, he hopped up on the narrow porch and went through the bat-wing doors and into the saloon.

"I'll talk to you later, Jake," he said in passing as he made straight for the kitchen.

Tillie turned from staring out the back door. "Well, hi there, Jim." She smiled at him. "I wasn't expectin' to see you for a while."

"Have you heard from Sage yet?" Jim wasted no words.

Tillie hesitated a minute before answering. "Yes. As a matter of fact, I got a letter from her yesterday. She wrote that she has found a singin' job that pays real well, and that she'll be comin' for Danny within the week."

"Where was the letter from, Tillie?" Jim watched her closely, ready to spot any lie she might tell.

Tillie averted her eyes from him as she answered, "There was no return address on the envelope."

"That could very well be, but you know damn well where she is. Now tell me."

Tillie turned angry eyes on him. "How come all of a sudden you want to know where she is? Your uncaring attitude toward her is what drove her away. Do you suddenly have the urge to sleep with her again?"

"No, I don't have the urge to sleep with her again!" Jim fairly shouted, a guilty flush on his cheeks. "I never led Sage on, Tillie. She knew from the beginning that I'm not the marrying kind."

"Why don't you leave her alone then? She's makin' herself a new life and new friends. She don't need you to be comin' and goin' in it."

"I think she's in grave danger from her brother-in-law, Tillie," he said gently, stopping the irate woman's tirade. "My guess is that Reba told him where she is."

"But Reba wouldn't know . . . unless . . . she overheard me and Sage talkin about her leavin'." Tillie sat down, her face pale. "Reba was always sneakin' around, listenin' to other people's conversations."

Jim nodded. "That's probably what happened. Now, tell me where Sage is, Tillie. Time is very important."

"She's in Cheyenne, Jim," Tillie answered hurriedly. "I didn't lie when I said there was no return address. But she's singin' in a place called the Gilded Cage.

"Hurry after her, Jim. That madman may kill her if he gets his hands on her."

Jim stood up. "Fix me enough trail grub for two days while I go to the livery to see about a mount. I wore Major out coming in."

There wasn't a decent horse in the stable; not one that could do more than ten or twelve miles a day, and that at a dog trot. "What I need," Jim muttered to himself, "is a broad-chested, long-legged animal that can run from dawn to dusk with only short intervals of rest."

He was swearing softly to himself when he spotted Rooster's big sorrel. He recognized the horse, and knew of its great endurance. It had outrun many a posse. Jim didn't hesitate to throw his saddle on the broad back. Rooster wouldn't mind that he had borrowed the animal.

He took the time, however, to tell the livery man that he was taking his friend's mount, and to be sure to tell Rooster who had him. Tillie was waiting at the end of the alley, a grub bag in her hand.

"Good luck, Jim," she said. "I'll be prayin' you get to Sage in time."

Jim took the bag and left Cottonwood on

the run, the strong mount's long legs eating up the miles. At dusk, when he made night camp, he figured he had covered at least 25 miles. As he removed the saddle and patted the sorrel's rump, dust ballooned from the animal's coat. He took a waterbag from the cantle and poured water into his hat, then sympathetically watched the animal drink. When he had removed the bit from the big horse's mouth he tethered him to a bush growing in a patch of lush grass. He turned to tend to his own needs.

As Jim built a campfire and started a pot of coffee to brewing, a wolf howled somewhere in the darkness, a melancholy sound. With wild, echoing howls, the animal began to call his pack to the chase.

He sighed his relief when the yowls faded away in the distance. They were running away from, not toward him. Nevertheless, he would keep a fire going all night. The sorrel would look very tempting to them should they come upon his camp.

Jim quickly ate the bread and meat Tillie had packed, and had two cups of coffee. The last flames of the fire were sending up a flickering light among the leaves of the cottonwood he'd made camp under. He tossed more wood, from the supply he had gathered, onto the fire; then he wrapped himself in his bedroll. He fell asleep instantly.

As soon as dawn began to streak the sky the next morning, Jim threw back his blanket and fumbled for his boots, the only articles of clothing he had removed. He warmed over the

remains of last night's coffee, ate a beef sandwich, and then continued on toward Cheyenne,
the mount readily taking the gallop asked
of him.

The afternoon coach to Cheyenne bounced
along the rutted road, dust swirling behind it.
It carried only one passenger: Reba, the madam
from Trail's End.

The aging whore hardly felt the jarring her
body was receiving. Her mind was too busy
thinking of her future. At last she had a future.
There would be no more taking on any man
who had the price.

She opened the small cloth bag hanging from
her wrist and looked inside it; then she quickly
pulled the drawstrings together. It was still
there: the big roll of money Harry Jones had
given her.

Reba leaned back in the hard seat and
stared out the window, thinking back to last
night.

She and Harry had gone to her room and she
had hurried out of her clothes. But when she
turned to her new lover, expecting him to be
in the same naked state, he was leaning against
the wall, fully clothed. She had walked up to
him and slid her arms around his neck and
shoulders. "Ain't you gonna get undressed?"
she'd asked him. She had been surprised when
he had pulled her arms away.

"I want to talk to you, Reba," he'd said, and
he sat down on the edge of the bed.

"Of course, Harry." Reba sat down beside
him. "What's on your mind?"

"That woman who used to sing downstairs—what happened to her?"

Angry jealousy gripped Reba. Was Sage Larkin on the mind of every man in Cottonwood? She shrugged her shoulders indifferently. "She went away."

"Went away? Where?"

Reba shrugged again. "No one knows. She caught a stage and left town."

Leland Larkin looked at the whore through narrowed lids. The bitch was lying; he could see it in her shifty eyes. He sighed inwardly. It was going to cost him to find out just where Sage had gone. He reached into his pocket, pulled out a thick roll of money, and laid it on the table beside the bed.

When Reba looked at it, avarice in her green eyes, Leland had said, "There's enough money there for you to start a new life in a new town if you can remember where Sage Larkin went."

Reba thought back to the conversation she'd overheard between Sage and Tillie. Her hand reached for the money. "She went to Cheyenne. She plans on gettin' a singin' job there."

Leland grabbed her wrist as her hand settled over the money. "If you're lying, I'll come back and put a bullet in your heart."

"I'm not lyin'," Reba whined. "I heard her tellin' Tillie that was where she was goin'."

The man who Reba had thought would marry her had left then, without another word.

Reba saw that the sun was ready to set as she came back to the present. Cheyenne lay sprawled in the distance. She would catch a train there and head for San Francisco, and her new life.

Shortly after Reba caught the stagecoach, Leland Larkin went to the livery stable and saddled his mount. He led the horse outside, swung onto its back, and turned it in the direction of Cheyenne.

"I'll get you this time, sister-in-law," he gritted through his teeth as he laid the whip to the horse. "At last you're gonna pay for all the pain you have caused me. When I'm finished with you you'll rue the day your mother ever gave you life."

Chapter Twenty-one

"Well, what do you think?" Ruby asked Sage as the two sat their hired horses, looking at a small house about a mile from Cheyenne.

"It looks good from the outside," Sage said, her eyes scanning the neat, compact, white-painted building, then surveying the forty acres that came with it.

"I've got the key to the front door," Reba said, sliding out of the saddle. "Let's take a look inside."

A friend of Ruby's mother sold land, and when she mentioned that a friend of hers was looking for a house, he had told her of this property that had just become vacant a week earlier.

"You can rent it or buy it," Ruby said, turning the key in the lock.

"I think I'll rent at first," caution prompted Sage to say. "See if Danny and I like it well enough to buy."

The size of the house was deceiving from

the outside. Inside, Sage and Ruby found four good-sized rooms. Two bedrooms, a parlor, and a kitchen. The walls were sound and the floors only squeaked a little. The place had been stripped of all furniture except for a kitchen range.

"We'll have to start scaring up some furniture for you," Ruby said, walking out of the smallest bedroom. "I'll bet Carey has some odds and ends stashed away in that big house of hers. And we could spread the word among the dancers. I doubt they have much, but they could ask a friend, who could ask a friend."

Sage wasn't too concerned about furnishing the house. She had enough money to buy what was immediately neccessary. Her main concern was, would Danny be happy here? She thought that perhaps he would as she gazed out the kitchen window at a shed where a horse could be kept, plus a good-sized fenced-in pasture. The open range stretched out beyond it, where Danny could ride as often as he pleased. Maybe he wouldn't miss the McBain ranch too much.

She turned and smiled at Ruby. "Let's pay the first month's rent, then go tell Carey."

"Carey is going to be happy for you, but she's gonna miss you."

"Yes," Sage agreed, "and I'm going to miss her. Of course we'll see each other often. I'm going to miss her walking me home every night, too," Sage added with a frown. "I don't look forward to making the trip out here alone every night."

"You could always ask Jefferson to see you home," Ruby said, a teasing twinkle in her eyes.

"I'm sure he'd jump at the chance."

"Hah! That fat buzzard. If I had a dog, I wouldn't let him walk it home."

The second night she performed at the Gilded Cage, Jefferson had entered her dressing room without bothering to knock. She was sitting in front of the mirror removing the paint and powder from her face, and her eyes narrowed warily as she watched his reflection come toward her.

Without asking her permission, he had pulled a chair up close to hers. Putting a hand on her knee, he had said through thick lips, "I could pay you more money if I had a mind to. Why don't we go to my hotel and discuss it?"

She had slapped his hand away and, eyeing Jefferson coldly, said in equally cold tones, "If you want me to continue singing in your theater, you'll never make that suggestion to me again."

"You misunderstand me," Jefferson blustered, jerking to his feet. "It was only a friendly offer."

"Keep your friendly offers to yourself from now on." Sage also stood up, her eyes sparking fire.

Miffed, the fat man stalked to the door, slamming it behind him. After that he was very careful how he treated her and what he said to her. Sage was a good calling card for his business and he didn't want to lose her.

Ruby told Sage later that Jefferson had approached most of the other girls with the same proposal. Some had taken him up on it, only to find an additional dollar in her pay envelope at the end of the week. No one had any affection for their boss.

Returning to town and leaving their hired mounts at the livery, Sage and Ruby walked to the land office, where Sage paid the first month's rent. She was given a receipt for her $25 and told she could move into the house whenever she pleased. Giving Ruby a big grin, she said, "Let's go tell Carey."

As Sage had thought she would, Carey greeted her news with mixed emotions. "I'm gonna miss you, girl, but I understand that you need to make a home for your nephew. You wouldn't want him playing in the streets of Cheyenne."

"My moving is going to present me with a couple of problems, though," Sage said after Ruby had left and she and Carey were having a cup of tea. "I'll have to find someone to stay with Danny while I sing, and there's the problem of me getting home at night. I don't look forward to making that trip alone in the dark."

"I know an Indian couple you could hire real cheap. They're a decent pair, in their mid-fifties. The man could drive you to and from work. He's a big feller. I don't think anyone would be anxious to tangle with him."

"That sounds fine, Carey. Would you get word to them as soon as possible?"

Carey nodded; then she said, "What you need, though, is to find a good man and marry him. That would solve all your problems."

Sage smiled thinly. "I'm beginning to wonder if such a man exists these days. My husband was a good man, but I haven't run into any others since his death."

There was a short silence; then Carey spoke. "I don't mean to pry into your private affairs, Sage, but did a man hurt you there in Cottonwood? Sometimes you look so sad, like your mind is a hundred miles away. I realize you could still be grievin' for your dead husband, but it doesn't seem like the kind of grief I see on your face when you think no one is watchin' you."

Sage shook her head. "To my shame, I only grieved a short time for Arthur. Sadly, he was the type of man easily forgotten." She fiddled with her spoon, tracing patterns on the table-cloth. She lifted her eyes to Carey; then she said, "There was a man in Cottonwood. A handsome devil who I foolishly thought had fallen in love with me; would ask me to marry him." She directed a scornful laugh at herself. "Like most men, he only wanted to get into my bed."

Sage sighed. "I shouldn't be surprised. He's forty-two years old and has been a bachelor all his life. He likes a variety of women too much to settle down with just one." She went back to playing with her spoon. "I'll never trust another man."

"Don't say that, Sage. There are a lot of good men out there. You just happened to pick a bad one."

Sage shrugged and finished her tea. "You may be right, but I'm not looking for one. I'm going to my room now and write to Tillie; tell her I'll be coming for Danny soon."

It was Sage's day off, as well as Ruby's. The two of them had been out most of the day, going from place to place, looking at offers of furniture. Most pieces shown to them should have been thrown on a trash heap years ago. But Sage was polite in her refusal of the articles. She wasn't doing too badly. An old woman had given her a nice, sturdy bed frame, minus the mattress. Then a friend of Ruby's had donated a dresser, and Ruby had given her a rocker from her own scantily furnished home.

"There are no ifs, ands or buts about it, Ruby," Sage said as she drove the lightweight rented wagon out to the small house. "I'll have to dip into my savings and buy whatever else I need."

Unfortunately, this past spring Carey had cleared out every piece of furniture she wasn't using. Sage wondered what a kitchen table and chairs, a bed set for Danny and a mattress for her would cost. It would be a skimpy household for a while, until she could gradually add pieces as her wages allowed her. She still had most of the money she had arrived with, but she intended to hang on to it as long as she could. She never wanted to be dependent on anyone again. It put a person at a disadvantage, lowered his self-value.

But as much as Sage hated to admit it, she still needed emotional security. She had felt loved and wanted ever since she could remember. She had thought that Jim would provide her that, had foolishly felt sure of it.

Her lips curled scornfully. That showed how little she knew of men. She had a lot to learn about the opposite sex, but she was in no hurry to educate herself further. She already knew that for the most part they weren't to be trusted, that they took but seldom gave of themselves.

When the wagon was pulled to a stop in front of the rented house Sage and Ruby pulled and tugged the few pieces of furniture off the wagon and carried them inside. As the rocker was placed in front of the fireplace, Sage realized that she also would have to see about getting wood to fuel it in the winter. A long, ragged sigh escaped her lips as she locked the door behind her and Ruby.

Sage didn't talk much on their way back to town. Now that she had started the wheels in motion to provide for her nephew, she was beginning to realize what a big undertaking it would be. In her mind the years stretched ahead, and she wondered if she could make it alone in this man's world.

With lips firmed, she reminded herself that she came from good, sturdy stock. By the time she pulled the team up in front of Ruby's place she had convinced herself that she could meet and overcome any obstacle put in her path.

As Ruby climbed out of the wagon, Sage looked at the run-down, weathered house and its sagging porch and rubble-filled yard. Her attention switched, then, to the two children who burst through the door, calling their mother's name as they threw their arms around her waist.

Pride shone in Ruby's eyes as she introduced the handsome little boy and the very pretty little girl. "I'm very happy to meet you, Ruth Ann and Jamie." She smiled down at the towheaded youngsters.

Jamie smiled back at her, but Ruth Ann shyly

hid behind her mother's back. There was a longing in Sage's eyes as she said, "You've been blessed with beautiful children, Ruby."

"Thank you, Sage. They're good children too."

"I give you so much credit for raising them alone. I hope I can do as well by Danny."

"It's not been easy. When their daddy walked out on me I was scared to death. I had no money, and there was very little food in the house. Ruth Ann was just a baby, and I couldn't have gone to work even if I could have found a job."

Ruby shook her head, as though still wondering at what had pulled her through until she could go to work. "My mom, who had sucked at a whiskey bottle ever since I could remember, sobered herself up and worked like a dog in the kitchen of a wealthy family living on the other side of town.

"Poor Mom. How hard that must have been on her—to stay sober so long. All through my growing-up years I had been convinced that she cared nothing for me. There were never any kisses or hugs, although she never hit me. But when she came through for me when I really needed her, I knew that she loved me after all."

Ruby laughed softly, affectionately. "I'll always look after her, the old soak."

A few minutes later, bouncing along alone in the wagon, Sage chastised herself for having doubts about her ability to raise Danny. Skinny little Ruby had been raising her children alone for five years, and doing a fine job of it. Surely

Sage Larkin could raise one young boy by herself.

Friday dawned gray and cloudy. When Sage awakened she found her nightgown clinging to her body in the humid air. It would rain before the day was over, she thought with satisfaction. According to the *Wyoming Tribune,* a good long rain was needed. The paper wrote that ranchers were becoming concerned that the rangeland was drying up, as well as some water holes. Their cattle were becoming gaunt, and the coming year looked lean for the cattlemen if it didn't rain soon.

Sage lazed around in her room, too lethargic in the hot, heavy air to get dressed. She dreaded going to work tonight. It would be unbearably hot in the theater, crowded with sweating humanity.

When she heard the men leave the boarding-house she drew on her robe and made her way to the kitchen. Carey looked up from a steaming pan of dishwater and drew an arm across her sweating forehead. "Ain't this humidity fierce?" she said in greeting. "It just saps the strength out of a body. We're in for a big storm."

Sage agreed and, listless, set a skillet on the stove to fry herself an egg. Later, as she ate her skimpy breakfast and drank a cup of coffee, Carey told her that she had gone through her linen closet and found a few things she could have. "I set aside two sets of sheets and pillowcases, and two blankets. I don't have any spare bedspreads or quilts."

"That's all right, Carey. I appreciate the linens.

I'll go to Jackson's Emporium and buy whatever else I need." Sage stood up and, taking her dirty plate, cup, and fork over to Carey, picked up a dishtowel and began drying the dishes draining in a rack.

The expected rain came around noon, accompanied by crackling lightning zigzagging across the sky and ominous thunder rolling behind it. Sage and Carey ran through the house, closing windows and doors; then they sat in the kitchen listening to the wind hurl the water against the house, sending rivulets down the window.

The storm raged for over an hour; then the lightning and thunder diminished, but the rain continued, soaking the scorched earth. Carey cracked the windows a couple of inches throughout the house, and the cool air that drifted in was a welcome relief from the heat.

The energy that had been sapped from Sage returned, as well as an enthusiasm for her new home. Day after tomorrow, she would catch the stagecoach to Cottonwood. From there Rooster could take her out to the McBain ranch to collect Danny.

She spent the rest of the day in her room going over her dresses; mending a hem, checking seams, looking for spots on skirts and bodices.

Then the gray and wet daylight deepened into dusk. By the time Sage ate supper and got dressed in her favorite green dimity it was time for Carey to walk her to the Gilded Cage.

"I'm sorry I can't come fetch you home tonight," Carey said when they arrived in front of the theater and Sage stepped from under the huge black umbrella the older woman held over their heads. "Are you sure there will be someone to walk you home after you've finished singing?"

Sage hurried to step under the theater awning. "Yes, I'm sure, Carey. Go sit with your sick friend and don't give me another thought. I'll be fine. I'll see you in the morning."

"Well, all right," Carey said, a worried frown still on her brow. "I don't feel good about it, though."

Carey stood for a moment after Sage had disappeared inside the big building; then, the worry still on her face, she turned and plodded off through the rain and mud.

As Sage walked through the dimly lit passageway to her and Ruby's dressing room, she could hear male voices shouting, "Bring on the songbird."

She had thought, considering all the rain, the audience would be small tonight. But a peek through the drawn drapes showed her that the house was packed as usual.

The jugglers were opening the show as Sage began to apply powder and paint to her face. The dancers were doing their number as she tried to do something with her hair. The dampness from the air had turned it into tight curls. She finally gave up trying to tame it, and left it as it was. Ruby was entering the dressing room then, the dancing act finished. She had only to wait for Madam Louise to sing her aria.

"It's hot as Hades out there," Ruby said, plopping herself into a chair and patting at her damp face with a handkerchief. "I wish we dancers didn't have to close the show. I'll be absolutely wilted by the time I finish another dance."

"Who's walking you home tonight, Ruby?" Sage asked her flushed friend.

"I don't know; one of the bouncers. Why?".

"Carey can't meet me tonight. She's with a sick friend. Do you think the man would walk me home too?"

"Of course. Just be ready when I finish."

Madam Louise's last trilling note sounded, followed by the usual polite clapping of the women in the audience. A moment later Sage parted the stage drapes and stepped out to a loud, hand-clapping, foot-stamping welcome.

The din lowered to a whisper as she climbed up on her stool and picked up the guitar. She smiled down at the faces gazing up at her, making each man there think that he was the only man receiving it. She sang her old songs, added a couple of new ones, and then left the stage, hearing behind her shouts of, "More, more!"

Back in her dressing room once more, Sage sat before the mirror removing the heavy paint from her face. She had just wiped away the last of it when, from the corners of her eyes, she saw the dressing room door leading to the alley ease open.

She whipped around in the chair and her heart stopped beating, frozen in terror. Leland Larkin stood in the doorway, a malignant smile on his face.

How had he found her? The question hammered in her brain. Only Tillie knew where she had gone, and she would die before she would divulge that information.

Don't let him know you're scared, her inner voice warned. *Stand up to him. Order him away.*

Her voice was controlled when she spoke, though she was shaking with panic inside. "What are you doing here, Leland? What do you want?"

"Now that's a stupid question, Sage." Larkin closed the door behind him and advanced on her. "What have I always wanted?"

"I thought I made it clear that I didn't want you when I married your brother," Sage said, thinking inanely that it must still be raining as water dripped off Larkin's slicker and puddled at his feet.

"You were a young girl then and didn't know what you wanted. You picked the wrong brother and put me through hell all those years. And if that wasn't enough, after I rid you of my weakling brother you turned to a half-breed."

At Sage's startled look, Larkin nodded his head. "Oh, yes, I know all about you and LaTour. I stood outside your window one night and watched the two of you wallowing in sin. The prim and proper Sage couldn't spread her legs fast enough for the breed to crawl between them."

Leland's face twisted demonically. "As I stood out there in the darkness, watching him thrusting inside you, I plotted my revenge. Before I kill you you're going to pay dearly for every pain you've made me suffer."

Before Sage could move, Larkin was upon

her, gripping her wrists with a strength that made her whimper with pain as the delicate bones were crushed. She opened her mouth to scream, and Larkin slapped her so hard across the face, it rocked her head, stunning her. Moving with lightning speed, he shoved a handkerchief in her mouth and bound her wrists together with a rope he took from his pocket.

Raising a taunting eyebrow at her, Larkin stepped back. "Scared?"

Sage glared at him, almost choking on the handkerchief. Yes, she was scared; scared half to death. This madman meant to kill her after he had tortured her in whatever way his sick mind had dreamed up.

Larkin had just jerked her to her feet and was preparing to sling her over his shoulder when the door from the passageway opened and Ruby stepped inside.

"What in the blue blazes do you think you're doing?" she screeched, and threw herself at Larkin.

He dropped Sage back into the chair, at the same time drawing a broad knife from its sheath at his waist. He brushed aside Ruby's flaying fists and grabbed her, flipping her over his shoulder. When she landed on her feet he whirled around and thrust the knife up between her narrow shoulders.

A stunned look came into the soft brown eyes; then blood gushed from her mouth. When her body went limp and folded over Larkin's arm he flung her away as though she was of no importance, a pesky fly he had killed.

Everything had happened so fast, Sage couldn't comprehend it all at once. Then her eyes fastened on the crumpled body of her little friend and she became white-faced with fury. She sprang from her chair and launched herself at her brother-in-law, using her tied hands as a club. Not only had she lost a dear friend, but two young children had lost their mother.

Larkin merely laughed at Sage's attack as he balled a fist and clipped her on the chin with it.

Sage tried to fight off the wavering darkness that crowded in on her. She could not. She was unaware of when she was tossed over Larkin's shoulder and carried out into the alley.

Chapter Twenty-two

Jim had no difficulty finding the Gilded Cage as he guided Rooster's horse down the main street of Cheyenne. A crowd of people was gathered in front of the two-story building, speaking in hushed tones. He was gripped with an apprehension that made his heart pound as he found a spot at the long hitching rail fronting the boardwalk. He knew with a certainty that Sage was the subject of the conversation going on.

Flipping the reins over the long, shiny post, he hurried to join the stunned, white-faced people milling about. He tapped a man on the shoulder and asked, "What's going on?"

"One of the girls who worked here was just murdered. Stabbed in the back."

Jim's face turned ashen; the bastard had got to Sage before he had. He felt sick with the pain that gripped him, was afraid he was going to vomit from it.

On the heels of his grief, Jim's muscles grew

taut and his eyes gleamed with cold fire. Leland Larkin would pay, pay in a manner that only an Indian could contrive.

He began pushing a path through the men and women, moving toward the theater. He would hold Sage again, look on her beautiful face one last time, then go hunting for her killer.

Jim's determined progress was halted when a middle-aged woman with a pale face and worried eyes blocked his path as she stood arguing with the town marshal. He walked around them and continued on toward the closed doors of the theater. When he grasped the brass doorknob the marshal left off talking with the woman and hurried to intercept him.

"You can't go in there, mister!" he called.

"You want to try stopping me?" Jim's hand dropped to the Colt hanging low on his right hip.

When the lawman stopped in momentary surprise Jim opened the big, heavy door and closed it behind him. He stood for a moment in the semigloom of a long hall, its only light coming from the sun as it tried to penetrate the ceiling-high windows, wondering where he went from here. A low murmur of voices came to him then, and he walked in that direction.

He burst into a small room just as a sheet was being drawn up over the face of a slender body. With an inarticulate cry he rushed to kneel beside the statue-still shape beneath the white cloth. With hands that trembled he took hold of a corner, bracing himself as he lifted it.

The two men who watched him curiously

started at the cry of thanksgiving Jim uttered.

A woman he had never seen before stared sightlessly at Jim. He dropped the sheet and bowed his head on his bent knee, reverently thanking God that it wasn't Sage lying there so still and cold.

"Do you know the woman?" The marshal had followed him into the small dressing room.

Jim shook his head and stood up. "I thought she was someone else." He noticed for the first time two young women who stood off by themselves, crying quietly. He stepped over to them. "Do either of you know Sage Larkin, and where I can find her?"

A tall blonde wiped her eyes, composed herself, and answered, "We don't know where Sage is. It's believed that whoever killed Ruby abducted her." When all the blood left Jim's face the woman said gently, "Her landlady, Carey Baker, is outside. She may know something."

Jim nodded his thanks, wheeled, and hurried outside. He stood on the boardwalk, his gaze skimming over the crowd that still hung around. Where was the older woman who had been talking to the marshal when he first arrived? He felt sure the woman had been Carey Baker.

She was not among those who waited. He turned around to reenter the theater to inquire where Sage's landlady lived, then turned back around. He had caught sight of a brightly flowered dress moving down the street. Carey Baker had worn such a garment. He hopped off the wooden sidewalk and hurried after her, praying that she could help him.

"Ma'am," he called after the matronly figure,

"could I have a few words with you?"

Tear-wet eyes gazed up at Jim when he caught up with the woman. "Say your few words, mister," she said quietly. "I've got worries on my mind today and I'm in no mood for idle chitchat."

"Neither am I," Jim said gently, knowing that the woman was suffering. "I think our worries are for the same person. I'm from Cottonwood and I'm looking for Sage Larkin."

"Why are you lookin' for Sage? What do you want with her?" The questions were asked suspiciously.

"I'm looking for her because I think she's in danger. And what I want with her is, I want to marry her, and take her back to Cottonwood where she belongs."

Carey's eyes spit fire at Jim. "Why did you let her leave there in the first place? She was a very unhappy woman when she first came here."

Jim looked down at the floor. He couldn't face the accusation in Carey's eyes. Every word she said was true. If he hadn't been a thick-headed fool, Sage would be his wife by now, safe from the man who had stalked her, killing four peolpe in his determination to have her.

He made himself look up at Carey. "Fool that I am, I let her go. But I swear to you, I didn't think I meant that much to her. Do you have any idea where she might be? Did she ever mention being afraid of a man named Larkin, her brother-in-law?"

"No," Carey answered thoughtfully. "She never talked about anyone but her nephew and a woman called Tillie . . . and a man who wasn't satisfied with just one woman." She gave Jim a censuring look. When he looked away again she asked, "Do you think this Larkin killed Ruby, then took Sage away?"

"As sure as I'm standing here, I think it. And God only knows what he intends to do with Sage."

"What do you mean to do?" Carey asked as they started walking down the boardwalk. "You'll try to find her?" The words were more an order than a question.

Jim glanced at the sun, ready to set. It would be dark in another hour, and he was desperately in need of sleep. And Rooster's horse, plodding along behind him, needed a good long rest. He *and* the horse had to be alert when they started looking for Leland Larkin.

"Just as soon as it's daylight tomorrow morning, and I can see to pick up the bastard's tracks, I'll start trailing him. And God help him if he harms one hair on Sage's head."

Jim had a feeling that Larkin would head back to the area he and Sage came from. Would he maybe find Sage dead somewhere along the trail? Jim shook his head, as though to dislodge the unbearable thought.

"You look beat to the bone, mister," Carey said as their boot heels rang out on the boards. "Let me fix you a bite to eat; then I'll find you a bed to sleep in."

It felt to Sage as if she had been riding all her life. But according to the position of the moon, probably only a couple of hours had passed since Leland had tossed her onto his stallion, then climbed up behind her before racing out of town.

Her jaws ached from the gag and her hands had long since grown numb, the ropes on her wrists so tight, they had cut off her circulation. Her back hurt from holding herself away from Leland, afraid that the touch of her body might arouse him.

So far, thank God, he hadn't touched her in a sexual way. But that didn't mean that he wouldn't once they stopped for the night or reached their destination, wherever that might be.

She had another fear as well. What would Leland do to her once he grew tired of tormenting her in whatever fashion his deranged mind dreamed up? Would he kill her? She knew now that he wouldn't hesitate at killing a woman.

Her little friend, Ruby, came to mind. Killed by this monster because she had tried to help her friend. What would happen to the dancer's children now? Would their grandmother stop drinking and raise them properly? She doubted it. The woman might want to, but she had been at the bottle for too many years.

And what about Danny if she didn't come out of this alive? Would Jonty and Cord keep him, raise him? She felt that they would.

Sage left off her disturbing thoughts when Leland pulled the stallion in and swung out of the saddle. "We'll stop here for the rest of the night," he said, jerking her to the ground. "Don't seem to be anyone following us." He shoved her toward a flat rock. "Go sit down over there and don't try to get away. You'd be a tasty morsel for the wolves that wander around in these woods."

Sage's hatred for the man was like a cancer inside her as she watched Leland build a fire, start coffee, and place a frying pan on the bed of red coals. Her eyes widened fractionally when he looked up and caught her glaring at him. He stood up and stalked over to her. Standing over her, he stroked his private parts through his trousers. "If you hadn't soiled yourself by sleeping with the breed, I'd put a different kind of look in those condemning eyes."

In her rage, Sage managed to spit the gag out of her mouth. "Never, not in a million years, would I allow you to touch me in that manner. I would feel unclean for the rest of my life."

His face twisted in rage, Leland sprang at Sage, coming down on his knees beside her. He grasped her delicate jaw with one hand while the other drew a knife from its sheath at his waist. Tightening his fingers on her tender flesh, he brought up the knife and laid its blade on her cheek, barely an inch below her right eye.

"You'd feel unclean, would you," he snarled. "Let's see how you feel about the touch of cold steel."

Sage felt only a small sting, but she also felt the warm blood that trickled down her cheek. The madman had cut her face. She closed her eyes to hide her terror. Would he cut her again?

A sigh of relief whistled through Sage's teeth when, with an oath, Leland released her with a hard shove, then went back to the fire. She struggled up from the ground where she had fallen and sat on the rock again. She knew now that Leland no longer desired her; he only wanted to torture her, make her suffer. And sooner or later, if no one came to her rescue, he would kill her.

Sage became conscious of the frying meat and brewing coffee permeating the area around the campfire. Her mouth watered; it smelled delicious. She hadn't eaten since having a light lunch with Carey. A few minutes later she couldn't believe it when Leland removed the pan from the fire and, squatting on his heels, carefully picked up a piece of the hot meat and bit into it. Swallowing her saliva, she watched him eat every scrap of the salt pork.

He doesn't intend for me to eat tonight, Sage thought in astonishment. Was that his plan? To starve her to death? She wanted to kill him with her bare hands when later, after swigging down two cups of coffee, he poured what remained in the pot onto the fire. He stood a moment, watching the curling wisps of smoke floating above the blackened coals; then he stalked over to her.

Sage tensed for more abuse, but all he did was tie a rope around her waist. Then he fastened its end to his own middle. "In case you decide to take a walk tonight," he sneered, "you'll be taking me with you." He took up his bedroll, unfolded it, and stretched out on top of it.

Sage swung between relief and anger: relief that she wasn't going to be bothered by him, but anger that he wouldn't even give her a blanket to sleep on. He was treating her like an animal.

Thankfully, the rope was long, giving her free movement in a six-foot area. She waited on tenterhooks for Leland's even breathing, telling her that he slept. She was squirming from the discomfort of a full bladder.

Finally snorting snores came from his blankets. The rain had stopped shortly after they left Cottonwood, and now in the damp darkness, Sage managed with her bound hands to hoist up her dress and petticoat, untie the ribbon of her drawers, and answer nature's call. Sighing, she moved about three feet from where she had wet the ground, lay down, and curled her body against the cool night air, dreading tomorrow.

Sage woke often during the night, aware of the cold and the discomfort of lying on the hard ground. But most of all she awakened because of the gnawing hunger in the pit of her stomach. It seemed like a hundred hours had passed since she had eaten.

A pink dawn was emerging from behind the eastern horizon when Sage was jerked awake by a sharp tug of the rope around her waist. "Sit up. Let me get this rope off you," Leland growled.

When he had rid her of the rope he put it down beside the saddle he had used as a pillow. He straightened up, and then, leering at her all the while, undid his fly and urinated on the ground, so close to her, the toes of her boots were splattered. She closed her eyes, afraid of what he might do next.

Evidently, he felt that he had humiliated her enough for the time being, for she heard his footsteps crunching away from her. She opened her eyes to see him kindling a fire over last night's ashes. A few minutes later she again smelled the wonderful aroma of frying meat and brewing coffee. She swallowed convulsively, her empty stomach roiling as once again Leland began to eat from the frying pan. She was more convinced than ever that he planned to starve her to death, to sit and watch her slowly die as she begged him for food.

A few minutes later she gave a start and was hard put not to cry out her thanksgiving when Leland walked toward her, the frying pan in his hand. Without speaking, he set the pan down and untied her. She could only stare at the few pieces of meat for several seconds as sensation returned to her fingers.

Never had anything tasted so good to Sage. She had to keep cautioning herself not to eat too fast, for fear her stomach would cramp.

She looked longingly at the coffeepot, but, like last night, whatever remained in it was thrown onto the fire.

She was allowed a drink of water from Leland's canteen before he tied her wrists together again. Then she was tossed onto the stallion's back, her skirt riding up past her knees.

The sun rose higher, and the day became hot, making the air muggy from the previous day's rain. Leland had not spoken since breaking camp, and that made her nervous. The farther they traveled, the more tension she sensed growing inside him.

Were they nearing the end of their journey?

Did his jumpiness have anything to do with her? she wondered, dread growing inside her. She knew that once they reached their destination her torture would begin, by what means she wouldn't let her mind imagine. She knew how cruel Leland could be. She had seen him abuse animals many times, not to mention the savage way he had beaten Arthur.

The sun moved westward and hunger pains began to rumble in Sage's stomach. Dusk would soon be upon them and he would make camp for the night. Would Leland let her eat, or would he make her wait for the morning meal?

An hour later dusk had come and gone, and still Leland kept the weary mount moving on. A pale moon rose, bathing the earth in a dim light, just enough for him to see where they were going. Sage was hanging on by sheer will alone, determined not to let her brother-in-law see any weakness in her. That he was trying to break her spirit, make her beg for mercy, was obvious. And she felt sure that once he had accomplished that, he would kill her.

Sage's back ached from holding it erect, and her legs were one solid ache from the long hours in the saddle. She was silently praying for the strength to keep from giving in to her body's weakness when she saw a pale, shimmering light ahead in the darkness. Were her eyes deceiving her? No—Lamplight was shining through a window, and they were riding toward it.

She thought of the three men who had killed her family, and a shiver ran down her spine. Were they sitting, waiting for Leland to deliver her to them? Were they the ones who would kill her? Panic gripped her. They wouldn't kill her outright; they would first take their pleasure of her body, the way the redheaded one had done to poor Mary.

A shack of a place loomed in front of them, and Leland drew the spent mount to a halt, shouting as he slipped out of the saddle, "Lisha, you lazy breed, get out here and take care of my horse."

As Leland jerked Sage out of the saddle, a ragged teenager burst from the shack and hurriedly gathered up the trailing reins and led the stallion away, dodging a kick from Leland as he went past him.

Sage staggered a bit on her numb feet as Leland grabbed her elbow and propelled her into the shack's single room. As he flung her onto the rickety chair, the young boy watched them, fear and dread in his eyes. He jumped when Leland ordered harshly, "Put supper on the table, you little bastard."

Turning to Sage, and seeing her staring at the boy, his eyes narrowed to pinpoints of anger. His hands shot out and fastened around her throat, his fingers biting into her flesh. "Yes," he grated out, "he came from my seed. And you, you bitch, could have saved me that shame if you hadn't chosen Arthur over me." He released her then, and walked away.

Leland's furious words had gone unnoticed by Sage. She remembered that Leland had hated Indians even before she and Arthur had married. Had he, way back then, had a squaw hidden away, giving her children? There was no doubt in her mind that the half-breed teenager who had taken charge of the mount had Leland's blood coursing through his veins. And the boy had to be all of fifteen.

She watched the other lad, who looked a little older than Danny, laying out his father's supper, and her heart went out to him. He was trying his best to escape Leland's attention.

It came to Sage that the hatred Leland claimed to have for Indians was really hatred of himself because he had lain with an Indian woman, had sired children on her. She wondered what had happened to the woman.

It struck Sage, too, that, if not blood-related, these two boys were her nephews through her marriage to Arthur. She felt an immediate kinship to the two unfortunate boys. She wanted to spring to the younger one's defense when Leland cuffed him alongside his head and demanded, "Did you read that chapter in the Bible like I told you to?"

"Yes, sir," the boy answered in a quivering voice, cowering.

"I'll question you on it later," Leland muttered, and he sat down at the table. As he shoveled meat and beans into his mouth, Sage stood up and walked outside, not caring if he came after her and beat her with his fists. She couldn't bear to look at him for another minute.

The two boys sat on tree stumps, their heads bent, their hands clasped between their knees. Sage walked over to them. "Why do you stay here?" She looked at Lisha.

"We have nowhere to go. When I was just a

baby our mother tried to go back to her village, but she was turned away because she had run off with him, bringing shame to her people."

He shrugged his thin shoulders. "At least he doesn't come here often. This past month, though, he's been here twice."

"How do you manage to live?"

"Larkin always leaves a rifle behind, for me to hunt with. Then there are the vegetables we raise in the summer, and we fish in the river. We get by. Better to go hungry once in a while than have him live with us all the time."

"I take it your mother is dead."

"Yes, three years ago. Giving birth to a dead baby."

Sage turned to the younger boy. "What's your name, son?"

"I'm called Benny, ma'am."

She smiled at the two youngsters. "You fellows can call me Aunt Sage if you want to. I was once married to your father's brother. In fact, you look an awful lot like your Uncle Arthur, Benny."

Both boys looked at Sage in stunned, pleased surprise. It was evident that they knew nothing about their father's people, had probably never even given any thought to the possibility that they might have white relatives.

"Did you leave Larkin's brother because he was mean?" Lisha asked.

"Oh, no. Your Uncle Arthur was the kindest man in the world. He was shot to death by outlaws this past spring." She wanted to add, "At your father's instruction," but caution held her tongue. It could be a hard blow to the boys to learn in one minute that there had been an uncle, and then be told in the next that their father had had his brother killed.

Sage opened her mouth to ask them to untie her; then she paused when she saw alarm leap into the boys' eyes. Leland's heavy hand fell on her arm. She wheeled around to look at him, her throat bone dry. In his hand he carried his wicked-looking knife. It had angered him that she had left the shack, and now he was going to kill her.

She closed her eyes, waiting, wanting to pray but too terror-stricken to form the words.

She felt the coldness of the blade on her flesh; then she gasped her relief when she felt the bindings on her wrist fall away. Leland gave a low, ugly laugh.

"You thought your time had come, didn't you?"

Before Sage could answer he grabbed her chin and ran the point of the blade along her jaw. A horrified look came over Benny and Lisha's faces as trickles of blood ran down her throat.

While Sage stared at him dumbly, so afraid she couldn't speak, Leland laughed harshly. "That is only the beginning, my beauty. You see, I have decided not to kill you, after all. I have a worse punishment in mind for you. I am going to disfigure that lovely face of yours. When I am finished slicing at it you will never attract another man again. The half-breed, LaTour, will turn from you in disgust."

Gripping her arm, he pulled her into the shack

and shoved her down at the table. "Eat," he ordered.

When she made no move to pick up her fork Leland taunted, "Aren't you hungry? Have you lost your appetite? It's a long time until breakfast."

Sage could only shake her head. She was beyond speech. Leland would do exactly what he threatened, and the consequences of such an act overwhelmed her. With a face so mutilated it would scare children, how was she to earn a living? How would she provide for Danny? She would no longer be able to stand in front of an audience and sing.

Dear Lord, she prayed silently, *help me to get away from this madman.*

Sage was weary to the bone as she sat on the small stool. She had been sitting there for over an hour, listening to and watching Leland as he stood over Lisha and Benny, quizzing them on the Bible. Every time a response wasn't precise in its wording, the unfortunate boy received a cuff to the head that knocked him half off his seat.

Rage boiled inside her. It was blasphemous for this black-souled murderer to stand over these children, beating the word of God into them. She asked herself why his Maker hadn't struck him dead a long time ago.

The questioning and answering continued, perverse pleasure twisting Leland's lips as he struck his sons at the slightest excuse.

Benny was picking himself up off the floor after receiving an exceptionally hard cuff when

Leland's name was shouted from outside. With a vile oath, Leland drew his six-shooter and spun the cylinder, checking to see if it was fully loaded. Then he slipped it beneath a dishtowel that lay on the table.

"Open the door," he snarled at Lisha.

When the door was open and his name was called again, Leland shouted, "What in the hell do you men want?"

"We heard in Cheyenne that Sage Larkin had been abducted and we reckoned it was you who grabbed her. So we're here to get the rest of the money comin' to us."

After a short pause Leland called, "Come on in."

Sage barely repressed a furious cry when she recognized the three men who clumped into the shack. They were the same three who had killed her family. She forced herself to remain quiet, caution warning her not to call attention to herself. If those three got it into their heads to use her, Leland might take evil pleasure in letting them do it.

In the dimness of the room, lit only by a stub of a candle, the three men sat down at the table with Leland. As they spoke in low tones, Sage's mind raced, thinking of ways of getting herself and the boys away from there. There were three mounts outside, and Leland's back was turned to her and his sons. Could they make a dash for the door, find the horses in the dark, mount them, and get away before Leland caught them?

It was certainly worth a try.

She squeezed a grubby hand on either side of

her and whispered, "When I stand up and dash to the door be ready to follow me as quickly as you can."

Their eyes sent back a message of agreement.

As the three of them waited, a violent argument erupted between Leland and the three men.

"You will, by hell." The redheaded man brought his fist down on the table, making the candleholder bounce. "That was the agreement. Half when we killed your brother and the Willises and the balance when you got the woman."

He leaned toward Leland. "Look," his voice was threatening, "you've got her now, and we want our money."

Rage glittering in his eyes, Leland said loudly, "Yes, I've got her, but through no help from you." His hand crept toward the crumpled towel. "You're not getting another dime from me."

"Then by God we'll just take her away from you, you tight-fisted bastard." The one with the red hair lunged to his feet. "We're the ones who tipped you off where she was."

All the time the argument was going on, Sage hadn't taken her eyes off Leland. She would know the instant his rage was ready to break into violence. If he went for the gun hidden under the towel, it would be the only chance she and the boys might have to make a break for freedom.

In the blink of an eye, Leland grabbed the gun, and everything erupted into total confusion. Guns blazed and chairs skittered across the floor as the other two outlaws surged to their feet.

"Now," Sage hissed and ran toward the door, the boys at her heels. They burst outside and spotted the mounts standing in the faint splash of the candle shining through the grimy window. The boys didn't have to be told to mount up.

All three hit the saddles at the same time. They slapped their heels against the animals' sides, sending them tearing away in a hard gallop. As they raced away, one last shot was heard from inside the cabin.

Chapter Twenty-three

It was barely daylight when Carey shook Jim awake. "Time to get up, Jim," she said in hushed tones, trying not to awaken her boarders. "I've got you some breakfast ready and some trail grub packed."

"Thank you, Carey." Jim sat up and swung his feet to the floor, anxious to get on Leland's trail. He had spent a restless night, his sleep interrupted with disturbing dreams of Sage. In his nightmares she needed him desperately and he couldn't get to her.

He stamped on his boots as Carey left the room; then he took his gun and holster off the bedrail and strapped it around his lean waist. Finding his hat where he had dropped it on a chair, he carried it in his hand as he walked through the house, making his way to the kitchen by the odor of fried bacon and fresh coffee.

Carey, clad in a robe that had seen many

washings, her graying hair hanging down her back in a single braid, looked up from the stove. "You can wash up over there." She jerked her head in the direction of a dry sink situated beneath a window. "Your bacon and eggs are ready when you are."

"If you don't mind, Carey, I'll forgo washing up," Jim said. He sat down at the table, making short work of the meal Carey had prepared for him,

Altogether not more than five minutes had passed since Carey had awakened Jim when he thanked her for her kindness to him and walked out the kitchen door to saddle the horse, which had been stabled in a small shed.

"My prayers are with you, Jim LaTour," Carey called from the doorway as he sent the sorrel galloping out of her backyard.

Unlike Leland, Jim didn't make camp when darkness fell, but rode on through the night. The man he followed already had too much of a head start on him.

Twice he came to a watering hole where he paused to let the horse drink. When he grew hungry he ate from the grub sack Carey had provided for him: beef sandwiches and cold fried chicken.

The path of single tracks he followed were easy to discern on the wet earth. Evidently, Larkin was confident that he wouldn't be followed; he had made no effort to cover his passing.

What was happening to Sage now? Was she at this very minute trying to fight Larkin off? He refused to think that she might be dead.

The sky lightened to a dull gray; then the east turned pink and daylight arrived. Jim discovered that the trail he followed was suddenly leading toward Cottonwood. In the darkness he hadn't noted it, all his attention being on the tracks.

Why would Larkin return to Cottonwood? Jim asked himself as the sun rose higher, a great red ball that warned it would be another scorcher. Was he going to collect Danny, to inflict more pain on Sage as he tortured the lad in some way?

Jim tightened his grip on Rooster's sorrel, urging him on. He had to catch up to Leland.

Twice Jim reined in the weary horse for a few minutes' rest before pushing on. He ate some of Carey's fried chicken; then, a couple of hours later, the sun disappeared and the gray of twilight quickly darkened into night. The weary horse slowed to a walk and Jim didn't have the heart to call more speed from him.

The moon rose and the mount plodded on. The tracks Jim had been following down a narrow valley suddenly changed direction, compelling them to climb to the top of a ridge. Jim halted there and looked down on a stand of cottonwood. His eyes moved slowly over it; then he was startled into giving it closer attention. Had he seen a spiral of blue smoke lifting among the trees?

He leaned forward over the saddle, his eyes squinted and peering. Had he also spotted a dim light? Naw, he thought; his eyes must be playing tricks on him. He sat a moment longer, not fully convinced that he hadn't seen a light among the trees. His eyes glued to the spot where he thought he had seen it, the light suddenly appeared again, as though a body had hidden it for a moment.

His heart began to thud as he lifted the reins, urging the horse forward. Would he find Sage down there? Would he find her alive?

He was halfway to the small timber when he heard a shot ring out. "Oh, dear God," he whispered, "am I too late?"

Jim checked the sorrel, stopping just within the shadow of the cottonwoods. He swung to the ground, letting the reins trail. The well-trained animal wouldn't move until he was ordered to do so.

He moved noiselessly through the large tree trunks until he almost walked into a rudely constructed shack not much larger than a storage shed. He paused there, watching the building intently. He could see through the small, grimy window the figure of a tall, bearded man moving about. Leland Larkin; he knew him beyond a doubt.

He saw Larkin bend over, then straighten up slightly, as though he were dragging something heavy. He lost sight of him for a moment, then saw him again as he backed out the door. The something heavy was the body of a man being dragged outside by its feet. As it was dragged into the tall weeds surrounding the shack, the moon shone on a head of red hair.

"Dick Harlan," Jim muttered, and wondered if the other two outlaws were inside, also dead.

He waited until Larkin went back inside the shack; then he slipped up to the window and peered inside. His eyes lit on Tex and Ed. Tex lay crumpled on the floor and Ed was sprawled over the table. Both were dead.

Jim's eyes scanned the room, looking for Sage. He saw no sign of her. Dear Lord, where was she?

Jim's eyes shifted back to Larkin, and when he saw the man bend over and grab Tex by the heels and start pulling him toward the door, he slipped around to the front of the house and stepped quietly through the open door.

"Hold it right there, Larkin." His voice came hard and cold.

Larkin's body stiffened and his hands released the booted feet. He turned slowly, blank stupefaction in his eyes, as he stared at Jim. "So," he said finally, "you've caught up with me, breed."

"Were you foolish enough to think that I wouldn't follow you to the ends of the earth if need be?"

"You're the fool," Larkin jeered. "You've followed me for nothing."

"No." Jim shook his head. "You've got her, and I'll not leave this hole until I've wrung it out of you where she is."

Larkin shot Jim a look of venomous hate; then he laughed harshly. "I'm quite willing to tell you where she is, breed. I killed her shortly after I took her and left her for the wolves and buzzards. By now only bones are left of the beautiful Sage."

A pain so intense it seemed to shatter his chest gripped Jim. His worst fear had been realized. A red film of rage mingled with anguish in his eyes as his hand, a blur of movement, swept down to the deadly Colt.

The gun spit fire and smoke, and a bullethole appeared between Larkin's horror-stricken eyes. A sigh rushed through his lips as he fell on top of Tex's limp body.

The acrid smell of gunsmoke stung Jim's eyes and nostrils, bringing back a semblance of sanity. His eyes swept over the carnage, of which he had added a part. His eyes dead, like those of the men who lay on the floor, he sheathed the Colt and left the shack, a broken man. He walked back to the horse hidden in the trees, stripped the animal of saddle and bridle, and lay down at its feet. Tomorrow morning he'd ride to his ranch. He couldn't face Tillie yet, couldn't tell her what had happened. He was drifting to sleep when he thought of Danny and groaned. How in the world was he going to bear telling the lad?

A rapid drumming of steel-shod hooves sounded in the quiet night as Sage and her two young companions raced along by the light of the moon. The outlaw's mounts were fresh and fleet of foot, quickly widening the distance between them and Leland.

Bending low over her mount's neck, the wind whipping her hair back like a banner held aloft, Sage prayed she and the boys were headed toward Cheyenne. She had chosen the direction by instinct and could be totally wrong in her decision. There was no use asking Lisha or Benny. She imagined those two poor children had never been farther than a five-mile radius from the place they called home.

They had been riding for close to an hour when Sage pulled her mount in, the boys quickly following her lead, to listen for the sound of pursuit. All was quiet, the only sound the heavy breathing of the horses.

"Where are we going, ma'am?" Lisha asked in a low voice.

"I'm hoping that we're traveling toward Cheyenne. There's a city marshal there, and we'll be safe from Leland," she said to soothe the boys.

Lisha looked up at the sky as though searching it. "The last two times Larkin visited us he came from that direction." He pointed to the right of them. "If he grabbed you in Cheyenne, then that's the way we should go."

Sage looked at Benny, at his scared face. "Are you all right, honey? Can you keep going?"

The youngster nodded. "I could ride for a week straight if in the end we'd be free of him."

"Let's go then." Sage turned her mount's head to the right.

Sage and the boys raced on, though they and the horses were tiring. Sage knew they would have to stop soon for a few hours' rest, but where? Her eyes searched the flat open country. She saw no place of concealment where they could hide themselves. Lisha, also aware that soon they must rest, called out and pointed ahead. Sage peered through the darkness and made out the silhouette of a stand of timber high on a ridge. She smiled at the teenager and nodded her head.

In twenty minutes they rode in among the

trees. If it had not been for Benny's sharp eyes they would have ridden past an old deserted cabin, well hidden in a growth of lodgepine, brush, and rock. If anyone found it, it would be by accident.

The perfect place to grab some rest and maybe a few hours of sleep, Sage thought, swinging to the needle-strewn ground. The boys followed her action. Lisha pushed open the sagging door and they trooped inside.

The cabin had the odor of a place that had been empty for a long time. Sand gritted underfoot, and dead flies and spiderwebs decorated the single window through which the bright moon shone. "I think we can safely stay here until morning," Sage said. "But first we must hide the horses."

The tired mounts were led to the back of the building, where a small, shallow stream trickled over a bed of smooth pebbles. The horses snorted, eager to get to the water. As they relieved the animals of saddles and bits, Sage and Lisha grinned at each other. Behind each cantle was a bedroll. They would not have to sleep on the floor.

"Check the saddlebags for some grub, boys," Sage said, flipping back the flap of the one she'd taken off her mount.

"I found some beef jerky," Benny exclaimed after a moment. "Did you find anything, Lisha?"

"Same as you; some jerk. What about you, ma'am?" Lisha walked over to Sage, who stared down at a flat paper-wrapped package in her hand.

"I only found this," she answered, "But I

don't think it's food of any kind. It's too soft." She stripped away the wrapping and all three gasped. Sage held a stack of greenbacks in her hand.

"It's money, isn't it, ma'am?" Benny asked in awed tones. "I saw Larkin give some to that redheaded man one time."

"Yes, it's money, Benny, and a lot of it." She fanned one end of the currency. "I'd say over a thousand dollars."

"That's probably the money Larkin gave Harlan to kill your family, ma'am," Lisha said quietly.

"I don't doubt it in the least," Sage choked out, the money suddenly burning her palm. She stared down at it. Had this stack of paper been the instrument of the death of her family? She hurriedly shoved it back into the saddlebag. "Don't forget to bring in the rifles," she said, picking up the one she had found on her own mount.

Back inside the shelter, they sat down on the floor and chewed slowly at the tough strips of dried beef. The boys made a necessary call outside, with Sage doing the same when they returned. She looked up through the canopy of leaves and prayed, "Please, God, see us safely to Cheyenne."

Lisha and Benny had unfolded the bedrolls in her absence, side by side in a row. Each boy was stretched out on an end one, leaving the middle one for Sage. She smiled softly to herself: her little protectors.

Chapter Twenty-four

The sun coming through the broken glass of the window scattered its rays on the three sleeping faces. Sage opened her eyes, blinked, and then raised an arm to shut out its brightness. She felt a warm pressure at her side and, turning her head, looked at Benny's young, freckled face.

Memories of the past two horror-filled days swept over her. She raised her head and looked around the room that had sheltered them through the night, half expecting to see Leland leering at her from some corner.

Other than her and the boys, the only occupant of the room was a little field mouse skittering across the floor. It disappeared into a hole in the wall.

But that doesn't mean Leland isn't out there somewhere, Sage thought, *trailing us like a demented bloodhound.*

She sat up and gently shook Lisha's thin shoulder. When he blinked up at her, a flash

of bewilderment in his eyes, she smiled at him
and said, "The sun is well up. We've got to get
going."

Lisha nodded as memory returned to him.
He rubbed the sleep from his eyes and then,
standing up, quickly rolled up his blankets.
Benny awakened at the sound of his brother's
and Sage's voices and stared uncomprehending-
ly at Sage for a moment. His eyes grew watery
as he remembered where he was and why.

"Come on, Benny, get up," Lisha ordered
gruffly. "We've got to saddle the horses and get
out of here. We don't want Larkin finding us."

That their father might come upon them
brought Benny to his feet and out the door
ahead of his brother. As Sage rolled up his
blankets, she shook her head, anger clouding
her eyes. A child shouldn't be that terrified of
his father.

Morning mists were still lifting from the long
valley when Sage and the boys rode away from
the old cabin, Lisha leading the way. Although
he was only fifteen, he was years older in
many ways. It had soon become evident to Sage
that he had been forced to grow up quickly;
to see to his mother and brother's welfare in
the long absences of his father. That he had
managed to keep their bodies and souls together
spoke of a wit and a determination that many
grown men didn't share.

A sense of security came over Sage. She was
sure in her mind that this hardened boy would
lead them safely to Cheyenne, to the little house
she had rented.

Nevertheless, she looked behind her often as

she brought up the tail end of their single-file line. She had lived in fear of her brother-in-law for too many months. If he was still alive, he would follow her, she knew for a certainty.

Sage didn't fully relax until they topped a rise and her rented house stood only a mile or so away. It was around four hours to sunset when she and the boys drew rein, and she pointed and said, "Lisha, Benny, down there is your new home."

There was a period of silence before Benny asked uneasily, "Will we be living alone, ma'am?"

"Of course not." Sage grinned at him. "You'll be living with me and my nephew, Danny. Danny's an orphan. His mother and father were killed a few months back.

"We may have a couple of other youngsters living with us," Sage added, lifting the reins and starting down the small hill. "They're orphans too. When we get settled in I'll ride into Cheyenne and see if they need a home. And one other thing: I think you'll be pleased to know that you also have a grandfather and a grandmother. Someday I'll take you to visit them."

"They won't want to see us," Lisha said bitterly.

"Of course they will. Why do you say that?"

"Our mother's parents wouldn't even look at us."

"Well, that won't be the case with these grandparents," Sage assured the brothers. "They'll love you dearly."

There was doubt and hope in Lisha's eyes,

but he made no response to Sage's declaration. He would wait and see, and make up his own mind.

The shack where four men lay dead was ten miles behind Jim when he roused himself and raised up to look through the leaves of a large cottonwood. The sky was sprinkled with stars.

He lay back down with a ragged sigh. Sage was dead. How was he going to continue living in a world where she didn't exist?

A shudder gripped his body as hot, bitter tears burned his eyes and throat.

Dawn slipped in as Jim cried out his misery, a wretchedness that left his face gaunt and his blue eyes shadowed. He had looked upon grief many times, had felt it before when he had learned of Cleo's death. But never had he experienced this gut-twisting, mind-destroying pain.

When for a moment he wished that he could just lie there and die, too, he pushed the thought away. There was his daughter to consider, as well as Sage's young nephew. He would take the boy and raise him, of course. Not only did he want to, but he owed it to Sage. She had loved the youngster devotedly. It would be like having a piece of her as Danny grew into manhood.

Jim sat up, pulled on his boots, and then rolled up his blankets, his movements slow, almost trancelike. When he had saddled Rooster's horse he slipped a foot into the stirrup and swung onto the animal's back. The horse moved out at his pressure on the reins.

Jim veered away from the direct route to Cheyenne. He couldn't face the woman, Carey, yet. His pain was still too fresh.

Nor could he face Tillie and tell her about Sage, he thought, cutting across country, heading toward his ranch. He knew that his cook and Jonty and Danny would be worrying and wondering by now about her long absence, but he had to accept her death first, and heal the open wound in his heart and mind.

It was midday when Jim arrived in his valley and looked down at the scene below. He pulled in the sorrel, pushed back his hat, and wiped the sweat off his face with his neckerchief as he gazed downward.

Cattle were scattered all over the floor of the basin, with riders moving among them. All his cowhands were slim and wiry, and he'd have it no other way; a heavy man was too hard on a horse. Jim put his hat back on his head when he saw a rider split off from the herd and come galloping toward him.

Rooster! Never had he needed a friend so badly.

Rooster's horse shot past Jim, wheeled, and rode alongside him. He was subjected to searching eyes; then Rooster said quietly, "You bring bad news."

Jim nodded. "The bastard killed her, Rooster." His voice was rough with his pain.

"You avenged her, of course."

"I shot the bastard right between the eyes."

"Too bad you didn't torture him first."

"I thought that later, but when the rabid wolf stood there and quietly and maliciously told me that he had shot her and left her to the buzzards, my Colt just seemed to jump into my hand and fire.

"What's been going on in my absence?" Jim asked as the two horses moved out.

"Well, your house is about finished. All Applegate has to do is paint it. It sure is a fine-lookin' place. You're gonna get lost in all them rooms, though. A place that big needs a lot of younguns runnin' around in it."

When Jim made no response, Rooster said, "Clem is gettin' ready to drive half the herd to the railroad in Laramie. He'd have been gone already, but he's been hangin' around, hopin' you'd show up."

Rooster slanted Jim a glance from the corners of his eyes. "Might do you good if you come along, Jim. Change of scenery; work your butt off; get your mind on somethin' else."

Rooster was right, Jim thought. Nothing could be better than to work himself to the bone every day, and fall into an exhausted sleep at the end of it.

"How long do you think we'd be gone?"

"Oh, I don't know." Rooster pushed his hat forward and scratched his head thoughtfully. "Three weeks to a month, I guess."

"Let's go talk to Clem. Tell him to be ready to pull out in the morning."

Sage left the livery, driving the same light-weight wagon she had hired only a week before to move donated furniture to her new residence. She had spent a busy hour and a half since riding into Cheyenne.

Her first stop had been at the boardinghouse,

riding down the alley and coming up behind the place. She couldn't rid herself of the fear that Leland was lurking around, ready to spring on her. She had startled poor Carey so, as she came through the kitchen door, the woman had dropped a pan of biscuits on the floor.

The biscuits had rolled across the floor unnoticed as the two women hugged each other, tears of thanksgiving running down Carey's cheeks. "Oh, Sage, it's so good to see you alive and unharmed." She hugged Sage tightly one more time before releasing her.

Carey took a step back, running her eyes over her, taking in the soiled, wrinkled dress Sage had worn to the theater that terrible night, the brown hair a tangled mess hanging around her shoulders. "You are all right, aren't you, honey?" she asked softly, scrutinizing Sage's dirty face, her eyes widening at the two long, red lines Leland's knife had put on her face.

Carey's hand came up to gently touch her cheek, and then her jaw. "He tortured you, didn't he, girl?" Carey dropped her hand. "Did he . . ."

"No, Carey, he didn't. Other than cutting my face, he did me no harm."

"How did you manage to get away from him, and who was he?"

"May I tell you all about it while I bathe and get into some clean clothing? I have much to tell you, and a lot of things to take care of before nightfall."

Carey had nodded, and the hip bath in her room was prepared. Sage sprinkled some bath salts in the water, then stripped off her filthy clothes and stepped into the rose-scented water. She leaned her head on the backrest, relaxing for a moment and feeling the stiffness and tiredness ease out of her body.

"Sit up," Carey ordered, "and I'll wash your hair for you. It looks like a rat's nest."

When the thick lather Carey had worked up in her curls had been rinsed away Sage took up the washcloth and bar of scented soap and began her bath. As she washed away the grime and sweat, she told her friend everything that had happened to her. She said that Leland's two sons waited for her at the rented house, and that she intended to take Ruby's two children there also.

"Ruby lost her life trying to help me. The least I can do is raise her little ones."

"It's a very honorable thing to do, Sage, but it will take every cent you earn to support four younguns . . . five, countin' your nephew. You'll never be able to buy that house you like so much."

"Maybe not." Sage stood up and began drying herself with the large towel Carey handed her. "I'm afraid it's going to be too small for all of us anyhow."

She had left the boardinghouse a short time later, going to the theater, where she was greeted warmly by Jefferson. After telling him the bare essentials of her capture and her escape, she told him that she would return to work the next night, then hurried away.

Her next stop was down the street to the grocer's, where she stocked up on staples, meat, and vegetables. Then she made a trip across the street to a clothing emporium. Lisha and Benny's shirts and trousers were practically rags, and she doubted they wore underwear. Certainly they had no shoes.

When she had chosen two sets of clothing for the boys, from the skin out, she moved to the table containing boots. For Benny she bought the size Danny wore; for Lisha she had to guess at the size by looking and judging what would fit him.

The teenager who did all the heavy work for Carey in the boardinghouse helped her to collect and stash all her packages and bundles into the wagon and then she was on her way to see Ruby's little boy and girl.

It was a pathetic sight that greeted Sage as she pulled up the horse in front of the run-down house where Ruby had lived and set the brakes on the wagon. Five-year-old Ruth Ann, her blonde hair a tangle of curls that looked as if they hadn't felt a brush since Ruby had died, sat on the sagging step leading off the dangerously canting porch. Her elbows were propped on her bent knees, supporting her dirty little tear-tracked face.

As Sage climbed down from the wagon and walked toward her, the child looked up with a woebegone expression. Recognition came into the blue eyes. *A friend of Mama's,* they seemed to say, as with a rush Ruth Ann's little legs came pounding toward her.

Sage stooped and caught the sobbing child in her arms and carried her back to the porch. She sat down on a rickety chair there, hoping it would hold both their weights.

She had never cuddled the soft body of a little girl before, and never had she experienced a mother's instinct so strongly. Even from the age of two Danny had felt all male, with a sturdy little back and muscular legs that squirmed to get away if you tried to hold him too long or too near you. She lovingly stroked the little body that couldn't seem to get close enough to her.

"I want my mommy, Auntie Sage," the little one hiccuped. "I miss her."

"I know, darling." Sage held the sorrowing child closer. "I miss her too. But she's in heaven now, and we're going to have to comfort each other." She stroked the silky head. "Do you think we can do that?"

"I guess so." The small head nodded on Sage's shoulder.

The screen door behind them scraped open, and Ruby's mother lurched onto the porch. "Oh, Miss Larkin, thank God you've come," she cried as young Jamie hurried to steady his grandmother. "The ladies from one of the churches are threatening to take the children away from me and put them in an orphanage. They say I'm not fit to raise them."

She plunked herself down on the edge of the porch, maudlin tears running down her seamed cheeks. "Maybe I'm not," she admitted, smoothing the soiled, wrinkled dress down over her knees. "But it would break the little ones' hearts to be separated now, just losing their mama and all."

Sage looked at Jamie, saw the scared look in his eyes, and reached out an arm to draw him to her side. "No one is putting these children in an orphanage," she said firmly. "They're coming home with me."

Such relief came into Jamie's eyes, Sage wanted to cry. The eight-year-old had been suffering even more than his sister had: He was old enough to know the meaning of an orphanage.

"God bless you, Miss Larkin." The grandmother tried twice to get to her feet but failed both times. She finally gave up the effort and folded her hands in her lap. "I tried to do my best for the little ones, but I guess it wasn't enough. The heart just seemed to go out of me when Ruby was killed."

Sage reached forward and patted the thin shoulder that shook with sobs. She had never doubted that she loved her daughter and grandchildren, but the years of drinking had rendered her incapable of helping anyone, including herself.

Sage put Ruth Ann off her lap and rose to her feet. "Come on, children. Let's go get your clothes together. I want to get home before dark."

The sun was setting behind the distant mountains, sending shadows reaching out on the flat country as the wagon rolled out of Cheyenne, Sage handling the reins and a child on either side of her. Tearful good-byes had been said to the bleary-eyed grandmother, with promises of visiting her real soon.

And I'll see to it that the promise is kept, Sage said to herself, flicking the horse's rump with her whip, hurrying it along. Twilight was almost upon them, and Lisha and Benny were probably getting a little nervous by now at her long absence.

It was dark inside the house when she pulled the wagon to a creaking halt outside the kitchen door, and so quiet she grew anxious. Had the boys grown uneasy and left? Had Leland followed them and taken his sons away?

She climbed out of the vehicle and turned to lift Ruth Ann off the high seat, leaving Jamie to scramble down by himself. "Wait here," she whispered to the children and stepped upon the narrow porch that ran the width of the house. She rapped on the door and laid an ear against it, listening for sounds inside. She heard nothing. Ready to go around to the front door and use her key, praying that she wouldn't find the door wide open, she saw the white blur of a face peering through the window at her.

Sage smiled her relief and called out, "Open the door, Lisha, and come give me a hand unloading the wagon."

An hour later Sage and the children were sitting on a blanket spread on the floor, eating their supper by the light of the lamp she had lit and placed up on the mantel.

As steak, fried potatoes, and string beans were consumed by hungry young appetites, Sage knew a contentment she hadn't experienced for a long time. She had a family again—children to fill the empty place her body had been unable to fill. When a small voice inside her whispered, *What about a man in your life?* she pushed away the image of Jim LaTour and thought of how happy Danny would be to have young companions to play with.

When the plates had been scraped clean Sage set the boys to cleaning up the kitchen while she made up the bed she and Ruth Ann would sleep in. The boys would sleep on the floor until she could have some beds built in the second bedroom.

There was laughter and a little horseplay as the boys spread out their bedrolls, Jamie smoothing out the one Sage had used as they fled Leland. But once tired bodies stretched out on the blankets they settled down and fell almost instantly asleep.

With an amused smile, Sage took down the lamp from the mantel and carried it into her bedroom, where Ruth Ann had crawled into the bed as soon as it had been made up. Picking up the pad of paper and pencil she had purchased at the mercantile, she sat down on the edge of the bed and wrote a letter to Tillie and Jonty, explaining the events that had kept her from coming for Danny. She wrote to Jonty that she would come for him as soon as possible.

She sealed the letters and was ready to blow out the lamp when she heard the low sound of sobbing; then Lisha whispered, "Shhh, Jamie, you're too big to cry."

Was that the Indian blood in Lisha speaking, Sage wondered, that ingrained belief that men never showed tender emotions, or had his hard life made him insensitive to others' human frailties?

She walked into the boys' room and said softly, "A man is never too old to cry if he has good reason to." She knelt down beside Jamie's curled body and, laying a hand on his shoulder, said gently, "Come and sleep with me and your sister tonight."

A few minutes later, lying in bed, Jamie cuddled up next to her. Sage smiled in the darkness when she heard Lisha say gruffly, "I guess a man has reason to cry for a dead mother."

Chapter Twenty-five

Rooster watched his friend from across the campfire. The creases that fanned from the corners of Jim's brooding eyes were deeper, and there was more gray in his black hair. There was a bleakness in the handsome face that he'd never seen before. Jim was hurting, he knew, and there was nothing he could do about it.

There had been times on the trail when he had wanted to caution his friend to slow down, to not drive himself so hard. He had kept his counsel to himself, however. Jim would resent him knowing how he bled inside. Time would dull the edge of Jim's pain, but he would never forget the woman who had sung in his saloon, of that Rooster felt sure.

Jim blinked his eyes, erasing Sage's face from the flames that danced before him. He wanted to swear at the cowhands who sat on a blanket, laughing and bantering as they played poker.

He wanted to stride over to the players and kick the cards flying, and demand "How can you be so happy while I'm slowly dying inside?"

He shook his head wearily. They'd think he was losing his mind. They didn't know that two weeks ago he had lost a part of himself. Only Rooster knew the pain that was tearing him apart.

Carey and Tillie's faces swam before him. Those two would know a part of his suffering when he told them that Sage was gone forever. His conscience stabbed at him. He should have gotten word to Carey about Sage; he should have taken the time to tell Tillie before starting on the cattle drive. His only excuse was that his pain had been too fresh then, too sharp to share.

Jim heaved himself to his feet and, saying good night to Rooster, stretched out on his blankets, spread some distance from the others. Tomorrow they would arrive at the stockyards, where buyers waited to take the herd off his hands. On his way home he would branch off to Cheyenne. Carey had been very fond of Sage; she had a right to know what had happened to her young friend.

Sage hurried about the kitchen, getting supper ready. Ordinarily she wouldn't be in such a hurry, but it had taken longer than she had thought to answer all the marshal's questions.

The posse had tracked Leland to the shack and found the dead bodies inside. They had figured out that Leland's pistol had killed the three outlaws, but Leland had been killed with a Colt. None of the men wore a Colt. Did she know who had killed the bearded man? the law officer had asked her.

Sage could only dumbly shake her head. Leland was dead, and bless the man who had killed him. At last she was free of him. No longer would she always be afraid, forever looking over her shoulder, dreading that she would see him coming after her.

"But you were there, Miz Larkin; surely you saw the gunman," the marshal prodded.

"All I know," Sage answered, a little impatiently, "is what I told you before. When the boys and I raced out of that shack Leland Larkin was alive, shooting at the three men. All I can add is that I'm grateful to whoever put an end to that evil man."

The lawman had studied her face and come to the conclusion that she was telling the truth, that she wasn't trying to protect anyone. He drew a sheet of paper across his desk—a legal-looking form—and dipped a pen into an inkwell. "As far as I can make out"—the pen scratched across the paper—"all four men deserved to die. I'll just put in my report that Larkin was shot by an unknown hand."

Sage had told him how he could get in touch with Leland's parents, her in-laws. When he said that the body would be taken to them she had left the small office and pushed her mount to its limit in her hurry to get home and tell Lisha and Benny her good news. For the first time in months she didn't cast a look over her shoulder.

Sage's attention was drawn to the open win-

dow. The boys were out by the corral, currying the horses, arguing over whose mount was
the strongest, had the most stamina, could run
faster and longer. She could have told them
that there wasn't that much difference in the
animals that had belonged to the outlaws. They
were all sturdy mounts, chosen for their speed
and durability. A strong, range-bred horse could
sometimes make the difference between life and
death to an outlaw being chased by the law.

It still amazed her how Lisha and Benny had
responded to the changes in their lives these
past few weeks. Both boys had fleshed out from
the regular, hearty meals they ate and hardly
looked like the same two youngsters who had
fled their father. Benny now laughed and played
as enthusiastically as Jamie, every day looking
more and more like Danny, his cousin.

And Lisha . . . there was a quiet happiness on
the teenager's high-cheeked face, the only sign
of his Indian blood, as he went about overseeing
the younger ones, breaking up an occasional
argument before it came to blows, seeing to
it that each boy did the chore he had allotted
to him.

As though it was his duty, the teenager, old
beyond his years, had taken up the role of head
of the house, his new family's protector. He was
firm with Benny and Jamie, gentle with Ruth
Ann. She had no fear that the children wouldn't
be all right under his care when she went off to
work each night.

Sage gazed unseeingly out the window. Only
one thing was missing in the contentment of

her days: Jim. If only he had returned her love. What was he doing tonight? she wondered. Had he moved into his new house yet? Had he taken Reba with him?

Stop it! she commanded herself. *Be thankful for the blessings you've received. You no longer have to fear Leland; thank God for that and forget that blue-eyed womanizer.*

Impatient with her thoughts, Sage gave the pot of venison stew a stir; then she began to set the table, firmly putting Jim out of her mind.

After a long discussion with Lisha one night, when the younger children were already asleep, they had decided that the money they had found in one of the saddlebags was payment Leland had given the outlaws to kill her family. Wasn't it poetic justice that the money should end up in their hands? Consequently, they had no compunction about using it.

The first two things the money bought for them was a kitchen range and a long table with eight chairs. "In case we have company sometime," she explained to Lisha, who looked a little bemused. The boys still slept on the floor, but she had made arrangements with a carpenter to build double beds for the other bedroom. Lisha and Benny didn't mind the present arrangements: They had slept on the floor all their young lives. And to Jamie it was a treat, like camping out, he'd said.

She went to call to the boys that supper was ready to be served. While they washed up on the back porch, she placed a big bowl of stew and a pan of cornbread, which she cut into thick slabs, on the table.

Lisha and Benny, never having been around a little girl before, were enthralled with Ruth Ann, fascinated with her doll-like face, blue eyes and blonde curls. From the beginning, even when they ate their meals on a blanket spread on the floor, the little girl sat between them. As Sage watched Lisha lift Ruth Ann up and gently place her in a chair whose seat had been raised by a board supported on two flat rocks, Sage told herself that if she didn't watch the teenager, he would spoil the child rotten.

The days were growing shorter, twilight already descending when Sage left the house to ride to the Gilded Cage. Lisha stood on the back porch, holding the bridle of her saddled mount. *What would I do without you, Lisha?* she thought as he laced his fingers together, forming a step to assist her into the saddle.

"Sing pretty tonight." He grinned up at her, handing her the reins. "And don't worry about the younguns. I'll keep a strict eye on them."

And he would, Sage knew, as she smiled down at him. Then she nudged the mount with her heel, sending him loping away.

Bawling and bellowing, the herd was driven into the stockyards by cowboy yells and swinging ropes. Jim sat with a buyer on the top rail of the tall corral, counting heads along with him. Dust swirled in the air, threatening to choke man and beast.

"I count an even five hundred, Mr. LaTour." The rotund buyer climbed down from his perch as the last longhorn was prodded into the enclosure and the big gate closed behind it.

"That's how many we started out with," Jim answered as his sweating companion pulled a pad of paper and a pencil from a vest pocket and began scribbling on it.

A few minutes later the top sheet of the pad was ripped off and handed to Jim. "This is what I came up with. Check it over."

Jim scanned the figures, and when he nodded that he agreed with the total a check was handed to him. They shook hands, and when the buyer walked briskly away Jim moved tiredly to where Rooster leaned against the corral, waiting for him.

"I don't know which I want first, Rooster," he said to his friend. "A shot of whiskey to cut the dust out of my throat or a bath to get the damned stuff off my body." He looked at Rooster's sweat-stained shirt, then examined his own stains. "We must smell like a couple of goats. I think a bath comes first. I don't think the lowest dive in Laramie would let us in the place in our present condition."

They handed their tired mounts over to one of the cowboys. Then, their saddlebags slung over their shoulders, they went in search of a Chinese bathhouse. An hour later, miles of dust, sweat, and grime scrubbed away, freshly shaven and wearing clean clothes, the pair made their way to a hotel, signed in, and walked into the establishment's barroom.

Each tossed down two shots of whiskey in rapid succession, then sipped the third one. "I wish the ride home was over," Rooster said.

"Not half as much as I do." Jim gazed into his glass of whiskey. "I have to make a side trip into Cheyenne. There's a woman there I must see, to tell her about Sage. I'd rather walk all the way back to the ranch than tell her that Sage is dead."

Rooster nodded his grizzled head. "I don't envy you having to tell that. It'll be worse tellin' Tillie, though. She was taken with Sage. Then there's the boy you have to break the news to."

With a bleakness in his eyes, Jim drank the rest of his whiskey and set the glass back on the bar. "I'm ready to catch some sleep. What about you?"

Rooster pushed away from the bar. "I was ready when we rode into town. A bed will sure feel good. My old bones don't like sleepin' on the ground anymore."

The second day on the trail, Jim drew Major in at around noon and waited for Rooster to come alongside him. "I'm gonna cut across country now, to Cheyenne. I'll see you back at the ranch in a couple of days."

"I'll be there. Ride easy, Jim."

The shadows of night were settling in when Jim rode into Cheyenne. He remembered that Carey's boardinghouse was two blocks down and one block over from the main street. When he came to the cross street, however, he rode on. He needed a shot of whiskey to help him face Carey, to tell her what he must.

Pain and bitterness gripped him like a vise as he approached the Gilded Cage and heard thunderous applause given to one of the entertainers. A singer, he imagined, the one who had replaced Sage. The new woman would not sing like his little songbird had, in a voice so sweet and clear it tugged at a man's very soul.

Jim was almost past the theater when the clapping died down and the words of "Beautiful Dreamer" wafted through the double doors and hit him in the chest with the impact of a bullet. "Sage," he whispered, with an incredulous joy, "you're alive!"

He pulled the stallion in and swung to the ground. His fingers trembled as he tethered Major to a hitching rack and pushed open the door of the theater.

Jim stood in the back, leaning against the wall, his eyes devouring the beautiful woman on the stage. Was it possible that she had grown more lovely than she had been when he had last seen her? His heart pounding, he waited until she had finished the song to a round of applause. Then he slipped outside and made his way to the back of the building.

When the alley door readily swung open Jim frowned. Although he was thankful that he could gain access to Sage so easily, so could any other man walking down the alley. He was amazed that after what had happened here a few weeks ago, more precautions for the women's protection hadn't been made.

He stepped into the narrow hall from which the dressing rooms branched off, telling himself that Sage would run no more risks in this place.

He was taking her back to Cottonwood, where she belonged.

Jim took two steps, then came to an abrupt halt. Sage had left the stage and was walking toward him. Their eyes met and held; hers full of surprise, his blazing with a blue light.

"Jim!" Sage's tongue was released first as she rushed toward him. "What are you doing here? Is anything wrong with Danny?"

"Danny's fine." He caught her by the elbows, drawing her against his hard body. "God, Sage," he said raggedly, "I thought you were dead."

Before Sage could respond to the pain-filled words, Jim's mouth captured hers in a kiss that, though tender, was all-consuming. "Oh, Sage," he whispered against her lips, "I died a hundred times thinking that you were gone from me forever. I'll never let you out of my sight again."

He raised his head and let his eyes feast on the face that had haunted his dreams. Trailing gentle fingers down her cheek, he said, "We'll stop at the boardinghouse, collect your clothes, and then head for home."

He lowered his head toward Sage again, but she turned her face away, refusing him her lips. "I'm sorry, Jim," she said in a low voice, "but I won't be going back to Cottonwood with you. I have made myself a home here. I have respect from everyone. I will not go back with you and be your whore."

"Sage!" Jim jerked her chin around so that he could glare into her eyes. "You know damn well that you were never my whore. You were my lover, which is vastly different." He ran a finger over her soft red lips. "I want you to be my wife, to live out our days together."

"Do you mean it, Jim?" Sage looked at him with wide green eyes. She was afraid she was dreaming, that she would wake up, her day filled with longing thoughts of him.

Jim's face softened. "I never meant anything so much in my life," he whispered and lowered his head again, this time to be met by eager red lips.

"Come on. Let's get out of here." Jim finally lifted his head, his loins aching, a stiff erection uncomfortably prodding the front of his trousers. "I've got to get you to a bed."

Sage hid an amused smile against his throat. He didn't know it, but it would be a while before he got her into a bed again. There were four children around who would keep him sleeping alone.

"I've got my own place a few miles out of town," she said, stepping out of his arms. "My horse is at the livery. Shall we go?"

"You bet." Jim grinned and wrapped his arm around her waist as they stepped out into the night.

"Hey, I know that horse," Jim exclaimed when the animal was led out to Sage. "That's Red Harlan's mount. How did you get a hold of him?"

"I'll tell you all about it on the way to my house," Sage answered as Jim lifted her into the saddle.

It was a beautiful moonlit night. As Sage and Jim rode along, she related all that had happened to her on that terrible night. Her voice wavered a bit when she spoke of Leland's cruelty to his squaw.

"I must have just missed you," Jim said when she finished telling how she had fled, but not mentioning the boys. That was her big surprise for him. "In case anyone wonders, or cares, I was the one who shot and killed the bastard. He told me that he had killed you and left your body for the wolves and buzzards.

"He died in his next heartbeat."

A short silence fell between them, each left with their own thoughts of that horrible time.

Sage spoke then. "There's my place up ahead."

Jim peered at the dim light shining in a window. An unbearable thought came to him as he remembered that she hadn't actually agreed to marry him. "Do you always leave a lamp burning, Sage, or has another man taken my place?" He turned Major in front of her mount, making her pull in. "Is there another man, Sage?" he rasped, his eyes piercing hers. Sage bit her tongue to hide her pleasure at Jim's jealousy. Let him feel the bite of it for a while, she told herself. God knew the emotion had gnawed at her many times.

Gazing back at him, she said softly, "You were gone a long time, Jim. How was I to know you would change your mind about me?"

"I'll throw the bastard out," Jim swore savagely. Spinning Major on his hocks, he raced away toward the little house.

Sage gazed after him, a wide smile on her face. She hoped he wouldn't scare the pants off Lisha. She kicked her heels into the horse and raced after Jim. When she burst into the kitchen seconds later she didn't know which face showed the most surprise. Jim looked like he'd been poleaxed and Lisha's face was pale and wide-eyed.

She giggled, and Jim spun around to glare at her. "You enjoy putting me through hell, don't you?"

Sage nodded. "A little." All levity left her face. "Women have spoiled you all your life, Jim LaTour. I want you to know up-front that I will not. If you stray one time after we marry I will cease to love you, and be long gone before you can do it a second time."

Jim looked at her, seeing the seriousness in her eyes. "I have no intentions of even looking at another woman again, Sage, let alone taking one to bed."

"Good." Sage smiled at him. "Now, I want you to meet Lisha Larkin." Jim shook the teenager's hand; then she motioned to a small figure sleeping on the floor. "And that is Benny, his brother. We're going to adopt them."

"We are?" Jim blinked in surprise.

"Yes, as well as the towhead sleeping next to Benny. His name is Jamie, and his five-year-old sister, Ruth Ann, is asleep in my bed. They're the children of the woman who Leland killed when she came to my defense. We'll be adopting them too."

"We will?" It seemed that two words strung together was all Jim could get across his lips.

"And then, there's Danny. Do you think . . ."

Jim's white teeth flashed in a wide smile.

"After I've adopted Danny, do you have any more hidden away?"

"Oh, Jim, I love you." Sage threw herself at him. "We'll have such a good life with our little family."

Jim's arms went around her. "Little family? Daddy to five youngsters—six, counting Jonty." He held Sage away from him and asked earnestly, "Do you think I'll make a good father? I haven't had a lick of experience with youngsters."

"You'll make the best father in the world, Jim."

Jim drew Sage back into his arms. "I guess I'd better buy more land, run more cattle. It's going to take a lot of grub to feed five growing children."

He looked at Lisha, who watched them with curious eyes. He had never before seen affection between a man and a woman. "Of course"—Jim smiled at the teenager—"I'll have a right-hand man helping me."

Lisha blushed with pleasure and ducked his head.

"Are you hungry?" Sage stepped away from Jim.

"For food?" He smiled at her crookedly.

Amusement twinkled in Sage's eyes. "I can fix you something before you spread your blankets on the floor with the boys."

Jim gave her a pleading look and she added, "You can't expect a little girl to sleep on the floor, now can you?"

Jim narrowed his eyes at her for a moment, and she was hard put to keep a serious look on her face. "Be ready to leave for my ranch in the morning. The house is built, and there are bedrooms for everybody."

When he stalked out the door to tend to his mount and bring in his bedroll the knowing smirk Lisha gave Sage made her laugh softly. The teenager knew what had been on Jim's mind.

Epilogue

The grass was wet with dew as Sage and Jim walked in the twilight. The night was cool, with a touch of frost in the air. Overhead, wild geese honked as they flew southward, a sure sign that winter•wasn't far off. Sage could hardly contain her happiness. So many good things had happened in the past month.

First, their wedding . . . in church, making eyebrows rise. Jonty and Rooster had stood up with them, while the children, Cord, and Tillie, looked on. Ruth Ann, crying because she had to sit with the boys, had to release the hand of the woman who was fast replacing her dead mother.

Sage remembered with a smile how the wedding party had gone to the restaurant after she and Jim had spoken their vows. Two tables had been pushed together to accommodate their large party. She couldn't determine who had stared the most, Lisha and Benny, awed by the bright lights and the opulence of the dining

417

room, or the other diners, who whispered among themselves.

When the remains of a beef roast and its side dishes had been removed from the table dessert had been served: a three-tier wedding cake with white frosting with pink roses on top. Jim had ordered it baked the day before to surprise his new wife.

The younger children were yawning when farewells were said to Jonty and her family and they all piled into the hired wagon. Jim slapped the reins on the team's broad backs and drove out of town, an arm around Sage's waist.

By the time they arrived at the ranch Ruth Ann had fallen asleep in Lisha's lap and Danny leaned heavily agaist Tillie, fighting to keep his eyes open. Jamie and Benny had lost the battle a mile out of town.

There had been a couple of rough spots at first as they settled in, Sage remembered. Ruth Ann had put up a howl, resenting Jim for taking her place in Sage's bed. Lisha hadn't liked losing his stature as head of the household to Jim and had gone around with a long face for a couple of days. Then Jim had wisely given the teenager the responsibility of looking after his eight brood mares and two stallions. All four boys, including Danny, who were starved for the attention of a father, very nearly worshiped Jim.

As she did. Sage hugged Jim's arm against her breast. Their nightly walk had taken them back to the house, and Jim paused at the bottom of the three broad steps that led to the wide porch that stretched along the front of the house. Jim swung Sage around to lean up against him.

"Did I detect a silent message just now?" His eyes gleamed hotly in the moonlight.

Sage slid a hand inside his pants, pleasuring him as she whispered, "I see you got the message."

"If I didn't before, I certainly have now," he groaned, "and if you don't remove your hand right now, I'll be making love to you on the porch."

Sage laughed softly, gave a gentle squeeze to the erection that was growing under her caressing fingers, and removed her hand. Jim swept her up into his arms and carried her into the house. There he set her on her feet, and together they climbed the winding staircase to their bedroom, at the end of the wide hall. Jim closed the door behind them and locked it . . . against Ruth Ann, who sometimes crept into their bed in the middle of the night.

They hurried out of their clothes, letting them drop heedlessly to the floor, then dove for the bed.

That article of furniture rocked and creaked long into the night, accompanied by low groans and soft, shuddering cries.

SPECIAL SNEAK PREVIEW!

A FIRE IN THE BLOOD

Shirl Henke

**Winner of the *Romantic Times*
Career Achievement Award!**

Author of more than six million books in print!

"Fast paced, sizzling, adventurous. A true Western historical romance with a strong-spirited heroine and a provocative, hot-blooded hero who will set you on fire. I'm in love with Jess Robbins!"

—Roseanne Bittner

*AVAILABLE NOW AT
BOOKSTORES AND NEWSSTANDS
EVERYWHERE!*

Chapter One

Miss Charlene Durbin's dressmaking shop was doing a land-office business on Wednesday morning. The weather had finally broken at the end of May and the lashing spring rains abated, allowing the wealthy ranchers' wives to flock to the capital city and gird themselves for the season of galas that always took place in cattle country after the spring roundup. Louella Wattson and her daughter Emmaline were cooing over a bolt of puce velvet, while Sissy Markham and her sister Kaddie searched pattern books with the avid interest of prospectors just handed the map for a motherlode.

"Does it fit comfortably, Miss Jacobson?" Charlene's assistant Clare asked timidly as she stood back to inspect her handiwork, made of yards and yards of bronze satin edged in cream lace. The colors were unusual, but so was Melissa Jacobson. Her pale ivory skin and fiery dark red hair were set off perfectly by the gown.

Lissa turned and inspected herself in the oval mirror standing in the middle of the large, crowded shop. She adjusted the rich lace gathered at the low-cut neckline and nodded to Clare.

"Ooh, look at *him!*" Julia Creed hissed, looking out the front window. "Bold as if he owned the capital—governor and all. I've never seen such insolence." As she had intended, a crowd of curious women quickly clustered around her and peered at the street below.

"He's a breed right enough," Lucy Moorhead said with the contempt only a woman raised in Sioux country could muster.

Louella Wattson shooed two of the younger women aside and squinted at the new arrival in town. "Why, it's a disgrace. Where is the marshal at a time like this?"

"Cowering in Professor McDaniel's saloon, or I miss my guess," Lucy replied.

"What's all the fuss about?" Lissa asked. Raising the satin skirts of her unfinished ball gown, she walked to the window and peered out. Her eyes fastened on him at once in spite of the noonday crowd on the street. Surrounded by crude cowboys and officious merchants, the rider on the big black stallion stood out like a mountain lion in a flock of woollybacks.

Lissa's eyes were riveted to the stranger as he rode slowly past, holding his reins carelessly in one hand with a negligent ease that belied the watchful expression on his hard, chiseled features. His other hand rested casually on the handle of the fancy Colt revolver strapped to his thigh. Although his wide black hat with a silver concho headband shaded his face from the sun, she could see that his features were exotically handsome in a bronzed, hawkish way. His nose was straight and prominent, his eyebrows thick and dark, and his mouth wide with sensuously shaped lips. She studied his firm jawline with the faint stubble of a dark beard growing on it. How would it feel to run her fingers across its scratchy surface, to touch those magnificent lips and stare into those slitted eyes? *What color are they, I wonder.*

She felt powerless to look away as he swung down from his horse at a hitching post across the street. His body was long and lean, with wide shoulders and narrow hips. He moved with the sinuous grace of a stalking puma. Pulling his hat from his head as he stepped into the shade, he ran his fingers through a shaggy head of night-black hair that lightly brushed his shirt collar.

Lissa continued to stare transfixed at the stranger, who affected her in a way no other man ever had. "That is the most sinfully dangerous man I've ever seen," she murmured breathlessly. *What possessed me to say that!*

Sissy Markham snorted disgustedly. "Yer pa'd be real pleased to see you makin' eyes at a dirty Injun."

"He looks neither dirty nor like any Indian I ever saw," Lissa replied dismissively. Sissy and her sister were vicious-tongued old maids.

"You'd best watch yourself, young lady," Lou-ella chimed in, her voice stern. "We all realize you've spent the past years back east in school, but you were born here. You should know what it means when a man has mixed blood. That odious stranger is not only a half-breed lowlife, but a hired killer as well. He's got a fearful reputation. Name's Jesse Robbins, and he hires out to wealthy stock growers who want to rid the range of squatters and rustlers. Why, he's little better than an outlaw himself."

Lissa arched her eyebrows as she glanced fleetingly at the fat old matron. "And how do you happen to know so much about this Mr. Robbins?"

"I overheard my Horace talking to Mr. Mathis just yesterday. Why, he was aghast at the sort of riffraff the Association was bringing in."

"Then Lemuel has hired him for the Association?" Lissa asked. Lemuel Mathis was president of the Wyoming Stock Growers Association and a suitor of hers, although she did not encourage him.

Louella looked a bit flustered. "Well, I'm not completely certain which one of the members is hiring him."

"But we all know he's no good—and so should you," Emmaline Wattson added in the patronizing, nasal voice that had grated on Lissa since they were children.

"I wonder who he's working for," Lissa said pensively.

Suddenly, the women's attention was again drawn to the street when one of the cowhands lounging against the wall of the saloon hauled himself up and stepped off the wooden walkway. He was young, slightly built, and looked purely mean. Spoiling for a fight, he spoke loudly so his voice carried the length of the muddy street.

"We don't cotton to no Injuns drinkin' our whiskey in Wyoming," he said in a heavy Texas drawl.

Robbins finished tying his horse to the hitching rail, then turned slowly and faced the youth.

"You yeller, gut-eater?" the half-drunk kid prodded as the other men around the saloon scooted out of the line of fire.

Robbins betrayed no emotion at the racial slur or the questioning of his courage. He just walked slowly around the young cowhand.

"You *are* yeller. A damned yeller gut-eating redskin." The boy moved in the tall stranger's path again.

"I never shoot a man for free, but I might make an exception because I'm trail weary and thirsty," Robbins said as he brushed the slight figure out of his way.

That was all the encouragement the boy needed to reach for the Navy Colt on his hip. Before he had it halfway out of the holster, the barrel of Robbins's double-action revolver came crashing down on his forehead.

"Would yew lookit thet," one tall, skinny Texas cowhand said with awe in his voice.

"Never even seen him pull it," another man added as the group watched the stranger step over the crumpled body of their companion.

At the dressmaker's across the street, the cluster of women watched Jesse Robbins disappear into the dark interior of the saloon. "Well, I do declare, a lady isn't safe on the streets of the territorial capital anymore. You really must move from this dreadful location, Charlene, or I shall just have to find another modiste," Louella pronounced to the chorused agreement of the others.

All but Lissa, who ignored the badgering of poor Charlene Durbin and glided across the cluttered shop to her dressing room. As she stripped off the satin gown, her thoughts were not of dresses or dances, but of the dark, dangerous stranger who worked for the Wyoming Stock Growers Association. She was dying to know who had hired Mr. Jesse Robbins.

Jess walked into the Metropolitan Hotel and stopped to look around. Classy place all right, with big, ugly, overstuffed chairs covered in maroon velvet sitting in clusters around the lobby, flanked by potted palms that were as big and showy as any he had seen in Algiers or Tunis. Maroon and dark-blue carpeting swallowed up the sound of his footfalls as he strolled to the big walnut counter beside the steep stairs.

He leaned his leather weapon case against the wall, then swung his saddlebags from his shoulder and laid them on the wide countertop. "I'd like a room and a hot bath."

The hotel clerk drew back as if his nostrils had just been assailed with scrapings from a livery stable floor. His thin lips puckered up, causing his chin to retreat even further into his neck. "I don't think you got the right place, cowboy. Rawlins's place on Eddy Street might give you a room."

"I want a room here . . . now," Jess said in a low, silky voice.

"We don't take in no breeds—hotel policy," the clerk added quickly, half-indignant, half-wary as he watched the stranger's cold gray eyes lighten to the color of boiling mercury.

"I'm making an adjustment in hotel policy," Jess said, reaching for the register and the pen lying beside it. Before the sputtering clerk could stop him, he signed his name and shoved the book across the counter.

"The owners'll fire me," the clerk whined, as Jess tossed a gold piece on the counter and picked up his bags. He walked around the counter and pulled a key from one of the small wooden compartments on the wall, then turned toward the stairs.

"You can't just . . . just . . ."

"Don't get your shirt full of fleas, Noah," a calm, stentorian voice interrupted. "The stranger works for me," a tall, elegant man with iron-gray hair and a thin, austere face informed the clerk.

"Mr. Jacobson. I didn't . . . I mean I didn't know—"

"It's all right, Noah. Go see that Chris fetches up some bathwater for Mr. Robbins. And put Lissa's things in her room as well," Jacobson commanded as he bypassed the desk and approached Jess.

Jess set down his bags and sized up Marcus

429

Jacobson. He was dressed in the plain rough clothes of a stockman who worked his own range. His hand, when he extended it, was callused from hard work, and his ice blue eyes were keen and incisive. Jess returned the handshake. "I'm a day early. Didn't think you'd be in town yet."

"Just arrived this afternoon. I'm going to the club to clean up before dinner."

Jess had heard of the famous Cheyenne Club, a private and very exclusive men's organization whose membership was restricted to the wealthiest of Wyoming cattlemen. He knew that no invitation would be extended to him to join Jacobson at that establishment. They did not even allow cowhands, much less Indians. "I look forward to a long, hot soak myself," he replied noncommittally.

"Good. I'll be back here around seven. We can have dinner in the hotel dining room and discuss the job I need to have done."

Within half an hour, Jess was luxuriating in a steamy tub. The boy who had filled it seemed as nervous as a half-broken mustang, but had said nothing, merely done his job, then stuttered his thanks for the coins Jess had tossed him. He dismissed the memory and laid his head back against the rim of the fancy copper tub. A half-breed gunman always made folks nervous, whether it was in Texas or Wyoming.

Looking around the small bathing room, Jess admitted his surprise about the accommodations, which were modern and elegant. A water closet sat in one corner, and on the other side of the partially closed door was a suite with a

430

parlor and a large, well-appointed bedroom. Purely by chance, he had helped himself to the fanciest setup in the place!

With almost ten thousand inhabitants, Cheyenne was more than a territorial capital. It was the main hub for the high plains cattle industry. The powerful Wyoming Stock Growers Association had its headquarters here, and the Union Pacific railroad shipped over one hundred thousand head of beef east every fall. Smiling to himself, Jess wondered how rich old Marcus Jacobson really was. He would soon find out. Jesse Robbins planned to charge a fearfully high fee for his services.

He had always spent his money as soon as he earned it, buying up more land and good breeding stock for his own small ranch in western Texas. The Double R would never be as big and fancy as the spreads of cattle barons like Jacobson, but it was home for Jess and his younger brother, Jonah. A home they had earned with blood and tears.

Pushing thoughts of the tragic past from his mind, Jess considered the terms of his deal with Jacobson and began to lather up.

Lissa tired of the gossiping women at the dressmaker's shop and left to meet her father at the hotel. By now he should have arranged for Chris to unload her baggage in her usual rooms and draw her a steamy bath.

When she entered the hotel, Noah was not at the front desk. Knowing the nasty-tempered little man's predilection for a late afternoon nip at the bottle, she considered herself fortunate.

She would be able to slip upstairs without having to deal with him. Hoping her bath was ready, she reached behind the desk for her key. The pocket marked #12 was empty.

"Chris must have taken it so he could fill my tub," she murmured to herself as she climbed the stairs. The door to suite #12 was indeed unlocked. She swept into the parlor.

Now where the devil are my bags? Nothing had been brought up yet. She muttered a small, unladylike oath about Noah Boswick, then stopped as she heard the sound of splashing water from the adjacent bathing room.

"Chris, put orange blossom bath salts in— ooh!" Lissa stood frozen in the doorway. *He* was in *her* bathtub! Naked! His bronzed shoulders rippled with muscles, and one long-fingered hand rested against the pelt of black hair on his chest, holding a bar of soap. His hair was wet and he shook his head to clear the water from his eyes. She could see the faint outline of his body beneath the water—but not too clearly, thank God. Then he opened those mysterious eyes that she had wondered about earlier. They made her heart stop beating. Fringed by long black lashes, they were pure silver. His sensuous mouth curved in an intimate smile that heated her blood. Then he spoke and her heart raced wildly.

"Orange blossom isn't exactly my fragrance," he said dryly. "You don't look like the hotel maid. Might I hope you're a present from my employer?"

Lissa was unable to tear her eyes from his gleaming wet skin. The tantalizing patterns of soap bubbles foaming on his shoulders fairly beckoned her hands to glide over the lean, hard muscles.

"What are you doing in my suite?" she finally managed to choke out.

"Your suite? I have the key." His voice was laced with laughter.

"Well, you certainly didn't use it!" she said indignantly as a flush scalded her cheeks. "The door was unlocked. This is the suite my father always reserves for me. I naturally assumed—".

"You naturally walked right in and opened the bathroom door when you heard me splashing," he interrupted ungraciously, still smiling. "Do you often spy on men in their baths?" Before she could sputter an answer, he started to rise out of the water, saying, "Sweetheart, hand me one of those towels as long as you're here."

She whirled and fled to the echoing sound of rich male laughter.

What a breathtaking little cat, he thought as he rinsed off and rubbed himself dry. Since it was unlikely that any other uninvited guest would be so lovely, Jess strolled into the lavishly appointed parlor, slipped the lock on the outer door, then returned to the steamy bathing room with his razor to complete his toilette. The uncharacteristic carelessness of the unlocked door niggled at the back of his mind.

As he pulled a clean shirt and pants from the armoire where the bellboy had hung them, Jess turned his thoughts to his fire-haired intruder. For certain no hotel maid. He had known that at a glance. Her tan linen traveling suit was far too expensively cut for her to be a mere servant, and her hands were too pale and soft to have endured any kind of manual labor. She might have been a very expensive whore, but he doubted it. The way she blushed gave away her lack of experience, but there was the matter of those hungry gold eyes. He chuckled. A she-wolf never eyed up a young maverick with any keener interest than the little redhead had shown while she studied him in that bathtub. She was ripe for the taking all right.

But before he accepted her unconscious invitation, he wanted to know who she was. A man of his background could get in a mountain of trouble over a rich white lady, even if she was the one who initiated the whole affair. Maybe after dinner he would head to the biggest saloon in town and ask around. A beauty with her unusual coloring would certainly be well-known in a territory with as few females as Wyoming.

He inspected his appearance in the mirror. The black homespun suit made him look like a preacher—or a politician. He considered wearing his .41-caliber double-action Colt Lightning, but decided against it. After all, this was the classiest hotel in Cheyenne and he was having dinner with one of the wealthiest cattlemen. There was an unwritten law on the plains about rich men. Seldom did anyone try any fireworks around them. They were too powerful, and the retribution for any disgruntled cowhand or outlaw was swift and terrible.

"Just in case the unlikely occurs," he muttered grimly and pulled open his gun case. He selected a single-action Colt pocket revolver and its specially-made shoulder holster. He strapped it on and shrugged into his suit coat, then glanced in the mirror one last time. He needed a haircut, but what the hell. It was not likely that Jacobson would bring his wife along, and even if he did, Jess was not interested in impressing Lissa Jacobson.

Lissa inspected her appearance in the mirror. Her hair had turned out rather well. How heavenly to have a hairdresser here in Cheyenne! The woman had fashioned it in an elegant bouffant style with a heavy chignon at the crown and soft wispy curls framing her face. "Now all I need to do is select a gown," she murmured, moving to her wardrobe, which overflowed with neatly pressed dresses in a rainbow of colors.

Dinner in a civilized dining room was quite an occasion after the endless winter months spent snowbound at the J Bar Ranch. The isolation had nearly driven her mad, with only her father and that hateful housekeeper for company. In desperation, she had often gone down to the bunkhouse to talk with Vinegar Joe, the crotchety old cook, and Moss, the ranch foreman. The young hands were not much company since they mostly tended to stare gape jawed at Marcus's beautiful daughter and shuffle around trying to please her. All the poor homely illiterates did was add to her sense of frustration.

Marcus had sent his only daughter east for an education when her mother died. Her Aunt Edith and Uncle Phineas had taken in the frightened girl and lavished everything on her

435

that a childless couple could give. She had spent brief summer vacations at J Bar, but her life had been in St. Louis.

When she was eighteen, Lissa had made her debut at the Veiled Prophet Ball, the most elegant social event of the aristocratic old city's season. Handsome, wealthy young men from all the best families had courted her. She had adored their attention, thinking that she would eventually marry one of them and settle down to be one of the social arbiters of the city, like Aunt Edith.

Then Marcus had swooped down and snatched her back here to this beastly wilderness the summer before last. His plans for his sole heir were quite different from hers. She was to marry an influential stockman who could run his empire. Together they would provide heirs to inherit the kingdom Marcus Jacobson had spent his life building.

As if that had not been bad enough, his first choice for the position was Lemuel Mathis, a well-to-do attorney in town and president of the Wyoming Stock Growers Association. Lemuel was, she supposed in all fairness, a fine-looking man for one approaching the advanced age of forty. Unfortunately, he was a crashing bore.

All Lemuel was interested in was the cattle industry. Of course, Marcus and all the rest of their friends shared the same single-minded interest. At least Lemuel did attempt to court her in his own punctilious way.

But Lemuel Mathis was the farthest thing from her mind as she prepared for dinner. All she could think about was the possibility of encountering the gunman again. Just thinking of that swarthy, hawkish face with the mocking silver eyes made her heart pound. He was an arrogant beast, no doubt of that, a mixed blood, forbidden to all decent women. Her mouth went dry, and she felt queerly faint and flushed just thinking about him naked in that tub. She could still envision the soap bubbles coating his dark skin, the cunning patterns of hair on his chest and forearms, the lean, sinuous rippling of his muscles. How would it feel to touch that hard body and run her fingertips along the contours of his heated flesh?

Lissa gave herself a mental shake and turned her attention to the gowns. They were cramped in this smaller room, which had fewer armoires and chests for her extensive wardrobe. Damn his insolence for taking *her* suite! She had to settle for a smaller room at the end of the hall.

She could not keep her wayward thoughts from trespassing to Jesse Robbins. There had been a great deal of trouble here lately with cattle and horses being stolen. She knew that her father and several of the other big ranchers like Cyrus Evers had been conferring about how to solve the problem. *Could Papa be the one who hired Robbins?*

Just thinking about it made her smile wickedly. If so, the presumptuous devil was in for quite a rude awakening. He would be Marcus's employee, and she would be the boss's daughter. Now that might just make him a bit more polite!

Just then a rap sounded at the door, and

her father's voice called out, "Are you there, Princess?"

"Come in, Papa. I was just deciding which gown to wear for dinner tonight. I thought the aqua, but perhaps the gold . . ."

Marcus turned his hat in his hands, fingering the leather headband nervously. "Princess, I know how you've been looking forward to dinner here in Cheyenne, but something has come up—"

"You promised, Papa! What could be more important? I'll wait if you have to have some boring old meeting over at the Association."

"I'm afraid that won't be possible, Lissa," he said placatingly.

"But I just had my hair done, and the hotel maid pressed all my gowns in a special rush. . . ." she wheedled.

His jaw was set in that stubborn way that she knew meant he would not be moved. Lissa recognized it because she too clenched her jaw the same way on frequent occasions.

"I'm sorry, Princess. I'm going to have to have a business dinner. A man I just hired has arrived a day early, and Lemuel and I need to discuss vital J Bar affairs with him."

Her heart skipped a beat. *Jesse Robbins!* "I don't see why I can't sit in. I promise to keep quiet and let you talk."

His blue eyes were glacial as he replied, "This man is not the sort that a lady would ever be seen socially with. He's a half-breed stock detective from Texas."

So it *was* he. "Oh, poo! What difference does that make to me? I only want to dress

438

up and have an elegant meal in a civilized place." She knew Marcus shared the Westerner's prejudices about good women associating with Indians or gunmen—and stock detectives were by definition gunmen. But the whole thing was narrow-minded and silly. She had half a mind to say so, but he gave her no opportunity.

"I know you've spent your formative years away from here, and for that reason I'll ignore that foolish remark," he said sternly. "I promise to take you to dinner tomorrow night. Now be a good girl and order whatever you want sent up from the hotel dining room for tonight." He walked over to her and placed a kiss on her forehead, then started for the door. He paused midway and said, with a twinkle softening his cold blue eyes, "Oh, Princess, your hair does look grand. Have the hairdresser come again tomorrow—and wear the gold dress."

After her father left, Lissa began to pace and scheme. If Lemuel was going to be present, too, then she could say she was so eager to see him that she just couldn't wait. Papa would be furious, but since he had been pushing Mathis at her for over a year, he could not stay mad. And he would never guess that her real motive for coming to the dining room was the silver-eyed gunman.

Lissa could not wait to see Jesse Robbins's face when she made her grand entrance and was introduced as Marcus Jacobson's daughter. "I bet he swallows his tongue!"

NORAH HESS
Kentucky Bride

"Norah Hess not only overwhelms you with characters who seem to be breathing right next to you, she transports you into their world!"
—Romantic Times

Fleeing her abusive uncle, D'lise Alexander trusts no man...until she is rescued by virile trapper Kane Devlin. His rugged strength and tender concern convince D'lise she will find a safe haven in his backwoods homestead. And beneath Kane's soul-stirring kisses she forgets everything except her longing to become his sweetest Kentucky bride.

_3253-8 $4.99 US/$5.99 CAN

LEISURE BOOKS
ATTN: Order Department
276 5th Avenue, New York, NY 10001

Please add $1.50 for shipping and handling for the first book and $.35 for each book thereafter. PA., N.Y.S. and N.Y.C. residents, please add appropriate sales tax. No cash, stamps, or C.O.D.s. All orders shipped within 6 weeks via postal service book rate. Canadian orders require $2.00 extra postage and must be paid in U.S. dollars through a U.S. banking facility.

Name _____

Address _____

City _____ State _____ Zip _____

I have enclosed $_____ in payment for the checked book(s).
Payment <u>must</u> accompany all orders.☐ Please send a free catalog.

Kentucky Woman
NORAH HESS

Winner of 5 *Romantic Times* Awards!

Norah Hess's historical romances are "delightful, tender and heartwarming reads from a special storyteller!"

—*Romantic Times*

Spencer Atkins wants no part of a wife and children while he can live in his pa's backwoods cabin as a carefree bachelor. Fresh from the poorhouse, Gretchen Ames will marry no man refusing her a home and a family. Although they are the unlikeliest couple, Spencer and Gretchen find themselves grudgingly sharing a cabin, working side by side, and fighting an attraction neither can deny.

_3518-9 $4.99 US/$5.99 CAN

LEISURE BOOKS
ATTN: Order Department
276 5th Avenue, New York, NY 10001

Please add $1.50 for shipping and handling for the first book and $.35 for each book thereafter. PA., N.Y.S. and N.Y.C. residents, please add appropriate sales tax. No cash, stamps, or C.O.D.s. All orders shipped within 6 weeks via postal service book rate. Canadian orders require $2.00 extra postage and must be paid in U.S. dollars through a U.S. banking facility.

Name _____

Address _____

City _____ State _____ Zip _____

I have enclosed $_____ in payment for the checked book(s).
Payment <u>must</u> accompany all orders. ☐ Please send a free catalog.

NORAH HESS

"Overwhelms you with characters who seem to be breathing right next to you and transports you into their world!"

—*Romantic Times*

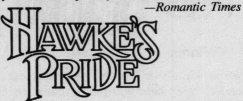

From the moment she laid eyes on him, Rue thought Hawke Masters was the most arrogant man she'd ever seen. But once he got her home to his ranch, after a shotgun marriage, she had second thoughts. Could he be the man she had dreamed of all her life — or was she simply blinded by the ecstasy she felt in his strong arms?

_3051-9 $4.50 US/$5.50 CAN

LEISURE BOOKS
ATTN: Order Department
276 5th Avenue, New York, NY 10001

Please add $1.50 for shipping and handling for the first book and $.35 for each book thereafter. PA., N.Y.S. and N.Y.C. residents, please add appropriate sales tax. No cash, stamps, or C.O.D.s. All orders shipped within 6 weeks via postal service book rate. Canadian orders require $2.00 extra postage and must be paid in U.S. dollars through a U.S. banking facility.

Name _____

Address _____.

City _____ State _____ Zip _____

I have enclosed $_____ in payment for the checked book(s).
Payment <u>must</u> accompany all orders. ☐ Please send a free catalog.

NORAH HESS

Best Western Frontier Romance
Award-Winner—*Romantic Times*

In the rugged solitude of the Wyoming wilderness, the lovely Jonty Rand lived life as a boy to protect her innocence from the likes of Cord McBain. So when her grandmother's dying wish made Cord Jonty's guardian, she despaired of ever revealing her true identity. Determined to change her into a rawhide-tough wrangler, Cord assigned Jonty all the hardest tasks on the ranch, making her life a torment. Then one stormy night he discovered that Jonty would never be a man, only the wildest, most willing woman he'd ever taken in his arms.

_2934-0 $4.50

LEISURE BOOKS
ATTN: Order Department
276 5th Avenue, New York, NY 10001

Please add $1.50 for shipping and handling for the first book and $.35 for each book thereafter. PA., N.Y.S. and N.Y.C. residents, please add appropriate sales tax. No cash, stamps, or C.O.D.s. All orders shipped within 6 weeks via postal service book rate. Canadian orders require $2.00 extra postage and must be paid in U.S. dollars through a U.S. banking facility.

Name _____

Address _____

City _____ State _____ Zip _____

I have enclosed $_____ in payment for the checked book(s). Payment **must** accompany all orders. ☐ Please send a free catalog.

A FRONTIER CHRISTMAS

Madeline Baker, Robin Lee Hatcher, Norah Hess, Connie Mason

Discover the joys of an old-fashioned Christmas with four stories by Leisure's most popular historical romance authors.

LOVING SARAH
By Madeline Baker

A white woman learns the true meaning of Christmas from the Apache brave who opens her heart to love.

A CHRISTMAS ANGEL
By Robin Lee Hatcher

A little girl's wish for a Christmas angel comes true when a beautiful stranger arrives at her father's Idaho farm.

THE HOMECOMING
By Norah Hess

An innocent bride finds special joy in the Christmas homecoming of a husband who married her on the rebound, then marched away from their Kentucky homestead to fight for his country's independence.

THE GREATEST GIFT OF ALL
By Connie Mason

A lovely young Colorado widow rediscovers the magic of love when her two children befriend a traveler who resembles St. Nicholas.

__3354-2 $4.99 US/$5.99 CAN

LEISURE BOOKS
ATTN: Order Department
276 5th Avenue, New York, NY 10001

Please add $1.50 for shipping and handling for the first book and $.35 for each book thereafter. PA., N.Y.S. and N.Y.C. residents, please add appropriate sales tax. No cash, stamps, or C.O.D.s. All orders shipped within 6 weeks via postal service book rate. Canadian orders require $2.00 extra postage and must be paid in U.S. dollars through a U.S. banking facility.

Name _____

Address _____

City _____ State _____ Zip _____

I have enclosed $_____ in payment for the checked book(s).

Payment <u>must</u> accompany all orders. ☐ Please send a free catalog.

A WILDERNESS CHRISTMAS

Madeline Baker, Elizabeth Chadwick, Norah Hess, Connie Mason

Discover the old-fashioned joys of a frontier Christmas with Leisure's leading ladies of love at their heartwarming best!

MADELINE BAKER
"Loving Devlin"

Love comes full circle as a half-breed helps his woman bring forth their own Christmas babe far from the comforts of civilization.

ELIZABETH CHADWICK
"The Fourth Gift"

Half her ranch sold to a Yankee, a determined woman fights to buy out the interloper until he fulfills the wishes dearest to her heart.

NORAH HESS
"Christmas Surprise"

For a lovelorn spinster, the dreary winter days become as bright and new as the Christmas surprise a handsome stranger brings her.

CONNIE MASON
"Christmas Star"

Following her own Christmas star through Colonial Virginia, a beautiful orphan makes three lonely people into a true family.

___3528-6 **A WILDERNESS CHRISTMAS (four stories in one volume)**

$4.99 US/$5.99 CAN

LEISURE BOOKS
ATTN: Order Department
276 5th Avenue, New York, NY 10001

Please add $1.50 for shipping and handling for the first book and $.35 for each book thereafter. PA., N.Y.S. and N.Y.C. residents, please add appropriate sales tax. No cash, stamps, or C.O.D.s. All orders shipped within 6 weeks via postal service book rate. Canadian orders require $2.00 extra postage and must be paid in U.S. dollars through a U.S. banking facility.

Name _____

Address _____

City _____ State _____ Zip _____

I have enclosed $_____ in payment for the checked book(s).

Payment <u>must</u> accompany all orders. ☐ Please send a free catalog.

WOMEN OF COURAGE...
WOMEN OF PASSION...

Share in this sweeping saga of the American frontier, and the indomitable men and women who pushed ever westward in search of their dreams.

A Promise of Thunder by Connie Mason. Storm Kennedy has lost her land claim to Grady Stryker, a handsome Cheyenne half-breed, and now finds herself forced to marry him in order to get her land back. She may be his legal wife, but Storm vows she'll deny him access to her last asset—the lush body Grady thinks is his for the taking.
_3444-1 $4.99 US/$5.99 CAN

Promised Sunrise by Robin Lee Hatcher. Together, Maggie Harris and Tucker Branigan face the hardships of the westward journey with a raw courage and passion for living that makes their unforgettable story a tribute to the human will and the power of love.
_3015-2 $4.50 US/$5.50 CAN

Beyond the Horizon by Connie Mason. The bronzed arms and searing kisses of half-breed scout Swift Blade are forbidden to her, yet Shannon Branigan senses that the untamed land that awaits her will give her the freedom to love the one man who can fulfill her wild desire.
_3029-2 $4.50 US/$5.50 CAN

LEISURE BOOKS
ATTN: Order Department
276 5th Avenue, New York, NY 10001

Please add $1.50 for shipping and handling for the first book and $.35 for each book thereafter. PA., N.Y.S. and N.Y.C. residents, please add appropriate sales tax. No cash, stamps, or C.O.D.s. All orders shipped within 6 weeks via postal service book rate. Canadian orders require $2.00 extra postage and must be paid in U.S. dollars through a U.S. banking facility.

Name _____

Address _____

City _____ State _____ Zip _____

I have enclosed $_____ in payment for the checked book(s).
Payment <u>must</u> accompany all orders. □ Please send a free catalog.

Top-selling Historical Romance
By Leisure's Leading Ladies of Love!

Savage Embers by Cassie Edwards. Before him in the silvery moonlight, she appears as if in a vision. And from that moment, a love like wildfire rushes through the warrior's blood. Not one to be denied, the mighty Arapaho chieftain will claim the woman. Yet even as Falcon Hawk shelters Maggie in his heated embrace, an enemy waits to smother their searing ecstasy, to leave them nothing but the embers of the love that might have been.

__3568-5 $4.99 US/$5.99 CAN

Winds Across Texas by Susan Tanner. Once the captive of a great warrior, Katherine Bellamy finds herself shunned by decent society, yet unable to return to the Indians who have accepted her as their own. Bitter over the murder of his wife and son, Slade will use anyone to get revenge. Both Katherine and Slade see in the other a means to escape misery—and nothing more. But as the sultry desert breezes caress their yearning bodies, neither can deny the sweet, soaring ecstasy of unexpected love.

__3582-0 $4.99 US/$5.99 CAN

LEISURE BOOKS
ATTN: Order Department
276 5th Avenue, New York, NY 10001

Please add $1.50 for shipping and handling for the first book and $.35 for each book thereafter. PA., N.Y.S. and N.Y.C. residents, please add appropriate sales tax. No cash, stamps, or C.O.D.s. All orders shipped within 6 weeks via postal service book rate. Canadian orders require $2.00 extra postage and must be paid in U.S. dollars through a U.S. banking facility.

Name _____

Address _____

City _____ State _____ Zip _____

I have enclosed $_____ in payment for the checked book(s).
Payment <u>must</u> accompany all orders.☐ Please send a free catalog.

DISCOVER A NEW WORLD OF HISTORICAL ROMANCE!

By Love Betrayed by Sandra DuBay. Rebecca Carlyle agrees to become a spy for the British to avenge her husband's death. But she never expects to find passion in the strong arms of American Beau McAllister. How can she remain true to her cause when all she wants to do is surrender to the ecstasy she has found in the tender caresses of the enemy?
_3282-1 $4.99 US/$5.99 CAN

Mistress of the Muse by Suzanne Hoos. When young Ashley Canell returns to the Muse, her family home, she is faced with dark secrets—secrets that somehow involve her handsome stepcousin, Evan Prescott. And even as she finds herself falling in love with Evan, Ashley fears he might be the one who is willing to do anything to stop her from unraveling the shocking mysteries of the Muse.
_3417-4 $4.50 US/$5.50 CAN

Island Flame by Karen Robards. Young and beautiful, Lady Catherine Aldley was raised by England's most proper governesses, but Jonathan Hale makes her feel like a common doxy. When the lustful pirate attacks Catherine's ship, he spares her life but takes her innocence in a night of savage longing.
_3414-X $4.99 US/$5.99 CAN

LEISURE BOOKS
ATTN: Order Department
276 5th Avenue, New York, NY 10001

Please add $1.50 for shipping and handling for the first book and $.35 for each book thereafter. PA., N.Y.S. and N.Y.C. residents, please add appropriate sales tax. No cash, stamps, or C.O.D.s. All orders shipped within 6 weeks via postal service book rate. Canadian orders require $2.00 extra postage and must be paid in U.S. dollars through a U.S. banking facility.

Name_____

Address_____

City _____ State _____ Zip _____

I have enclosed $_____in payment for the checked book(s).
Payment <u>must</u> accompany all orders.☐ Please send a free catalog.